GW00504014

9

....
COUNTY COUNCIL
This book has been
withdrawn from the
County Library stock
Price:

0 7 DEC 2004

Through The Years

Katherine Sinclair

BUCKS. COUNTY LIBRARY

ASK 337754

B11 196 642 6

S

PIATKUS

Copyright © 1994 by Katherine Sinclair

First published in Great Britain in 1995 by
Judy Piatkus (Publishers) Ltd of
5 Windmill Street, London W1

**The moral right of the author
has been asserted**

*A catalogue record for this book is available
from the British Library*

ISBN 0–7499–0289–2

Printed and bound in Great Britain by
Mackays of Chatham PLC, Chatham, Kent

For Allison Dial

Chapter 1

*

MAGGIE

The midday din muffled the urgent knocking on Maggie Nesbitt's door. Horse-drawn carts rumbled past her basement window with its worm's-eye view of the sidewalk, shrieking children spilled out of the crowded tenements across the street, costermongers yelled their wares, and from the harbor came the mournful wail of a departing ship.

Reluctantly Maggie laid down her pen and went to the door.

A young woman stood on the bottom step, shivering in the December chill despite her fur-trimmed cloak, which did not quite conceal her advanced pregnancy. She was tall, held her head proudly, and smooth hair the color of cornsilk was visible beneath a fashionable hat. Compelling lavender-blue eyes regarded Maggie through a veil of pain. She spoke in a low voice with a hint of an accent Maggie could not place. "Does the midwife live here?"

"Well, I—"

"Fetch her. Quickly." Her tone was now imperious.

Maggie explained patiently, as she had to others. "My mother was a midwife. She died a year ago. I helped her a few times, but I've only delivered a couple of babies by myself."

"Then I've no choice but to place myself in your hands."

"Why don't you go home?" Maggie suggested gently. "Your family—"

"I can pay you."

"I didn't ask for money. Who sent you to me?"

"The first woman I asked when I got off the horsecar at the corner of the street. Please . . . I—oh!" She clutched her abdomen and looked down at the liquid trickling from beneath her skirt to the well-scrubbed doorstep.

Maggie helped her into the room. "Are the pains coming close together?"

The woman nodded, biting her lip to hold back a moan of agony.

"Your water broke, it's all right. I'll help you. What's your name?"

"Delia."

No surname, but Maggie hadn't expected one. "Sit on the bed, Delia, and let's take off your clothes."

Unlike some of her mother's patients, who reacted with alarm to having to remove their clothing in front of a stranger, Delia expressed no false modesty. As she unpinned her hat, Maggie bent to unbutton a pair of soft kid-leather shoes. Her fingers touched delicate silk-stockinged feet.

Under the cloak Delia gripped a bulging reticule, which she kept in one hand as with the other she began to unfasten a fine wool jacket.

"I won't steal your money," Maggie said brusquely, "but put your purse under the pillow if you're worried about it."

To Maggie's chagrin, Delia did push her reticule under the pillow. Another contraction ripped through her slender frame, but she bore it in stoic silence.

Maggie deftly dealt with buttons and hooks, stripping her charge down to her chemise. Delia pulled off her own pantalettes before lying on the narrow bed. Maggie drew a sheet up over her, then added a blanket.

"If anyone comes looking for me, please don't tell them I'm here."

She didn't wear a wedding ring, so apparently there was no husband to pursue her. She probably feared an irate father might arrive. Maggie carefully folded the expensive clothes and placed them on a chair. Of her mother's furniture, only the chairs, gate-leg table, bed, and tallboy had escaped the secondhand dealer. Maggie had sold everything else in order to pay the doctor and funeral expenses.

As Maggie lit the stove and put a kettle of water on to boil, she heard Delia panting and said reassuringly, "Try to relax. Don't push yet. Ride the wave of the pain as it comes."

After laying out towels and scissors, she went back to the bed. "I'll try not to hurt you, but I must see if your baby's in the right position. I shall have to look between your legs, too, then we'll know how long your labor might be."

Carefully palpating Delia's abdomen, then examining the birth canal, Maggie hid her dismay at Delia's narrow hips and the fact that although her contractions were only minutes apart, there was very little dilation. Most troubling of all, the baby was in a breech position.

Delia endured her ministrations with quiet fortitude, her classically beautiful features registering no emotion, but Maggie could see the pain in her eyes.

Covering her again, Maggie said in as matter-of-fact a tone as she could muster, "The babies I delivered were straightforward births to women who had other children." She paused. "I think I'd better see if a doctor will come and look at you."

"No!" Beads of perspiration now glistened on Delia's brow and her lips were bitten raw, but her voice was firm. "You are *not* to tell anyone I'm here. No one, I implore you."

"But I don't have the experience or the skill—"

"It will be all right. We'll manage." Delia attempted an encouraging smile; Maggie felt as if their roles were subtly being reversed.

An early twilight fell, and frost formed on the windowpane. Maggie mopped Delia's fevered forehead and gripped her hands as the contractions grew stronger.

Moved by her courage and endurance, Maggie said, "For God's sake, cry out! Don't hold back."

Delia's lips barely mouthed her reply, "Will it help? I don't think so." Then her head twisted from side to side, and she writhed as the next contraction began to build.

As the pain eased, to Maggie's amazement Delia began to sing. Her contralto voice had a heartbreaking quality that was such a contrast to her dispassionate demeanor that Maggie listened in spellbound silence for a minute before realizing that Delia was singing in French. There was also a hint of tethered power to her voice, as if she might easily raise the rafters if she chose.

When the words faltered as she was again caught in the throes of a rising contraction, Maggie said, "What a beautiful singing voice you have. Are you French?"

By way of response, Delia started to sing again, this time

a rousing German drinking song, gasping out the words as her body was convulsed with pain.

Bitter cold crept in around the ill-fitting door and window, and the basement room, never adequately heated, grew frigid as a tomb. Maggie pulled a woollen shawl around her own shoulders, but Delia threw aside her blanket in her fevered writhing.

As darkness fell Delia grew weaker, but more inclined to talk, whispered comments that were punctuated by fierce pains. "It's New Year's Eve." She sounded surprised to discover this.

"Yes. Your child's going to arrive in a brand-new century."

"No, he's going to be born in the last year of the *old* century," Delia corrected. "The new century won't begin until nineteen hundred and one. It's a common error."

"Well, nineteen hundred *sounds* like a new century. How do you know it's going to be a boy?"

Delia responded with quiet ferocity, "It *must* be a boy. I do not wish to be responsible for bringing a girl into the world, to suffer like this."

Maggie put her hands to Delia's abdomen again. "Delia—I have to fetch a doctor. Your baby has to be turned—I think if the head was in the right position, you could deliver now."

"No . . . doctors." Her voice was husky with fatigue now. "Can you do it?"

"I saw my mother do this once." Maggie hesitated. "No. I can't. I'll be back as soon as I can."

"If you leave me I shall crawl into the street and throw myself under the first horsecar." There was no doubting the resolve in her tone, nor the determination in eyes that were suddenly glacial.

Maggie murmured a prayer as she rolled up her sleeves and prepared to attempt to turn the obstinate baby.

The surprisingly healthy girl arrived at one minute past midnight. Her exhausted mother and midwife knew that the new year had arrived because of the revelry on the street outside. Several merrymakers from the heavily Scottish and Irish immigrant neighborhood rapped on the door clamoring to be "first foot" in the household, but Maggie ignored them, so they moved off in search of other donations of bread, coal, and hot toddies.

Maggie sat at the foot of the bed holding the baby, who slept peacefully, oblivious to the turmoil her arrival had caused. Delia did not ask to hold her. Delia was like a rag doll, Maggie thought, limp and lifeless, yet her pale blue eyes burned with a light that was mesmerizing in its intensity. Most new mothers escaped gratefully into deep sleep, but Delia seemed more inclined to talk. She was euphoric that together they had triumphed in a life-and-death struggle.

"You were wonderful, Maggie," she said in a throaty whisper that was more commanding than a shout. "No doctor could have done more. I shall never forget what you did for me this night."

Maggie looked down at the baby in her arms, loving the soft warmth of her, and was troubled that Delia seemed to have forgotten that she was now a mother. "You did all the work," she said. "Oh, Delia, she's beautiful. Perfect. What will you call her?"

"*He* was to be named Victor—" She broke off abruptly, as if she had been about to say a second name but stopped herself. She finished, "I shall have to think about it."

"Is there anyone I should send word to? Somebody is surely worrying about you."

"No. There is no one."

"How do you intend to take care of an infant and yourself without help? Look at your hands—you've never lifted a finger to do anything for yourself since the day you were born. And your clothes—I could eat for a year for the price of that cloak."

Delia's gaze flickered about the spartan room and came to rest on the table, where Maggie's ink bottle, pen, brushes, and paper still lay. "You're an artist?"

"It's just a hobby," Maggie answered defensively, echoes of her father's complaints that she wasted time and paper with her scribbling returning. "I have a job in a garment factory."

"You're not married?"

"Are you?"

Delia regarded her with half-closed eyes, a small smile curving her lips, her expression aloof, amused. There was a hint of decadence about her, Maggie thought, that was both intriguing and intimidating. For all her youth, here was a woman who would never play by others' rules. "No, thank God, I am not."

Maggie said, "I was married and widowed before I was twenty. He was lost at sea and I shall mourn him all the days of my life."

"That seems a waste of a young, attractive woman, unless like me your ambition lies elsewhere."

"I hope your ambition includes a way to take care of this baby," Maggie said. She couldn't take her eyes off the child. A tiny perfect human being, so sweet and helpless. She supposed she ought to place the infant in her mother's arms.

Looking up she saw that Delia was fast asleep.

Maggie lined a drawer with a blanket, then cut up one of her petticoats to swaddle the baby. She used her softest shawl as a receiving blanket. Placing the infant in the makeshift crib, Maggie curled up beside it on the floor.

Sometime during the night she awoke to the sound of a lullaby. Her groping hand found the infant was still in the drawer beside her, sleeping peacefully. In the dark room Delia lay in her bed singing a lullaby in the saddest, sweetest voice Maggie had ever heard. She felt a tear well up at the sheer haunting beauty of the human voice and was about to ask if Delia would like to have the baby beside her, when the singing stopped and Delia's deep, even breathing indicated she had again fallen asleep.

"Put the baby to your breast," Maggie ordered the next morning. Beyond the basement window the city street was still in the way only a busy place can be following the night's revelry. "Your milk isn't in yet, but the baby's suckling will help it come in."

Delia gave a faint grimace of distaste but opened her shift and allowed Maggie to put the infant to her breast. "And what if it doesn't come in? What shall we feed her?"

Maggie lit the stove and reached for a cast-iron skillet hanging on the wall. "We'll find a wet nurse. Babies don't do well on cow's milk. But your milk will come in, I'm sure."

"I'm very hungry."

"Good. There'll be eggs and fried bread in a minute, then

I must be off. I'll leave a sandwich by your bed, and I'll try
to get home early tonight."

"The baby's asleep. Where shall I put her?"

Maggie looked at her curiously. "Don't you want to hold
her?"

"She slept in that drawer over there, did she?"

Before she realized what Delia was about to do, she was
out of bed hobbling over to the makeshift crib.

"What are you doing? Get back into bed before you start
to hemorrhage."

Delia placed the sleeping baby in the drawer and straightened up, rubbing her lower back with her hands. "I'd rather
get up. Your bed is hard."

"You need a lying-in period. You're not a coolie giving
birth in a rice paddy."

Ignoring her, Delia slipped her fur-trimmed cloak around
her shoulders to ward off the morning chill, pulled a chair
close to the table, and slid into it. In the morning light almost
iridescent threads of lavender had appeared in her eyes, and
her hair was a halo of pale gold. Maggie had never before
seen such coloring. She had to ignore an urge to get out her
watercolors and try to capture Delia's image on paper.

"Did you say you had to leave?" Delia asked. "Don't you
have the day off? It's New Year's Day, or had you forgotten?"

"I work part-time as a maid for a rich family uptown when
they need extra help. They're receiving all day today."

Delia picked up one of Maggie's sketches. An India ink
and charcoal portrait of the old woman who sold needles and
thimbles on the street. "This is very good."

Maggie placed Delia's breakfast plate in front of her. "Did
you make any preparations for this baby at all? A layette?
Anything?"

She had to wait for an answer until Delia had taken several
bites of her food. "I suppose I never believed it was true.
That an infant would actually arrive."

"Well, she's here and she needs a layette. We can't buy
anything today, so we'll have to manage with my petticoat
and shawl. Tomorrow—if you have any money, because I
don't—I'll buy what she needs."

Maggie put on her coat and eased her calloused fingers into knitted wool gloves.

Delia glanced at her. "Aren't you going to have breakfast?"

"No time. Put the baby to your breast if she cries. She'll get some nourishment even before your milk comes in. You might sing her a lullaby, too. I don't believe I've ever heard a voice like yours. I'll see you this evening. Please try to rest."

The first day of the nineteen hundreds passed swiftly for Maggie. The family for whom she worked celebrated the New Year with a day-long open house, and she was kept busy. It was nearly eight o'clock that evening before she wearily made her way back to her basement room.

She began to feel uneasy when no glimmer of light showed through the window blinds. Unlocking the door, she stepped into the dark room. "Delia?"

There was no response from Delia, but at the sound of her voice a baby's hungry wail filled the air.

Stumbling in the direction of the cry, Maggie berated herself for not seeing all the signs that had been plainly in view. Delia had arrived with no layette for the infant, no change of clothing for herself. She'd given no surname, no information about who she was or where she came from. She had shown little interest in nursing her daughter. This morning she had insisted upon getting up. Delia had undoubtedly intended to abandon her baby all along. How long had she been gone? An hour? All day?

Maggie scooped up the baby and rocked her back and forth. The tiny girl quieted down. She felt very cold, so Maggie put her inside her coat next to her heart and massaged the tiny hands and feet.

It was awkward lighting the gas mantel with one hand, but she didn't want to put the baby down again. When the amber light filled the room, she looked first at the table. Her sketches lay at one end, Delia's breakfast plate, scraped clean, at the other. There was no note, no instructions.

The room was neat and Delia had made the bed. Maggie thought of those icy lavender-blue eyes, the silent stoicism with which Delia had endured a hellish labor, and shivered.

The baby in her arms whimpered again, and Maggie went

over in her mind the list of neighbors currently nursing infants. Most of them would urge her to take the abandoned baby to the nearest orphanage. But there was one who might be willing to give the poor mite a start in life. Hallie McDougall, who cheerfully dealt with a rambunctious brood of seven in addition to a new baby. The McDougalls occupied a first-floor apartment in the same brownstone where Maggie rented the basement room. Maggie's mother had delivered several of their babies, Maggie herself having delivered the last one.

Yes, Hallie would help out. But before taking the baby upstairs, she'd need dry swaddling.

Placing the baby on the bed in order to change her makeshift diaper, Maggie noticed a narrow leather strap dangling from beneath the pillow.

Delia's reticule. So, she had left something behind besides her baby.

Maggie pulled the reticule from beneath the pillow. As she had guessed, it was stuffed full of crisp banknotes.

Chapter 2

*

Hallie McDougall, a buxom redhead with a merry laugh
and twinkling hazel eyes, appeared oblivious to the loud but
good-natured squabbling of her brood as they set the dinner
table. Her four boys and three girls, all of whom had inherited her own flaming hair, ranged in age from fourteen down
to the newest addition, who suckled with noisy satisfaction at
her breast. At her other breast Delia's abandoned baby took
her feeding with dainty concentration.

"Will your husband mind?" Maggie asked anxiously,
glancing at the wall clock over Hallie's head to see how soon
the burly Drew McDougall might arrive home from his steve-
dore's job.

Hallie's infectious laugh rang out. "Go on with yer bother!
He'll never notice another one!"

Her own plump boy occupied most of her lap, while Delia's little girl curled under Hallie's well-rounded arm. The
newborn had delicate features and a soft sheen of fair hair
that would surely rub off within days. Drew McDougall
would have to be blind not to notice there was an interloper
in the nest, but Maggie made no comment. Hallie had leaped
at the opportunity to repay her for delivering her last baby six
months earlier.

"What kind of woman abandons a bairn as bonny as this
one?" she asked indignantly now.

"The most icily composed one I've ever seen," Maggie replied. "She never cried out once, never even whimpered. A
true stoic. Perhaps it takes someone that cold to be so brave."

Hallie regarded her admiringly, temporarily forgetting the
subject of their conversation. "You're so nicely spoken,
Maggie. Just like your ma was. Educated, she was, wasn't
she? A real lady. How'd she ever end up a midwife?"

Maggie was not about to explain that her mother, seduced and abandoned by her father, had stayed with the midwife who had delivered her, and, with no way to support herself and her baby, had remained to learn the ancient profession from her aging mentor. By the time Maggie's father returned, out of work and now ready to marry a woman who would support him, the old midwife was dead and her mother had a thriving practice. Ignoring the question, Maggie said, "Oh, I'll never be the lady my mother was, Hallie."

"Ah, but there's something about you, lass. Breeding is what I think it is. You got it from your ma. Your pa, now, he was a diamond in the rough."

"To say the least," Maggie murmured.

"Will you keep the bairn yourself, then? Och, I'll be glad to feed her for you, but you've got your job and you'll need your sleep at night. I could keep her during the day, but Drew can scarcely put up with this lot of his own when he comes home." She cast a rolling glance at her boisterous brood, who were slicing bread and placing a circle of chipped bowls around the table to receive the nearly meatless stew presently simmering on the stove. At least four of the children would stand for their meal, since the McDougalls did not own enough chairs to seat them all.

"Perhaps Delia will come back," Maggie said doubtfully. "Hallie—there's something else. She left a purse full of money. I don't know what to do with it."

Hallie snorted indelicately. "Keep it, that's what. Buy the bairn some clothes and a cradle."

"But there's over two hundred dollars!"

For possibly the first time in her life, Hallie was speechless. Drew was lucky to earn as much in a year.

"Something else is worrying me," Maggie went on. "Delia said she'd taken a horsecar here on New Year's Eve, but Mrs. O'Reilly next door told me that she'd heard Mrs. Lonnigan took in a boarder about three months ago, a fair-haired girl in the family way, who never left her room. She'd asked Mrs. Lonnigan if there was a midwife on the street."

"Delia?"

"More than likely. She left nothing behind in her room, so evidently didn't intend to go back, and she brought nothing with her when she came to me, so I don't know what happened to her belongings. But the frightening thing is—Mrs. O'Reilly heard that a well-dressed man arrived in a private carriage and went storming into Mrs. Lonnigan's demanding to know where his wife was. She said he scared Mrs. L. out of her wits, threatening to have her charged with harboring a fugitive."

Hallie pursed her lips. "Phew! You think the money's stolen?"

"I don't know. But if Delia *is* his wife—although she wasn't wearing a wedding ring—she obviously didn't want him to find her and the baby. I think I'll just bide my time and see if she comes back. And if the money's his, I think you're right. Their child deserves a layette, at least."

"Good girl," Hallie said approvingly. "Now let's hope nobody told the gent where you live."

The bleak days of January fell into a pattern for Maggie. She deposited the baby with Hallie before leaving for work, picked her up each evening, paying a small sum for this service. She had to give up her part-time maid's job, which meant money was tight as the new foreman at the factory had spitefully found ways to dock her wages after she refused to go out with him. Still, she resolutely left Delia's money intact except for buying baby clothes and a secondhand cradle.

Delia's baby seemed to have inherited not only her mother's pale hair and blue eyes, but also her fortitude. Hallie remarked wonderingly that she'd never seen such a "good" baby, who never cried or fussed despite the fact that she slept less than other infants.

It was Hallie who insisted upon naming her. "Patience, because that's what the sweet little mite is. She waits patiently for her turn. Not like that little hooligan of mine. Maggie, we have to call her something, so why not Patience?"

"Her mother was counting on a boy and had picked out the name Victor," Maggie answered. "Perhaps we should call her Victoria?"

"After that auld biddy on the throne?" Hallie grimaced. The McDougalls had been fervent proponents of Scottish home rule before emigrating. "*I*'m going to call her Patience."

Maggie grinned. "So be it."

At first every footfall to her doorstep caused Maggie to look up hoping Delia had come back, but as the days passed, long-suppressed maternal yearnings Maggie had not even known she possessed surfaced, and she began to feel ambivalent about Delia's return, since it would mean she would have to give up the baby. She found herself growing more attached to the tiny girl and dreading the day she would have to give her up.

People who saw her with the baby were quick to mention the difference in their coloring, the unspoken question being whether the fair-haired, blue-eyed baby could have come from a dark-haired, dark-eyed mother. Maggie usually muttered something about being a nanny.

But one day when she was in the butcher's shop, with Patience as usual the object of much admiration, to her own complete surprise Maggie answered, "Oh, my husband had sandy hair and blue eyes."

Will Nesbitt had indeed had sandy hair and blue eyes, and had been in his watery grave more than seven years. Her response said less about her incomplete marriage than about her feelings for the baby. She realized that she had secretly begun to hope Delia would not return.

January slipped away and February brought even more frigid weather. All of Hallie's children, then Patience, came down with colds. Maggie came home one night to find the tiny girl coughing and wheezing. Rushing her from the Mc-Dougalls' apartment to her own small room, Maggie quickly lit the stove and put on a pan of water in order to fill the room with warm steam. She walked the floor all night with Patience in her arms, making sure she could breathe.

At dawn she bundled the baby in blankets and reluctantly took her upstairs to Hallie. "You will watch her closely, won't you, Hallie? I think her cough is looser this morning, but you won't let her get chilled, will you? I'd stay home with her, but I daren't give Montrose any reason to fire me."

"That auld sod," Hallie said, taking the baby from her. "Is he still after ye, then?"

"No, now he just tries to make my life a misery to me because I had the nerve to refuse him."

Hallie sighed. "They think a pretty young widow is fair game, Maggie. Ye should take another husband."

"If I ever found one who compared to Will, I would. But I'd rather be on my own than put up with most of the men I know. Must go, Hallie. Take good care of Patience for me."

Slushy snow on the streets slowed the horsecar, and Maggie was late. The roar of sewing machines assailed her as she walked into the long barrackslike room of the garment factory.

Montrose, the foreman, blocked her way. He regarded her with a malevolent stare. A big man with a pasty complexion contrasting sharply with a red-veined nose, he had a slack mouth that seemed to have settled into a permanent leer. Since the factory's owners rarely put in an appearance, Montrose was lord and master over the fifty women who labored in the unheated room at the closely packed machines, working the treadles with ill-shod feet, coaxing coarse material beneath stabbing needles with fingers swollen with chilblains, or risking amputation from the lethally sharp cutting machines.

Montrose pulled out his pocket watch and studied it.

Maggie said breathlessly, "I'm sorry I'm late—the snow—"

"Second time since Christmas," he observed, frowning and shaking his head as if confronted by a crime too heinous to ignore.

"I'll stay and make up the time tonight," Maggie said quickly, although the thought of being alone with him after hours was frightening. "I'm ten minutes late—I'll stay twenty, will that be all right?"

How she hated to beg, but knowing he could hire a dozen women willing to take her place left her little choice. He took his time before replying, "Very well. But this is your last warning. And today you'll pick up pins."

Maggie bit back a protest. The piecework sewing was poorly paid, but picking up pins, sorting scraps of cloth, sweeping floors, was the work of apprentice girls and earned only a pittance.

The day dragged interminably by. Maggie wished there was a way to get in touch with Hallie to see how the baby was faring, but the women were given only a ten-minute midday break.

Eventually the twelve-hour day ended, and one by one the

sewing machines were shut down and the women began to leave. Maggie worked at breakneck pace, hoping that if she picked up every pin, swept every inch of the floor clean, and boxed away the scraps, Montrose might take pity on her and only keep her behind for the ten minutes she'd missed that morning.

The foreman strode slowly down the narrow aisles between the machines, searching for any particle of lint or pin she might have missed, then nodded, satisfied. "You can clean my office now. And then, Little Miss High-and-Mighty who thinks she's better than everybody else can add up the time cards for me."

Out of the corner of her eye she saw the last of the other women leave. She didn't look at her boss as she went into his cramped office and began to sweep the floor. He followed, perched on the edge of his cluttered desk, and watched her. She avoided getting too close to him, knowing he would surely touch her if she did. There had been many other occasions when she had met him on one of the narrow aisles and he had deliberately pressed against her, or allowed his hand or elbow to brush across her breasts or hip. Since this had been in full view of the other women, Maggie daren't contemplate what he might do now they were alone. Her only hope, she decided, was to try to occupy the twenty minutes with busy work that might keep him at bay.

Glancing at the time cards carelessly tossed onto his desk, she said, "Maybe I should total them up before I dust off the furniture."

Without waiting for an answer, she went around to the back of his desk and sat down. She kept her head bent as she added the total of each woman's output, marking cents earned against pieces of work finished and adding the totals. She completed the last card and looked up at the clock on the wall. "I believe I've stayed twenty minutes now, Mr. Montrose. May I go?"

Slowly he rose from his perch on the edge of the desk.

Maggie covertly measured the distance to the door. If she could distract him for the time it would take to walk half a dozen steps ... "How's your wife, Mr. Montrose?" she asked, easing out of his chair and moving cautiously around the desk.

"My wife's none of your concern."

As if she hadn't heard, Maggie went on, "Expect Mrs. Montrose and the children are tired of the cold weather, aren't they? A lot of colds and coughs going around, too. I hope they're all keeping well."

She had almost reached the door when he caught her, one sinewy arm snaking around her waist and pulling her back against the hard thrust of his erection.

Desperately she grabbed the brass knob and tried to wrench open the door. Montrose's breath was hot against the nape of her neck, and the more she struggled, the tighter she was wedged between him and the door, making it impossible to pull it open.

He laughed unpleasantly as one of his hands gripped her breast, and she winced with pain. His other hand fumbled with her skirts. Maggie was angry as well as afraid. He was so much stronger than she, and since he was behind her, she couldn't rake his face with her fingernails.

The bodice of her gown tore under his relentless grappling, and as her breasts were freed, he greedily grabbed them in both hands.

Releasing the doorknob, Maggie jabbed backward with her elbows and had the satisfaction of connecting with his flabby stomach. He grunted, winded, and she spun around, shoving him away from her.

A second later she had the office door open and was racing through the workroom.

Montrose caught up with her as she opened the door to the street. She cried, "Oh, Mrs. Montrose—how nice to see you! Your husband's just leaving."

His footsteps skidded to a stop behind her. She sped out onto the street, not looking back as Montrose realized he'd been tricked and cursed her soundly.

Waiting for the horsecar that would take her home, she wondered miserably what would happen when she went to work the following day.

There was little cheer at the McDougall house, either, as the baby boy was howling at the top of his lungs, the next two up the stair-step family were screaming and punching, and the older five arguing about whose turn it was to wash the dishes. There was no sign of Hallie or Delia's baby.

Maggie looked around, a knot of fear forming. "Where's Patience? Where's your mother? Oh, dear lord, is the baby all right?"

Hallie's oldest son, a lanky freckle-faced lad named Duncan, detached himself from the melee. "Och, not to get yerself in a bother, Miz Nesbitt. Ma's just gone next door to get some syrup of figs for the wee one's cough."

"She took the baby out in this weather, at this time of night?" Maggie asked, angry and fearful. "She'll catch pneumonia!"

"Och, away with yer! She's well wrapped up."

"Pick up your baby brother and comfort him," Maggie called over her shoulder as she ran from the room.

Out on the stoop an icy wind took her breath away. Oh, God, she prayed, don't let Patience get pneumonia! Why couldn't Hallie have sent one of the older children for the syrup of figs?

Blinking, Maggie now saw that a closed carriage had parked in front of the brownstone. Since there was no sign of a visitor approaching the stoop, she looked down at the basement door to her own room.

A tall, well-dressed man wearing a black hat and black coat with an astrakhan collar stood on the bottom step. As she watched he raised an ebony cane with a silver knob and pounded on her door.

She called, "Who are you and what do you want?"

He looked up at her, and she was struck first by a pair of keenly penetrating eyes, a much darker blue than Delia's, but unlike her aloof gaze, this man's stare seemed to take in every detail of Maggie's appearance—indeed, she had the uneasy feeling he could see all the way through her.

Sweeping off his hat to reveal a high forehead and smooth dark hair, he announced, "I am Hugo Van Courtland. I wish to speak to Cordelia."

Chapter 3

*

Standing beside Van Courtland on the doorstep, Maggie realized just how tall he was. Well over six feet, she decided, with muscular bulk to his shoulders and chest. An imposing presence; confident, commanding, and more than a little intimidating. He waited for her to answer his question, or perhaps expected her to invite him inside.

She said calmly, "I have no idea where Cordelia is, or if I even know her."

"Oh, I believe you do." His voice was deep, resonant, well modulated.

When she didn't respond, he added, "You *are* Mrs. Nesbitt, are you not?"

She nodded.

"I was told that you delivered Cordelia's baby on New Year's Eve. May I speak to her?"

Maggie thought rapidly. She could not produce Delia and didn't want anyone to know she had the baby. Perhaps she could distract him with the money Delia had left behind.

"Wait here." Maggie unlocked her door and went inside. A moment later she returned with Delia's reticule.

"She left this behind. I . . . took a small sum from it, but the rest is here. She left the next day—New Year's—and I haven't seen her since. That, sir, is God's truth."

He glanced at the reticule, but did not take it from her. "She didn't tell you where she was going?"

"No, she didn't. Nor where she came from. Are you going to take her money from me or not?"

"If she left it behind, she no doubt intended it to be her payment to you for your services. Keep it. I am only interested in finding her."

Maggie cleared her throat. "Are you related to her?"

He paused. "No." Reaching into his inside pocket, he withdrew a slim leather wallet and a gold fountain pen. Extracting a card, he wrote something on it and handed it to her. "If you think of anything she said—anything at all—that might indicate where she was going, please let me know. I shall be at the hotel for a couple of weeks before returning home."

Maggie took the card and began to close the door. He started up the steps, then turned to look down at her. "The child—what was it? A boy or a girl?"

He had, of course, assumed that Delia had taken the baby with her. "A girl," Maggie replied, praying that Hallie would not suddenly appear with Patience in her arms.

Van Courtland's expression showed no reaction to this news. He put on his hat and went up the street. His coachman leaped to open the carriage door for him.

Maggie looked down at the card in her hand. Inscribed in gold following his name was an address in New Orleans, under which he had written the hotel and room number where he was staying in New York.

Heart thumping, she closed her door and slowly let out her breath.

Minutes later Hallie arrived, the baby in her arms. "Has he been here? Has he gone?"

"Yes. How did you know about him? Is that why you took the baby—how is she? Oh, give her to me, please."

"I kept the blanket over her face so she wouldn't breathe the cold air. Mrs. O'Reilly came and told me he was at the Lonnigans'. I thought it must be the gent who was there before. Then Duncan saw him at your door—he was here twice before you got home. I was terrified we'd be had up for kidnapping the bairn and afraid he might come knocking on my door, too."

"Thank you, Hallie. You did the right thing." Maggie put Delia's reticule on the table and took Patience from Hallie's arms. "I tried to give him the money, but he wouldn't take it. He said he wanted to find somebody named Cordelia. His name is Hugo Van Courtland, so I suppose that's her name. He didn't carry on or threaten me. I'm surprised Mrs. Lonnigan was so afraid of him."

She pulled the blanket away from the baby's face and

gasped. Patience was limp and dull-eyed, her skin a bluish tint, her breathing shallow.

Hallie said, "I'll go and fetch the doctor."

Maggie kept watch over the baby for the twenty-four hours it took for her to reach the crisis, not daring to sleep more than a few minutes at a time. The doctor diagnosed severe bronchitis verging on pneumonia and prescribed warm steam, a poultice for the tiny chest, cough syrup, and keeping the baby propped up to help her breathe.

During those hours Maggie gave little thought to anything but saving the baby's life. She sent word with one of the other women who worked at the garment factory that she was sick and would be back in a day or so.

On the morning of the third day the doctor returned, listened with his stethoscope to Patience's breathing, and pronounced her out of danger.

After the doctor departed, along with ten dollars from Delia's reticule, Maggie contemplated taking Patience up to Hallie and going to work, but she was reluctant to leave the baby and was so exhausted herself she doubted she would be able to sew even a minimum quota for the day. She decided to stay home one more day.

Late that afternoon Maggie, half-asleep, sat beside the baby's cradle and faced the fact that she had no intention of ever giving the child up. The decision brought a great sense of relief. Now she could make plans for their future.

The first order of business would be to move to a place where neither Delia nor Hugo could find them. Maggie still felt uncomfortable using the money Delia had left, but judging by her clothes and carelessness with money, she could well afford to give her child a start in life. Maggie decided to forfeit the balance of the rent she'd already paid, find another room, and hire someone to move her furniture right away. She wouldn't go too far, since she wanted Hallie to continue to care for the baby. The main thing would be to be sure the Van Courtlands didn't suspect that the midwife still had the baby.

While Patience slept, Maggie began to pack. She would have to go back to work tomorrow and hoped she could find a room the following evening. She was wrapping her mother's china cups in tea towels when a loud knocking on the door awoke the baby.

Without thinking, Maggie opened the door.

Montrose stood on the threshold, and before she could recover from her surprise, he pushed past her into the room.

Fearing the effect of the icy blast of wind on the sick baby, Maggie closed the door and faced him.

He glanced about the room, his small cunning eyes lingering for a moment on the whimpering infant, then he grinned at Maggie. "Sick, are you? Giving birth to a bastard, I'd say."

"You know that isn't true. . . ." Maggie began.

"Whose baby is it, then?"

"That's none of your business," Maggie said. "If you've come to fire me for being absent, then do it."

"Absenteeism is certainly grounds. An illegitimate child won't go over well with the boss, either. But maybe if you're nice to me, I'll let you come back to work."

"Get out," Maggie said. "You have no right to come in here."

He took a step toward her. She backed behind a chair. The room was small. If she fought him there was a danger of crashing into the baby's cradle. Perhaps she could persuade him to leave peacefully.

Forcing a smile, she said wheedlingly, "The baby's very sick. The doctor says it might be contagious. I didn't want to bring the sickness to you and the others."

Snorting in derision, Montrose reached for her.

Maggie lifted the solid wood chair and, with a strength she hadn't known she possessed, hurled it at him. He staggered for a moment, spinning dazedly, then crashed to the floor. Maggie bent and scooped up the baby and fled.

Minutes later she was pounding on Hallie's door.

"Go and find a policeman," she told Duncan. "Tell him there's a man in my room."

"Dear lord in heaven!" Hallie exclaimed. "Van Courtland, is it?" She gave Duncan, who stood with his mouth hanging open, a sharp push. "Away with ye, ye great lout. Get the copper!"

"Montrose," Maggie said breathlessly, sinking into the chair Hallie offered and rocking the baby to soothe her. "I've lost my job for sure now, Hallie."

"Lucky for you you've got the money Delia left. That's more than enough to tide you over."

Maggie jumped to her feet in alarm. "Oh, no! The money—it's still in her reticule lying in plain sight on the tallboy. I was packing and I—here, Hallie, take the baby. I must go back before Montrose sees it."

She sped from the room, and Hallie yelled for her next oldest son to go with her and watch out for her.

Maggie's door gaped open, and she went into her room with a sinking heart. Although less than five minutes had elapsed, Montrose had left. Delia's reticule was also gone.

Despair washed over Maggie. Even if she reported the theft to the police, Montrose would deny he was ever there. It would be her word against his. The enormity of her dilemma assailed her. Jobs were so hard to get, and in the past Montrose had made sure any woman who angered him did not get a job in any of the other garment factories. The only other alternative was domestic service, but no household would hire a live-in servant with an infant, and they couldn't survive on occasional day work.

Maggie made her way slowly back up to Hallie's apartment to pick up Patience. Of one thing she was certain. She would never give up the baby.

Chapter 4

*

DELIA

There were three brothers, you see. One desired me, one loved me, and, I fear, one hated me.

Delia opened her eyes and looked into the impersonal gaze of a stout middle-aged woman wearing a starched white uniform. Behind her a small room with a high barred window on one wall came slowly into focus. Her wrists were tied with gauze strips to the steel rails enclosing her narrow bed.

Blinking against the sudden onslaught of daylight, Delia attempted to speak, but her parched mouth could not seem to form the words. Her mind was filled with blurred, half-recalled images she strove to capture and study, but the effort was too great.

How weak she was! She could not even summon the strength to tug at the restraints on her wrists. She felt fiery hot and icy cold at the same time, and every bone in her body must surely protrude from her shrunken flesh, so that it seemed only her skeleton lay on the hard mattress.

"So you're awake at last," the white-uniformed woman said. "You've been very ill."

She dipped a cloth in a bowl of water on the bedside table and wiped Delia's mouth. The moisture against her cracked lips was like nectar, and Delia eagerly opened her mouth to lick the cloth, but it was snatched away.

"The doctor will be in to see you shortly," the nurse said.

Delia wanted to beg her for a drink of water, and to please untie her wrists, but could manage only a dry croak.

Alone again, Delia tried to organize her thoughts and memories into recognizable order. But recent events eluded her, and only echoes from the past penetrated the fog....

God doesn't know where we live, Delia, so don't bother asking Him for help.

Don't you think I'd stop the babies coming if I could? Do you think I like hearing them wail with hunger, watching the rickets start?

Who is that singing? By the saints, woman, you should put her to sing on the street corner with a hat in front of her.

Oh, God, oh, dear God, help us, he's dead! What will become of us now? Delia, if you run and hide I'll tell them you did it. You're only his stepdaughter, and everybody knows he beat you worse than any of us. I can't go to prison. Who'll take care of the babies? Just for a week or two, pet, until we can find somewhere to go.

No use looking for your ma, Delia, she's dead and gone. Not three days after your pa. Your little brothers? Scattered to orphanages and parish homes.

You duck down behind somebody with a big suitcase, see, then slip on the train and keep two cars ahead of the conductor.

How old is she? She has a child's body, but her eyes are ancient. He will only pay for a virgin.

I can make you the toast of two continents.

You can't waste your talent, Delia. Damn it to hell, I won't allow you to throw yourself away.

Is it Hugo's? Damn, why am I asking? Of course it's Hugo's.

A man wearing a soiled white coat, a stethoscope dangling from his neck, entered the room. He had a carefully clinical expression and wore gold-rimmed glasses. He pressed the stethoscope to her chest briefly, then told the nurse to untie her wrists.

"May I have a drink of water, please?" Delia's voice cracked horribly.

The doctor nodded, and the nurse poured water from a chipped pitcher on the bedside table. Delia attempted to sit up but was too weak. The nurse slipped her hand under her head and held a metal cup to her lips.

Sinking back onto her pillow, Delia surreptitiously slipped her hand under the sheet to feel her abdomen. It felt curiously slack and empty, despite a tightly wrapped binder. So it was true. It was all over. The months of growing a new life inside her had indeed come to an end. The pain of her labor had not been a nightmare.

Try as she might, Delia could not picture the baby's face. She looked up at the doctor. "Am I in an asylum?"

"No, not at all. This is a private nursing home. We had to restrain you because you were delirious with fever. You've had a severe case of toxemia. You're a very lucky young woman to have survived it. Nurse Markham will bathe you and bring you a tray shortly. But first we must tell your husband you're feeling better. He's been here every single day. I'll send him in."

Delia closed her eyes. *Her husband.* Naturally Julian would say she was his wife. She willed herself to face him calmly.

Both the doctor and the nurse withdrew. Delia waited. It would be Julian's style to delay his grand entrance, in order to build suspense and dread. The ploy worked with most people, but Delia had long ago taught herself never to show fear, nor even discomfort. She'd learned at a very early age that if the tyrants of the world were denied the spectacle of their victims cowering or pleading for mercy, then their victory was a hollow one.

At least ten minutes dragged slowly by before Julian strode into the room. As always, he was impeccably dressed. He handed his hat, gloves, and cane to the nurse who followed as though she were a valet, and said brusquely, "You may go."

He stood beside the bed, surveying Delia with a slight frown. His features weren't as perfectly balanced as those of his brothers and perhaps reflected a coarser sensuality. His hooded eyes, cynical expression, and the sprinkling of gray in his dark hair made him look older than his thirty-two years.

"You look like a scarecrow," he said at length.

"And you look like what you are. The devil incarnate," she rejoined, meeting his stare unblinkingly. "One day I will probably kill you, Julian."

He smiled. "Good. The old Delia hasn't been completely obliterated by motherhood. I feared a softening of the hard edges."

"I suppose you took the baby to Hugo. What did he say?"

"What did you expect him to say?"

"Do you know how infuriating it is when you answer a question with another question?"

"You mean, as you just did?" Julian chuckled.

"I'm too weak to spar with you, Julian. I'm ravenously hungry. Will you order some food? Then tell the wardress I must bathe."

"Of course." He turned to leave and then looked back and said, "In two days we'll be aboard our private railroad car, and you, my sweet, will be on your way to fulfilling your destiny."

Nurse Markham handed her two gauze pads to place over her oozing nipples. "Your milk will dry up in a day or two. Try not to drink too much. I must tighten your binder now."

The nurse's fingers were ice cold. She pulled the flannel binder cruelly taut across Delia's stomach and pinned it in place. Delia welcomed the twinge of physical pain. It helped alleviate another yearning that unexpectedly surfaced.

"You must do this for yourself when you leave tomorrow. You're thin as a stick, but you must tighten up those stomach muscles if you want to get your figure back. Wear the binder for at least six weeks."

"Nurse ... when Mr. Van Courtland brought me here— was the baby with me? Did you see her? Was she all right?"

The older woman gave her a guarded, almost frightened glance. "I wasn't on duty that night." She gathered up the wash basin and towels and left.

Delia steeled herself to roll to the edge of the bed. She sat up and lowered her feet to the floor. She waited until the room stopped spinning, then stood up slowly. A squeezing sensation behind her eyes, a wave of nausea, and she was flat on her back on the bed again.

She lay still for a minute, then tried again. This time she managed to walk to the door. Panting, she tried the knob. The door was locked. It took all of her remaining strength to return to the bed. Lying limply, shivering but too weak to pull the covers over her, she accepted the fact that it would be impossible to get in touch with Hugo before she left.

Some of the blanks in her memory had filled in. She now recalled the tortuous path she had taken to the basement room of the midwife. What was her name? Maggie something.

Large, grave eyes, richly brown, and great masses of hair the color of a sleek sorrel racehorse the Van Courtlands owned. Capable hands, a compassionate voice, more educated than she would have imagined a midwife to be. A lovely complexion. She had been shocked by Maggie's youth, having expected a wrinkled crone who would bully her. But of course, Maggie had only been the daughter of the midwife.

Looking back, Delia realized she had felt stronger the day after she gave birth than she did now. According to Markham, she'd been here more than a week, the first days lost in a delirium of fever that also blotted out some of the details of giving birth and the first day of the new year.

She struggled to recall what had happened, knowing that she had intended to be gone before Maggie returned that day, indeed had been preparing to leave when Julian arrived. She remembered going to answer the door, the sudden blast of icy wind, the tall Van Courtland figure looming over her, the stinging slap to her cheek . . . and then everything became confused.

Angry words, the baby crying, threats and recriminations, her own voice swearing to keep her part of the bargain if he would take the baby to Hugo. She remembered Julian's hooded gaze, his rage at seeing the proof of her perfidy, the names he had called her, and how she had flown at him, raking his arrogant face with her fingernails. He had pushed her away, and she stumbled and fell. She recalled sudden violent pain and a rush of warm blood from inside her, then oblivion. After that there had been only fever dreams.

Tomorrow they would board the Van Courtland private railroad car for the long journey across the country to San Francisco. She supposed it was meant to be. She wasn't strong enough to go to Hugo today. Rosy fantasies of Hugo seeing her with the baby and declaring he could not let her go away with his brother faded before the reality of her physical limitations. Besides, she couldn't risk Julian carrying out his threats against the people she cared most about in the world.

She attempted to direct her thoughts to the fame and fortune Julian swore awaited her, but knew in her heart that she would sacrifice it all to stay with Hugo. Had she seriously expected him to take her and the baby under his wing, that he would somehow make everything right again? There was no hope of that kind of a miracle.

But surely he would care for the child. He must. After all, he was the only one capable of dealing with the hereditary quirks that would undoubtedly manifest themselves in her daughter, as they had in two previous generations.

Chapter 5

*

Delia had been twelve when Julian Van Courtland and several of his student friends heard her singing beneath the wrought-iron balcony of the Cajun Club in the French Quarter of New Orleans.

"My God! Will you listen to that!" Julian had stopped dead in his headlong dash up the stairs to the girls' rooms. On the ground floor of the club black musicians played their new melodies, creating an oddly appealing harmony that some called "ragged." Delia shaped her songs to accompany the ragtime.

"Oh, come on, Julian, it's just some ragamuffin begging in the gutter. There are girls waiting to be jazzed."

"Go on up without me," Julian said, peering into the shadows where Delia crouched, a battered felt hat upturned on the cracked pavement in front of her.

The sweet, sad song faltered as he moved closer. He dropped a silver dollar into the hat, and startled by the princely sum, she stammered, "Ooh . . . thank you, sir."

"Where did you learn to sing like that, little girl?"

"I've got a lot of baby brothers. I used to sing to them when they were hungry and wouldn't sleep."

"That was no lullaby. That was a torch song. Who taught you that?"

Sensing danger, she grabbed the hat and squirmed back into the shadows. "I dunno, mister. You go 'way and leave me now or I'll yell for my ma."

"Your mother is upstairs?" He jerked his head upward toward the balcony.

Delia nodded. She greatly admired the ladies who worked in the rooms above the club, with their exotic looks and fancy clothes, and would have been proud to claim kinship with any of them.

She inched along the wall toward the Cajun Club's courtyard and was poised to make a dash into the club when he seized her arm and stopped her.

"Not so fast. I'm not going to hurt you. I'm curious about you. I happen to know that all the girls upstairs are high yellows. You didn't get that pale hair and magnolia skin from one of them. Who are you, and where did you come from?"

She was almost frightened enough to scream the truth. *I came from New York 'cos there was a terrible fight and my pa got dead and my ma told me to run, though we were both hitting him 'cos he was drunk and going to throw the new baby out the window. Ma said if I ran they'd put the blame on me on account I was only his stepdaughter, and then she'd be able to take care of the little brothers. But she died, too, and I didn't want to go to an orphanage. I sneaked on a train and ended up in St. Louis.*

The memory of the interval between St. Louis and her arrival on the streets of New Orleans intruded then and she shivered. She shouted, "Let me go," and kicked him in the shins.

Caught by surprise, he grunted with pain and released her. She ran through the courtyard into the club, dodging between the tightly packed benches, trying to disappear in the blue swirls of tobacco smoke.

The following night he came back. This time he stood a respectful distance away and waved another dollar at her. "Just talk to me for a minute—"

Delia fled, but he cut her off at the entrance to the club. She wheeled around and raced up the wrought-iron stairs to the balcony.

Stumbling onto the balcony, Delia was caught in a pair of silken-smooth arms and found herself crushed to a perfumed bosom. "Whoa! Hold up there, honey! You cain't come up here!"

Heavy footsteps clattered up the iron stairs.

"Please don't let him get me," Delia begged.

As her pursuer reached the top of the stairs, her rescuer pushed her through a French door into a darkened room.

Delia scrunched herself under a bed covered with a satin

quilt, aware of spicy scents and the muted murmur of laughter and other sounds, some baffling, that penetrated the walls. Out on the balcony the woman engaged the man in conversation, snatches of which Delia caught.

". . . oughta be ashamed. Just a chile . . ."

"With the voice of a sophisticated chanteuse."

"She's long gone. Hey, you want a little fun, baby? Y'all go next door . . . I'm fixin' to take a break right now."

"Just tell me who she is. Can you imagine that voice with training . . ."

"You'd better go now, mister."

"Don't tell me she belongs to you—you're not old enough. Or to any of the other girls for that matter—she's too fair."

"If'n y'all don't leave right this minute, I'll yell for the bouncer."

The voices faded into the night.

Minutes later the French door opened, and Delia was aware of the perfumed swish of a filmy negligee. A lamp was lit, and high-arched feet in feather-trimmed mules appeared beside the bed. "Where you hidin', honey? You kin' come out now. He's gone."

Cautiously Delia crawled out from under the bed. She looked up at the most beautiful woman she had ever seen. A shiny black curtain of hair fell to an exquisitely tiny waist, large amber eyes fringed with lustrous lashes slanted above high-chiseled cheekbones, generously full lips curved into a reassuring smile. Although the man had said all of the Cajun Club girls were high yellows, Delia had been in New Orleans long enough to recognize that she was looking at a woman more Creole than Mulatto.

"Thank you for letting me in," Delia said.

"What's your name, sugar?" The singing lilt of a Caribbean island lingered in her speech, overlaid with the local patois she had no doubt picked up from the other girls.

"Delia. It's short for Cordelia." She paused, reluctant to give her last name in case the police were still looking for her, then, seeking a reasonable sounding alias as a surname, used the name of the square below. "Delia Jackson."

"I'm Mignon Chamond. Where's your folks, Delia?"

"Don't have none."

"You ain't from these parts. You run away from home?"

"No. I told you. I don't have a home."

"Where you been sleeping?"

Delia shrugged.

"I'm gonna give you a blanket and a pillow. Y'all curl up out there on the balcony until I get off work, then you can come home with me."

Disappointed, Delia asked, "You don't live here?" The lamplight had revealed, to her eyes, a most luxurious room, with gold flocked wallpaper, yards of lace adorning a handsome four-poster bed, and an elegant china bowl and pitcher on the marble-topped washstand.

Mignon chuckled softly. "No, honey, this is where I work."

Unaccustomed to the warmth and comfort of a blanket and pillow, Delia promptly fell asleep and was awakened by Mignon gently shaking her. A pink-silver dawn was breaking over the now quiet city. "Come on, honey, time to go home."

Delia was never sure about the exact relationship of all of the people who lived in the ramshackle frame house on a misty bayou downriver from the city. They were all ages, all colors. The elite of the household were, or had been, entertainers and musicians. Some now eked out a living fishing, others scavenging or dealing in secondhand goods. She suspected a few of them occasionally made their living by other less legal means. Some were boarders, who came and went, others seemed to be family. They cheerfully rearranged pallets and belongings to stretch sleeping space to the maximum, tossing more beans into the gumbo and squabbling noisily about who got to collect the rent from each new arrival. The patriarch of the clan was a venerable octagenerian named Daddy Lou, who, Mignon informed her, had formerly worked on the riverboats and could blow a horn like Gabriel himself.

When Mignon dragged home the skinny little blond waif, she announced, "I done found this one sleeping on the street outside the club. And y'all know what'll happen to her if she catches the eye of one of the gentleman callers."

"What can she do to earn her keep?" The question came from a tall, statuesque woman with a complexion the color of creamy coffee and features that might have graced an Egyptian coin. The extended family and their boarders, Delia noted, came in every shade, from the Creole-pale Mignon to coal-black Daddy Lou.

Delia shyly produced the thirty-five cents she had collected in her hat outside the Cajun Club the evening before. "I can sing."

"This girl's got a voice that sends shivers down your spine, Eulie," Mignon said, adding with some glee, "She'll give you a run for your money someday."

Eulie, whom Delia decided had to be an Egyptian princess, narrowed her eyes. "We don't need no chillun to care for, 'specially no white girl-chile. Who knows who'll come looking for her?"

"She's an orphan. Let her stay until we can find someplace else for her," Mignon pleaded. "Go on, honey, sing for them."

Eulie folded her arms across her ample bosom and gave Delia a show-me stare.

Delia began to sing, hesitantly at first and barely able to make herself heard above the clatter of dishes and conversation from what seemed to be dozens of people.

Gradually the room fell silent, and when the last notes drifted away in the humid air, there was a long moment when no one uttered a sound. They stared at the fragile girl as though she were a mirage.

Then Daddy Lou slowly got to his feet and shuffled over to her. He reached out with a hand that now trembled with age and touched her pale hair. "Make room for this chile, she'll be staying with us for a spell."

Nobody questioned the decision.

Although Mignon had taken Delia under her wing, it soon became obvious that the two people who were going to be the strongest influence on her future were Daddy Lou and Eulie, although in Eulie's case the help was given reluctantly.

The evening of her arrival Delia asked Mignon to take her back to town with her so she could sing in Jackson Square, but Daddy Lou said, "Y'all won't be going to N'Orleans tonight, Delia. You and me and Eulie got work to do."

"But ... if I don't go and sing on the square, I won't be able to pay to stay here."

"Don't worry 'bout that none. We got some work to do before you sing agin." He turned and boomed, "Eulie, y'all get on in here."

Eulie appeared in the doorway, her tall impressive figure clad in a brightly colored cotton gown, a red bandanna on her head, necklaces and bracelets of wooden beads clicking as she moved.

"Now, Delia," Daddy Lou said, "Eulie here sings the gospel, and I been a horn player all my life, and we'ins is fixin' to teach you all we know. See, sugar, you got a big talent already, but it needs to grow. Y'all think of a seed in the ground—it's gotta have water and sun, don't it? Eulie and me, we's going to be your water and sun."

"Not me," Eulie said flatly. "After I done made my pralines and hawked 'em round town, I barely got time for choir practice."

"Y'all kin give up some choir practice."

"You're a crazy old man to let that child stay. How'd you know she ain't got family looking for her? You want us all to go to jail?"

"Hush yo' mouth, woman. She done tole us she's an orphan. While this chile is heah, we'll teach her what we know."

"Well, I cain't start now. I'm singing solo tonight."

Daddy Lou's sunken eyes gleamed ominously. "Sure you can, Eulie. Take her with you. Her first lesson can be to hear the gospel sung lak only you can do it."

Eulie hesitated, then crossed the room in three angry strides, looked down contemptuously at Delia and said, "She's ingrained with filth. I doubt I'll get her clean in time."

An hour later, scrubbed within an inch of her life, clad in a hastily cut-down print cotton frock, her damp hair wrapped in a blue bandanna, Delia accompanied Eulie and Daddy Lou to the First Baptist Chapel of the Saints and listened, spellbound, to Eulie's rich contralto lead the choir.

The rafters shook and the floor bounced as feet stamped and hands clapped in unison with the voices raised in joyful praise of the Lord. Wide-eyed, Delia watched and listened. How different this service was from the somber ritual of the Catholic Church!

"See how Eulie's voice is stronger than all the others?" Daddy Lou whispered in her ear. "Y'all know why? It's on account she knows how to *breathe*. She uses her voice like an instrument, see—jes' like I blow my horn. That's what you're gonna learn, sugar."

When they returned home, Eulie complained she was all wore out and in no mood to mess around with singing lessons. Daddy Lou fixed her with a stern stare until she dropped into a chair and motioned for Delia to approach her.

Delia did so with some trepidation.

Eulie's hand connected, not gently, with her midsection. It would be some time before Delia would identify it as her diaphragm.

"Right there is where your voice starts. Let me feel you breathe." Delia took a breath. Eulie snorted derisively and gave her a slight shove.

"Come here, sugar," Daddy Lou said. He was removing a gleaming brass trumpet from a battered leather case. After wiping off the mouthpiece with his sleeve, he handed it to her. "Blow me a note, baby."

To her mortification, although she blew with all her strength, no sound came from the trumpet.

"That's all right, honey. Eulie and me, we're going show you how."

"She's too thin," Eulie said grumpily. "She ain't never going to be a singer. Ain't got no power in that stick body."

"You're jes' jealous," Daddy Lou said. He winked at Delia.

It was unusual for everyone to leave the house simultaneously, but several weeks after her arrival, Delia arose one morning to find only Daddy Lou prowling around the house closing the shutters.

There was a peculiar tension in the air, and the sky was an angry copper color.

"Big storm coming," Daddy Lou said, and he sounded worried. "The others they's seeing to the boats. Mignon stayed in town last night, and Eulie's over to the church to help out there. Y'all grab some food and git on upstairs. I'll be up soon."

Delia found some hush puppies left over from the previous night's meal, some cold grits from Daddy Lou's breakfast, and several pralines Eulie had been unable to sell the previous day. She placed the food in a basket, then added half a bottle of milk from the big old wooden ice box and climbed the stairs, feeling excited, like she was going on a picnic.

Daddy Lou had not yet shuttered the landing window, so she put the basket down and peered through the mottled glass.

As she watched, the storm swept up the river. The first gust of wind shrieked toward them, bending the trees double, tearing strands of Spanish moss loose so that they swirled aloft like ghosts.

The gale struck the house with such force that it shook on its foundations. The rain followed the wind, a deluge such as Delia had never seen, and she quickly realized why Daddy Lou had sent her upstairs. The river was already high, and would surely flood its banks under the onslaught of rain as heavy as this.

"Git away from that glass!" Daddy Lou's voice yelled up to her as he started up the stairs.

Delia leaped back as the window rattled under the onslaught of the storm. Wind and rain were tearing the world asunder in a violent symphony of destruction that was somehow wildly beautiful. The doomsday music of the hurricane made her skin tingle and excitement surge along her veins. Her last view of the outside world was of gray moss standing up straight on the cypresses like plumes of smoke and the river already splashing toward the porch.

"Up to the attic," Daddy Lou's breath wheezed alarmingly, and he gasped out the words as he slammed the shutters closed.

They huddled together in the attic with the rain pelting the roof and unseen objects thudding into the house. She felt afraid now because she could not see what was happening outside and the din prevented conversation. But Daddy Lou kept his arm around her shoulders reassuringly.

Then all at once, as though silenced by the baton of some almighty orchestra leader, everything stopped. Only the dripping of water from the eaves could be heard.

"What happened?" Delia whispered.

"We's in the eye," Daddy Lou answered. "Pretty soon the other side of the storm will catch up with us." He climbed stiffly to his feet. "You wait here, sugar. I'm going downstairs to fetch up some more vittles before the water gits too high."

"I'll go help you—"

"No," he said sharply. "Stay here. I can heah water sloshing around down there. No telling what come in with it."

She felt very alone and frightened after his footsteps faded into the eerie silence. She stood up and walked around the attic, which was the bedroom of a pair of boarders who surely must have to stoop beneath the sloping ceiling.

After a while she went to the door and leaned down into the stairwell. "Daddy Lou? When are you coming back up?"

There was no response.

A moment later the storm resumed in all its fury. From somewhere below came the sound of shattering glass as windows exploded under the onslaught of the wind. Delia cried out in fright.

What had happened to Daddy Lou? She began to worry. He was old and not steady on his feet. At length, unable to bear the suspense, she climbed down the attic ladder and started down the staircase.

Brackish water was already lapping halfway up the stairs. She paused, peering through the banisters. Soggy sofa cushions and bric-a-brac floated by. The windowpanes and shutters had given way. River water had flooded the rooms, bringing with it broken branches and several dead birds.

"Daddy Lou?" Delia shouted over the roar of the wind. She thought she heard a faint response, from the direction of the kitchen.

Shivering with fear, she lowered herself gingerly into the water, which was waist-high and rising. Reaching the kitchen door she saw that the wooden icebox had fallen across the corner of the room, pinning Daddy Lou to the wall. Only his head and one arm protruded above the capsized icebox.

Catching sight of her, he yelled, "Go back upstairs! Stay up there. I cain't git my leg free, so I'll just bide here. Don't worry none. I'll be all right. Go on, git!"

She held on to the doorjamb, wondering what to do, feeling the rush of water try to take her feet out from under her. She clearly wasn't strong enough to move the icebox. But what if the water rose over Daddy Lou's head?

Something moved between them in the dark water, swimming frantically, coiling toward the icebox. Delia's cry of alarm was lost in the howling wind. A snake . . . oh, dear Jesus, a cottonmouth!

Kitchen towels still hung from a rail on the wall, and almost without thinking, Delia grabbed the largest towel and plunged toward the snake. Holding two corners of the towel in each hand, she flung it over the snake's head and pulled the reptile into a writhing bundle.

Holding it as far away from her body as she could, she struggled back into the living room. Windows on both sides of the room had now blown out, and the river poured through the front and out through the back in a swift current. She tossed the towel with its lethal cargo into the rushing water and watched it disappear, then went back to the kitchen.

"You hold on, Daddy Lou!" she shouted. "I'm going for help!"

Afterward, she was never sure how she made her way through the buffeting wind and soaking rain, dodging floating logs, clinging to the roots of cypress, ever fearful of encountering more cottonmouths. She saw swamp rabbits and even a bobcat crouched in the kneelike root of a cypress, looking wet and stunned, oblivious of the easy prey nearby.

A shrimp boat tossed violently at its moorings but appeared to be intact. Several splintered planks testified to the fact that other boats had not been spared. There was no sign of any of the men. She struggled on, knowing their nearest neighbor was around the next bend in the river, under normal circumstances not a great distance, but a daunting journey through what was surely a tempest.

Then, without warning, there was no ground under her feet. She was swimming for her life.

"Holy Mary, Mother of God, help me," she prayed desperately, feeling the current pick her up and carry her.

Debris swirled around her in the water, poking and prodding and tearing her skin.

A log floated by and she seized a protruding branch and held on. She was black and blue, gasping for breath, by the time the log caught on a tangle of fallen trees and the smashed wooden porch of their neighbor's house.

She screamed at the top of her lungs but had little hope of making herself heard inside the shuttered house over the howling storm.

Her hair clung wetly to her face, and she choked as a huge clump of moss wrapped itself around her head. Then all at once strong arms grasped her and pulled her from the log. "It's all right, you're safe," a deep voice said close to her ear. "Let's get you into the house."

"No, no! Daddy Lou's trapped—the icebox fell and he's going to drown. You've got to help him!" she shrieked, then promptly fainted.

She opened her eyes and looked into Mignon's concerned gaze. The first thing that struck her was the silence. No more howling wind and rattling rain. They were in Mignon's upstairs bedroom. "Daddy Lou?" Delia asked, struggling to sit up.

"He's all right—sleeping right now. Got a busted leg and some bruises, but he's a tough old critter. He'll be just fine. He's so proud of you, honey. Says you saved his life. He saw you grab that cottonmouth, and if you hadn't fetched Big Jim to move that icebox, the old man would've drowned."

Relieved that the old man was safe, Delia turned her attention to the state of her own health. "I never passed out before. What ails me?"

"I 'spects all that's wrong with you, sugar, is that you missed breakfast, had a lot of excitement, and had to swim for your life. I got some nice soup ready for you, that'll fix you up."

"You sure Daddy Lou's all right? Can I go see?"

"Sure, baby. I don't guess nothing's gonna wake him."

Delia jumped out of bed. Her leg crumpled under her, and she sprawled on the floor. Baffled, she looked up at Mignon, who quickly dropped to her knees beside her. Her fingers went to Delia's ankle. "Guess the doc missed this. Looks like you sprained it."

Delia looked at her puffy black-and-blue ankle with interest. Guiltily she hoped she would now be allowed to stay until it healed. Downstairs might be under water, windows and doors were gone, and the house had been ramshackle to begin with, but Delia had never felt more safe than she did here.

Chapter 6

*

The entire Van Courtland family burst into Delia's life three months after she moved in with Daddy Lou, Eulie, Mignon, and the others. The occasion was what Mignon grandly referred to later as Delia's "debut," and it came about by a whim of fate.

"The Van Courtlands' butler done passed over," Daddy Lou announced early one morning.

To Delia he explained, "Mr. Van Courtland senior and his butler Henry used to come up to St. Louis on the paddle wheeler when I played on the river years ago. Old gempum's been dead and gone for years, but Henry, he stayed on. He's a member of our church. Mr. Hugo Van Courtland wants me to lead Henry's parade and Eulie to sing at the service."

Delia knew all about the colorful funeral parades through the streets of New Orleans. The marching musicians played a mournful dirge on the way to the cemetery but a cheerful on-to-glory for the departed on their return. "Who's Mr. Hugo Van Courtland?"

"Owns half of N'Orleans," Mignon said. "Carpetbaggers who come in from Europe during the war. I ain't never laid eyes on any of 'em, but I heard plenty." She was buffing her long fingernails to a fine sheen, sitting with her slender legs curled under her on a faded cretonne-covered couch that still smelled faintly of swamp water from the soaking it had suffered in the hurricane.

"Well, now, ole Henry said they owns barges and boats and a whole mess of property, *in*cluding the Courtland Concert Hall that weren't doing so good so it's shut down right now. The second Mrs. Van Courtland fancied herself what they call a patron of the arts before her husband passed on. She and her boys don't spend much time in town these days. Only Mr.

Hugo keeps a place in N'Orleans and takes care of the family business. He's the first wife's son," Daddy Lou said. "The ole man done bought one of them plantation houses 'way out on a bayou. Folks say he wanted a place where that youngest son of his could be hid."

"Why?" Delia asked, intrigued. "What's wrong with him?"

Daddy Lou shrugged. "He's strange in the head, they say. And the other one's as wild as they come. Reckon Mr. Hugo, he's had his hands full keeping them two brothers of his out of trouble."

"You cain't lead no parade," Eulie put in. "How you going to lean on your stick and blow your horn at the same time?"

Daddy Lou gave her a sly grin. "Don't need no stick any more. My shinbone's all mended up. Good as new."

"Why, you old rascal!" Mignon exclaimed. "You just been using it to play on our sympathy, huh?"

Delia, listening and observing, knew that the leg Daddy Lou had broken, and which had only recently been released from its plaster of paris prison, was far from good as new. When he was tired he relied on the walking stick to get about. She decided that leading Henry's funeral parade must be very important to Daddy Lou.

Since the funeral was to take place in two days, both Daddy Lou and Eulie immediately began to practice. Daddy Lou's trumpet would wail his own tribute to the departed Henry as he followed the casket, and play "When the Saints Go Marching In" on the return journey. But Delia listened most closely to Eulie's rich contralto rehearsing "Swing Low, Sweet Chariot," to be sung at graveside.

Delia hid behind the sofa when Eulie practiced, because Eulie had never, as she put it, "cottoned to her." Still, Delia had learned a great deal by observation and imitation. Daddy Lou and his horn had taught her how to breathe, and how to listen, really listen, to music; but from Eulie she learned control, timing, presentation.

Then on the morning of the funeral, disaster struck. Eulie awoke clutching her throat, unable to speak, let alone sing. The hastily summoned doctor diagnosed quinsies. The abcess would have to run its course. There was nothing to be done but apply hot poultices and hope it would burst.

Daddy Lou drew Delia to one side. "The Van Courtlands,

they're expecting a song when we get to the cemetery. Sugar, nobody else but you—"

"I know the words!" Delia exclaimed, excited. "I can do it."

The dead were interred above ground in New Orleans, due to the marshland upon which the city was built, and to Delia the cemeteries were little cities of the dead, with the "passed over" occupying miniature stone houses, often gaily decorated with beads and colored stones and memorabilia from the departed's life.

Henry's parade to the cemetery had drawn a large crowd, and Daddy Lou, resplendent in a tall silk hat and white silk scarf, rose to the occasion by blowing his horn so magnificently that Delia was certain the angel Garbiel would immediately open the gates of heaven. Daddy Lou favored the leg he had broken when the icebox fell on it, but for his age he kept a steady but solemn pace as he led the musicians and mourners through the narrow streets.

The Van Courtland family, who had evidently been very fond of their butler Henry, did not walk in the parade, but they were waiting at the cemetery for the graveside service.

Delia caught a glimpse of three men in white linen suits who swept their Panama hats from their heads as the coffin arrived. She stood between Daddy Lou and Mignon and covertly glanced at the fabled Van Courtland brothers as the minister's melodious voice intoned, "Ashes to ashes, dust to dust . . ."

The oldest son, that would be Hugo, stood slightly apart from his brothers. They were all well over six feet tall, but Hugo had more bulk to his shoulders and chest, and seemed more physically powerful than the other two. They all had smooth dark hair, but she saw no distinct family resemblance of features, although she supposed all three could be described as handsome.

Then her gaze met that of the man standing farthest from her, and she jumped, startled. He was staring at her, perhaps wondering where he had seen her before. Delia had no problem remembering him. He was the man who had chased her up to the balcony of the Cajun Club and into the arms of Mignon. Delia looked away quickly.

The sun blazed from a pallid sky, and the humid air was heavy and still. The minister droned on, and Delia shifted from one foot to the other restlessly until Mignon's hand descended on her shoulder in gentle reprimand.

At last the minister finished speaking. Daddy Lou raised his trumpet to his lips and softly blew the first notes of the melody, then as the sound of the horn faded Delia began to sing.

She didn't look at the Van Cortlands as she sang, or at anyone else. Something magical happened, as it always did. It was as if the words and the music swept her away to some new and glorious place that only the sound of her voice could create. When she sang she felt she moved beyond the reach of harm or despair or ugliness. It was as if each note took with it a tiny piece of her earthly self and sent it soaring up into the heavens to sparkle with every sunbeam, dance on the clouds, and ride on rainbows.

When she finished Mignon took her hand and led her away. Delia felt the eyes of all three Van Courtlands follow her.

The summons to the Van Courtlands' mansion on the bayou came within the week. Daddy Lou's tired old eyes looked thoughtful, and he seemed to be choosing his words carefully as he told her, "They want you to sing at a musical evening they're having at the Willows. Sugar, you don't have to go if'n you don't want to, but I believe it would be good for you."

"I don't want to," she said promptly.

"Oh, baby, don't be so hasty," Mignon said. "They're mighty influential people. You never know where this might lead."

"Mignon—that man who was chasing me the night you took me in—he's one of them."

Mignon bit her lip. "I know that, honey. But Mrs. Van Courtland is giving a real big soiree, and everybody will be there."

"He has a wife?" Delia asked hopefully, feeling this would make him seem less menacing. The prospect of singing before a large assembly was appealing.

"Mrs. Van Courtland is the mother of the youngest two brothers," Daddy Lou answered.

"Honey, if you accept, they said one of us can go along with y'all to accompany you on the piano," Mignon put in, clearly beside herself with anticipation, since the only piano players present were the ailing Eulie and herself.

"Ain't gwine be you," Daddy Lou said coldly. Delia had become aware that he disapproved of Mignon's way of life, despite the fact that she insisted that the Cajun Club was just part-time and temporary until she fulfilled her dream of becoming an actress.

"Eulie's too sick," Mignon countered. "You going to take her yourself, Daddy Lou? Won't look good, an old black man taking a little white girl. 'Sides, your fingers are too stiff to play."

His wrinkled frown deepened. "Makes no never mind. The chile said she don't want to go."

Seeing the disappointment on Mignon's face, Delia decided to overcome her apprehension about the Van Courtlands. After all, she owed all of her present good fortune to Mignon. "I'll sing for them if Mignon can go with me."

The entire house was in an uproar in the days preceding their departure to the Willows. Clothes were selected, discarded, the songs she would sing had to be chosen and practiced; she was instructed from all sides, often to the accompaniment of much arguing about etiquette. The denizens of the house were nothing if not opinionated. Even Eulie, still unable to speak or hardly swallow, roused herself long enough to mime her approval or disapproval of each suggestion.

On Saturday morning the Van Courtlands' carriage arrived, and Delia and Mignon were whisked away by a dignified looking coachman, his stark white hair a fine contrast to his dark face.

Delia felt like Cinderella in her new white frock and shiny black shoes. Mignon had wrapped her damp hair in rags the previous night so that today it fell in golden ringlets beneath her new straw boater with the long blue velvet ribbons. She had worried about the expense and how she would ever pay them back, but knew if she brought up the matter she would

receive the same reply Daddy Lou always gave her when she
suggested it was time she began to earn her keep: that one
day she would understand that what they were doing was to
invest in her wonderful gift. She didn't understand, but knew
that life with her colorful companions was far preferable to a
lonely existence on the street.

Mignon, under pressure from Daddy Lou and Eulie, had
toned down her usual flamboyant style of dress. She normally
favored vivid colors and liked to clothe herself from head to
toe in a single shade—usually bright red or rich purple. Today, however, she wore a demure chocolate brown gown with
a soft lace jabot fastened with a a cameo brooch at the throat,
and a gossamer light silk shawl draped about her shoulders.
They packed clean underwear, night attire, and their evening
gowns in an ancient carpetbag Daddy Lou produced and
which undoubtedly had sailed up and down the river with
him in his paddle-wheeler days.

The carriage bore them through the streets of the Vieux
Carre, past the proud Spanish design buildings, arches, court-
yards and balconies that had been old when Andrew Jackson's ragtag army had marched triumphantly beneath them.
Street vendors attached to flocks of brightly colored balloons
or pushing carts of ripe fruit, and grinning hawkers waving
garish voodoo dolls paused to glance admiringly at the
gleaming carriage and its occupants. Had she not been sick,
Eulie might have been strolling down Bourbon Street or
along Dumaine carrying her tray of homemade pralines. Mignon could not resist waving majestically to the crowd, as if
she were a visiting queen.

Leaving the city streets behind, they journeyed into the ee-
rily beautiful Louisiana swampland, catching glimpses of
shrimp boats moored to front porches and skiffs darting along
the shallow passes that were the streets of the bayou country.

It was midday when they reached the Willows, which lay
behind a dense barricade of trees dominated by weeping willows and moss-draped oaks. Only confetti sprinkles of sunlight penetrated the dense foliage overhead as the carriage
made its way along a gravel drive to the rear entrance. The
front of the house faced the bayou, and when Delia later saw
the gracious white column and broad terrace and asked why

it was so situated, she was told that in the past most of the
visitors had arrived by pirogue rather than carriage.

Not that the rear entrance was modest by any means. They
were met by a young black man in a white jacket who was
undoubtedly Henry's replacement, and he conducted them
along a broad corridor to a drawing room to wait until a maid
was summoned to take them upstairs.

Delia scampered through their adjoining bedrooms, ex-
claiming in wonder at the canopied beds, the elegant dressing
tables, and the flower-filled urns. The maid placed Daddy
Lou's battered carpetbag on a tapestry bench and began to
unpack it, while Mignon stood in front of an oval mirror on
a carved rosewood stand and calmly unpinned her hat, as
though she were accustomed to such luxury, although Delia
knew that not even the Cajun Club could boast such time-
lessly beautiful appointments. In fact, Delia now recognized
instinctively the difference between quality furniture and its
tawdry imitation.

"Miz Van Courtland thought you could rest and then join
her for tea about four o'clock," the maid told them. "Y'all
can pull this heah cord when you're ready."

They were far too keyed up to rest. Delia would have liked
to explore the house, or at least the grounds, but Mignon said
that would be a serious breach of etiquette. Mignon herself
worried that they had not brought afternoon gowns and would
have to go to tea in their traveling clothes. She insisted they
both disrobe and hang their dresses out to "air."

At five minutes to four, dressed again, Mignon pulled the
bell cord, and the maid reappeared to conduct them to an
even larger drawing room with a wall of windows overlooking a carefully tended flower garden. Delia was so eager
to meet her hostess that she didn't realize until she was well
inside the room that Mignon and the maid had not followed.

Finding herself suddenly alone with an expanse of polished
wood floor stretching interminably toward an elegant brocade
sofa, Delia looked back in time to see the maid closing the
doors.

"Come in child, you'll see Miss Chamond again shortly."
The voice was soft and melodious.

Mrs. Van Courtland sat on the brocade sofa, a silver teapot
poised over a delicate china cup. Before her a low table held

the tea service and an array of tiny triangular sandwiches and iced cakes.

Delia approached cautiously, uneasy that Mignon had been mysteriously whisked away. She perched awkwardly on the edge of a chair facing the woman on the sofa.

"My sons inform me that you have a most extraordinary singing voice, my dear." Her own voice was as sweet as warm honey, and she was lovely in a flowery, faded sort of way, with silvery hair and the very pale complexion so prized by Southern women. Her gown was a soft gray with white lace framing the neckline. "I wanted this opportunity to meet you alone so that we might have a little chat."

Delia cleared her throat nervously and made her rehearsed speech. "Thank you for inviting me."

Mrs. Van Courtland smiled. "Thank *you* for coming. Would you like a sandwich, or one of the *petits fours*? Do you drink tea or would you prefer milk? I suppose I should have ordered lemonade, I didn't think. It's been so long since we had a child in the house. I dismissed the maid and thought we'd help ourselves." She motioned for Delia to select one of the delicacies before her.

Delia was far too uncomfortable to eat or drink, but picked up a miniature sandwich and accepted the china plate she was offered. She hoped she would not be forced to take a cup of tea since she had no idea how she would manage with both hands full.

But Mrs. Van Courtland had apparently forgotten as she leaned forward and pounced. "Now tell me, what is a young white girl doing living with a passel of no-account colored folk?"

Outrage and anger momentarily tied Delia's tongue in a knot. She jumped to her feet, sending both plate and sandwich flying. "They are *not* no account! They're not." Quivering with rage, she added as an afterthought, "How'd you like it if I said nasty things about your family?"

"Are you telling me you are the *daughter* of one of those women? Which one, the Chamond chit who brought you?" She knitted her pale brows and murmured, as if speaking to herself, "I suppose it's possible, her complexion is very light and you could have had a white father. The mixing of the races in New Orleans has always been a disgraceful problem, and one that certainly would not be countenanced anywhere else."

Delia already had her mouth open to defend all of her friends, but some inner wisdom caused her to stop and think. She could not speak of her real family in New York, for fear of being sent back there to face the law over her stepfather's death, and if she didn't have a satisfactory explanation as to where she came from, Mrs. Van Courtland might well get suspicious and call in the authorities. But asking if Mignon was her mother was, of course, a trick. Mignon was barely nineteen, certainly not old enough to have a twelve-year-old daughter.

"No, ma'am," Delia said slowly. "My ma is Eulie."

Mrs. Van Courtland's eyes narrowed slightly. "Your father must have been very fair. Swedish, perhaps? Or you are a throwback—I've heard of such things, of course." She leaned back against the high sofa back and said, "Very well. You may go. We shall see how you conduct yourself this evening before coming to any rash decisions."

Decisions about what? Delia wondered as Mignon fussed with her hair that evening, weaving ribbons and flowers into the drooping ringlets. Delia had not shared the details of her meeting with their hostess with Mignon, who apparently had been to tea with the housekeeper and butler.

"Mignon, could we go home right after I sing?"

"Whatever for, honey? Don't you want to spend the night in this lovely room?"

"Maybe we could go right now? Tell you the truth, I didn't like that ole Mrs. Van Courtland. I think she's up to something."

Mignon laughed. "We don't have to worry none about her, sugar. I heard tell nobody does nothing unless Mr. Hugo says so. But listen, it's Mr. Julian we've got to butter up, on account of his mother is gonna let him reopen the concert hall. Maybe he'll let you sing there one day."

There was no time for further explanations as they were summoned to yet another drawing room, this one large enough to accommodate what appeared to be dozens of guests. A cellist and a harpist had just finished playing. An expectant hush fell as Mignon sat down on the piano stool and Delia took her place in front of the grand piano. The program Daddy Lou had selected began with a ballad that had been popular during the war that he'd heard was a favorite of the family, then she would sing "My Sunbeam from the South," and would end with a Negro spiritual. If an encore was requested she would sing "Creole Belle."

Mignon played the introduction, but Delia faltered on the first note. For the first time she was very much aware of her surroundings. Mignon repeated the introduction and Delia began to sing, but could not soar away with the song as she usually did. The combined penetrating gazes of the Van Courtlands kept her trapped in the room. She feared her performance suffered in consequence.

But the assembled guests applauded enthusiastically after each number, and several cried, "Bravo! Bravo!"

The youngest brother, Marcus, sat closest to the piano. He wore a strangely disturbing expression and watched her from beneath half-lowered lids. She noticed his long graceful fingers moved in time with the music, as if caressing the piano keys. His dark hair was ruffled, untidy, and his shirt was unbuttoned at the throat, giving him a careless appearance that seemed to make the statement that he cared little about what people thought of him.

Julian, who surely recalled first seeing her as a singing beggar in Jackson Square, sprawled on a sofa next to a lovely young woman. He pinned Delia to the spot with the intensity of his stare, and she had the uncomfortable feeling that he listened to her not for his own pleasure, but for some more practical reason, or at least one that might benefit him.

But it was toward Hugo that Delia's own gaze kept drifting. He leaned against a marble pillar, his arms folded across his broad chest, his dark blue eyes crinkled at the corners and a small smile of appreciation on his lips. Of the three brothers only he seemed to be enjoying her singing for its own sake.

Mrs. Van Courtland smiled benignly until Delia began to sing the sweet sad strains of the Negro spiritual that was to be her finale, then the smile vanished and was replaced by a glare. The older woman snapped open an ivory-handled fan and batted the air in front of her face. Mignon must have seen the gesture, for she abruptly stopped playing the melody and indicated with several chords that the recital was over.

Delia curtsied as Eulie had taught her to polite applause
but no calls for an encore. The recital seemed to have concluded on an awkward note, in contrast to the earlier enthusiasm of the guests. She was about to escape from the room
when Julian Van Courtland cut her off.

He grinned and ruffled Delia's ringlets. "We have met before, haven't we? You've improved greatly since then, but
you've a way to go yet. Still, very nice, very nice indeed."

The youngest brother, Marcus, appeared at her side so
abruptly that she jumped. She looked into his strangely
brooding gaze, and a shiver rippled down her spine. This was
the brother who was "strange in the head," according to
Daddy Lou.

Marcus leaned so close to her ear that she felt his breath
against her cheek. *"I thought the sparrow's note from heaven,
Singing at dawn on the alder bough, I brought him home, in
his nest, at even, He sings his song, but it cheers not now—"*

"Shut up, Marc," Julian drawled. "Ignore him, Cordelia,
he's quoting a poem, and it has nothing to do with you. He's
annoyed because you brought your own accompanist. He
wanted everyone to beg him to play so that he'd have the
pleasure of refusing."

Following the Van Courtlands' lead, several other guests
approached, pressing close and causing Delia to feel an inexplicable stab of panic. Then over the babble of compliments
and questions one resonant voice made itself heard.

"Thank you all very much, but please, give the child room
to breathe. Come, Cordelia, let's get you some refreshments.
Julian, will you fetch something for Miss Chamond?"

Hugo's large hand closed around Delia's, and she was led
to a long buffet table in an adjacent room. Hugo filled a crystal cup with punch and handed it to her solemnly, then his
face broke into a smile that surely lit up the room. "You are
a very talented young lady. Your voice is beautiful. As indeed, so are you. How old are you, child?"

"Twelve," Delia answered shyly.

"Do you go to school?"

Delia's eyes darted nervously around the room, seeking either a reasonable answer or escape. "I . . . hurt my ankle. It's
only just strong enough to walk on."

"I see. Well, slake your thirst and we'll go and find Mother. She wants to thank you for entertaining our guests."

But Mrs. Van Courtland, in a lowered voice that no one else overheard, did not thank her. She hissed, "You are never to sing those darky songs in my house again, do you understand?"

Delia was glad to go back to Daddy Lou's house the next day. They arrived so late that she fell into bed exhausted as Mignon described to the eager throng their experiences with the Van Courtlands.

She awoke to find Mignon gently shaking her. "Get up, sugar. We need you downstairs. Here, put on my robe."

Sunlight flooded the room. Delia rubbed her eyes. She had slept late. She stumbled after Mignon down the stairs, dragging Mignon's white satin robe like a bridal train behind her.

In the living room Daddy Lou, Eulie, and Julian Van Courtland sat around the table like a tribunal.

"Couldn't you have dressed her in something else?" Daddy Lou muttered.

Mignon tossed her hair back over her shoulder and shrugged. "You said to bring her right down."

Daddy Lou looked at Delia, his tired old eyes twitching in that way he had when he was worried about something. "Chile, Mr. Julian here has come—"

"On behalf of my mother," Julian interrupted. "This is her idea."

"Yessir, well, chile, he done come to ask your ma"—he glanced in Eulie's direction as if to remind himself of the role into which she had unwittingly been cast, then fixed an accusing stare first on Delia, then on Mignon, to make sure they both understood he disapproved of the deception—"if she will let them send you off to school."

"A very special school, Delia," Julian put in, "where your voice would be trained."

Still half-asleep, Delia looked from one to the other, not fully comprehending what was happening. Eulie, who was still unable to speak due to her bout with quinsies, gave her a baleful look.

Delia stammered, "No, no, I don't want to go away. I want to stay here."

Eulie's frown etched itself deeper.

Julian leaned forward. "Your . . . mother has already given her complete approval, Delia. In fact, she's eager for you to accept my family's sponsorship. Surely you want the same opportunities that have been given to your brother?"

Delia blinked. "My brother?"

Julian's expression was that of one whose baited hook had just been taken. He answered with elaborate indifference, "Isn't Thaddeous in Paris with his father?"

There was an awkward silence as Delia looked from one to the other, seeking guidance. No one had ever mentioned that Eulie had a son, nor had she ever spoken of him.

Mignon hastily put in, "Delia ain't never been around Thad. His pa took him away when he was a baby."

Eulie promptly rose and lurched from the room, slamming the door behind her. Daddy Lou fixed a reproving gaze on Julian and muttered, "Ain't no call to upset folks, Mr. Van Courtland. Ah done told you we'd take care of this."

Julian stood up. "Very well. The rest is up to you. You know how to get in touch with me." He picked up his Panama hat and walked out.

Mignon slipped her arm around Delia's shoulder. "Don't look so worried, honey. Nobody's gonna make you do nothing you don't wanna do. But why did you tell Mrs. Van Courtland Eulie was your ma?"

"Because you're too young to be," Delia said miserably. "Now I've made Eulie mad. How come her son doesn't live with her?"

"It's a long story, honey. His pa had more to offer him, I reckon—"

"Hush yo' mouth, Mignon," Daddy Lou said. "Ain't none of your business. Go on, git out of here. Let me talk to the chile."

After Mignon left the room, Daddy Lou said, "Sugar, you know how I make the ragtime music with my horn?"

Delia nodded. "You make it up as you go along."

"There's a big word for it. Im-pro-vise."

"Improvise," Delia repeated, wondering what this had to do with the Van Courtlands' wanting to send her to school.

"See, sugar, that's what most folks have to do with their lives. Ain't no good playing the same ole melodies in the same ole way. What I'm trying to tell you, honey, is that it ain't good to slam too many doors shut, or forever stay on one track. 'Cos if'n we do, why, we's never gonna make any magic."

Delia shuffled her feet and tugged at the sash to Mignon's robe uncomfortably, sensing another great upheaval looming in her life.

"What this ole darky is trying to tell you, sugar, is that you got to grab any opportunities that come along. Don't say, my life is gonna be this way and no other, these are my plans and I ain't gonna change 'em. Improvise, Delia."

Chapter 7

HUGO

Had I known at the outset of all the machinations and deceptions involved in our family's patronage of Delia, I would not, of course, have permitted her within a hundred miles of us. But then . . . how drab life would have been.

"There's a young woman asking for you at the desk," the bellboy told Hugo when he opened his hotel room door. "She has one of your cards and said you might be expecting her. She says her name is Mrs. Margaret Nesbitt."

Hugo searched his memory for the name. He had finished his business in New York and was impatient to leave. "Did she say what she wants to see me about?"

"No, sir. But . . ."

"Yes?"

"She has a baby with her."

Hugo snapped his valise shut. "Tell her I'll see her in the lobby in a few minutes."

When the bellboy departed, Hugo tapped his fingers on the top of his valise thoughtfully. He remembered now. Maggie Nesbitt was the name of the midwife who had delivered Delia's baby. But there had been no sign of either Delia or the infant at the midwife's lodgings. He considered this fact as he went down to the lobby.

Maggie Nesbitt sat in a corner, a black wool shawl wrapped around herself and the baby. Her clothes were shabby and her face pinched, her large brown eyes anxious. Hugo had seen hunger before and recognized it now.

She jumped to her feet as he approached, and he said quickly, "Please, sit down." She did so with a grateful smile. He remained standing.

"I trust you've come to tell me you remember something

Cordelia said that might indicate where she went?" He wasn't sure why he referred to Delia by her full name. He supposed it was a way of reprimanding her in absentia for the worry she'd caused.

"I'm sorry, no." Maggie drew a deep breath. "Mr. Van Courtland, I came to you because I didn't know where else to turn. You see, this is Delia's baby. She abandoned her. I should have told you when you came, but I thought I could manage. I hoped she'd come back, but then I lost my job and we've nowhere to go."

There had been too many tricksters in his past, too many people with schemes to appropriate some of the Van Courtland wealth. "Do you really expect me to believe that is Cordelia's child? It's been almost three weeks since I visited you, and there was no baby in evidence then."

"Look at her," Maggie urged, pulling back the shawl.

He glanced at the infant. A sweet face, soft down of fair hair. "Mrs. Nebitt, one infant looks much like another. What exactly do you want from me?"

"I . . . I thought you'd help us. Take care of Patience— that's what I call her. Perhaps even keep me on as a nanny."

"And why would you expect that?"

She blushed as she whispered her response, "Are you not the father? I couldn't imagine any other reason for you to be searching for Delia."

"But Cordelia did not tell you that I was."

"No."

"Did she tell you anything about me, or my family?"

"Nothing, no. But you see, she was only with me over-night, and she was in labor for most of that time. I had to work on New Year's Day, and she was gone when I got home. She left her baby."

There was a blazing honesty in the young midwife's eyes that breached his skepticism. Perhaps she was telling the truth and this truly was Delia's baby, Julian's wire notwithstanding. The implications, if that were the case, were chilling.

How much did Maggie Nesbitt know? How much was she holding back? Delia could have told her a great deal during the hours of her labor, and even if she hadn't, he himself had foolishly given Maggie his card, which could lead her to the Willows. If he refused to help her, would that be her next stop? Perhaps it would be better for him to take charge of the situation now and prevent further complications.

While he was considering his options, Maggie said with quiet desperation, "I'm destitute. I've spent every penny I have. My landlord locked us out because I couldn't pay my rent. The baby was ill, you see, and we had to have a doctor. Mr. Van Courtland, I've grown to love her so. I didn't want to put her into an orphanage, and it will break my heart to give her up, but I realize I've been selfish trying to hold on to her when she isn't mine. Please, if you won't help us, will you at least tell me if Delia has anyone who will?"

He said carefully, "Delia was a protégé of my family. We took a personal interest in her, educated her, and in return . . . well, let's just say that she caused a great deal of upheaval in our family. However, I will not turn my back on her now. While I endeavor to find her to learn whether or not this child is hers, I will see to it that the infant is cared for."

"Please . . . please may I take care of her? She knows me, you see."

"I shall have to look into your background before I make a decision about employing you."

All of the hope died in the young woman's eyes. She said heavily, "Then I might as well tell you I was dismissed from the garment factory where I worked. There's no telling what the foreman will tell you about me. There's a chance he may even say I was discharged for having an illegitimate child."

"The child in your arms, I presume?"

"I have friends and neighbors who will swear to you that she is not mine. And you know from Mrs. Lonnigan that Delia was expecting and came to me to deliver her baby."

He walked over to the window and looked down at the street, several possibilities occurring to him. "I will find a place for you and the child, Mrs. Nesbitt, if in return you will agree to allow everyone to believe the infant is yours."

Surprised, Maggie said, "Gladly!"

"I don't suppose you've registered the birth?"

She shook her head. "I was waiting for Delia to come back."

"We shall register her as Patience Nesbitt, then."

Maggie appeared to be momentarily taken aback. "My husband was lost at sea and presumed dead years ago."

"His body was never returned? You have no death certificate?"

"No."

"Then his name will be given as the father."

Doubt claimed her expression. "But if you find Delia . . ."

"Mrs. Nesbitt, I can make life much easier for both you and the infant. Are you going to argue, or are you going to agree to my terms?"

"I have no choice," Maggie said quietly, her arms tightening almost imperceptibly around the baby.

After some deliberation Hugo decided to take Maggie and the baby to Natchez. He wanted them close enough to keep an eye on the situation, but not in New Orleans where the Van Courtlands were well known. And heaven forbid they ever found the Willows.

Van Courtland barges hauled cargos between Natchez and New Orleans. In addition they still owned a paddle wheeler, the *Dixie Belle*, an indulgence of his late father who never forgot that his fortune began in his riverboat gambling days, albeit assisted by blockade running and black marketeering on both sides of the Mason-Dixon line during the War Between the States.

Maggie Nesbitt was clearly dazzled by the gracious city high on the verdant bluffs above the Mississippi. Hugo took them to their new home himself, and as the carriage bore them along tree-lined streets, Maggie gazed upon the Creole-style houses of Greek and Palladian influence surrounded by formal gardens and murmured, "How beautiful it is."

He glanced at her. "Yes. The atmosphere of antebellum elegance is well preserved. However, Natchez is also an important trade and shipping center."

"How mild the climate is. I'm sure Patience will recover completely here. Do you live here, Mr. Van Courtland?"

"No. I shall give you the name of an attorney here whom you may contact if you need anything."

At the small house on Palmetto Street, Jemmie awaited them, her dusky features wreathed in smiles at the sight of the baby. Jemmie had been nursemaid to both Julian and Marcus, and although now in her sixties, she was delighted to have an infant to care for again. It had seemed prudent also that Jemmie should be the one to watch over Delia's child, in view of his suspicions. Jemmie would certainly recognize any inherited traits.

Hugo was not a man who, having made a decision, harbored doubts that he might have made a mistake. But his last vision of Jemmie holding Delia's baby lingered in his mind as he journeyed back to the Willows.

If only there was a way to find Delia and make her tell him, truthfully, who the father was. Would that settle everything? Or simply complicate the situation beyond solution? And which would be the lesser of the evils? To learn that the infant was a Van Courtland, or a Bouchet? In either case, the child had entered the world bearing a heavy burden.

Why did it have to be another girl-child? Unbidden, memories of a skinny little girl in a made-over frock singing her heart out in a New Orleans cemetery returned. At the time Delia had seemed to be all voice and wide, seeking eyes.

He doubted he would have thought about her again had it not been for coming upon his brothers engaged in a heated argument about her the day after Henry's funeral.

"I'll prove to you she has as much talent as you have, Marcus!" Julian was shouting. "And I'll give hers to the world. Yours is locked inside you, and you're not willing to let it out."

"You're a fool, Julian, a fool and a parasite. You've nothing to give yourself, so you prey on those who do. If you know what's good for you, you'll say nothing to Hugo or Mother about reopening the hall. Let your little songbird fly away."

"I'll do no such thing. I'll persuade Mother to invite her to sing at the musical evening, and when she hears her—"

"Trouble, *trouble*, if you bring her here! I observed that little girl. I was privy to her thoughts. I knew how she felt when she sang at the cemetery—it's an elusive, indefinable state that few mortals attain, and it won't stand up to mass scrutiny. I feel the same way when I sit down at the piano—"

Julian snorted. "In the middle of the night, with no one to hear. What sense does that make?"

"How would you know the torment? How *could* you? Do you think it won't happen to her, too? Better beware, Julian.

You've hooked an exotic fish, but landing it might be beyond you."

"We'll see about that—ah, here's Hugo. Let's see what he says. Hugo, I really feel I can recognize budding genius when I see it. That little girl who sang at Henry's funeral is going to be the songbird of the century. I feel it in my bones. I'm thinking of asking Mother if we can bring her here to sing for our guests next weekend. What do you think?"

"Fleur will never agree," Hugo said absently, overlooking Julian's undeniable charm and influence on his mother when he wanted something. But at the same time there were other things on Hugo's mind. Not least of which was his impending marriage.

Chapter 8

*

Upon his return to the Willows, Hugo went straight to his stepmother's sitting room, which adjoined her bedroom.

Fleur Van Courtland lay on a white satin *chaise longue*, her embroidery hoop untouched on her lap. She turned her head slowly, as if it were a great effort. Her eyes were sunken and smudged with shadows. Perhaps this time she was really ill, he thought.

She murmured, "You're back. Is Julian with you?"

Hugo shook his head. "He and Delia might as well have dropped off the face of the earth."

"But you believe Julian found her—that they're together?"

"Yes, I think so." There was no need for her to know about the baby until she felt stronger. "How is Marcus?"

"He still refuses to speak to anyone. He hasn't said a single word since that dreadful woman left. How I hate her! She has robbed me of not just one, but two of my sons."

"Marcus will come around, he always does. After all, this isn't the first time he's withdrawn from us. It's unfair to blame Delia. Anything could have brought this episode on."

"But the last words he uttered were to ask why Delia did not come down to dinner and when I told him she'd gone for good he stormed up to his room and locked the door."

"I'll talk to him later. What about you, Fleur, how are you feeling?"

She shrugged thin shoulders. "I shall feel better when I hear from Julian. How I miss him. Oh, Hugo, what mischief you wrought when you allowed that woman to come into our home. She caused a wound that will never heal."

Hugo bit back an angry response to his stepmother's convenient memory lapse. No purpose would be served in pointing out that from the very beginning he had argued against their involvement with Cordelia. Julian had been the only one who had wanted to bring her into the family and Julian always managed to get his own way with his mother. He was, after all, her favorite. Her firstborn son. And she would spend her every waking minute attempting to make up to him for the fact that she'd had the poor judgment to marry a widower with a son and heir, thereby depriving her own sons of the bulk of the Van Courtland wealth.

He could also have pointed out that Cordelia was installed at the Willows while he, Hugo, was touring Europe with his new bride. How long ago that seemed now, yet it was only—what? Six or seven years? He considered asking her about Gabrielle, but decided he was too weary. The query would only precipitate another tirade. He was in no mood to do battle with Fleur's denial over Gabrielle's culpability in their farce of a marriage.

The union between Hugo and Gabrielle Marchand, only daughter of one of the oldest and most aristocratic of Louisiana planter families, and the Van Courtland heir had been his father's hope and dream from the time Hugo was a boy. "We have the money," his father used to tell him. "They have the name, the bloodline."

"What's wrong with our name?" Hugo had asked.

His father had chuckled and responded, "You mean, apart from the fact that I chose it rather than being born with it? Oh, not to worry, it's legal now. But we're outsiders, Hugo. Carpetbaggers. The old guard are not going to accept us in my lifetime. It will be up to you to make us respectable by marrying into the right family."

Hugo hadn't concerned himself with his father's obsession, turning a deaf ear to examples of various lesser European royal houses pairing their offspring with more powerful neighboring countries, ignoring urgings to call on Gabrielle. Hugo danced with her occasionally at cotillions, conversed briefly at garden parties and barbecues, but backed away when she began to flirt with him. She was pretty, with sparkling green eyes and dark hair, vivacious, popular; but he was intent upon completing his education, learning all there was to know about his father's various enterprises, and, more important, creating some of his own.

At the time he made it, the deathbed promise had seemed merely a device, a loving gesture to ease his father's passage to whatever lay beyond the grave.

The old man had gripped his hand with surprising force. "You're my firstborn, Hugo. My immortality. Hell, sometimes I wonder how I could have sired the other two. You'll inherit everything. Cut Julian loose as soon as you can, but you'll have to take care of Fleur and Marcus. I trust you to do the right thing. But you've got to promise me . . . swear . . ."

His father's eyes stared into some far-off place, and Hugo wondered whether he was looking back or searching for a future he'd never see.

"I'll take care of them, don't worry," Hugo assured him.

"Hugo, you must acquire the one thing I never could. You know what it is . . . our grand alliance, Hugo. The Van Courtlands and the Marchands. Marry Gabrielle. Promise me, so I can go in peace." His father's eyes had burned into his, despite the fact that it was clear the old man's life was rapidly ebbing.

"I hadn't planned to marry for a few years," Hugo answered cautiously. "I still have a year of university, and then I'd like to see something of the world."

"After your tour, then. Swear it."

That would be at least two years into the future. By then Gabrielle would surely be married to one of the county's young blades who panted after her. Hugo felt safe in making the promise.

But Gabrielle had not selected one of her many suitors. She had waited for Hugo. Furthermore, she and her staunchest ally, Fleur, made sure that everyone in the county was aware that Gabrielle and Hugo had an "understanding." Since Gabrielle had a younger sister, Monique, who would be of marriageable age when Marcus was ready for a bride, Fleur's interest in keeping the Marchands happy was double-edged.

Still, it was his deathbed promise to his father that weighed most heavily on Hugo's conscience. He called on Gabrielle, noted that she was lovelier than ever, that some of her youthful coquettishness had disappeared, and decided that marriage to her would certainly not be a hardship to any man.

There had been women in his life, but none who had come

close to causing that spark the poets ranted about. Hugo did not believe in the durability of passion. Certainly it was no basis for a lifelong partnership. Perhaps the old man had been right about the importance of bloodlines. It didn't make sense to take infinite care breeding horses and then leave the propagation of humans to chance.

And so the die was cast. If only he could have foreseen the cruel jaws of the trap he was setting for himself. Had the first hint come on his wedding day, when Julian smuggled in among the invited guests his skinny little waif and secretly arranged for her to sing before the ceremony?

The entire county was excited about what they were calling the wedding of the year. Hugo was glad to leave all the arrangements to Fleur and the Marchands. Since he was now caretaker of all the Van Courtlands' holdings, he had little time to involve himself with the preparations. They would be married at the Willows because the Marchands' country house was in a rather sorry state of disrepair, and Gabrielle's parents would not hear of accepting his financial assistance until after the wedding; a quirk of their code of etiquette that Hugo found baffling. He busied himself at his office in New Orleans and spent as little time at the Willows as possible.

Then all at once it was the day of the wedding, and guests were tucked into every spare room, and carriages began to arrive at dawn. Hugo awoke to find the household in a flurry of preparations.

Angry clouds hovered in an ominously sullen sky, and the humidity hung like a sodden cloak, threatening rain before the day was over. Although alternate arrangements to move the outdoor wedding into the house had been made, anxious eyes watched the sky, and there were muttered prayers that the rain would hold off, to avoid the impossible task of packing legions of guests into the drawing room. Fleur fussed and complained that everyone would be cramped for space, some guests would have to be relegated to the hallway, and there was nothing more forlorn than an outdoor wedding moved inside.

But the rain held off, and, miraculously, as the guests assembled on the broad, sweeping lawn on the south side of the house, the clouds parted and fitful sunshine shone through.

Waiting for his bride before an archway of rambling roses and camelias that emitted an almost overpowering scent, Hugo squinted skyward and hoped they would not all be drenched before Gabrielle officially became Mrs. Hugo Van Courtland. He wondered idly if his father would now rest in peace.

Then all at once the clouds retreated. The victorious sun shone brilliantly, and there was Julian's towheaded little waif standing off on the sidelines beneath a weeping willow, singing in her hauntingly true voice a ballad of love.

Hugo felt a thrill ripple down his spine as he listened. All conversation stopped, and it seemed even the birds fell silent, as though awed by the beauty of the human voice. Delia sang without accompaniment, and none was needed.

Watching her, Hugo was aware of a curious feeling seeping into his consciousness. Something about the girl touched him deeply. He felt protective, fearful for her safety, concerned for her welfare, curious about what she felt as she raised her voice to the heavens and held every creature within hearing spellbound.

This was the third time he had seen her, but he had not realized previously that despite the malnourished body and hunger-pinched features, Delia's face held the promise of great beauty; and those eyes, startlingly blue with hints of iridescent lavender in their depths, were almost as mesmerizing as her voice. Who was she? Where had she come from? What could have happened to a child that would give her the voice of an adult?

The ballad ended, and impulsively many of the guests leaped to their feet to applaud—inappropriately, according to the dismayed expressions of Fleur and the Marchands, who had taken their places on the front row of the lawn chairs just before Delia started to sing.

Someone called *"Encore!"* Delia shook her head, obviously not expecting this. She clearly believed she would sing only once, as she had at the funeral, without reaction from the guests. For an instant she hesitated, then turned and fled, disappearing around the corner of the house.

When the excited murmur of wonder faded and the guests resumed their seats, there was a moment's pause, as if everyone had temporarily forgotten the real purpose of the assembly. Then Fleur frantically signaled to the musicians in the gazebo to begin the bridal march.

A seemingly endless parade of bridesmaids, hooped and parasoled, approached two by two. Hugo heard the minister clear his throat, saw Julian, his best man, pat his pocket to assure himself he still had the ring. Marcus, looking scornful, sat next to his mother, having refused to take any active part in what he called a ridiculous ritual.

Gabrielle appeared at last, a vision in a white crinoline, a lacy wide-brimmed hat trailing yards of tulle. Hugo watched as she came toward him on the arm of her father. How lovely she was, how gracefully she moved.

But as she drew closer he noticed something disconcerting. Could he be mistaken, or was that a look of triumph in her green eyes? He had no time to speculate what that particular look meant, however, as at that moment the sun vanished, the clouds rushed back, the heavens opened, and rain came down in a solid sheet.

In the ensuing chaos as guests ran for shelter, chairs were overturned, the archway toppled. Hugo fought his way through the shrieking bridesmaids to Gabrielle, swept her up into his arms, and carried her to the house.

Two hours later in the main drawing room, having changed into her first-day dress, Gabrielle recited her marriage vows in a tight, angry voice, glaring at Hugo as though the rain were all his fault. The rain drummed against the windows and gloom crept through the house, accompanied by the musty odor of damp clothes and imminent mildew.

Hugo did not learn the exact cause of Gabrielle's anger until their wedding night, when she faced him with glittering green eyes.

"How dare you have that little girl sing without my permission? Do you realize that we were *ready and waiting* when she started singing? Why, we could have finished the ceremony while she was wailing. It's all her fault—and yours—that my wedding was ruined!"

Chapter 9

*

Hugo did not learn Julian's plans for Cordelia until he and Gabrielle returned from their honeymoon in Europe by which time his bride's rage over her ruined wedding had dissipated. But Julian's plans for his protégé, Hugo feared, would undoubtedly precipitate another tantrum.

"We're going to send her to school in Philadelphia," Julian said excitedly, "where she'll not only study music and have her voice trained, but we hope acquire poise. However, we can't inflict her upon a decent school until she loses some of her rougher edges. So Mother agreed to allow her to come to the Willows periodically this summer. She'll just stay for two or three days at a time. Then in the fall she'll go to Philadelphia."

Hugo eyed his half brother suspiciously. "Isn't she a little young, even for you? What are you up to, Julian?"

"I'm going to reopen the concert hall—restore it, renovate it, and some day our little nightingale is going to step onto the stage and sing, and I shall be acclaimed as her patron. The most famous artists in the world will beg to perform here—you'll see. Who can tell, perhaps even young Marcus will break out of his self-imposed cocoon and allow the world to applaud his genius. Someone has to develop talent, Hugo, and perhaps that person is even more essential than the artist himself. I now see my place in the grand design."

"Do you, now? I suppose as an avocation it's preferable to your former exclusive pursuit of whores. But I'm uneasy about your bringing her here. Why not just hire a governess?"

"That wouldn't be the same. Delia would still be living in a hell house, learning the Lord knows what in the way of manners and morals. Here she'll be surrounded by examples of how to speak, how to act—Mother has promised to spend time with her."

Hugo considered pointing out that the Willows had been left to him, and that he now had a bride who was mistress of the house. But he had never been particularly fond of the old plantation house on the bayou, in which an inescapable atmosphere of sadness and despair seemed to linger. The Willows was not, after all, the Van Courtland family estate. Their father had acquired it only a year or so before his death. Hugo preferred the houses in New Orleans and Natchez, where he had grown up.

As if reading at least some of his thoughts, Julian put in, "Come on, Hugo, you don't spend much time here anyway. Don't tell me you're going to take up residence with your bride here. It's too damn close to your in-laws' place, for one thing. Do you really want old man Marchand as a neighbor?"

It was true, the Marchands' rapidly deteriorating antebellum mansion was just a short distance down the river, much too close for comfort. He shrugged. "It sounds as though the Delia situation is a *fait accompli* anyway. But what have you learned of her background? You don't really believe she's related to any of the people who have been taking care of her, do you?"

Julian grinned. "Not for a minute. I've pretty well pieced together her story. Delia ran away from home, or perhaps an orphanage. From her accent, she was probably originally from an immigrant family who came to New York not too long ago. I don't know how she came to be in New Orleans, but I do know she was singing in Jackson Square outside the Cajun Club a few months before we found her in that boardinghouse of Daddy Lou's. I asked some of the merchants, and they said a little blond girl had been seen around the square for several weeks, but never with any of the Cajun Club girls until the night I heard her sing and tried to talk to her."

"Then how did she come to be living with Daddy Lou?"

"I figure Mignon took her home with her. Delia claimed Eulie was her mother, but I checked—Eulie has only one child—a son who lives in Paris with his French father. She and Mignon originally came from one of the Caribbean islands, but the boy has never lived with his mother."

"Gabrielle wants to stay here for a week or two," Hugo

told him. "Until the painters are finished with the house in town and the new furniture is delivered. So I hope you haven't invited your little nightingale for a visit right away—my wife is still somewhat peeved about her singing delaying our wedding."

Julian chuckled. "What a comedy of errors that was! I never saw so many drowned rats assembled in one place before. Actually, I wasn't expecting you back for another couple of weeks and even as we speak, Joshua is fetching Delia. They should be arriving at any minute."

Hugo sighed. "Try to keep her out of sight as much as possible, will you?"

"How is she going to learn to live like a civilized creature if I lock her away? Be reasonable, Hugo."

Was it his bride's undisguised hostility toward the child that caused Hugo to be protective of her? Or his stepmother's constant humiliation of Delia? Fleur seemed to believe that berating the little girl for any minor mispronunciation of a word or slip in table manners was the way to teach her. He found himself, much to Julian's amusement, rising to Delia's defense.

Having endured Gabrielle's tirade upon learning the little girl was to be seated at their first family dinner the day they returned, Hugo then found himself listening with rising impatience to Fleur's harping about Delia's accent and manners.

At last, unable to bear the way she seemed to be paralyzed with embarrassment, he snapped, "For heaven's sake, Fleur, let the child eat her meal in peace. You've filled her head with enough instructions to drill an army. Let some of them sink in."

Delia flashed him a grateful if tentative smile that faded when Gabrielle said, "Darling, Fleur is right to correct her. I for one find it most unappetizing to eat with a little savage." She turned to Fleur. "Perhaps it would have been wiser to start her off in the servants' dining room?"

"Absolutely not," Julian said. "Mother—you promised."

"I'm sure we'll do better tomorrow, won't we Cordelia?" Fleur said. The little girl nodded but looked so desolate that Hugo's heart went out to her.

Marcus merely watched with malevolent amusement, as

though a melodrama were unfolding for his entertainment alone.

When the meal came to an end and Delia was excused from the table, Hugo also arose and followed, leaving Gabrielle in conversation with the others. He caught up with the little girl as she was about to slip out through the trades-men's entrance to the kitchen garden.

"Whoa—wait a moment. I'd like to have a word with you."

She looked up at him expectantly. Her extraordinary eyes were filled with lavender shadows in the twilight. He was re-lieved to see some of the fear had gone from her gaze.

"I'm afraid this isn't a good time to walk outside," he said as gently as he knew how. "At dusk there will be swarms of mosquitoes rising from the bayou. But if you want to get away by yourself, let me show you the place."

He took her to the solarium, which was the only addition his father had made to the house. It had been built around the south and west corners of the main house and filled with a profusion of ferns and orchids. Wrought-iron chairs and benches, lit by oil lanterns atop lampposts, and rough plank decking between the densely packed plants gave the illusion of being in a park. Two walls of windows protruded outward, topped by a glass roof that revealed the first stars glittering in the rapidly darkening sky.

Delia gasped with delight as he turned up the nearest lamp. "Ooh! What a lovely place. The flowers look like fairy prin-cesses! I never saw any like them before. What are they?"

"Orchids. My father brought them from a South American rain forest. I suspect my father's youth was deprived. He was always much impressed with the trappings of wealth, the ex-otic and the unusual. He tended to surround himself with pretty but useless things."

The child regarded him with solemn but knowing eyes, and he wondered if she was reflecting upon the next generation of Van Courtlands' penchant for pretty but useless women, but decided she was too young for such thoughts.

"You can come here any time to be by yourself. Only the gardeners come in here nowadays, and then only in the morn-ing."

With the frankness of youth, Delia asked, "Why do you keep it if nobody uses it?"

He paused, considering how to answer. The solarium had become his own private retreat when he was forced to spend any time at the Willows. He felt close to his father here and safe from intrusion, since Fleur and his brothers thought the maintenance of the rare varieties of orchids was foolish and the space could better be used to convert an adjacent room into a ballroom. Hugo had taken perverse satisfaction in refusing, on the grounds that the solarium was a private memorial to his father. Besides, its upkeep was far less of an expense than some of his father's other indulgences, such as the paddle wheeler, or the opulent eighty-foot private railroad car that was a veritable mansion on wheels, or the racehorses in Kentucky.

Delia was watching him in an oddly empathetic way for one so young, almost as if she could sense his ambivalence toward his father's various legacies. Hugo said quickly, "As a matter of fact, I sometimes come in here when I'm staying at the Willows."

"Isn't this where you live?"

"No. I have a house in New Orleans. I come here only occasionally. Delia, I haven't had any experience dealing with little girls, but I want you to come to me if anyone upsets you, or hurts your feelings. Remember, they don't own you. You are your own person."

She smiled shyly, then suddenly cocked her head on one side, and her lips parted in wonder as the first notes of a sonata, played as only Marcus could render it, drifted through the house.

Hugo was surprised. His half brother usually performed his solitary concerts in the small hours of the morning, when the household was asleep. The delicately precise piano notes at this early evening hour almost sounded like a summons. But for whom?

Chapter 10

*

JULIAN

There were times when I didn't want to share her with the world, I wanted to carry her off and shut her away from lustful eyes. Then there were times when I felt my own destiny was so utterly dependent upon her success that I dare not see her as a mere woman. To me, Delia was the Stradivarius that I, the master craftsman, was fashioning.

Of course, there were also times when I wanted to strangle her.

The endless vistas of the great prairie had at last given way to wooded foothills, and as the train snaked westward in the distance they could see snowcapped peaks carving a jagged line across the pale sky.

In the private car attached to the rear of the train, Julian put aside the history of San Francisco he was reading in order to observe both the view and Delia's reaction to it.

She sat up, leaning forward to look out of the window, and he knew she was forcing aching muscles to obey her brain's command. He could almost hear his mother's voice echoing around Delia's mind. Head up, shoulders back, don't slouch. Yet she must long to collapse into herself. He knew she tried to conceal her malaise. He'd seen her hand creep surreptitiously to her side, seen the fatigue in her eyes in the instant before she lowered those lustrously fringed eyelids to shut him out. Delia had never been strong, and he was angered by the way childbirth and its aftermath had ravaged her frail body.

Neither of them had mentioned her baby since leaving New York, and they both knew the discussion was long overdue. It was not for lack of privacy, since the eighty-foot car had separate crew's quarters for a cook, two waiters, and a conductor. There was a master stateroom, a bathroom complete with tub, and a guest bedroom. In the dining salon and drawing room there were gold plush divans, tasseled and fringed draperies, velvet portieres, inlaid woodwork, and wall-to-wall Turkey carpets. There were bottled-gas lamps with reliable coal oil in reserve. There was even a parlor organ in the dining salon.

Noting that Delia was again gazing at the mountains, Julian said, "Those are the Sierras. California at last."

She turned away indifferently, a gesture that he knew said more about her feelings toward him than any lack of interest in their destination.

"Delia—we should discuss—"

Abruptly she jumped to her feet.

He picked up her shawl and followed her out onto the observation platform, where she gripped the brass rail and looked back down the tracks. He pushed aside the thought that she might be seeing the tracks as her last tenuous connection to all he was forcing her to leave behind.

Slipping her shawl over her shoulders, he said, "It's cool out here. You don't want to catch a chill."

"We certainly can't let your investment perish of pneumonia, can we?" Delia responded bitterly. "I'm curious, Julian. How did you talk Hugo into letting you use his private railroad car?"

"It was my father's car before it was Hugo's," he answered shortly. The terms of his father's will were still a source of resentment. The pittance he had been left in a trust fund barely covered his living expenses, and his earnings the past few years had never quite matched his spending. "Hugo never uses it."

"In other words, you simply took it?"

"Somebody should get some use out of it. My father was a flamboyant old rogue who loved to flaunt his wealth. Hugo goes to the other extreme."

"From what I've seen, Hugo is generous to a fault. He certainly indulges you. You're always crying poverty and borrowing from him. I can't believe you paid for my education and my studies in Europe out of your own trust fund. And your various theatrical enterprises couldn't have paid our travel expenses, let alone have supported your lavish spending habits. Hugo paid my way, didn't he?"

Julian decided to cut off those speculations immediately. The last thing he needed was for her to learn the truth about who had really been her benefactor. "Perhaps you should lie down for a while. Get all the rest you can, while you can. Once we arrive you'll be busy with dress fittings and rehearsals and meetings with people who can help launch your career. Your first booking is less than two weeks away. When I made the arrangements, I didn't know you were expecting a baby. I had counted on you to keep your word."

"I promised not to marry." Delia's tone was ironic. "And I have not married."

Abruptly she went back inside the car and disappeared into the bathroom. For most of the journey she had ignored him, whether because she needed all of her concentration to recuperate from the ordeal of childbirth and her subsequent illness, or out of resentment that she was being forced to honor her agreement, he didn't know. A little of both, perhaps.

A few minutes later she returned and took her seat by the window. "You did let Hugo know where we'll be staying? How long will it take for a letter from him to arrive? Did he know you had taken me to the nursing home? Did you tell him? He was in New York at the time, but he didn't come to see me—"

"I suppose that's why you decided to go to New York to give birth, because you knew Hugo goes there frequently," he interrupted, hearing the malice in his tone but unable to disguise it.

She silently gave him that ice-cold Delia stare she had perfected. The same one she had given in response to his first angry demand that she confirm his suspicion that she was carrying a child and if so admit that Hugo was the father.

The latter accusation had brought an impassioned declaration. "Hugo is a gentleman. Unlike you, he's honorable. He's faithful to his wife. There is no possibility that I, or anyone other than Gabrielle, might be carrying his child."

Knowing his brother, it was possible that Hugo had been able to resist temptation, despite the fact that Delia had done everything but throw herself at him. Still, she *had* run off to New York to give birth and must have calculated that the child was due about the time Hugo would be there on business. He had to consider Hugo as one of two possible culprits. The other being Thaddeous Bouchet.

Julian decided to take another tack. "What did you think, that Hugo would believe the child was mine? After all, you could hardly go running to your colored friends, could you? That would have been too obvious a clue as to who fathered your child."

For an instant her eyes blazed, and he thought he'd at last goaded her into an admission, but then her mask descended and she asked quietly, "Where is he, Julian? Will you at least tell me what happened to Thad? I don't believe he went back to France, not for a minute. I do believe you caused him to disappear."

"Why couldn't you have been honest with me from the start?" he flashed back. "Why did you conceal the fact that you were *enceinte*? Even when I asked you point-blank, you denied it. By the saints, I believe you would have denied it right up until the moment I found you at the midwife's, had it not been for the fact that your baby was there, sleeping in a drawer."

She made no response, but she blinked rapidly like one awakening from a deep sleep and attempting to reconnect with reality.

He wondered if she was trying to remember what had happened before she fell. Good God, surely she didn't believe he had meant to hurt her? A little slap on the cheek, that was all, when he saw that she had indeed given birth to an illegitimate child. He'd goaded her, yes, trying to get her to admit that either Hugo or Thaddeous was the father.

But it was she who flew at him like a wildcat, raking his face with her fingernails. He'd merely held up his arm to ward her off and she'd tripped and fallen. He remembered the sick horror he'd felt when he saw her lying at his feet, blood spreading in what seemed to be an unending pool. In his blind panic he had gathered her up into his arms and rushed her to the private nursing home. He hadn't even thought about the baby as he paced the floor while they fought to save Delia's life.

When at last he remembered the child he had gone back to the midwife's room, only to find the infant was gone. Undoubtedly the midwife had returned and taken her to an orphanage, which, in view of the child's bloodline, and the effect her presence would have on Delia's career, was just as well.

"Do you know what stung the most, Delia?" he asked.

She shook her head.

"When you came to your senses, your first thought was that one day you would probably kill me. Your second was to suppose that I'd taken your child to Hugo and wonder about his reaction."

She stiffened, clutching the arms of her chair for support as the train began a steeply banked curve. "You *did* take her to Hugo? Julian, please don't torture me. Please tell me my child is safe with Hugo."

Julian knew that he had to tell her then. He could no longer put it off. He stood up, took a moment to get his balance in the swaying car, then kneeled before her and took her hands in his.

Even before he spoke, the abject fear in her eyes almost deterred him, but he told himself this was the only course of action he could follow, there simply was no other way out of the dilemma. It was for her own good. In the end she would be grateful.

"Delia . . . I didn't take the baby to Hugo—no! Wait, listen to me. I couldn't tell you the truth before, you were too ill yourself. I took the baby to the nursing home. You were close to death, and the infant became ill, also. They did all they could, but they weren't able to save her. . . ."

Catching her arms as she began to flail and scream, Julian allowed himself a moment of regret that he had not dealt with Thaddeous Bouchet when he first turned up in New Orleans.

As he tried to comfort her, his thoughts whirled back to his first meeting with Bouchet.

Julian had gone to collect Delia to take her to the Willows for her last visit prior to leaving for the boarding school in Philadelphia. He wasn't expected until the following morning, but decided to see if that old watchdog, Daddy Lou, would let them leave that evening.

He heard the music long before he reached the ramshackle old house on the bayou. The sound of Daddy Lou's horn, soaring above the mournful wail of a clarinet and the happy tap dance of piano keys, burst through the moss-draped trees and echoed across the still water. He could also hear clapping hands, stamping feet, laughter and conversation.

A party was evidently in progress.

Julian stood in the shadow of an ancient cypress and observed the house for a moment. All the doors and windows were open, and there were people everywhere, the overflow from the house sitting on the porch swing and steps, or perched on the rickety rail.

Then he caught a glimpse of light gold hair in the sea of dark heads and made his way to Delia's side. She was smiling, her expression happy and animated. Until she saw him. He stifled a twinge of annoyance that his arrival caused the joy to leave her face.

"What's all this?"

"Eulie's son—Thaddeous—is here."

"Your brother, you mean?" He winked.

She looked him in the eye. "He isn't my brother."

"Your half brother?"

"No, not that either. Eulie isn't my mother."

"You don't say!"

"So now you know I didn't tell you the truth, maybe you don't want to send me away to school?" She regarded him hopefully.

"On the contrary. Getting you away from here is essential."

"I'll probably run away from school."

"No, you won't. If you do I'll have Daddy Lou and Eulie and all of them put in jail."

She squinted through the gathering dusk. "You can't do that."

"Oh, yes, I can. You'll see, if you don't behave."

Mignon pushed through the crowd as the music ended. She was clad in a brilliant red silk gown, cut provocatively low, her long curtain of hair cascading over her shoulders. He stared at the swell of her bosom and tiny waist, feeling a surge of desire that distracted him and allowed Delia to slip away.

" 'Evenin' Mr. Van Courtland," Mignon said, dimpling. She was well aware of her effect on him. "We weren't 'specting you tonight."

"I was in town, so I thought I'd pick up Delia now, save

me a trip tomorrow." He wrenched his eyes away from Mignon and looked around to see where Delia had gone.

She was standing on the porch, in conversation with someone who stood in the shadows. Julian could see only a slim male silhouette holding an instrument at his side.

"Who is the clarinet player?" Julian asked Mignon.

"Eulie's boy. He's visiting her for a spell."

"Excuse me." He made his way quickly to the porch and was irritated that neither Delia nor Thaddeous saw him coming, as they were so engrossed with each other.

The boy was perhaps sixteen or seventeen and, other than the tightly curled dark hair and honey-colored skin, appeared to have inherited Caucasian rather than African features. His chiseled cheekbones and aquiline nose must have come from his French father. Julian noted the flashing dark eyes and a wide smile and grudgingly acknowledged that the boy was handsome. Delia was laughing at something he had just said.

Sensing Julian's approach, Delia turned then and saw him. She made a somewhat stiff introduction, in the manner his mother had taught her.

To Julian's astonishment, the boy offered his hand for a handshake. He clearly had lived abroad too long.

Ignoring the outstretched hand, Julian murmured, "How do you do," then added condescendingly, "You play the clarinet very well. Are you a musician in . . . Paris, isn't it?"

Thaddeous lowered his hand but smiled warmly. "Thank you, sir. No, the clarinet is just a hobby. I'm a student at the Sorbonne. My father is urging me toward a career in science, but I'm leaning toward the law."

Julian's surprise increased, although it scarcely registered that the boy was attending an ancient and world-famed university. What startled Julian was that Thaddeous Bouchet spoke like a white man, and his slight French accent only seemed to emphasize the fact. There was also an ease of bearing, a frank and inquisitive look in his eyes that indicated not only was he educated, but he had never learned the proper humility a black man needed to survive in a white society.

"How long are you staying in America?" Julian asked.

"I shall be visiting my mother for three weeks."

Julian wondered later why he hadn't recognized that he had received an evasive and incomplete answer? Probably because about that time several people clamored for more music, and Thaddeous was dragged away to rejoin Daddy Lou and Eulie.

Still, Delia could have mentioned that this was Thaddeous's first visit to the United States. His father had taken him from Martinique to Paris when he was less than a year old, leaving Eulie behind. More important, that after visiting with his mother, Thaddeous was to sail up the Mississippi and then tour all the major cities of the Northeast, including Philadelphia.

Julian had lost no time in removing Delia to the Willows, with the curt explanation that there were further preparations to be made for the journey to Philadelphia the following day.

How she fought against going! Right up until the last minute. When the tearful goodbyes to Daddy Lou and Mignon and the others were at last over and they were in the carriage traveling through the deep blue bayou twilight, Delia made her last desperate plea to be allowed to sacrifice her future.

"If you knew I'd done something really, really bad . . . you wouldn't want me to go to that fancy school, would you? If I tell you a secret, will you let me stay with Daddy Lou?"

"That depends. What did you do?"

"You won't send me to jail, will you?"

"Ah, I have a felon on my hands."

He felt her shiver, despite the soggy heat, and took pity on her. "I don't want to hear your reasons for running away from wherever you ran away from, Delia. But I am curious as to how you made your way from New York all the way to New Orleans."

"How did you know I came from New York?"

He chuckled. "You just told me, but let's say I suspected it from the start, by the way you spoke."

She considered this for a moment and then declared, "I'm going to learn how to speak so that nobody will ever be able to tell where I came from."

"Good idea."

"I was in St. Louis for a while," she said in a low voice. "I met a man and a lady on a train, and they said they wanted me to be a companion for their daughter, on account of she was sick. But they lied. They didn't have a daughter. They had a lot of girls like me and—"

Julian felt cold. "What happened to you there, Delia?"

She was silent for a moment, and he wondered if she was telling the truth when she replied, "Nothing. I ran away again. But I . . . stole some money from them. So you see, I'm a thief. You won't send me to jail, will you? I swear I'll pay them back as soon as I have the money. But I don't think those people at the fancy school would want me there if they knew, do you?"

"Now, you listen to me, Delia. Someday you'll thank me for giving you an opportunity in life that few people are given. You *will* go to school. You will do everything you're told. You will study until I tell you your education is complete. I may send you to Europe to study music with one of the masters later, I haven't decided yet. After that you will allow me to direct your career for at least five years. You will not marry during that time, unless, of course, I decide to marry you myself."

He laughed to show he was joking, then went on: "In return, I guarantee that nothing you did in your past will ever come back to haunt you. Further, your friends Daddy Lou and the others will not be charged with kidnapping you, or keeping you in an immoral house. You see, your friend Mignon does what those girls in St. Louis were doing. But she'll be safe, too. If you care about your friends, then you must always remember that their fate is in your hands. Now I want you to solemnly swear that you agree to all I have said."

She sat silently beside him for several minutes, undoubtedly attempting to think of a way to avoid making the complete commitment he was insisting upon. At length she answered in a low voice, "I swear. I'll do all you said, as long as you keep your word about Daddy Lou and the others."

Chapter 11

*

Julian had given the master stateroom to Delia, and that night he remained awake in the guest room for hours, listening in vain for the sound of grief. But Delia did not cry. Around three in the morning he heard her singing softly. He couldn't distinguish what she sang as the words were lost in the rhythmic grinding of wheels on the track.

Why didn't she cry for her lost child?

Illegitimacy and tainted blood notwithstanding, how could any woman who had given birth not shed a tear for a baby she had held in her arms? Delia had screamed and railed at him, but she had *not shed a tear.*

Her rage had been directed at him, for not telling her before they left New York that her baby was dead. But had there been any true grief in that outburst? Or merely anger? Within minutes she had been in control again, which surely showed her ambivalence about the child.

Delia had always been good at hiding her feelings, and Julian wondered if she would maintain that icy stoicism right up to the moment she plunged a dagger into his heart. But her reaction to the death of the baby troubled him greatly. Either a volcano of pent-up emotions would one day erupt, or she did not believe his story that the infant had died; or the woman who was his whole life was an empty shell, devoid of feelings, compassion, unable to care about anything or anyone. Julian wasn't sure which explanation disturbed him the most.

She had asked only, "Does Hugo know about the baby?"

"I believe he suspected. But I took care of that. I sent him a wire: FEARS UNFOUNDED—DELIA EXHAUSTED TAKING HOLIDAY."

"So you didn't tell him where we were going?"

"Why should I? We're not answerable to Hugo."

She had not uttered another sound until he heard her singing during the night. Perhaps she was emulating Marcus. Since early childhood his brother had gone to the piano during the night when he was troubled. Delia had always been intrigued by Marcus's nocturnal concerts. Julian had warned her never to go to his brother at night, since he played to exorcise his demons and approaching him then would be akin to suddenly awakening a sleepwalker, but Julian suspected Delia had not heeded the warning.

Perhaps her nocturnal song was a substitute for tears? It was a rationalization that troubled Julian less than the other possibilities.

The following day as they drew near their destination, she was again completely in control of her emotions. He had selected San Francisco for her first American performance, despite his eagerness to renovate Courtland Hall and have her appear there, in order to put three thousand miles between her and all of her previous connections. By the time they returned to New Orleans, there should be an adequate buffer between Delia and her past.

Arriving at their hotel, Julian accompanied Delia to her room. He stood at her window. "You have a view of the bay and the cable cars climbing the hill. You'll find this an interesting city. It's not New Orleans, of course, and will seem young and uncouth, perhaps even ugly by contrast, but it is quite unique. Settlers came here from all over the world, and they're creating a blending of cultures that—"

"I'm aware of the city's brief history, Julian," Delia interrupted. "It's a raucous one, to say the least."

He shrugged. "You'll find the climate is cool to downright chilly. You must dress accordingly, and don't go out in the fog, it will affect your throat."

"What I don't understand is how you got this booking at the Grand Opera House. How much of Hugo's money did you use to put me on the program? I've never auditioned, so you must have bribed somebody. Which opera will I be in and what part am I singing?"

"Well, now, I've been meaning to explain about the Opera House. It's one of the oldest theaters in San Francisco, but it fell on hard times and was shut down in 1885 because business started moving off Mission Street. It stood empty for years, then stooped to vaudeville—"

"What?" Delia shrieked, "I won't—"

"Oh, calm down. They then started booking independent theatrical companies who were touring in defiance of the theater trust. But I've heard Mission Street is reviving and soon the Opera House will again house grand opera. Not that it will matter to us, because we'll return to New Orleans as soon as you've made a name for yourself. Besides, the touring company you'll be appearing with will present a musical program that includes a famous coloratura and a fairly well-known tenor, so you'll share the bill with artists who will draw a crowd."

"I should have stayed in Europe," Delia said. "I could have done *La Bohème.*"

"You think as an understudy you'd ever have gone on stage? You were only offered the chance because the maestro was lusting after you."

"According to you, every man who sees me is lusting after me."

"In view of recent events, I'd say my concerns were well founded." As soon as he uttered the words, he wished he could take them back. He added quickly, "Besides, I'm not sure that you should tie yourself down to grand opera. You would have to make your name in Europe and I want to create in you a uniquely American performer."

"There are American opera companies. And if I was not to sing opera, then why did you send me to Paris to study?"

"For the discipline. But I wouldn't have, had I known Bouchet was there. I believed he was in Martinique." Damn, again his mouth had run away with him.

She sighed. "We always come back to Thad, don't we? Julian, we're three thousand miles across the country now. Will you at least tell me what happened between you and Thad?"

"Nothing happened. I never saw him again."

"You're lying."

He shrugged. "Believe what you will. Incidentally, while you're appearing here, I thought that in addition to operatic arias you might occasionally sing modern American pieces. We want to appeal to as wide an audience as possible. You'll sing opera for your first performance. After that I may select other pieces."

Her full lower lip curled slightly. "In other words, I'll do as I'm told, as usual."

"Exactly." It was always better to play the stern taskmaster with her, because that was what she expected from him. He added, "I'll see you at dinner. You'd better rest now."

In his own room Julian brooded over Delia's involvement with Bouchet. He didn't know for certain what had become of him, but he had a pretty good idea. New Orleans tended to be considerably more colorblind than the rest of the South, and Bouchet had never had the sense to realize that. Probably thanks to that French father of his, who educated him abroad and brought him up to believe he was as good as anyone else. Bouchet had broken the strictest of Southern taboos by associating with a white woman. He got away with it in New Orleans and possibly up North, but if there were other white women in his life and they were daughters of the South, then Bouchet could very well have ended up on the end of a lynch mob's rope. But there was another explanation for Bouchet's disappearance that Julian dared not discount. Nor did he particularly want to explore it. Still, better to know for sure. Perhaps a wire to the Pinkerton agency in New Orleans would be in order. While at Western Union he could also wire his mother. He'd kept quiet about the San Francisco trip to avoid her tearful tirades. Or would it be better to wait until he could send news of Delia's success? Nobody on earth wanted Delia to fail more than his mother, with the possible exception of Marcus.

Marcus had taken an instant dislike to Delia and never disguised his resentment of her. Yet even that had an interesting side benefit, since it inspired him to spend more time at the piano, not always in the small hours of the morning, and Julian knew that his brother was again composing music.

Julian had always been protective of his younger brother, despite their youthful bickering. When Marcus went into one of his black moods, Julian had been the only one occasionally able to coax him out of it. And when Marcus became violent, as he had a few times, Julian had both the inclination and the strength to subdue him. Hugo could have flattened both of them simultaneously had he chosen to, but Hugo, like Fleur, was convinced that Marcus was too fragile to be manhandled into giving up unacceptable behavior. Julian had no such compunctions.

During the first visits Delia made to the Willows, Marcus watched with malicious glee as Fleur attempted to civilize her, predicting that Julian had set her an impossible task. But Delia learned quickly, no one had to tell her anything twice, and this disappointed Marcus.

On her third visit Julian came upon Marcus standing at an open window above the terrace watching Delia serve afternoon tea to Fleur and Gabrielle.

Leaning close to his brother's ear, Julian whispered, "If you're so interested in tea with the ladies, why don't you join them?"

Marcus faced him sullenly. "This isn't going to take, you know. She'll revert back to the savage she is the minute our backs are turned."

"Why do you dislike her so, Marc? I'm genuinely curious. She hasn't done anything to you. I should think you of all people would appreciate her talent."

Scowling, his brother moved away from the window. "You aren't comparing her talent to mine? She parrots what she hears, with her singing as with everything else. I create. Even when I play music composed by others I put upon it the stamp of my own uniqueness by my arrangements. But more than that, I *create*. Do you have any idea what it's like to compose a brand-new piece? Try building a bridge in thin air. Try making a flower grow out of barren rock."

His voice had risen and Julian jerked his head in the direction of the open window. "Quiet, they'll hear you."

Marcus smirked. "Gabrielle hates her, you know. Because your waif follows every move Hugo makes, watches him like a lovesick puppy. Tell me, Julian, why doesn't she look at you like that? After all, aren't you, not Hugo, her self-proclaimed savior?"

"Hugo and Gabrielle will be leaving as soon as the town house is finished," Julian answered shortly.

"Gabrielle is beautiful, but she doesn't love Hugo, so she'll be a dog in the manger. Doesn't want him herself but won't let anyone else have him."

"She can hardly regard a child of Delia's age as a potential rival," Julian said.

Marcus raised his hands and rolled his eyes in one of the exaggeratedly dramatic gestures he gave when he felt he was being confronted by stupidity. "I wash my hands of you, Julian. Five or six years from now when your songbird returns to perform at the Courtland Hall, her body will have matured to the same degree as her mind."

"What do you mean?"

"Have you ever looked into those eyes of hers? She has ancient eyes, Julian. When her body catches up, no man will be able to resist her. Not even Hugo. And Gabrielle's female intuition already tells her that. You can be so blind, Julian. You've become obsessed with justifying your existence, and that's why Delia is sitting down there on the terrace pouring tea and arousing great waves of jealousy in Hugo's bride. Haven't you noticed that Hugo is almost nauseatingly kind to Delia?"

"No. But if he is, it's surely more than offset by how unpleasant you are to her."

As Julian expected, this remark caused Marcus to storm from the room.

Troubled by his brother's remarks, Julian went back to the window to observe the tea party. Marcus had always marched to a different drummer. He was unpredictable, volatile, given to frightening extremes of mood, but frequently he was almost uncannily perceptive.

Below on the terrace his mother and Gabrielle were looking at each other and laughing helplessly. Delia sat frozen in her chair, a dull flush staining her cheeks. Julian resisted the urge to rush down and ask what had transpired. After all, the two women were not necessarily laughing *at* Delia. Perhaps what amused them was above the child's head? Instead he went in search of Hugo.

He found Hugo in their father's study. Although the old man had been dead for years, Julian still thought of the study as his and, recalling being summoned there during his college days for stern lectures, never felt comfortable in the room.

Hugo was seated at the massive mahogany desk, a stack of documents in front of him. He glanced up. "I'm afraid I'm never going to get caught up. I may spend the rest of my married life making up for the honeymoon. I don't suppose you'd care to learn anything about moving cargoes down the river?"

"I'd really rather get started with the renovations of the hall," Julian replied cautiously. "That's what I wanted to talk to you about. I have some preliminary estimates—"

"No," Hugo interrupted. "Not on the strength of your hopes for Delia. You're going to have to earn the right to pour money into that white elephant of a concert hall, Julian."

"What do you mean?"

"You know nothing about music, about handling singers or any other performers, about any kind of show production, and certainly nothing about the business of owning and running the hall. You will first learn all of these things. When I'm satisfied you know what you're doing, I'll advance the money to renovate the hall and get you started."

"And just how am I supposed to learn all these things?"

"I suggest you go to New York. Take any kind of a show-business-related job you can get. I can introduce you to several people who might help, but after that you're on your own."

"New York?" Julian repeated, dismayed. "Why not New Orleans?"

"You'll see when you start working there. You may also want to go to London and Paris. In the meantime Delia can be educated and receive her musical training—that is, if she doesn't run away again."

"Don't worry, she won't."

"Now, as you haven't asked me to pay for Delia's schooling, I assume you've talked your mother into footing the bill. But if you agree to my terms, I'll pay Delia's expenses."

"There's no need for that," Julian said stiffly. "I've already taken care of it."

"Out of your trust?" Hugo was obviously both surprised and impressed. "You must have been living very frugally lately."

Julian decided to change the subject. "What about the renovations to the town house? When will you and Gabrielle be moving in?"

"Soon, I hope. But each time I think we're ready, my wife decides she wants something changed. I'm beginning to think she likes living here at the Willows. She and your mother certainly seem to get along well, and of course, she's only a short distance from Fontenay here."

Hugo paused, frowning slightly, and Julian wondered if it had dawned on his brother that his wife seemed more interested in renovating her ancestral home than moving into her own house.

Julian murmured noncommitally. Hugo might have inherited all of the Van Courtland wealth and power, but the price he'd paid was dear. The old man had chosen a wife for him. Marcus had said that Gabrielle didn't love Hugo. Perhaps he was right. But she certainly loved Hugo's wealth. She was spending money like water.

The memory of an episode that had occurred shortly before Hugo's wedding flashed into Julian's mind. Hugo had been in New Orleans attending to business as Gabrielle's family gathered in readiness for the wedding. With Hugo gone, most of the task of coordinating all of the details of the wedding fell to Julian as his best man and this necessitated frequent trips between the Willows and Fontenay, Gabrielle's home.

Two days before the wedding Julian realized, late one evening, that no one had mentioned where the newly married couple would spend their wedding night. They were to sail for Europe the following day, but was the first night to be spent at the Willows or at a hotel in New Orleans? If the latter, a suite must be reserved.

The moon was up, it was a pleasant night, and Julian decided to take one of the boats and row down to Fontenay to ask Gabrielle about her wedding-night accommodations.

The boathouse contained several skiffs, canoes, a couple of fishing boats, even an antique pirogue. When the Van Courtlands first came to the Willows, he and Hugo had used the boats often, but Marcus had always been deathly afraid of water. Nowadays Hugo was too busy, so only Julian used the boats.

Gliding silently over the dark water, he heard muffled voices and then, distinctly, a girl's laughter drifting from the dense growth of cottonwoods and dogwoods that marked the boundaries of Fontenay.

He recognized the distinctive laughter immediately. Only Gabrielle's laughter sounded like pealing bells.

As he drew closer he heard a man's voice speaking softly. Julian couldn't make out the words, but the intimacy of the tone caused him to stop paddling and catch an overhanging branch to stop the progress of the boat.

Had Hugo returned? But that surely didn't sound like Hugo's voice. In fact, although he couldn't be sure, it sounded as if the man had a slight lisp.

Gabrielle might be simply enjoying a late evening stroll with one of her visiting relatives, but then again, she might also be having a last-minute fling with a lover. Julian couldn't help but hope for the latter. It would serve old holier-than-thou Hugo right to acquire a soiled bride.

Julian quickly turned the boat and headed back toward the Willows.

The following day he was so busy that when several newly arrived Marchands were presented to him, it didn't at first register that Gabrielle's first cousin, Alain Marchand, fresh from the University of Georgia, spoke with a slight lisp.

Chapter 12

*

Julian slammed the newspaper down on Delia's dressing table and pounded it with his fist. "Damn him to hell for this!"

Peering over his shoulder, Delia scanned the heading above the piece in the entertainment section of the paper. "Serves you right, Julian. You're the one who dropped all the dark hints."

"Dark? They were not dark. I hinted that you *might* be an estranged member of a European royal family, emerging from a tragic past and performing under an assumed name. It was a device to get your name known before the concert."

Delia eased the newspaper out from under his hand and read:

" 'A Woman with a Past: Mystery singer to perform at the Opera House. Patrons attending next week's performance will note that on the bill is a singer who uses the single name Cordelia. The lack of a second name, which at first glance seems arrogant, might intrigue audiences if her voice matches her looks.' "

She looked up at Julian. "I'd say we're lucky they didn't print that drivel you ladled out to them verbatim. You actually said I'd recently completed a triumphant European tour. What if anyone checks?"

"They won't. Besides, by the time word returns from Europe, you'll be the toast of this town. We've only two more days before the concert. What worries me is that woman-with-a-past label."

"What did you expect, with all that nonsense about my tragic past and royal connections?"

"Damn, we should have changed your name completely. I still like the idea of using only one name, but what if—at the height of your fame—someone connects Cordelia to her real past?"

Delia's eyes glittered, but her expression remained derisive. "Perhaps you should have told them that I'm a fallen woman, a soiled dove—that I've trod the primrose path? That might then distract them from my other past—the one that you used to get me to do your every bidding."

Julian wasn't listening. He mentally reviewed the chances of anyone learning she had given birth to an illegitimate child. The only person who could connect her definitely to the birth was the midwife, Maggie Nesbitt, who also knew where the baby had been taken. When Delia became famous, as he had no doubt she would, would Maggie Nesbitt rise up to haunt them? Perhaps it would be prudent to find out. After all, the midwife and the baby might lead the inquisitive back to Thaddeous Bouchet and the others.

Turning from the newspaper, Julian asked, "Did the seamstress come? Did you have your final fitting?"

"The waist is too tight and the neckline too low. I'll probably pop right out of it with my first high note."

"The gown is exactly right for you. You aren't the ingenue type, my sweet. Part of your allure is your don't-give-a-damn attitude. You are the classic *femme fatale* and should dress accordingly. No prim little frocks and drab colors for you. You're going to flaunt your seductiveness."

"You complain that I'm too thin, then tell me I'm seductive. Isn't that a contradiction?"

"You *are* thin. The ravages of childbirth, no doubt. But your breasts are now more womanly. We should take advantage of that."

He turned abruptly to face her and found she was standing closer than he expected. Her eyes met his, and there was something enigmatic and disturbing in their depths, a challenge perhaps. Instinct urged him to take her in his arms and kiss her, thoroughly, savagely, mercilessly, and to hell with the consequences. The feeling was raw, primitive, and exhilarating.

As if sensing danger, Delia calmly moved out of range.

Julian blinked. He'd had that same urge before, many times. Indeed had acted upon it a couple of times. Her reaction was always the same. She simply went limp in his arms.

She didn't fight, or resist in any way. It was as if she were able to slip out of her body and escape to some unreachable place. He clenched his fists at his side and forced his mind to ignore his body's message.

As his surge of desire passed, he felt overwhelming rage. The man who had impregnated her—had she reacted to him in the same way? Offering a lifeless body rather than sweet surrender? Julian hardly thought so. Surely no man alive would want to make love to a corpse.

Not trusting himself to remain close to her, Julian said, "I'm going to find out who will be reviewing your performance for this paper and see if I can get him to write something that will make the readers forget this mystery woman nonsense. The trouble with mysteries is that someone always wants to solve them."

But the newspaper informed him that there was no specific music or theater reviewer. The task fell to whoever had the time or inclination to attend opening night.

Julian spent the next two days in an agony of suspense. He had no fear that Delia would be a success, but he did worry that he had not adequately covered her tracks. Her attitude worried him, also. Even for Delia, she was unnaturally calm, yet at the same time secretive. He had known many performers during the last few years but had never encountered one who was not either a mass of nerves or impossibly demanding just prior to opening night. Would she develop stage fright? Not likely. Was she planning to run away again? In all fairness, he had to admit that the only time she had broken her word and run away had been to conceal her pregnancy. But she had something planned, he was certain. He wished he knew what.

To his vast relief there were no catastrophes before opening night. He began to relax. Delia insisted that he take his front-row seat rather than remain with her in her dressing room. He didn't argue with her since she was not due on stage until just before the intermission, and he wanted to compare the other performances. She maintained her icy calm, but that enigmatic gleam in her eyes suggested she knew something he did not.

The program consisted of a variety of musical offerings to appeal to a wider audience than full-scale opera, while at the same time introducing opera to some of San Francisco's less musically sophisticated citizens who would be drawn by the appearance of a well-known vaudeville performer who would sing a medley of popular songs. Julian hadn't told Delia about the vaudeville performer until the last possible minute, and it still worried him that she had taken the news so calmly.

An accomplished, if aging, coloratura soprano opened the program. She sang two arias from *Aida*. She sang well, but the audience was restless, no doubt impatient for the appearance of the vaudeville performer.

Julian had his first qualm. If the crowd didn't want to sit still for an excellent rendition by the coloratura, what would they do to the unknown Cordelia, who would also sing operatic arias? He had worked himself up into a state of acute anxiety by the time Delia was due to take the stage.

The curtain rose and she stood alone on center stage. His breath stopped in his throat as he stared in stunned disbelief at the apparition before him.

If he could have groaned he would have. How could she do this to him? Had she planned her revenge all along? He had forced her to perform, but she was going to comply on her own terms. Obviously her career was doomed.

He tried to rise from his seat but was paralyzed. Besides, what could he do? It was too late, the audience had seen her. A hush fell as they regarded the singer's startling costume.

Scorning the gown he had had made for her, dismissing the hairdresser engaged to create an elaborate coiffure, Delia stood on the stage clad in a man's black frock coat over tailored pin-striped trousers, her hair dragged severely back from her face, which showed not a trace of greasepaint and was almost luminously pale under the stage lights.

Julian closed his eyes in an attempt to shut out the apparition that was Delia, certain that at any moment the audience would burst out laughing.

But almost instantly the orchestra struck up the opening bars, and Julian had his second shock of the evening. Instead of playing the introduction to an aria from *La Traviata* he had selected for her opening number, the musicians were playing the opening bars of an old German drinking song.

As he watched in horror, Delia raised a tankard in a toast to the audience and began to sing.

With training, her voice, always superb, had acquired power and control and gave a magical gloss to even this flimsy piece. All the shuffling and coughing and whispers in the auditorium were stilled, but Julian wasn't sure if the hush was caused by admiration or astonishment at Delia's clothes and choice of song.

She sang in German and he was thankful for that at least, since not many people would understand the ribald lyrics. Delia had shown a flair for languages—not only could she sing in French, German, and Italian, but she was also fluent in all three languages.

She strutted about the stage in her close-fitting trousers, loosened her cravat and then pulled it from her throat and tossed it into the orchestra pit. And all the while her magnificent voice held the audience spellbound.

At the end of the song there was a burst of applause, cut short when she silenced the house again by immediately beginning to sing, this time an old French ballad, a lament for a lost love. There was no need for anyone to understand the words, the heartbreak was in Delia's voice for everyone to hear. Julian saw a woman seated nearby surreptitiously wipe a tear from her eye.

A stagehand brought out a stool, and Delia perched on it and handed her frock coat and tankard to him. She unbuttoned the top button of her linen shirt as she finished the song, ending with just a hint of bravado. The poet's love might have departed, but the poet would survive.

The applause this time was deafening, along with shouts for an encore, and at last she sang in English, a song he was certain he had never heard before but which sounded vaguely familiar. Had someone written new, somewhat cynical lyrics about the battle of the sexes, to an old melody? The words were ironically amusing and the men in the audience hooted with appreciation while squirming with embarrassed recognition of their own shortcomings in their dealings with women. The women began to applaud enthusiastically before the last note faded.

There was pandemonium as Delia bowed and left the stage. The audience was on its feet, clapping and calling repeatedly for encores. Delia returned briefly to bow again and then disappeared into the wings.

Julian sat limply in his seat. She was a success. Despite the male attire and severe hairstyle, despite the inappropriate songs, despite defying him at every turn, *she was a success*.

He had to fight his way into her dressing room, which was packed with well-wishers. Shouldering his way to her side, Julian saw that she looked pale and weary, unmoved by the adoration, oblivious to her triumph. She merely nodded and murmured thank you in response to the gushing compliments, and dutifully signed programs. Seeing Julian, she raised her eyebrows questioningly.

He glared at her. "Your little scheme backfired, didn't it? You thought you'd be laughed off the stage and I'd release you from your agreement so you could go running back to—" He stopped himself as he realized those standing near were listening.

"Please—everyone—" he called out. "You must leave now. Intermission will soon be over. Allow her to change clothes." He seized the arms of the two nearest men and used them to herd the others from the dressing room, then locked the door and turned to face her.

"That was your intent, wasn't it? That this be your one and only performance?"

She sat down and began to unlace her man's shoes. "If that interpretation of my performance pleases you, then by all means believe it. You've always wanted to believe that I would never succeed as a singer unless you pushed and drove and goaded me to it. It never occurred to you that I had ambitions of my own, did it? That I had hopes and dreams of my own? That I might have succeeded without you?"

He was too taken aback by the sudden passion in her voice to comment.

She went on: "I could have gone on tonight in your harlot's garish gown and sung operatic selections that might not have been as well received as the coloratura soprano's were. I could have repeated what any one of dozens of singers have done before me and gone on to the same obscurity. Or I could be an original. I could set my own style. And damn it, Julian, that's what I decided to do."

What could he say in rebuttal? She had received a standing ovation for her very first performance. Who could argue with that? He asked lamely, "That last song you sang—what was it? Since you didn't follow the program, I'll need the title to give to the reviewers."

Her eyes met his, and unaccountably, he shivered. There was something in those blue-lavender depths that chilled his soul. He felt as if he were sinking into an ice-bound arctic sea.

She answered in a strangely detached tone. "Oh, you've heard the music before, many times. It's one of Marcus's compositions. He used to play it in the middle of the night." She paused. "I wrote the lyrics myself."

Julian stared at her. *Marcus?* She had composed lyrics to Marcus's music and had sung the piece to an audience? Julian wanted to say, *But why? You and Marcus hate each other*, how could you have created any kind of harmony together? But somehow the words stuck in his throat.

Chapter 13

*

MAGGIE

Surely I don't deserve such happiness. Delia is going to come and take her baby, and Hugo will send me packing. But, oh, while we're here, how glorious life is!

Maggie sat in the rear garden of the house on Palmetto Street in Natchez with Delia's baby on her lap, enjoying the lazy summer breeze that murmured in the magnolia branches overhead and surrounded them with the scent of blossoms.

Patience was thriving, gaining weight, eating well, her tiny lungs free of the chronic cough that had plagued her early weeks of life.

Jemmie came out of the house, shuffling toward them on arthritic limbs, carrying a tray containing a pitcher of lemonade and tall glasses.

"Oh, Jemmie! I would have come in for that," Maggie protested. She felt guilty that the old woman seemed to anticipate every need, as well as taking care of all the chores.

Jemmie's cocoa-brown face broke into her usual happy smile. "Y'all jes' go on playing with that baby."

She set the tray down on the white-painted wrought-iron table on a brick terrace adjoining the house and began to pour the lemonade into a glass. Jemmie had never by word or deed hinted that she harbored any curiosity about the baby, or Maggie, or their connection to Hugo Van Courtland. But sometimes Maggie longed to confide in her, especially on perfect days such as this when some melancholy stirring deep inside her warned that such peace and contentment could not last.

Jemmie looked up, her lively dark eyes darting to the gate that led from the front garden to the rear. "Why, heah's Mr.

Hugo come to visit. Afternoon, suh. Y'all's jes' in time for lemonade."

If a lightning bolt had descended from the clear blue sky, Maggie would not have been more startled by the unexpected visitor. Hugo had not come to the house since bringing them to Natchez. Cold dread gripped her. He could only have come to tell her that Delia had returned to claim her child. For one mad moment Maggie considered fleeing with Patience in her arms.

Reason prevailed as she silently wondered what her chances would be of Delia keeping her on as a nanny. Hugo might even recommend she do so. Maggie had been puzzled by Hugo Van Courtland from the start, since he seemed to bear little resemblance to the man who had terrorized Mrs. Lonnigan and Mrs. O'Reilly in New York. To Maggie, he had seemed to be shrewd, but kind and generous. Certainly not as they had portrayed him, a raving tyrant determined to track down Delia and deal harshly with anyone who stood in his way.

"Why, Mr. Van Courtland . . ." she stammered, jumping to her feet.

"Please, don't get up," he said and, turning to Jemmie, added, "Thank you, Jemmie, some cold lemonade sounds good. How are you?"

"Tolerable well, Mr. Hugo, 'cept for the rheumatics," Jemmie replied. She brought two glasses to them and then tactfully held out her arms for the baby.

When Maggie hesitated, Hugo said, "Let Jemmie take her. I want to talk to you."

Maggie reluctantly handed Patience to Jemmie and took a nervous sip of her lemonade.

Hugo pulled a chair closer and sat down. "Is everything satisfactory? According to Mr. Hepple you haven't requested anything, so I assume the housekeeping allowance has been adequate?"

"Oh, yes, more than adequate. In fact, I tried to return some of the money to your lawyer, but he said to keep it for emergencies, in case we couldn't get hold of him."

"And you and the infant are well? But that's a foolish question, since you both look extremely healthy—much better than when I first laid eyes on you."

Maggie could stand the suspense no longer. "She's come back, hasn't she? She's going to take Patience away from me?"

"No," he said quickly, "Delia hasn't returned." He reached inside his white linen jacket and pulled out an envelope, which he handed to her. "I thought you might be interested in this."

The envelope contained several newspaper clippings, and the first thing that leaped from the printed page was a photograph of Delia.

"Oh, my!" Maggie exclaimed. "What on earth is she wearing? It looks like a man's jacket and cravat."

"That's exactly what it is. Why don't you read the articles? It seems a chanteuse who calls herself simply Cordelia is the toast of San Francisco. Those are reviews of her performances, and each and every one raves about her voice, her range and versatility, and about her outrageous attire."

Maggie murmured, "I heard her sing—while she was in labor. When the pain was more than she could bear—when any other woman would have shrieked in agony, Delia began to sing."

"Yes, I've seen her cover her pain that way in the past."

Maggie was rapidly reading the clippings. The reviews were indeed one accolade after another, but Maggie found a recurring question equally intriguing, as without exception every journalist speculated on Cordelia's background. Where had she come from? How could a performer so talented, so unique, have sprung fully formed upon a San Francisco stage? She was a mystery woman without a past. Yet she must have a past. Was it true that she might be connected to European nobility? What about the rumor that she had been a reluctant royal bride who had run away from a loveless marriage? She was known to speak several languages. Her English was flawless, perhaps too perfect for a native daughter of either England or her colonies, or the United States.

Then Maggie came to a name that stopped her short. She read: *Cordelia's business manager, or whatever Julian Van Courtland's position is, refuses to answer any questions about her, even to divulging her place of birth.*

Maggie looked up. "*Julian* Van Courtland?"

"My brother—well, technically, my half brother. I have two. The other is Marcus. Didn't Jemmie tell you?"

"No. Jemmie has been close-mouthed about all of you."

"Dear old Jemmie. You can't buy that kind of loyalty."

The light dawned for Maggie. "So it was *Julian* who found out where Delia was staying in New York and then found me? He was the one who terrified everybody—I thought that was you."

"Julian can be somewhat overbearing."

"Has she written to you? I mean, it's none of my business, but if you intend to send Patience all the way across the country—"

"No, Delia hasn't written and neither has my brother, unless you count those news clippings, which I'm sure he sent. I don't intend to send the infant to her. Obviously Delia and Julian are attempting to sever all of her ties to the past. They certainly will not wish to have an illegitimate child pop up and ruin a promising career. That's what I came to talk to you about. I would like you to continue caring for the baby. I wanted to be open with you about her mother, because you may not have intended to stay on indefinitely in the role of nanny."

"*Patience,*" Maggie said.

"I beg your pardon?"

"Her name is Patience. You never call her by her name."

"I wasn't aware."

"I will take care of Patience for as long as she needs me."

"Mrs. Nesbitt—may I call you Maggie?"

She nodded.

"You are young and ... if I may say so, attractive. I'm sure sooner or later you will remarry. I need your word that if that happens, you will tell your husband that the inf—that Patience is your natural child. If you are unable to give your word, then I'd prefer to replace you immediately, while the—while Patience is still small enough to adjust to someone else. You see, I know what it's like to have the dearest person on earth disappear without warning from one's life. My mother died when I was a child."

Maggie felt an instant rush of sympathy and warmth toward him. "I shan't remarry, but yes, I'll give you my word. If I could, I'd adopt Patience as my very own. I love her so."

His gaze softened. "How lucky she is. Now, I should like to look at her. At this age they change so rapidly, don't they?"

She led the way into the house, and they found Jemmie sitting in the rocking chair in the nursery, Patience on her lap.

The room was filled with sunshine, and the baby's face, framed by pale gold hair, lay against Jemmie's arm, a contrast of light and dark skin that Hugo studied for a moment before speaking. Then he said softly, "She's very fair-skinned, isn't she."

Jemmie gave him a stern glance and muttered something under her breath that Maggie didn't catch. Hugo merely remarked, "You're too sensitive, Jemmie. I implied nothing of the sort. I was commenting on her fair skin as I might also have mentioned her eyes—what are they, blue or violet?"

Then, to Maggie's complete surprise, he asked, "May I hold her?" He took the baby gently from Jemmie, who appeared slightly mollified by the gesture.

How tiny Patience looked in those strong arms! He held her with the awkwardness of a male unaccustomed to babies, yet he must have conveyed trust by his touch, as Patience looked up at him fearlessly, her tiny fingers curled around his thumb, and then, wonder of wonders, she smiled.

Both Maggie and Jemmie gasped.

"Why, Mr. Hugo, suh," Jemmie exclaimed. "That chile done gave y'all her very first smile!"

"I believe," Hugo said solemnly, "Patience and I are going to be great friends."

After he left them, with the promise that he would visit whenever he was in Natchez, Jemmie broke her long silence about the Van Courtlands and confided to Maggie, "Mr. Hugo, he should have chillun of his own. He'd be a good father. Ah specks he'd like strong sons and pretty little daughters, too, only Miz Gabrielle she don't want no chilluns."

"Oh, every woman wants children," Maggie said. "But it isn't easy for some. Perhaps she wants children as much as he does."

"Well, she ain't never gwine git none lessen she sleeps in her husband's bed," Jemmie declared darkly. She clapped her hand to her mouth, apparently realizing that she was guilty of passing along servants' gossip, and added quickly, "Ah must be gittin' old, Maggie. My tongue is running away with me. Ain't none of my business. But I watched that boy grow up, and there ain't no finer man walks this earth."

Maggie was still thinking about how he had held the baby with awkward tenderness and about how handsome and stalwart he looked. Later she wondered if that was the moment she fell in love with Hugo Van Courtland.

Chapter 14

*

Maggie was so engrossed in the sketch she was working on that she wasn't aware they had a visitor until she heard Jemmie greeting Hugo.

The baby was taking her afternoon nap, the house was immaculately clean, and there was no reason for Maggie to feel guilty about using her free time in any way she chose, but she attempted to gather up her sketching materials before Jemmie showed him into the dining room. Maggie had chosen the dining room for its good light and large sturdy table upon which she could work.

But it was too late to hide what she had been doing. Hugo walked into the room. "Hello, Maggie. I brought a few things for the baby."

His gaze flickered over the contents of the table, and he picked up one of her sketches of Patience. "This is very good. You have captured perfectly the innocence of a baby's wide-eyed curiosity."

"You can have the sketch if you like," Maggie said shyly.

His jaw moved slightly. "I might have trouble explaining it to my wife."

Maggie felt herself flush crimson. "Oh, I'm sorry! What a fool I am!"

"Not at all. I'm sure you wonder why I have not told my wife about the child. Perhaps I should explain that Gabrielle doesn't particularly care for Delia and resents my family's involvement with her."

He paused, then added ruefully, "That's probably putting it too mildly. But I would prefer to keep Patience's existence secret, at least for the time being."

He picked up several of her other sketches and studied them, stopping at one of the dress designs and raising his eyes to look at what Maggie was wearing. "You designed and made your gown?"

Maggie nodded. It was a simple day dress of printed cotton, but she had added interest by using smocking at the waist and shoulders to give shape without restricting movement. "Clothes are so expensive and some of the ready-made fashions are hot and uncomfortable for summers here."

"No need to justify making your own clothes to me," Hugo said. "I admire both your thrift and your enterprise. I see Jemmie is also wearing one of your designs, and you have sketches of infant gowns."

Maggie knew she couldn't go on hiding what she'd been doing indefinitely, and he had given her the perfect opening to confide in him. She had grown more comfortable with him during the past few months. He had visited several times, usually bringing something for the baby, spending an hour or so in the small house on Palmetto Street enjoying Jemmie's lemonade or a mint julep if the afternoon hour was late. He was keenly interested in each stage of the baby's development, and often played with her, showing none of the embarrassment most childless men exhibited around infants.

She drew a deep breath and began, "Mr. Van Courtland—"

"Do you think we're now well enough acquainted that you might call me Hugo?"

"Oh ... yes." She was far from comfortable with the idea but was unsure why, so plunged on: "You see, I found a sewing machine up in the attic and decided to make some clothes for Patience and myself. Then one day I was buying fabric, and the shop's proprietor happened to recognize the material of the dress I was wearing as having come from her shop, and she complimented me on my work and asked if I would be interested in making a gown for a friend of hers who wanted something unusual for a garden party. Well, one thing led to another and I was given several orders by other ladies. I don't want you to think I've been neglecting the baby while I've been doing this—"

"Maggie, Patience is obviously well cared for, and I'm glad you have something fulfilling to occupy yourself with—I regret to say the old adage about Satan finding mischief for idle hands has been demonstrated to me many times."

"Actually, I'm hoping that sewing my own designs will turn out to be more than just a pastime," Maggie went on. "I believe I could turn it into a business. I worked in the garment factories of New York for years, I've a lot of experience. My goal is to make enough money to support Patience and myself. I feel so guilty taking money from you and depriving you of Jemmie, although she's wonderful and I—"

Hugo held up his hand. "Please! Not so fast! Let me respond. First of all, Jemmie has been retired from service to my family for several years but was delighted to be back in harness. She has grown very fond of you and Patience, and I'm sure would be heartbroken to be put out to pasture again. I can understand your desire to be self-sufficient, but please don't burn all your bridges too soon. It takes time to establish any new business, and while you're doing so why not stay here in this house and keep Jemmie on to help you? You'd be doing all of us a great favor. An unoccupied house quickly deteriorates, and I've never been able to bring myself to either sell or rent this one."

He saw her hesitation and went on: "You see, I spent many happy hours here as a boy. To me, this was a vacation house, a place for play rather than schoolwork. Our main house was in New Orleans, and my father bought this place in order to have somewhere to live when he came to Natchez on business. I only came with him during the school holidays. The fondest memories of my childhood were made here, when there was just my father and me. Since you and Patience moved in, it's almost like coming home. You've brought the house back to life."

"But deprived you of a place to stay in Natchez," Maggie pointed out.

"No, I never used the cottage. I found it more convenient to stay at a hotel, especially since I now have a good agent here and rarely visit Natchez. I closed the cottage after my father's death. I would like you to stay."

"That's very kind of you, Mr. Van . . . Hugo, and we'd love to go on living here, but I can't run a business from this charming house. I thought I'd rent a storefront and perhaps live on the premises."

"By all means rent your place of business, but live here, please."

"Well, I suppose it would be all right for a little while longer."

"Good. Now, another old adage my late father lived by was that all work and no play made Jack a dull boy. I'm going to be in Natchez for several days with nothing but business to occupy me. Would you and Patience take pity on me and accompany me on a picnic tomorrow?"

Maggie felt herself flush with pleasure. "Oh, that would be lovely."

"I'll be here with a carriage and hamper tomorrow morning after breakfast."

Maggie spent the rest of the day in a happy daze, but told herself the invitation meant nothing and she should not read anything beyond his interest in Patience in it. Still the prospect of spending the day with Hugo delighted her.

Jemmie did not share her enthusiasm. "Ah, doan' know, Maggie. Mr. Hugo, he's a married man," she said, a worried frown creasing her brow.

"Oh, he's just taking me along as Patience's nanny," Maggie protested.

"He sure done took to that chile," Jemmie muttered, her frown deepening.

"What are you suggesting?" Maggie asked sharply. "That he is the baby's father? He isn't."

"Folks is going to talk. That's what I'm saying."

"I can't cancel the picnic now, I've already told him we'd go."

"Seems to me lak' Mr. Hugo's been coming to Natchez a heap more'n he used to, and I done seen him looking at you when you wasn't noticing. Trouble's brewing is what I think."

"Oh, Jemmie, what nonsense!" Maggie had to turn away to hide her flaming cheeks.

"Be it on your own head," Jemmie declared darkly, and shuffled off to the nursery, muttering all the way.

The following morning Maggie was up before dawn, anxiously scanning the sky for any hint of rain, selecting and discarding clothes for both herself and Patience.

She was too nervous to eat breakfast, and paced restlessly even when the sun rose in a clear blue sky and her mirror told her that she looked pretty in her newest gown, a cool celery-colored muslin trimmed with white broderie anglais. She had washed her hair and copper glints now appeared in the sorrel waves that she had skewered into a coil on top of her head, but from which wandering tendrils were already escaping.

Jemmie placed a white cotton bonnet on Patience's pale gold hair and glanced sideways at Maggie. "If'n you want folks to think you is a nanny, maybe you should wear a pinafore and cap 'stead of that dress.'

"You know Mr. Hugo would hate that."

"Maybe so. But it would be proper."

"If it will make you happy, I'll ask him when he gets here. In fact, I'll go further than that. I'll tell him you think we might cause gossip and see if he wants to change his mind about taking us for a picnic."

"Ain't no call for you to bring trouble to these old bones. Ain't my place to say what Mr. Hugo cain't do." Jemmie finished tying the ribbons beneath Patience's chin and said, "There now, my li'l angel looks pretty as a picture."

Maggie laid her hand gently on Jemmie's arm. "You know I would never do anything to hurt Mr. Hugo, don't you? I owe him everything."

Jemmie didn't respond, but her anxious expression spoke volumes. She watched for Hugo's arrival from the parlor window and when the carriage turned the corner of Palmetto Street she called to Maggie. "He's heah and he ain't got no driver. He's driving the carriage himself."

She had obviously been hoping for a chaperone in the guise of a coachman, Maggie thought, and wondered if perhaps she should say something to Hugo—maybe even suggest that Jemmie go along with them. But she was beginning to learn from Jemmie a little of the strict code of behavior that existed between master and servant, and even in the hierarchy of servants themselves. She knew therefore that even if Hugo agreed, Jemmie would be scandalized by such a suggestion.

Minutes later Hugo was at the door and Maggie found her heart was beating too rapidly to say much of anything.

"How pretty and cool you both look," he said, sweeping the baby up into his arms. Patience cooed delightedly, as she always did when he visited. "It's going to be hot today, but

I thought we'd go to a wooded spot near the river that was a favorite of my father's and mine. In fact, it's where he taught me to swim and to fish. We shan't be late, Jemmie. I'll have them back by midafternoon."

The place he had chosen for the picnic was a picture of tranquility. A grassy bank, shaded by a dense canopy of branches, sloped gently to the water where sunbeams danced like fireflies on the indigo surface. It was like being in a cool green cathedral, hushed and sepulchral, with a window opening to a dazzling vista of light and endless motion as the river journeyed on to the sea, as it had for countless generations.

They spread a blanket and, with Patience lying between them, sat for a time in companionable silence watching the flowing water. Maggie had never felt more content or at peace, yet at the same time was disturbed by the realization that she was acutely aware of the presence of the man beside her. She could faintly smell the bay rum he had used after shaving, and out of the corner of her eye could see his profile and the way his dark hair ruffled slightly as a breeze drifted from the river. She couldn't see his expression, yet knew no matter what else would be written on his face and in his expressive dark blue eyes, there would also be that underlying sadness that never seemed to leave him. Not for the first time, she wondered about his Gabrielle. Oh, to have a man such as he for a husband and allow him to feel such melancholy. To Maggie, it was inconceivable.

"Did you always want to design dresses?" he asked after a while.

"I always loved to draw and to paint, yes. Living in New York I was able to go to the galleries and museums sometimes, and I read every book ever written about the great artists. But I didn't really consider designing dresses until I came here and needed something cool to wear."

"Did you go to school in New York?"

"No. My mother taught me at home. She was a Scottish schoolteacher who came here with the intention of going West to teach, but she met a man, a sailor on the ship bringing her to America."

"And you followed her example by marrying a sailor, also."

"Will Nesbitt was nothing like my father," Maggie said shortly.

"Ah," Hugo said quietly, and she wondered at the depth of understanding in that simple utterance.

Patience lifted tiny starlike hands to try to catch a butterfly that hovered briefly over her head before going to seek the sunlight, and they both turned to watch the baby for a moment.

"So here we are," Hugo said, "watching over Delia's child, while she . . ." His voice trailed away. "Maggie, have you considered, as I have, the consequences of what we are doing? I mean, the emotional consequences. I must admit it is something that had not occurred to me when you first brought Patience to me. I did not foresee that it was possible to become attached to a small scrap of humanity, although in fairness you told me that you already loved her. But I always believed that men were somehow immune to such feelings— that fathers merely tolerated their offspring until they were old enough to be companions. It's strange that I feel this fierce protectiveness—possessiveness perhaps—toward a child who is not even my own."

"Why, I think that's very touching," Maggie answered. "What a wonderful father you'll make to your own children."

Although she had not answered his question, he stood up and abruptly announced, "I'll fetch the hamper."

When he returned with a large wicker hamper, Maggie said, "You asked if I had thought about the consequences of our taking care of Patience. Yes, I have. Not a day goes by that I don't worry that Delia will return and whisk her away. Yet she hasn't cared enough even to inquire about her baby."

Hugo spread a checkered tablecloth on the grass and looked at her. "She doesn't know we have the baby."

Maggie felt her mouth drop open. "You didn't write to tell her?"

"No. As you know, she is with my brother. He and I both suspected she was with child before she ran off to New York. But then he sent me a message implying that it had been a false alarm. That's why I was skeptical when you appeared with the baby."

"But you do believe now that Patience is Delia's child?"

"Oh, yes, there's no doubt in my mind. However, until

Delia and Julian return and I learn the whole story, I thought it best just to wait and see what happens."

"I shouldn't ask—but do you believe your brother Julian is Patience's father?"

"No," Hugo said firmly. "He definitely is not. Had not Patience been conceived while Julian was abroad, I might have thought so, since Julian is not above lying about such things. But there is no possibility he could be the father."

"So we wait and see," Maggie said. "How difficult that is. So much easier to act—to do something. You know, I dream about Delia sometimes. Her icy courage, the way she sang a beautiful lullaby yet wouldn't hold her baby."

"She wouldn't?" he asked sharply, his eyes narrowed speculatively.

"No. In fact, she seemed reluctant to touch her. Almost as though she were ashamed. I supposed because she had given birth out of wedlock."

"No," Hugo said slowly, a strange expression on his face, "Delia wouldn't feel shame for having an illegitimate child. I think perhaps there is another explanation for her not wanting her baby, and since Julian denies there even is a baby—" He broke off, his gaze focusing on Maggie again. "Someday I'll explain. Now, I'm hungry, are you?"

He began to unload the hamper, producing cold roast chicken and thick slices of ham, crusty bread, fresh peaches, and strawberries, and spreading the feast before her.

They ate heartily and gave the baby a scraped clean chicken bone to suck on, which kept her happy for a long time. Then Maggie gave her a bottle of sugar water to drink, since she had been afraid a bottle of milk might spoil. "I must get back soon, as she'll need her milk and a nap," she said.

Hugo was watching her as she cradled the baby in her arms and held the curved bottle with its rubber teat to her lips. "You should have children of your own, Maggie. Perhaps it is even more imperative for you now, to avoid the heartbreak of parting from Patience."

"I keep hoping that won't happen. But in any case, there is no man in my life that I could . . ." Her voice trailed away as her eyes locked with his, and in that blinding second she recognized the lie of her words. There was indeed a man in her life that she could easily love. The trouble was, he belonged to someone else.

"Then we must remedy that situation," Hugo said quickly. "I have several personable young men working for me. I'll introduce you to some of them. We can't let a pretty young widow . . ."

Maggie didn't hear the rest of what he said as the word *pretty* echoed around her mind. He thought she was pretty.

They packed away the dishes and remains of their lunch, and then Hugo picked up the baby and suggested they go for a stroll along the riverbank. He directed their conversation away from personal matters to art, and astonished her with his knowledge of the great masters. He also amused her with some wry comments on the fashion foibles of both men and women. Then, as a heavily laden barge moved down the river, he told her a little of the history of the Mississippi.

Maggie felt enough at ease with him then to inquire if he was native born, and he replied, "Yes. In New Orleans. My father came here during the War Between the States, and after it was over he sent for my mother." He looked down at the baby in his arms and said, "Look, she's asleep. We probably should start back."

Later, after they were back in the small house on Palmetto Street, Maggie relived every moment of the time she spent with Hugo while Jemmie cast reproachful glances in her direction.

The following day Hugo returned, bringing several books. One contained reproductions of famous paintings. Another followed fashion trends throughout the centuries. And there was a collection of biographical sketches of several lesser-known artists. He presented them to her almost apologetically. "Please accept these as a token of my gratitude."

Astonished, she exclaimed, "But I am the one who is grateful to you!"

"Maggie, like others whose path Delia crossed, I know your life was thrown into turmoil. Because of her you lost your job, your home. You gave up everything to care for her child, at tremendous cost to yourself. I feel responsible for Delia's actions and grateful to you for doing what you did."

Not knowing what else to say, Maggie stammered her thanks for the books.

He added, "I'm leaving for New Orleans today. Don't hesitate to call on Mr. Hepple if you need anything."

Still clutching the books, she saw him to the door and watched him walk to the garden gate. He turned and waved. Maggie went back into the house, feeling bereft.

Maggie was so inundated with orders for gowns during the following days that the time passed swiftly. Her bank account was growing, and she would have liked to start looking for a vacant shop, but was too busy. She tried to arrange appointments for fittings and used the sewing machine only while Patience was napping, but found the baby loved to watch while she worked on the designs, so she made a fairly rigid pillow and propped the tiny girl on the dining table beside her sketchpad.

Two weeks after Hugo returned to New Orleans, Maggie received an invitation to a dinner party at the home of Mr. and Mrs. Walter Hepple, the attorney who represented Hugo in Natchez.

There was a handwritten note on the bottom of the engraved invitation:

Just a small gathering of friends, we hope you will come, Mrs. Nesbitt.

Maggie concluded that the Hepples' invitation must be Hugo's doing. She recalled him saying he would have to arrange for her to meet eligible men. The realization both disappointed and angered her. What did he think? That he must safely marry her off to any man willing to take her, in order to protect his own reputation?

The more she thought about this, the angrier she became. He didn't have to compromise himself by calling on her, by taking her on a picnic or buying her gifts. He could have treated her as nothing more than a children's nurse. Nor did he have to provide a house and a servant, as if she were his mistress and Patience his bastard.

That thought brought her up short. Where had that image come from? Surely not her own mind? But where else? She was attracted to him, after all. But wasn't what she felt only gratitude for his kindness? There could never be anything more between them. She had always loathed those pathetic women who coveted other women's husbands.

She had met Mr. Hepple only when he called to pick up the household bills to be paid and to give her housekeeping money. He was middle-aged, with a pale nearsighted gaze, and although he was always courteous, there was a hint of condescension in his tone. Maggie was quite sure he would never have invited her to dine at his home unless ordered to do so.

That evening, still undecided as to whether or not to accept the Hepples' invitation, Maggie sat in the nursery, rocking Patience in the big old wooden rocker that had perhaps been there when Hugo was a boy. She often imagined a dark-haired, inquisitive little boy romping through those rooms, perhaps sliding down the banister, or curled up with a favorite book in front of the parlor fireplace. But tonight her thoughts were taking her in another direction.

All day long Maggie had been unable to concentrate on her work as her mind wrestled with several questions that had begun to trouble her.

She kept returning to the fact that Hugo had brought her and Patience to this cottage in Natchez, although he lived in New Orleans. Where in New Orleans, she didn't know. He had said Delia had been a ward of his family, so presumably she had lived with them at one time. But neither he nor Jemmie had ever mentioned exactly where the Van Courtlands lived.

Maggie's curiosity about Hugo's home and family grew stronger. When Patience curled sweetly limp against her shoulder, Maggie put the sleeping baby down and went in search of Jemmie.

The old woman was in the kitchen, sitting at the table polishing the cutlery. Maggie took a chair opposite to her and picked up a cloth and a silver fork to polish. "I've been invited to dinner at the Hepples'."

Jemmie nodded to acknowledge she had heard, but made no comment.

"I believe it's Mr. Hugo's doing. He wants me to meet eligible men."

Jemmie polished silver furiously, her mouth making chewing motions as though she were eating words.

"Perhaps I'll go. I haven't decided yet."

This brought a response. "Seems lak' if'n Mr. Hugo wants

you to go, then you should go. He doan ask much, but he gives a whole heap."

"That's true," Maggie said. "Why do you think he does?"

"Ain't for me to say."

Several minutes passed in silence.

Then Maggie said, "You knew Delia, I suppose?"

"Yes'm."

"You know I hate it when you address me like that. I thought we'd agreed on first names? Am I still to be punished for going on the picnic?"

"Weren't fittin'. Best you go to Mrs. Hepple's dinner and doan go no place with Mr. Hugo." Jemmie looked up suddenly. "Lan'sakes! I sure hope Mr. Hugo he ain't planning to be at the Hepples'."

That was a tantalizing possibility, Maggie thought. She hoped Jemmie didn't see the way the color flared to her cheeks. She said quickly, "Tell me about Delia, please."

"She can sing lak' an angel."

"Did she live with the Van Courtlands?"

"She stayed at the Willows when she weren't away at school."

Maggie had to bend over the serving spoon she was polishing in order to hide the elation in her expression at this slip of Jemmie's tongue. "That's the name of their house in New Orleans, isn't it?" she asked casually.

"No, it ain't. The Willows is a big ole plantation house upriver from N'Orleans and doan you go asking me no questions I ain't supposed to answer."

"I'm sorry. Perhaps you'd care to ask me a question. To even things up, that is."

Jemmie's deepset eyes gleamed. "Patience is Delia's baby, ain't she? Nobody else could've given her those eyes and that hair."

"I suppose there's no use denying it. But, Jemmie, we mustn't tell anyone else."

Jemmie looked hurt that she would even suggest such a possibility. She stood up, old bones creaking, and put away the cutlery tray and silver polish. "Good night, Maggie. I be gwine to bed now."

"Good night, Jemmie." At least their rift seemed to have healed, she thought, as Jemmie had used her given name again. Maggie was relieved. The older woman's respect and counsel were important to her.

Maggie found it difficult to sleep that night. What if Hugo was indeed to be one of the other guests at the Hepples' dinner party? Oh, Maggie, she whispered to herself in the darkness of her room, you've never given a second glance to any man since Will sailed away and never came back. Why now, why this one? He's forbidden.

Still, she could not stop thinking about him, and when she finally slept, he was in all her dreams.

The following morning Maggie was expecting a customer to arrive for a fitting, so when the doorbell rang just as she was about to go upstairs she called, "I'll go, Jemmie. I'm right here in the hall."

Throwing the door open wide, Maggie saw their visitor was not her client, but a complete stranger. And what a stunning stranger she was to be sure. A petite woman with raven hair and flashing green eyes stood on the doorstep. She was dressed in a beautifully tailored linen suit, which seemed to emphasise her softly feminine curves. Her exquisite features, delicate as a china doll's, were marred only by a slight downward tilt to her mouth.

Before Maggie could speak, the green eyes flicked over her in undisguised appraisal, and the unexpected visitor spoke in a low purr. "You are Mrs. Nesbitt, I presume?"

"Yes, I am. Is there something—"

The interruption was rapier swift. "I am Mrs. Hugo Van Courtland."

Chapter 15

*

For a moment Maggie was too taken aback to speak. She knew a host of emotions must be showing on her face, ranging from shock to guilt.

Hugo's wife said coolly, "Perhaps we should go inside?"

"Oh . . . yes, please come in." Maggie led the way into the parlor, and at the same time Patience awoke and began to cry for her morning bottle.

At the sound of the baby's cry, her visitor's eyes glittered and her lips compressed. "I don't have much time to waste on this matter. Let Jemmie take care of her."

Maggie nodded, her thoughts racing. Obviously Gabrielle knew about Hugo's arrangements for Patience and herself, but did she know that the baby was Delia's? Maggie decided she must remain calm and be careful what she said until her unexpected caller revealed the purpose of her visit. Clearing her throat nervously, Maggie said, "Would you like to sit down?"

Gabrielle's eyes flickered over the antique furniture in the parlor, as though she were seeing it for the first time and found it not to her taste. "What I have to say won't take long. I am aware that my husband is "—she paused, as though searching for an appropriate word—"maintaining his mistress and his bastard here—"

Aghast, Maggie interrupted, "No! That isn't true."

A perfectly arched black eyebrow rose slightly. "No? You are here, are you not? A baby cried, did she not? And is that baby not yours? Oh, I know there is a birth certificate claiming your husband is the father, but wasn't he reported missing at sea seven years ago? Perhaps you are going to tell me there was a ghostly conception?"

"Your husband isn't the father," Maggie said quietly.

"Then who is?"

Maggie's mouth clamped shut.

Gabrielle's expression was disdainful. "This house belongs to my husband. Jemmie is an old family retainer who has been with the Van Courtlands since she was freed from slavery at the end of the war. Tell me why you and the child are here if not because you are my husband's mistress."

"I think you should ask your husband these questions," Maggie said guardedly.

"I do not need answers. I know all I need to know about you and your child. I came to tell you that I want you out of this house and out of my husband's life. Now, since I'm well aware that men are gullible fools in such matters, I insist that you be the architect of this. He is not to know I came to see you. You will move out. Tell him you do not wish to see him again. Make it very clear that your affair is over, finished."

"But I can't—" Maggie began.

"Yes, you can. If you do not he will be ruined, I promise you. I will make the affair and the fact that he sired a bastard public knowledge. The wives of his business associates, all of his friends and family, will be outraged. He will be ruined, Mrs. Nesbitt, both socially and in all aspects of his business. If this is what you want, then continue as you have in the past. If you profess to have any feelings for him, then quietly exit his life."

"Mrs. Van Courtland, won't you please talk to your husband about this? I'm sure he will explain—"

"Are you dim-witted? Am I not making myself clear? There is to be no further discussion. I want you out of this house before the week is over. If you comply with my wishes, and if you sign a document I have prepared stating that you guarantee to end your affair with my husband, I will pay you the sum of one thousand dollars."

Maggie controlled her anger with difficulty. "I am employed by Mr. Van Courtland. I will leave when he tells me he no longer requires my services."

Gabrielle carried a small parasol, now folded, and for an instant Maggie thought she might strike her with it. Instead she snapped, "Think over the consequences of your actions before making any hasty decisions, Mrs. Nesbitt," and flounced out of the room.

Seconds later the front door slammed. Maggie turned to the window and watched Hugo's wife depart, tiny feet taking rapid little steps toward the garden gate.

Now Maggie saw an open carriage waiting at the gate. A slightly built man jumped down as Gabrielle approached. He was handsome in a delicate sort of way, with the unhealthy pallor of one who suffers from a chronic illness. He was also far too well dressed to be a carriage driver and, from the familiar way he placed his hands around Gabrielle's tiny waist, must surely be related to her. A brother, perhaps, since they were both dark-haired and diminutive, and as Maggie's last glimpse of the two of them in profile confirmed, they did bear a distinct resemblance to each other.

There was a discreet cough behind her, and Maggie turned from the window to find Jemmie, the baby in her arms, standing in the doorway.

"I suppose you heard everything?" Maggie asked.

Jemmie gave her a blank stare.

"Oh, for heaven's sake," Maggie snapped, "I know there's nothing wrong with your hearing. Jemmie, I need your help now. I must get in touch with Mr. Hugo right away, and I don't want to go through Mr. Hepple to do it. You must tell me where I can find him."

"Ah doan know—" Jemmie began.

"Yes, you do. Will I find him at the Willows?"

A look of fear claimed the old woman's dusky features, and she shook her head violently. "I weren't supposed to tell you 'bout the Willows. You mustn't go, there, Maggie."

"The New Orleans house then? Or perhaps his office? I must go to him, Jemmie. He has a right to know of his wife's threats."

Jemmie shook her head helplessly. "Y'all will do more harm than good. Listen to this ole darky's advice, Maggie. Mr. Hugo, he's got family problems lak' you cain't imagine. This heah chile is the least of them. Now, ah knowed she was Delia's the minute ah laid these ole eyes on her. But if'n y'all go telling folks that, why Mr. Hugo's problems, they's gonna get a whole heap worse. Best to jes' do lak Miz Gabrielle says and move on out."

"Without a word of explanation to Mr. Hugo? After he's been so kind to us?"

"Tell Mr. Hepple you can manage on your own now, on account you is gwine in the sewing business. 'Sides, you'll have that thousand dollars Miz Gabrielle offered you."

"I wouldn't take a penny from her," Maggie declared. She paced restlessly around the small parlor.

"Don't make no more trouble for Mr. Hugo," Jemmie pleaded. "Miz Gabrielle, she's a very determined woman, and she weren't making no idle threats. Y'all defy her, and it won't only be Mr. Hugo who suffers, there'll be others, and maybe you, too."

"Me? What have I done? I've done nothing wrong . . ." Her voice trailed away. The old specter of losing Patience loomed again. She supposed she could move out, rent a storefront as she had planned, and although it would be a pinch for a while, with her growing list of customers she believed she could now support Patience and herself. Gabrielle Van Courtland's ultimatum had merely changed her timetable, not her plans.

Maggie held out her arms for the baby. "I suppose I could inform Mr. Hepple, and he could tell Mr. Hugo how to find Patience when he comes back to Natchez. You could stay on here until then. Or would you prefer to go back to the Willows? I shall miss you, Jemmie. I wish I could afford to hire you."

"I is a free woman," Jemmie said with dignity. "I reckon I can work without pay if'n I want to."

"Do you mean it? Oh, I'd be so grateful, and of course, I'll pay you as soon as I can."

For the first time since Hugo's wife appeared, Jemmie beamed happily.

"Let's start packing," Maggie said. Sooner or later Hugo would find out what happened, and, Maggie was sure, would tell his family the truth, thereby clearing up the whole situation. Then perhaps he would again come to visit Patience.

As they began to sort out Maggie's belongings, she glanced at Jemmie and asked, "The man who accompanied Mrs. Van Courtland but waited in the carriage, did you see him? Who was he?"

Jemmie didn't meet her eye, but after a moment she answered in what sounded like a studiedly offhand man-

ner, "Why, that was Miz Gabrielle's cousin. Mr. Alain
Marchand."

There was a moment's silence that to Maggie seemed
weighted with the possibility of an important revelation.
Jemmie probably knew almost as much about Gabrielle and
her family as she did about the Van Courtlands. But she offered no further information.

Maggie said, "They looked almost as much alike as brother
and sister."

"Well, they was raised together when they was chilluns, 'til
Mr. Alain went off to college." Jemmie's scowl indicated
clearly she would say no more on the subject.

"You know, it just occurred to me that Mr. Hepple's dinner
party will be held this coming Saturday. Perhaps I should go,
in case Mr. Hugo is there. I could tell him of our plans to
move then."

Now it was Maggie's turn to avoid the knowing glance
Jemmie gave her.

By the evening of the Hepples' dinner party Maggie felt
she had accomplished a great deal. She had found and rented
an empty store with living quarters over it. They would be
cramped, but with Patience sharing the single bedroom with
Maggie and Jemmie sleeping in a small parlor, they could
manage. There was even some furniture. Table, chairs, a bed,
a sofa. They could take the baby's cradle from Hugo's house,
but Maggie was determined not to remove anything else.

"But y'all need a sewing machine," Jemmie said. "Mr.
Hugo wouldn't mind if you borrowed the one you been using."

"No. I think I'll have enough to buy a secondhand machine. Mrs. Mowbray at the fabric store said she knows
where I can buy one fairly reasonably, and I went to the lum-
ber yard and they've got off-cuts of wood I can pick up to
make a worktable and shelves. Mrs. Mowbray said she'd
send her handyman over."

Maggie found she was excited and brimming with confidence at the challenge of becoming independent from Hugo,
while at the same time hoping somehow he would continue to
be a part of her life. After all, he would want to keep track
of Delia's child.

It was Jemmie who suggested Maggie take some time to make herself an evening dress for the Hepples' party. "You is gwine meet some ladies who might order clothes from you. Best wear something that'll catch their eye, and when they compliment you, tell them 'bout your business."

Maggie was at first doubtful. "I surely can't hawk my business at a private dinner party. I think it would be a terrible breach of etiquette." She paused, then grinned. "But if someone insisted on knowing where my gown came from, I suppose it wouldn't hurt to be truthful."

She had never owned an evening gown before, and although she winced at the cost of a beautiful length of fabric, an iridescent-shot taffeta in forest green that mysteriously shimmered amber and gold under the play of the light, she decided the result was worth the money.

She designed the neckline and small puffed sleeves in intricate ruffles edged with gold braid, which appeared to stand away from her body, creating a soft frame for her throat, shoulders, and a daring amount of cleavage. The bodice and draped skirt were plain, the shot taffeta needing no enhancement, and the waist was cinched as tight as she could bear. Jemmie would help her lace her whalebone corset.

The low neckline of her gown begged for a necklace, but Maggie had sold all of her own and her mother's jewelry to pay Patience's medical bills in New York. But when she came downstairs to show off the finished gown to Jemmie on the night of the party, Jemmie had a surprise waiting.

Smiling broadly, the old woman said, "Ah doan know who's mo' beautiful, you or the gown, Maggie, and you got the creamiest, plumpest, prettiest shoulders and neck I ever did see. But you need a neck ornament." She paused, then brought her hand from behind her back.

"Oh, Jemmie! How sweet of you." Maggie looked at a dark green velvet ribbon, to which Jemmie had pinned a lovely cameo brooch. "But you can't give me your brooch. I will borrow it for tonight, though, and do thank you."

Jemmie then held out her palm. "Figured you'd need earbobs too, so I done made these. Ain't much, but . . ."

Maggie exclaimed with delight as she saw Jemmie had fashioned the earbobs from tiny bird feathers, shimmering and iridescent like her gown, in shades of green and deep pansy purple, fastening the delicate feathers to gold wires. "Oh, Jemmie! How clever and artistic you are! I had no idea you had such talent. They're lovely."

Impulsively Maggie threw her arms around Jemmie and hugged her. Jemmie drew back, embarrassed but obviously pleased by the gesture.

The Hepples had sent a note offering to send a carriage for her, and Maggie gladly accepted. "I feel like Cinderella off to the ball," she told Jemmie as she departed.

The old woman grinned. "Only you ain't gwine turn into no pumpkin at midnight."

"I think it was the carriage that turned into the pumpkin," Maggie answered. "And Cinderella lost a slipper—I'll try not to do that, either."

She did indeed feel like Cinderella as she was borne through the twilit streets of Natchez to a gracious house on a tree-lined street. *Please let Hugo be here.* The thought—or was it a prayer?—came unbidden as she was shown into a crowded drawing room.

Mr. Hepple led a tiny birdlike woman in a rather unbecoming brown satin gown trimmed with drooping ecru lace over to Maggie. He said stiffly, "Abigail, this is Mr. Hugo Van Courtland's friend, Mrs. Nesbitt."

Surprised that the attorney would describe her as a friend, Maggie decided to clear up any confusion. "How do you do, Mrs. Hepple. Actually, I am a former employee of Mr. Van Courtland. I am about to embark upon my own business."

Mrs. Hepple had bright, lively eyes that twinkled in a friendly way, offsetting her husband's cold tone. "Welcome to our home, Mrs. Nesbitt, and congratulations upon becoming a businesswoman. Come to the punch bowl and you can tell me all about your endeavor."

"Please call me Maggie, and I'm afraid I'm making my business sound more important than it really is. I'm just a seamstress, but I will be opening my own establishment—designing as well as making clothes for women and children."

"If you tell me you made that gorgeous gown you're wearing, I shall shriek with joy and give you an order at once!" Mrs. Hepple cried, taking her elbow to lead her through the guests with a murmured promise to introduce her to them as

soon as she had assured herself of a first-in-line spot for
Maggie's services.

Hugo was not present, Maggie noted, disappointed. But the
guests did seem to be awaiting a late arrival before being
seated in the dining room, so perhaps there was hope that
Hugo would come.

She was introduced to the other couples and two young
lawyers who appeared to be single, confirming her suspicion
that Hugo had asked Hepple to pair her off with eligible
bachelors. She gave neither of them more than a passing
glance. Then a late arrival appeared.

Maggie looked across the room to see Mr. Hepple fawning
over a stunning vision in a burgundy gown that set off her
magnolia-pale skin and darker than midnight hair. Maggie's
spirits sank as she prepared to face Gabrielle Van Courtland
for the second time within a week.

Everyone present apparently knew her, as she was greeted
by a chorus of compliments and cries that she had stayed
away from Natchez far too long. Hugo's wife, obviously accustomed to being the center of attention, accepted that
homage with cool smiles and airy gestures.

Hepple paused only briefly beside Maggie to say, "I understand you have met Mrs. Van Courtland?"

Gabrielle's glance flickered over Maggie's gown, and as
the dinner gong sounded she murmured, too low for anyone
to overhear, "I deposited the promised sum in your bank yesterday."

"I don't want your money—" Maggie began, but Gabrielle
was already slipping her arm through Hepple's to go in to
dinner.

Maggie was seated beside one of the unattached lawyers,
Gabrielle with the other, and it was soon clear from the table
conversation that Hugo was in New York on business.

Observing his wife, Maggie felt grudging admiration for
her poise, her vivid beauty, and above all, her lively conversation. Everyone, it seemed, hung on her every word.

Gabrielle addressed Maggie directly only once during the
course of the evening. As dessert was served, she looked
across the table and said, "You must feel quite proud of your
elevated position in the world, Mrs. Nesbitt. Being a seam-

stress must be quite a step forward from" she paused delicately and finished—"your previous occupation."

There was an awkward pause, and everyone seemed to be concentrating on the crystal bowls of poached pears being placed before them.

Maggie felt herself flush. "I am not ashamed that I was employed as a nanny. Surely caring for a child is the noblest profession of all."

"A *nanny*," Gabrielle repeated. "Is that what you call it?"

Mrs. Hepple quickly picked up a spoon and tapped her bowl, the ringing crystal sounding like a warning bell. To a hovering maid she said, "You haven't forgotten the whipped cream, have you? Now, since Gabrielle has brought up the subject of Mrs. Nesbitt's enterprise, I'd like to propose a toast to her success, which judging by the gown she's wearing— which is one of her own designs—is assured."

Catching the frosty glance she was receiving from her husband, Mrs. Hepple added defiantly, "We're in a new century, Walter, and I for one believe it's time we rid ourselves of old-fashioned ideas about women in business."

"I agree," one of the younger women said. "How I'd love to be a journalist on Father's paper, but of course, he won't hear of it."

"And neither will I," her male companion said pompously. "No wife of mine is going to work outside our home."

"We aren't married yet," was the tart response, with a smile in Maggie's direction.

The whipped cream arrived and was ladled onto the poached pears, and when dessert was finished Mrs. Hepple asked the ladies to join her in the drawing room while the men had their coffee and cigars.

Maggie was quickly surrounded by women admiring her gown and her earbobs, wanting to know the address of her shop and asking about the latest trends in fashion. Maggie was grateful to Abigail Hepple, who with a few well-chosen words had somehow elevated her from seamstress to fashion expert.

Gabrielle remained aloof, taking a seat in a window alcove as far from the circle around Maggie as she could. Her hostess politely joined her.

When at last the clamor of questions quieted, Maggie

caught a snatch of conversation between Mrs. Hepple and Gabrielle.

"My dear, you are so kind to take care of your poor dear cousin, but do you think it's wise to be seen alone in his company? I heard you two rode through town in an open carriage last week."

"Alain is my first cousin, we are closer than brother and sister—indeed, we were raised together," Gabrielle flashed back. "Until I married Hugo, we had the same last name. How could anyone gossip about us?"

"Oh, you know how people are. You are not children any longer, and your husband is not traveling with you."

"Alain isn't well. He came to Natchez to consult a new doctor. He might even have to return to the sanitarium."

"I'm so sorry. Forgive me, dear. I didn't realize—"

The men were now drifting back into the drawing room, and Maggie was immediately monopolized by her dinner companion, whose name was Lucas Stone. He had russet brown hair that nearly matched her own, pale blue eyes, and an engagingly shy smile. He was, he informed her, newly employed by Mr. Hepple, and was originally from Savannah. "I've never been invited here before," he added, glancing around the luxuriously appointed drawing room. "Quite an honor for the lowest man on the totem pole."

"How do you think a mere seamstress feels?" Maggie asked. "I expect one of us was invited to be the dinner companion of the other."

"In that case, may I seize the opportunity to ask if I may call on you ... I mean, I did understand that you are a widow, didn't I?"

Maggie hesitated, then answered, "Yes, that would be nice. Although I must warn you that between setting up shop and caring for the baby, I don't have much free time."

"The baby," he repeated, clearly surprised.

Maggie merely smiled.

Across the room Gabrielle, in conversation with Mr. Hepple, suddenly shot a venomous green glance in her direction. Maggie shivered involuntarily, knowing that Hugo's wife was not finished with her.

Chapter 16

*

GABRIELLE

I had loved my first cousin, Alain Marchand, since we were children. We grew up together, and it was the most natural thing in the world. We didn't know that our love was forbidden, or that it was my destiny to rescue my impoverished family by marrying Hugo Van Courtland.

Gabrielle tiptoed into the sickroom at Fontenay and looked down at her sleeping mother. She looked peaceful, but her illness had ravaged her once beautiful features, leaving gossamer skin stretched tautly over fragile bones. Tiny clawlike fingers lay limply atop a pale satin coverlet. Her hair, once raven black like Gabrielle's own, was now reduced to smoky wisps through which her pale pink scalp showed.

Her eyes flickered open and a hint of a welcoming smile curved her mouth, quickly replaced by a grimace of pain.

Gabrielle sat carefully on the edge of the bed and picked up her mother's hand. "Oh, Mama! If I could bear the pain for you, I would."

"I would not want you to, my darling. Did you see the woman and the infant?"

Gabrielle nodded. "She wouldn't sign the document we prepared. But Hepple says the fact that we placed a thousand dollars in her bank account should be sufficient to implicate Hugo, should the need arise."

"And did she argue that the baby was not hers?"

"No. How could she? We've seen the birth certificate."

"Your husband was quite clever in that regard, wasn't he? But not clever enough. He might have diverted attention from the real mother, but not the real father."

Gabrielle felt a knife twist in her heart, but she managed to reply calmly, "Hepple says there's little doubt it's Delia's child. The same coloring and already a hint that she will have that strange composure—that untouchableness—that Delia has."

"You must be careful not to overplay your hand now, *ma cherie*. Wait and see what Hugo intends to do before you disclose the thousand-dollar payment to his mistress. Do you think she is, by the way, or merely a nursemaid?"

Gabrielle shrugged. "I don't know, nor do I care." That was not true, but it was the answer her mother wanted to hear. Gabrielle's natural competitiveness railed against the possibility of her husband finding the charms of any other woman comparable to her own. But she had always known who her real rival was. She added grudgingly, "The Nesbitt woman is quite attractive and didn't speak like a servant. I was surprised when Hepple told me she had moved from Palmetto Street so quickly. Jemmie has gone with her."

"No doubt to keep an eye on her for Hugo."

"He's torturing me, Mama. This waiting is worse than anything he could do. If only he'd said something—*anything*—before he left."

"He caught you in the arms of your lover, my pet. You were lucky he didn't shoot both of you. Perhaps when he returns from New York, he will listen to reason. After all, a divorce would tarnish him, also. The stigma is not one-sided. Besides, we now have our own ammunition—a veritable cannon. But we must save Delia's baby as a last resort."

Gabrielle stood up and moved restlessly around the room. It was warm and stuffy, and the sickroom smell overpowered the faint scent of potpourri set out in tiny china bowls. She would have liked to fling open the windows, but the doctors had cautioned against letting in the night air lest her mother catch a chill to further overburden her ailing body.

At least her mother was now surrounded by beautiful things; indeed, all of Fontenay had been transformed during the years of her marriage to Hugo. What a pity her father had sold off most of the plantation land before Hugo's wealth saved them. They were left with only the house now, but it was enough to make her mother's final days contented.

"Mama, I may not have to tell him I know the baby is Delia's. Hepple says Hugo visited Mrs. Nesbitt several times, even took her on a picnic one day. Hepple says we could accuse Hugo of infidelity, even threaten to sue the woman for alienation of affections. I like that idea. I hate the possibility of any connection between us and Delia. She and Julian have run off, and she apparently has abandoned the child to Hugo's care."

"I'm surprised that Julian would continue with her, in view of her bearing Hugo's child."

"Oh, Julian has always been besotted by her, you know that."

Her mother sighed. "Poor, dear Fleur. What a trial her sons have been to her."

"Well, apparently Julian has succeeded in his quest of making Delia the toast of San Francisco. He sent Hugo some glowing reviews of her performances."

"Then we must wish them both continued success on that distant coast and hope that they remain there."

Her mother was suddenly gripped by waves of pain that racked her fragile body. She bit her lip and twisted her head from side to side, trying to escape the agony.

Gabrielle watched helplessly until the pale lips gasped. "My laudanum—in the nightstand drawer."

Gabrielle fumbled in the drawer for the amber-colored bottle and attempted to stifle a stab of fear that her mother might soon leave her. She depended upon her wise counsel so. Everyone loved her mother, everyone respected her. Indeed, had it not been for the fact that Walter Hepple had long ago been in love with her mother, he certainly would not be presently keeping them informed of Hugo's activities.

The dose of laudanum gradually took effect, and her mother lay still. Her blue-veined eyelids flickered. "Darling, I'm rather tired. Perhaps in the morning . . ."

"Yes, of course. I'm wearing you out. Good night, dear." She kissed the frail cheek, which felt like brittle rice paper under the tentative touch of her lips.

"Gabrielle . . . you will be careful, won't you? Don't see Alain alone again, ever. Hugo might overlook this one episode, but he's not a man who will take being cuckolded twice. Indeed, if he allows you to get away with it once."

When his tuberculosis was in remission and he was not languishing in a sanatorium, Alain Marchand lived in a single

room above a café in the French Quarter, where he eked out
a precarious living as an amanuensis. Gabrielle had begged
him to allow her to help him financially, but he had always
stubbornly refused. She agonized over his health, his living
conditions, his fierce pride that was surely killing him.

Alain had been orphaned as a young boy and raised by
Gabrielle's parents. A small inheritance from his father had
paid for his education, and after leaving for university, he
never returned to live at Fontenay again. Gabrielle suspected
this was at her father's insistence.

Not far from Alain's room in the Quarter, the Van
Courtland's townhouse was located in a quiet neighborhood.
Some of Gabrielle's friends had at first looked with disdain
on the house, suggesting it was too modestly appointed, considering Hugo's wealth. But she had renovated, redecorated,
and refurnished and the result was extravagantly luxurious, if
more feminine then her husband would have preferred.

After visiting her parents at Fontenay, Gabrielle returned to
New Orleans and, with Hugo still safely in New York, visited
Alain the following evening. She ignored a twinge of conscience that her mother had begged her not to see her cousin
alone again by telling herself that she had not actually promised she would not do so.

She heard Alain coughing as she reached his door. How
unfair it was that the two people she loved most on earth
were stricken with incurable diseases, and how she secretly
railed at the cruel God who selected innocent victims. Her
mother would have been appalled had she known of
Gabrielle's lack of faith.

Pushing open the door, Gabrielle stepped into the cramped
room, with its shabby furnishings and stacks of books. Alain
struggled to his feet to greet her, and she was enclosed by
those dear arms.

"You shouldn't have come," he whispered. "But, oh, my
darling, how glad I am to see you. Let me turn up the lamp.
I must feast my eyes on your lovely face."

Her heart sank as the light revealed the dark shadows
under his eyes, the sunken cheeks, the telltale smear of blood
on the handkerchief he quickly slipped into his jacket pocket.
Only a few days earlier, when he had gallantly accompanied
her to Natchez, he had seemed reasonably well.

She drew him down beside her on his threadbare sofa and placed her hands on his cheeks. "You're burning with fever again, my dearest. I'll fetch the doctor. Have you eaten anything? We must—"

Alain touched her lips with his fingertip to silence her. "I'm all right, just a little tired. The journey to Natchez overtaxed my strength, I'm afraid. A few days' rest and I shall be fine."

"We must find a sanatorium in the mountains—I read that the mountain air is what you need." Her voice was sharp with fear.

Alain stroked her hair and murmured. "Ah, Gabrielle, you worry too much about me and not enough about yourself."

She nestled closer as he unpinned her hair and let it cascade through his fingers like a dark waterfall. His breathing was far too labored for her to hope for more than this comforting closeness of two bodies so perfectly in tune with two minds that they might have been a single entity, and so she loosened her bodice so that he might rest his cheek against the soft flesh of her bosom.

"Hugo isn't back yet?" Alain asked.

"No."

"Don't worry—I'm sure he'll listen to reason." His voice was heavy with fatigue.

Gabrielle tried to hold back tears as she recalled the dashing Alain of old, before his illness. They had not been truly intimate for months now. He simply wasn't strong enough. Perhaps that was why they had been so careless that evening at the Willows.

She stroked an errant lock of dark hair from his brow. How she missed his tender lovemaking!

As Alain drifted off to a laudanum-induced slumber against her breast, Gabrielle allowed her memory to take her back to that magical moment so long ago when he first made love to her.

It had been a lazy afternoon in early summer, the year before he left for the university. Gabrielle was fifteen and, according to Alain, lovelier than a rose. They had played croquet, strolled through the overgrown grounds of Fontenay, discussed punting down the river and decided it was too hot, so they would read poetry together in the shade of the massive old live oak that stood like a sentinel between the house and the river.

All afternoon Gabrielle had been aware of a peculiar tension between Alain and herself. She felt restless, aware of her skin in a way she had not been before, hearing formerly hidden nuances and meanings in the words of their favorite poets. By the time Alain began to read, in his husky, breathless voice that had acquired a slight but attractive lisp due to his already weakening lungs, she found she could hardly sit still.

He read the *Sonnets from the Portuguese*, and she crept closer and laid her head upon his shoulder, hearing the dearly familiar words in a new and thrilling context. Elizabeth Barrett had yearned for Robert Browning, longed for him body and soul with an intensity that eclipsed everything—her poor health, her unyielding father. And Robert Browning had swept her away from the damp moors of England to a life of sunshine and love and passion in Italy. Somehow their story, in Gabrielle's mind, became the story of Alain and herself.

Long ago she and Alain had instinctively known they were kindred souls, needing no one but each other. Together they had created a perfect world, filled with gentle pursuits and harmonious words. But soon Alain would be leaving for university, and their parting loomed specterlike, adding to the tension of that sultry summer afternoon. Once, months previously, when Gabrielle had impulsively kissed his mouth, Alain had reprimanded her, and she had protested, "But I love you."

"And I love you," he responded. "The love we feel is pure, Gabrielle. It is spiritual, not of the flesh. We are first cousins, but closer than that really. We could never marry, you see, yet will always share something beyond the reach of a husband and wife. Do you understand?"

"No, I do not," she muttered, because even then she knew she wanted to marry him. He had merely laughed and ruffled her hair.

So time had passed and apart from casual contact, a peck on the cheek, a chaste hug, an occasional rough-and-tumble quickly cut short by Alain, they had indeed remained locked in a pure and spiritual bonding.

But as he read the sonnets that afternoon, he allowed her

head to remain on his shoulder, and she felt his breath stirring her hair and warm against her brow, and his arm crept around her.

She held her breath as his fingers lightly caressed her bare arm. Then, as a sudden breeze caught her hair and whipped it across her face, Alain brushed the long silky strands behind her ear, and his hand came to rest in the hollow of her neck.

As he read on, his voice now husky with the same yearning she felt as acutely, his fingers drifted downward from her throat toward the soft swelling of her breast, and she squirmed against him, hoping to bring his tentative touch to the now exquisitely tender bud that pressed against her shift.

A moment later his fingers were inside her shift, closing ever so gently over her breast. She felt her diamond-hard nipple rise against his palm, and, panting now, she turned her face upward toward his.

For an instant he hesitated, then his mouth was on hers and they were kissing, in a way she could never have imagined, with a passion that took her breath away.

Feeling imprisoned by her clothes, hating the barrier of his, Gabrielle tore at the laces of her shift, grabbed feverishly at his shirt buttons. Somehow they were half undressed, her petticoats were up around her waist, and she was lying back on the grass, making small whimpering sounds, parting her thighs, writhing with a need so great nothing but its fulfillment mattered. She didn't even care if they were caught.

Alain gasped, "Gabrielle, we can't—we mustn't . . ."

But it was too late to turn back. If his mind told him to stop, his body would not, could not, be restrained. He rolled over on top of her, and she felt his manhood strain toward her.

Arching her back, she gave a cry of delight as their loins connected and seconds later they were one. She felt a twinge of pain, which was quickly replaced by pleasure, and for an instant they stared at each other in surprise. Then Alain's lips were on hers again, and his face blotted out the world so that she could see only him, feel only him. Her only awareness was of the rhythmic movement inside her, ever deeper, ever more exciting, building toward some pinnacle of bliss that even as she strove to reach it with the wild whirling of her hips, she also tried to delay it, because she never wanted this ecstasy to end.

When at last Alain shuddered, a great spasm passing through his body, Gabrielle felt herself crashing over the edge of a precipice with him, falling, weightless amid a thousand stars.

For an instant she was too filled with wonder to speak, then she said, "Oh, my dearest darling! I love you to distraction, beyond any love that ever existed before or ever will again."

Alain was suddenly silent. He rolled away from her, and they lay limply side by side. Then he clapped his hand to his forehead and groaned, "Oh, my God, what have I done?"

The pain in his voice jolted her from the misty sea of pleasure in which she floated. "Alain, we came together because we love each other. Please, my dearest, tell me that you love me. I couldn't bear it if you didn't."

" 'I love thee not, I dare not love thee! Go—' "

She recognized the lines, also written by Elizabeth Barrett Browning, and although she didn't want to hear the rest, he went on quoting:

"In silence; drop my hand
If thou seek roses, seek them where they blow
In garden alleys, not in desert sand."

"You can't deny our love, Alain," she whispered miserably. "That would be too cruel."

"Of course I love you. More than life itself. But our love cannot be of the flesh."

"Why not? Would we feel such longing if it was wrong? Could we feel such ecstasy with anyone else? No, my darling, only with each other. I won't believe what we did is wrong or forbidden, and you mustn't, either."

"But they would never let us marry."

"There must be somewhere on earth where we can marry."

He sat up. "You're such a child sometimes. A beautiful spoiled, wilful child, who thinks that simply wanting something is enough. It isn't. There are rules we must live by, or face the consequences."

"I don't care about stupid rules and consequences. I will love you until I die," Gabrielle said.

Alan merely sighed deeply and gathered her into his arms, holding her close enough that their hearts beat in unison.

"Tell me you love me," Gabrielle begged.

"I love you, oh, my dearest, how I love you. But I must be strong for both of us. I must resist temptation until fall, and then I'll go away to university and you'll forget me."

She had laughed at the ridiculousness of such a possibility, and, of course, they had not resisted temptation. That summer was the most perfect, carefree time of their lives, and when he left in the autumn Gabrielle was desolate.

Chapter 17

*

Delia was never a child. She was a witch, casting a spell on every male who saw her. There was no defense against her. Hugo and I might have had a chance together, had it not been for Delia.

The evening before Gabrielle was to marry Hugo, her mother had found her weeping in her room.

"Oh, *ma cherie*, don't! Please, don't." She gathered her daughter into her arms and rocked her back and forth as she had when she was a child.

"I can't marry him, Mama, I can't."

"Yes, you can. You must," her mother said quietly. "Listen to me, Gabrielle. You must not confuse marriage with love. The two are incompatible."

Gabrielle raised her tear-stained face in surprise.

"Marriage," her mother said firmly, "is a lifelong arrangement between a man and a woman from which each receives certain benefits in return for certain obligations. The primary purpose of marriage is the procreation and protection of children, the establishment of a home. We must examine the strengths and assets of a prospective partner as objectively as if we were entering a business agreement and should never marry someone we cannot respect. Now, contrast this to the enchantment of a love affair that is heady, ecstatic, uninhibited, and far removed from reality . . . because, *ma cherie*, the object of one's passion can be completely unsuitable."

She paused. "Do you understand to whom I refer, Gabrielle?"

"You know?"

"About you and your cousin? Yes. I realized the summer it began what was happening."

Gabrielle felt the hot color flare to her cheeks. "Does Father—"

"No. He would have sent Alain packing instantly. Men tend to stick together in these matters."

"But you never said anything to me."

"You were so happy, how could I spoil that for you? I could see that you and Alain were sharing something that few people are privileged to have. I knew, too, that he would be gentle with you, that your initiation into womanhood would not be the brutal deflowering inflicted by some lout of a husband concerned mostly with his own satisfaction."

Gabrielle was not shocked by her mother's frankness. They had always spoken openly of such matters, unlike most of her friends and their mothers.

Her mother went on: "But to be honest, I thought your passion would swiftly burn itself out because of its sheer intensity, and I didn't wish to deprive you of your memories. Many otherwise mundane lives are made bearable by memories."

"But I don't want to live on my memories, like some old woman. I want to marry Alain. But he won't marry me. Oh, Mama, how can I make him marry me?"

"He can't marry you. He's your first cousin. You are too closely related by blood. Apart from the poor health that has plagued our family that might be exacerbated by intermarriage, you would run the risk of mental aberration. A marriage of first cousins is a *mésalliance* of the worst kind, because of the risk of producing idiot offspring. This is why the law forbids it."

"Then Alain and I won't have children."

"And would you defy the teachings of your church in that regard? I think not. It is one thing to practice birth control during an *amourette* and quite another in marriage."

Gabrielle buried her face against her mother's comforting shoulder and sobbed. Alain himself had said much the same thing, adding that not only they, but their entire family, would be ostracized. There would be whispers of incest, he said, because their respective fathers had been brothers and he and Gabrielle had been raised in the same household.

Her mother continued: "Besides, if you don't marry Hugo, we shall be penniless, your father and I and Monique. We are hanging by a thread. All of your father's investments have failed, he has sold everything of value, including virtually all of our land. Even the house has been mortgaged to pay for your wedding."

"Then I shall marry him and, when Father is out of debt, kill myself."

"Oh, my darling, how dramatic you are! Stop and think for a moment. As Mrs. Hugo Van Courtland, you will have far more freedom and power than you do now. You will have almost unlimited wealth at your disposal and a handsome husband—"

"I don't think he's handsome," Gabrielle sniffed. "He's so big and muscular and . . . and not a gentleman."

"Like Alain, you mean? Actually, I believe Hugo is as much a gentleman, although perhaps not an intellectual. But, dear, Hugo has a far-flung industrial empire—his demands on your time will of necessity be limited." Her mother paused, then added, "*Think* about that, my darling."

Gabrielle considered her mother's statement carefully. She was surely telling her that marriage to Hugo did not mean her love affair with Alain must end. Since her mother had orchestrated her romance with Hugo from the beginning and it now transpired that she had known all along about Alain . . . what other interpretation of her remark could there be?

Over her mother's shoulder she could see her wedding gown, hanging over the armoire door, and her veil was draped across her *chaise longue*, looking vaguely, disturbingly, like a shroud. Gabrielle shivered, but murmured, "I'll marry Hugo tomorrow, Mama."

Until her wedding day Gabrielle had not given much thought to Julian's protégé. She had heard Julian had found a white child living with colored folks, and that she could sing and he had some grandiose plans for her. Julian had always been frustrated that his younger brother refused to perform in public, and no doubt his interest in the girl had something to do with Marcus and his music.

Then came the disastrous moment when Gabrielle stood on the terrace at the Willows waiting with her father for the bridal march to begin. Her young sister, Monique, a frail child born after her mother had suffered a number of miscarriages, was poised to lead the procession across the lawn, scattering flower petals in her path. The bridesmaids were paired and giggling on the terrace steps. Her father squeezed Gabrielle's hand reassuringly, and she slipped her arm through his. Her maid of honor handed her her bouquet.

Then Delia began to sing.

From where she stood, Gabrielle had a clear view of Hugo. The rapt look on his face as the scrawny little waif began to sing stunned her. Surely he had never looked at his bride-to-be with such utter absorption?

Gabrielle didn't pause to consider that she was only marrying Hugo for his money and didn't care a fig about him. Her natural competitiveness flared. How dare he be intrigued by a mere voice? How dare he even notice anyone else on the day he was to marry the prettiest, most sought-after girl in the county?

By the time she and her father were walking between the rows of lawn chairs toward her bridegroom, Gabrielle was fuming. Then the heavens opened, and torrential rain completed the disaster.

Somehow she remained calm during the hurried indoor wedding and reception, and she and Hugo left for their hotel in New Orleans. The following day they would board a ship bound for Cherbourg, en route to Paris.

Late that evening she sat in the cramped dressing room of their hotel suite, angrily pulling pins from her hair. She could hear Hugo moving around in the adjacent bedroom. He was probably removing his clothes and pouring the champagne he'd ordered. He would expect her to creep timidly into the marriage bed to submit to his lovemaking.

Ignoring the lace-trimmed nightgown of fine lawn that her mother had given her for her wedding night, Gabrielle unpacked a flannelette gown she wore only on cool nights and buttoned it tightly under her chin. She plaited her hair and tossed the dark braid over her shoulder, then stood up and opened the dressing room door.

Hugo had not undressed. Nor had he opened the champagne. He had unpacked his toilet articles and night attire and laid them out. He was sitting in an armchair studying what appeared to be a map and was so engrossed that he didn't even hear the dressing room door open.

Gabrielle's rage was near flashpoint. This was her ardent, eager bridegroom? How dare he be so casual about their wedding night!

She strode into the room and slammed the door behind her, jumped into bed, and pulled the covers up to her chin.

Hugo glanced up, his expression solicitous. "You must be exhausted. It's been a trying day for you. I didn't open the champagne. I think we both had enough at the reception."

Perversely, she now wanted the champagne. "I did not have enough at that miserable reception. I could never drink enough wine to make me forgot this dreadful day. The worst day of my entire life. You ruined my wedding day, Hugo, the only wedding day I shall ever have, and you *ruined* it."

His expression changed to one of bemusement. "I'm afraid I have no control over the weather, Gabrielle."

"I'm not talking about the rain. I'm talking about that horrid little girl showing off and delaying the ceremony. You knew we had planned every step, rehearsed it all. She wasn't supposed to sing."

"Delia's song was a surprise to me, too, but come on, let's be fair, her song did set a romantic mood, and if it hadn't started to rain—"

"You should have stopped her. Why didn't you stop her?"

"You're being unreasonable, Gabrielle."

"We could have finished the ceremony during the time she was singing. My beautiful dress wouldn't have been soaked, the guests wouldn't have been drenched. All anyone is going to remember about my wedding is that we all huddled in the drawing room and hall like drowned rats—"

"But Delia's song took only a few minutes." Hugo stood up and came to the bed.

She turned away from him. "I hate her, and I hate Julian for forcing her on us, and I shall never forgive you for not preventing what was surely a fiasco." She was close to tears again. "And I had to get married in my first day dress instead of my white gown, and people are going to remember I wasn't married in white, and you know what that means. . . ."

It occurred to her then to wonder, with a stab of superstitious guilt, whether a vengeful God had punished her for donning the undeserved virginal white. She also remembered that her mother had given her a tiny bottle of cochineal, concealed inside a lavender sachet, which she had been instructed to push up the sleeve of her nightgown. After the marriage had been consummated, she was supposed to surreptitiously open the bottle and make a red stain with the cochineal. "Be sure your husband sees it, *cherie*," her mother had said. "Men always look for proof of virginity."

Unfortunately, she had left the sachet containing the substitute blood in the pocket of her robe, which was now hanging in the dressing room. Gabrielle buried her face in the pillow and wept with anger and frustration. Nothing had gone right. This was truly the worst day of her life.

She felt Hugo's hand touch her shoulder, and she stiffened.

He said gently, "I'm sorry our wedding wasn't all you expected, Gabrielle. But we exchanged spiritual vows today, to love and honor and cherish each other all of our lives, and nothing else really matters. I care very deeply for you, Gabrielle, and am going to do my best to make you happy."

She kept her head turned to the wall and sniffed, refusing to be mollified.

Outside, the rain drummed relentlessly against the windows, and the humid air made the bedsheets feel damp and heavy, like cold clay. She would have liked to fling the covers aside and unfasten the neck buttons of her nightgown, but such an action might be construed by Hugo as an invitation to intimacies she was not yet ready to share. Let him grovel first and beg her to forgive him.

A moment later she felt Hugo's lips brush her hair, and he whispered, "Go to sleep now. Everything will seem better in the morning."

Then, to her astonishment, the lamp was turned very low, and she heard the door open and softly close. She sat up. Her husband had gone. He had left her alone on her wedding night. Mortified, she sank back on the pillow. It was a long time before she slept.

When she awoke the following morning the first thing she saw was a single red rose, lying on the pillow next to her. The rain had stopped and the room was filled with sunshine, spilling in from the open French doors that led to a trellised balcony.

Hugo was seated at a small table on the balcony, watching her. He smiled. "Good morning, Mrs. Van Courtland." He rose and came to the bed, bent and kissed her. "You are just as beautiful when you sleep. What a pleasure it is to look at you, Gabrielle. Now, while you dress, I shall personally select our breakfast."

Once again she found herself alone in the room. She glanced at her travel clock on the bedside table and saw there were less than two hours until embarkation time. Without her maid to help her, she would have to lace her own corset and attend to her own hair. Her irritation returned. She wouldn't have slept so late had not Hugo caused her to lie awake last night. Oh, if only it was her beloved Alain who was here with her!

She scrambled out of bed and flew into the dressing room, where, miraculously, hot water waited in a pitcher and scented soap and towels were laid out.

She had finished her ablutions and, clad in her underwear and robe, was struggling with her hair when Hugo returned. He put the tray on the balcony table and called to her, "Come and have breakfast while the coffee's hot. A ladies' maid will be here shortly to help you dress."

Gabrielle felt some of her tension dissipate, but wasn't yet ready to show any warmth toward her new husband. Joining him on the balcony, she saw he had brought a selection of fresh fruit, delicate crepes, and a bowl of whipped cream. She was surprised. He had a hearty appetite, she knew from having dined with him, and expected he would have brought ham and eggs and grits.

He watched her so closely as she ate that at last she cried, "You are embarrassing me, watching every bite I take."

"I'm sorry. It's just that you look so lovely, with your hair loose like that—I can't take my eyes off you." The explanation satisfied her. After all, he was supposed to be gazing at her adoringly. She decided to accept his homage graciously. He made a pretense of eating, but soon she felt his eyes on her again.

After breakfast the maid arrived as promised and swiftly put up her hair and helped her dress. Gabrielle began to feel a little more kindly disposed toward Hugo.

They traveled by carriage to the steamship and, after briefly inspecting their stateroom, went up on deck to join in the excitement of the departure.

The ship's orchestra played and streamers flew, passengers waved to those on the quay, and Gabrielle couldn't help but notice that more than one female glance stole in the direction of her husband. He had been right. Everything *did* seem much brighter today.

The day passed in a heady whirl of activity, exploring the ship, listening to an afternoon concert on deck, playing shuffleboard, enjoying the drinks and delicacies constantly being delivered by white-clad stewards. There was barely enough time for her to take a nap before changing for dinner.

She hadn't asked Hugo where he spent the previous night, and it would have pleased her to learn he might have slipped back into their room after she fell asleep and then sat up all night, but she knew it was unlikely. Still, tonight there would be no escaping the consummation of their marriage, for either of them.

Curiously, as they danced in the grand saloon after a sumptuous seven-course dinner, Gabrielle found herself growing excited by the prospect of taming this great hulk of a husband. It would be a personal triumph to bring him to that state of humble gratitude and blind adoration that Alain always reached after they made love.

Hugo's arm around her waist and his hand holding hers felt very strong and secure, despite the rolling motion of the deck. She felt tiny and feminine and protected. Furthermore, she soon noted that although all of the first-class passengers were treated royally by the crew, Hugo seemed to receive special deference. Stewards jumped to anticipate every command; sailors from the captain down snapped to attention when he appeared. She commented on this as her husband led her from the dance floor to their table.

He gave her one of his somewhat cynical half smiles. "Perhaps the fact that I have shares in the shipping company that owns this vessel has something to do with it."

Gabrielle knew little and cared even less about his various enterprises, but it certainly was comforting to know that she was now very, very rich. She sighed contentedly as he pulled out a chair for her. He gave her a quick glance, and something quite thrilling flickered in his dark blue eyes, causing a shiver to ripple down her spine. She lowered her eyes demurely and snapped open her fan.

"Would you like to go to our stateroom now?" Hugo asked. "We could open our wedding night champagne."

Gabrielle nodded, her heart fluttering in the cage of her ribs.

"Why don't you go ahead, I'll join you in a few minutes."

He was giving her time to undress in privacy, she knew. Tonight she could be sure to slip the sachet containing the bottle of cochineal into the sleeve of her nightgown. Excited and confident, she hurried to her cabin.

When Hugo arrived she was lying in bed, her hair spread carefully on the pillow, a touch of kohl emphasizing her eyes, her body perfumed, and, to her surprise, tingling with anticipation.

He still wore that expression she had seen earlier and which now appeared to her to be raw hunger. Crossing the stateroom in a few quick strides, he sat beside her and gathered her into his arms.

She had permitted chaste kisses during their engagement, which he had bestowed without the pulsing need she had always felt when Alain—and several other eager suitors—kissed her. Hugo, by contrast, had seemed almost indifferent. But tonight his kiss was so breathtakingly passionate that she felt she might swoon.

As his mouth explored hers, his hands sought the most intimate parts of her body, caressing her breasts, finding her inner thighs, and his touch was firm and sure. This was no tentative boy, but a man well versed in the art of making love. She felt swept away by the force of his desire; it carried her along at such a dizzying pace that she scarcely knew what she was doing. She felt herself melting, so eager for consummation that she forgot her mother's instructions to lie stiffly, playing the part of the timid, terrified and shame-filled virgin submitting to her husband. Instead she was a wild thing, returning his kisses, writhing beneath his touch.

When he pulled away in order to remove his clothes, instead of demurely averting her gaze, she watched him. How muscular he was! How powerful his shoulders and arms were. Nor did she turn away when he stood naked before her. A husband was supposed to don a nightshirt and never expose himself to his wife, but Hugo was far too ardent to pause for such niceties. For one thrilling instant in his passionate frenzy she thought he might tear her own nightgown from her body, and she quivered with excitement. Then she remembered the cochineal in her sleeve and drew back in alarm.

"Dearest wife," Hugo murmured and began to kiss her again. At the same time he slowly inched her nightgown upward until her lower body was exposed, then, carefully propping his weight on his elbows, he positioned himself between her legs.

At the moment he entered her, Gabrielle recalled in time that she must cry out in pain. It was not easy, as she wanted to moan with pleasure. His thrust was swift and sure and like nothing she had ever experienced with Alain. But this was something she realized much later, as at that moment all she could think of was the exciting fusion of Hugo's flesh with her own.

She had thought that she could never enjoy coupling physically with anyone else, believed that a woman must love the man she surrendered to—certainly had never dreamed that it was possible to feel such incredible pleasure from lovemaking with a man she didn't even particularly like.

Although she attempted to conceal the searing climax to which he brought her, her body gave her away, and as the spasms of release passed through her, she was unable to bite back her gasps and cries.

Lying in her husband's arms in a state of satiety and wonder, all sense of time and place, all thought, seemed to desert her. She was a creature comprised only of sensation, every nerve ending still tingled, her mind seemed to be filled with a rosy haze. She was vaguely aware of Hugo's murmured endearments, his compliments ... did he say he loved her? Gabrielle wasn't sure. It didn't matter. She was so engrossed in her own pleasurable feelings that she wasn't really listening to what he said.

A little while later he became aroused again, and this time he unbuttoned her nightgown and began to slide it down her body. "Let me see you as God made you, my darling. There is no need to feel shame with me. We're truly man and wife now, and nothing we do is forbidden."

She didn't respond as his lips had moved down her throat to encircle her nipple and she felt her own desire surge again.

Then, as his hand tugged the sleeve of her nightgown down her arm, he suddenly stopped. "Why, what's this?"

Gabrielle froze.

He held the sachet she had concealed in her sleeve, and even as her eyes widened in dismay, the tiny bottle of cochineal slipped from the sachet and landed on the bed beside her.

Hugo picked up the bottle and held it for a moment, then looked at her with eyes that seemed to pierce her. He asked, in a deceptively low tone, "Did you really think I would be fooled by this?"

Abruptly he rose from the bed, threw the cochineal bottle down beside her, and began to dress.

She cowered in the disarray of the bed. "Hugo, I—"

Buttoning his shirt as he spoke, he said, "More than anything else, I resent the dishonesty of that damned device. Do you know the one creature on earth I despise the most? It's a liar. Never lie to me, Gabrielle."

Then he left the stateroom, and shivering, she pulled the sheet up. She felt frightened and bereft. How she wished he had never found the stupid cochineal, which she hadn't used anyway. Where had he gone? To walk around the deck? Why, he had taken his pleasure and left her like some paid fancy woman. The humiliation stung like a thousand bees. She buried her face in her pillow and wept.

Hugo never mentioned the cochineal to her again. Apart from leaving her alone that first night at sea he did not allow the incident to mar their honeymoon. He was a lively and energetic companion and an ardent lover, and in spite of herself, she enjoyed his company so much that as the days of their honeymoon dwindled, she found she was not looking forward to his resuming his business activities and leaving her alone.

Back in New Orleans, the first day she found herself at a loose end, Gabrielle went to Alain, newly installed in a room over a café in the Quarter.

Her cousin was aghast. "Gaby, darling, what are you thinking of? We can't see each other alone again. You're married now. No, I insist upon taking you home. Come on, before anyone sees you."

To her chagrin, he had been adamant.

Hugo's house in New Orleans, partially remodeled during their absence, was now ready for paint and wallpaper. Since Fontenay was also in the throes of renovation, Gabrielle and Hugo were forced to take up temporary residence at the Willows. Unfortunately, Julian's protégé was also visiting.

Delia's atrocious manners, her scrawny appearance, and above all, her searingly abrasive accent grated on Gabrielle from the start. It seemed to her that anyone who could sing without a trace of an accent should also be able to speak in a reasonably civilized manner. But it was Hugo's protectiveness toward Delia that enraged Gabrielle most. It seemed that either Hugo was away on business, or, when he deigned to visit the Willows, he spent his time having fatherly chats with the child. Gabrielle's ardent bridegroom no longer placed her in the center of his universe.

Gabrielle found herself snapping at him, pretending to sleep when he came to their bed at night, and becoming so filled with resentment that she knew she was acting like a wicked stepmother toward Delia, and couldn't seem to stop.

One day even the strange and reclusive Marcus cornered Gabrielle and said, "You're making a mistake, sister-in-law. You should be kind to the child. The more you resent her, the more your husband will rise to her defense."

She replied indignantly, "You of all people have no cause to criticize me. You are rude to everyone, including her."

He shrugged, his eyes hooded and mysterious. "You'll be sorry when she takes her revenge."

"What do you mean?"

"I mean that one day she will take Hugo away from you. You just wait and see."

That night Gabrielle had a nightmare that she was in a speeding carriage plunging over a cliff into dense darkness. She was screaming for Hugo to save her, but he didn't come.

She announced the next day that since Hugo was busy in New Orleans, she was going to Fontenay. One wing of the house had been finished, and although her parents and Monique had not yet returned, she could use one of the finished rooms and would enjoy supervising the remainder of the refurbishment of her old home. She had, she decided, a real flair for this, and after all, it was her husband's money that was being spent.

It was, of course, fate that Alain should return while she was there, to pick up some books he had left behind years ago when he went away to college. They found themselves alone in the great house, with workmen who would soon be gone from their lives forever, and only a minimum staff of servants who would not dare spy on them.

"I didn't know you'd be here—" Alain stammered.

"Nor I you. Isn't it exciting? Oh, Alain, I've missed you so. Hugo is so mean to me."

He was immediately concerned. "He hasn't hurt you in any way? By the saints, I'll kill him if he has."

"No, no, he simply ignores me. I'm no more important to him than one of his stupid companies—less, in fact. He only comes to see me when he wants to satisfy his depraved lust."

She felt a little guilty about this falsehood, especially since she always welcomed Hugo's advances, but as Alain took her into his arms to comfort her, she decided the benefits of telling men what they wanted to hear were worth the resulting twinges of guilt. She could always confess to the priest that she had told a small white lie, recite a few Hail Marys, and be forgiven.

Whimpering pitifully, she delivered the *coup de gras*: "If you would have taken me away, I wouldn't have to endure this horrible marriage to a man I don't even like."

"Oh, Gaby dearest," Alain said miserably, stroking her hair. "I can hardly support myself. I couldn't let you live in poverty. But apart from that, you know we can never marry."

"Hold me closer," she begged. "I need your gentleness, your kindness. I need to know someone cares about me. . . ."

Although it was late afternoon and the workmen had departed for the day, the servants were in their quarters and could appear any second. "Dearest," Alain whispered anxiously, "we can't talk here. Let's go for a walk along the riverbank."

But at that moment a clap of thunder reverberated through the house and rain came down in a deluge.

"Come on," Gabrielle said. "They've finished work on the east wing. We won't be disturbed there."

They crept through the deserted rooms, past the shrouded furniture and silent walls, and slipped into one of the bedrooms. There, dizzy with the smell of paint and varnish, they clung to each other, pouring out their hearts, reliving every moment of that magical summer when they had been young and carefree, and inevitably the memories overcame Alain's reticence.

Soon they were making love with an abandon that was surely intensified by their long abstinence, for he had refused to touch her from the time her engagement to Hugo was announced. Even when she had lured him down to the river-bank just before her marriage, they had only talked longingly of their childhoods and ended up crying in each other's arms.

Lying nestled against her beloved Alain after they made love that rainy afternoon at Fontenay, Gabrielle said happily, "It will be weeks before the workmen finish and the family returns. We can meet here any time we wish."

"Darling," Alain asked faintly, "what about your husband?"

"I told you. He's so busy catering to his business and to that little heathen Julian took home that he's scarcely aware I exist."

"The little heathen who sang at your wedding? Tell me more."

How good it was to have someone to confide in, to whom she could reveal all her worst fears and petty jealousies with no fear of being diminished in his eyes. Alain loved her unconditionally, and, smarting from her perceived rejection by Hugo, Gabrielle wallowed in Alain's adoration.

When she was eventually forced to move into Hugo's house in New Orleans, the pattern was too deeply entrenched to abandon. Gabrielle visited Alain whenever Hugo was away, and always after she and her husband had quarreled. It was her way of paying Hugo back for being mean to her, or slighting her in some way. She salved her conscience by telling herself that, in a way, Alain was actually helping her stay married to Hugo.

Then her sister Monique unwittingly became the means by which Gabrielle could visit Alain openly.

Their mother asked if Monique could stay in New Orleans with her while being tutored by Alain. "She's failing history and English literature and I'm afraid she won't be accepted by a decent finishing school if she doesn't improve. You know how clever Alain is, how well read, and he's so patient he'll be able to help her. Now, dear, I know this is an imposition, with you and Hugo being newlyweds, but . . ."

Gabrielle quickly saw the possibilities. The twelve-year-old Monique would either have to be taken to Alain's quarters for lessons, or Alain would have to visit the house to tutor her. In either case, she would be able to see him more often.

Since she and Monique were not close in age, Gabrielle being almost seven years older than her sister, they had never been particularly close. Monique was a shy, timid girl who seemed always to be suffering from vague, unspecified ailments. Gabrielle was healthy as a horse and anything but shy or timid. She had to remind herself not to show impatience with her little sister.

What she had not expected was that following Alain's first lesson, during which Gabrielle had remained in the study to listen to the hypnotic sound of her cousin's voice, that Monique would come to her later and, although shaking with nervousness, blurt out, "Gaby, I . . . I wish you wouldn't stay while I have my lesson."

"Why not?" Gabrielle asked sharply. "I didn't interrupt in any way. I didn't say a word."

"I know, but—" Monique bit her lip. "When you and Alain are in the same room, you . . . I can't explain. You shut out everybody else somehow. It's like you're alone in the world, even if you don't speak to each other. I felt like an intruder. I couldn't concentrate on what he was saying."

"What nonsense," Gabrielle muttered.

"No, it isn't," Monique said earnestly. "Afterward, when we were all having dinner, I noticed that Hugo got very quiet, and I saw him look at you and then at Alain and I know he was feeling the same thing I did."

Gabrielle decided regretfully that she would not invite Alain to stay for dinner after the lessons in the future. Instead she would switch the lessons to the morning and have him stay for lunch, when Hugo would be gone.

The incident should have warned her, of course, that the day would come when Hugo would call her to account for her relationship with her cousin.

Chapter 18

*

Gabrielle heard Hugo arrive but did not go downstairs to greet him. She heard him ask their butler if she was home, or still visiting Fontenay, and the soft response, "Miz Gabrielle, she's heah, suh. Taking her afternoon nap."

She heard Hugo's heavy footsteps coming up the stairs and braced herself for the confrontation. But the footsteps, although they paused briefly at her bedroom door, continued down the hall to his room. She glanced in the direction of the connecting door between the two rooms, thinking perhaps he would change clothes and then come to her. But the door remained stubbornly closed.

Letting out her breath slowly, Gabrielle sat down at her dressing table and stared at her reflection. She was clad in a sheer peignoir, her hair loose about her shoulders in the way he liked, and she had dabbed perfume to her wrists, behind her ears, even on her inner thighs.

You have two choices, Hugo, she thought grimly. You can forgive and forget, or I shall confront you with your own perfidy.

Her nerves were shredded, from the dread of the forthcoming confrontation with Hugo, from worry about her mother and about Alain, above all from not knowing what her husband intended to do. He had come upon her during a party at the Willows clasped in Alain's arms, their lips almost, but not quite, touching. How could they have guessed he, or anyone else, would follow them into the solarium, where only the silent orchids watched? Hugo had simply turned and left without a word. He did not come to their room that night and had left the Willows before she arose the following morning.

Terrified about what he intended to do, she fled to Fontenay and hid in her room there until her mother insisted she return to her own home. By the time she arrived at their New Orleans house, he had already departed on another business trip.

They had, of course, had a stormy marriage from the start, but this was the worst crisis they had faced. Despite their frequent quarrels and Hugo's even more frequent absences, there had been one arena in which they met where both emerged victorious; their connubial bed. Gabrielle often marveled that two people so much at odds in every other aspect of their lives could enjoy the physical part of marriage so completely. It was almost as if two different people made love.

She did not see any contradiction in the fact that she also enjoyed her affair with her cousin. Her double life was enhanced both by the contrast between the two men and the danger of discovery. That she eagerly awaited Hugo's return to her bed was not something she pondered over, accepting the fact that although she disliked him because he was domineering and opinionated and not at all sensitive like Alain, he was an entertaining companion and a persuasive and powerful lover.

Then, three years after they were married, disaster struck. She discovered she was pregnant, but had no idea whether the baby was Hugo's or Alain's.

At Fontenay her sister Monique was ready to go to the expensive finishing school that Gabrielle and their mother had both attended and her father was again in financial trouble, in spite of Hugo having bailed him out on several previous occasions.

Gabrielle had to face the prospect of giving birth to a child that might be recognized as not having been fathered by her husband. Not only that, but there was also the possibility of dire consequences if first cousins produced offspring. Her decision was quickly made. She simply couldn't risk the collapse of her marriage.

As always, she took her dilemma to her mother.

"Oh, *cherie*!" her mother exclaimed. "Surely you practiced birth control with Alain? It cannot be his."

"I used birth control with *both* of them," Gabrielle replied tearfully. "I didn't want to bear children yet. I didn't want to lose my figure and have a fat waist like a matron."

Her mother's expression was shocked. "You defied the

church's edicts? You committed a cardinal sin? *Mon dieu!* I cannot believe this, Gabrielle."

Gabrielle knew that the sin to which her mother referred was not that she had been unfaithful to her husband, but that she had attempted to prevent conception of his child.

After a stern lecture about her wifely duties, and the suggestion that it might be time to break off her affair with Alain, her mother solved the problem for her by arranging a visit to a discreet doctor in Baton Rouge.

All might have been well and her secret might have been safe had it not been for the fact that upon her return to New Orleans, Gabrielle fell into a state of languor and depression. She didn't want to get up in the morning, didn't want to see anyone, not even her beloved Alain. Especially not Alain, and certainly not Hugo, one of whom was surely responsible for her humiliating, painful, and disgusting experience in Baton Rouge, and for her malaise afterward.

Hugo had been away on business when she went to Baton Rouge, and, not wanting to see him when he was due to return, she aroused herself sufficiently to travel to Fontenay to be with her mother. Here another unpleasant surprise awaited her. Her sister, who was supposed to be ensconced in finishing school, had been stricken with rheumatic fever and was confined to her bed. Her mother, beside herself with worry about Monique, spent every moment at her younger daughter's bedside and had little time for Gabrielle or her problems.

Disconsolate, she returned home to New Orleans and took to her bed, where Hugo found her upon his return.

He came straight to the bedroom—in those days they still shared the same room—promptly dragged the curtains back, and flung open the windows.

"Come on, Gabrielle, it's almost noon, get up," he ordered, not unkindly. "You won't sleep tonight if you sleep all day."

"I feel too blue to get up," she muttered, blinking.

"It's a nice day. I'll take you for a ride down to the river, and we'll watch the paddle wheelers leave. You know how the sound of the caliope and the colored steam always cheers you up. We could take a short trip up the river if you like; I have nothing pressing to attend to for a few days. The *Dixie Belle* has a new pianist who plays ragtime."

She covered her eyes with her hand to shut out the light and groaned softly. "I'm not well, Hugo. I need to rest."

He came to the bed and sat down, his penetrating gaze scanning her face. After a moment he drew a sharp breath. Picking up her hand, he said quietly, "You lost the baby." It was a statement rather than a question.

Stunned, she could only whisper, "How did you know I was with child?"

He folded her into an embrace and held her for a moment, stroking her matted hair. "I'm so sorry, my dear," he said at length. "I suspected before I left—I saw you rush from the breakfast table looking rather green about the gills a couple of times, and heard you vomiting one morning. I thought you might tell me—and I certainly would have canceled the trip if you had—but you said nothing, and I surmised you were waiting to be absolutely sure. Then—well, we quarreled over your visiting your cousin in that rat hole where he lives and you informed me you couldn't wait until I left, that you were only happy when I was gone ... Forgive me, Gabrielle, I should have known something was wrong and stayed with you."

There were genuine emotions in his voice, deep sympathy, regret, remorse, and the pain of loss.

Unwilling to let go of her resentment toward him, Gabrielle wriggled free of his embrace. "Please don't touch me. I still hurt all over."

He released her instantly. "You have seen a doctor, I hope?"

"Yes. Leave me now, Hugo. I must rest."

"Are you sure lying in bed isn't adding to your miseries?"

"I'm sure. Go now ... and Hugo, do you think you could sleep in the spare room tonight?"

He stared at her for an interminable moment, his eyes searching her face as though seeking her true motives for the request. She looked away guiltily.

"I'll have the houseman put a bed in the adjoining room," he said stiffly. "If you need me during the night, I'll just be through that connecting door."

The following day she had his clothes transferred to the adjacent room and never invited him back. Nor did he ever ask to return. There had been occasions, many of them, when he

visited her room and made love to her. But he never stayed
the night. Although she loved falling asleep curled up in his
arms after lovemaking and wanted him to remain with her,
she was too stubborn to ask.

Less than a year after her trip to Baton Rouge, Alain was
diagnosed as being in the early stages of consumption.
Gabrielle was convinced they were both being punished for
their sins, but she continued to see him. How could she desert
him in his hour of need?

With the passing years, although she discontinued practicing birth control with her husband, she did not conceive again
and this, too, became a thorn in Hugo's side. Although he
never reproached her, she was well aware that he longed for
children. She saw the unspoken yearning in his face whenever he saw children at play.

As she waited now for Hugo to come through the connecting door, she could not help but feel it was so unfair that
Hugo had caught her in a harmless embrace with Alain when
there had been so many times in the past that he could have
discovered them in far more damning circumstances.

Minutes ticked by. Hugo did not come to her. She paced
the floor, brushed her hair again, changed into a demure
white satin dressing gown, then changed back to the peignoir.
Every few minutes she stared at the connecting door, willing
it to open.

At last, unable to bear the tension any longer, she went to
the door and opened it. The room beyond was empty. Hugo's
luggage lay on the floor waiting to be unpacked by his valet,
his traveling clothes had been tossed onto the bench at the
foot of his bed. She could faintly smell the bay rum he used
after shaving. Ridiculously, she felt an urge to go and pick up
the shirt he had been wearing and inhale his scent.

She turned away, closed the connecting door, and rang for
her maid, who appeared almost at once.

"The green moire gown trimmed with black braid,"
Gabrielle said. "And a plain French twist for my hair. I want
to look businesslike and *formidable*." She gave the word the
French pronunciation she had learned from her French-born
mother.

When Hugo returned from a trip, they usually had aperitifs
before dinner on the balcony overlooking the city. She would

tell him what she had been doing, and whom she had seen, while he related amusing anecdotes about the places he visited and people he met. But tonight, although she waited on the balcony, clad in the most severe gown she owned, her hair so tightly drawn from her face it was giving her a headache, he didn't appear.

At length she went to the dining room. He was not there, either. She looked up as their butler brought a soup tureen to the sideboard. "Didn't I hear Mr. Hugo arrive earlier?"

"Yes'm, he done tole me to tell you . . ." The man spoke so slowly she wanted to shake him, "that he had to go to his office and ya'll shouldn't wait on him."

Although she wanted to hurl the tureen and the soup into the butler's smug black face, she contained her anger. The servants must have seen her waiting like a fool on the balcony for a husband who had already left the house. She was well aware that while everyone who worked for Hugo gave him absolute devotion and loyalty, she was merely tolerated.

She picked angrily at her food and retired to her room.

Awakening with a start in the darkness, she heard sounds in the adjoining bedroom. Jumping from the bed, she turned up the lamp and glanced at the clock. Past midnight. Damn him, where had he been until now?

Pulling on her satin dressing gown, she went to the connecting door and threw it open.

Hugo was fully dressed, sprawled on his bed, his hands behind his head, staring morosely in the general direction of her room.

"Why, what an unexpected honor, my dear." He stood up and bowed mockingly. "Welcome to my lair. I do believe this is the first time you have ever come to me of your own accord. It seems I must always pursue you into your silken nest. Have I ever told you how much I dislike all the frills and frippery of your room? Your taste in furniture would do credit to an eighteenth-century courtesan."

Gabrielle tilted her chin and folded her arms. At moments such as this she always longed to be much, much taller. She gave him her most defiant look. "I didn't come to discuss furnishings, Hugo."

"No, I didn't think so. You've come to demand your conjugal rights, is that it?"

"You know damn well why I'm here," she snapped.

"Why, Gabrielle! Such language. You shock me."

"What do you intend to do, Hugo?"

"About what?"

"If you don't stop playing this cat-and-mouse game immediately, I'm going to—to—"

"Yes?"

"Damn you, I'll fetch your pistol and force you to talk to me."

He laughed softly. "I've always admired your spirit, Gabrielle. I knew when I married you I wasn't getting a shrinking violet, but I had no idea I must try to tame a tigress."

He gestured toward the pair of armchairs placed at either side of his fireplace. "Please, sit down. You know you always get a knot in your neck from glaring up at me."

"I don't want to sit. I want you to answer my question."

"You want to know if I am going to send my seconds to call on your poor, ailing cousin, is that it? The answer is no. I'm not about to duel with a dying man. Besides, Alain came to see me."

"When?" Her hand crept nervously to her throat. "What did he say?"

"After the unfortunate incident in the solarium at the Willows, of course, to apologize and explain that when I caught the two of you in that compromising situation he had merely taken you there in order to speak to you privately about his funeral arrangements."

Gabrielle swayed unsteadily on her feet. She felt a scream rising in her throat. Then reason prevailed. Alain was not really near death, he had simply fabricated this story to protect her.

". . . and he didn't want to upset other members of the family, so took the opportunity to speak to you at the Willows," Hugo continued. "Naturally, you were overcome with sadness, and he was holding you in his arms to comfort you."

Hugo paused, watching her closely. She always worried at such moments that he could read her mind.

She swallowed a hard lump in her throat and regarded him as brazenly as she dared. One thought hammered at the back of her mind. If what Hugo was saying were true, then why hadn't Alain told her he had spoken with her husband? Alain had accompanied her to Natchez, and she had visited him in the Quarter only days ago. They had both agonized over what Hugo would do when he returned. The only conclusion she could draw was that Alain had met with Hugo today.

He was waiting for her to speak, watching her in that infuriatingly superior way that made her want to rake her fingernails down his arrogant face. Had his tone been sarcastic when he told of Alain's explanation? Had he believed Alain's story?

She tossed her hair back over her shoulder, wishing it were still drawn into the tight French twist, and replied cautiously, "Naturally I am very worried about my cousin."

"Of course," he drawled solicitously.

"You've never liked Alain, have you?" she asked recklessly, although she knew it would be prudent not to pursue the subject.

His eyes were hooded, his expression dangerously benign. "I've always pitied him."

She was outraged. "Pity? How dare you pity him! Alain is the sweetest, gentlest, kindest, most noble soul who ever lived. His body may have let him down, but his mind is so far above yours that even if he died today he would have brought more beauty and joy to those around him than you could if you lived to be a hundred."

For an instant she thought she saw fury in her husband's eyes, and almost hoped he would slap her. Then they could make love and put this unfortunate incident behind them. But he said sarcastically, "Such loyalty! Such adoration! Ah, would that I—a mere mortal man—could inspire such worship. But, of course, I am only your husband. Alain is . . ." Hugo paused and it seemed the air between them crackled. "Surely more than just your cousin?"

"What are you implying? That there is something between us? He is my first cousin, but we were brought up as brother and sister, and yes, I love and adore him and always will. He loves me purely and selflessly—he asks nothing of me. Damn you, Hugo, you have an evil mind. You suspect us because you cannot conceive of a man and a woman loving each other chastely. You judge us by your own standards—and it's well known that the Van Courtland men have the morals of alley cats."

Suddenly there was no protective space between them. He moved with surprising swiftness for a man of his size and seized her shoulders. "You asked what I was implying. I'll tell you. Your attachment to your cousin is unhealthy. Oh, I can see how it happened—he's older, you had a schoolgirl crush on him, his Byronesque charm and Old World gentility captivated you. No doubt he catered to you, listened to you, flattered you. But do you know what you really like about him? It's that you can dominate him completely. Oddly enough, it's also what draws him to you. That type of man needs to be absolved from guilt, and since you pursue him, he can throw up his hands helplessly and tell himself that whatever happens, it's not his fault."

"*Nothing* happened. What are you saying? We just went into the solarium to talk."

His grip on her shoulders tightened. "Do you think I'm a fool, Gabrielle? I've watched you when he and I are in the same room, and known how the wheels were turning in that conniving little mind of yours. Your expression is too transparent, my sweet, you should learn to play poker so that you could disguise it. You look at the two of us and wish that you could exchange us, one for the other."

Releasing her, he pushed her away from him and mimicked her slightly husky voice, " '*If only* Alain were not my first cousin, and not poor as a church mouse, if only *he* were my husband.' Do you think I don't know that when I make love to you, you wish it were Alain in your bed?"

She was too stunned to reply. She had never, not once, even *thought* of Alain when Hugo made love to her. How could he imagine such a thing? Hugo's lovemaking swept her away, overwhelmed all other sensations. Besides, her feelings for Alain were separate and apart from anything that happened between herself and her husband.

The injustice of Hugo's accusation outraged her. "You don't know what I think, Hugo, or what I feel. How arrogant of you to believe you do. How dare you accuse me of . . . of—"

"Adultery? Incest?" he suggested softly.

The words were like a whip, galvanizing her to action, and

she flew at him like a wildcat. Her attack caught him off guard. Her fingernails raked his cheek, and her fists were pounding on his chest before he grabbed her wrists to restrain her.

She struggled, attempting to kick him, screaming every obscenity she knew; all the while knowing the battle was futile. Within seconds he had pinned her arms to her sides, pushed her down on the bed, and used his body to keep her there. She stopped struggling and looked up at him, feeling the stirring of well-remembered desire.

Her nightgown had slipped from her shoulders during the struggle, exposing her breasts, which now rose and fell against his chest. She could feel the warmth of his flesh through his linen shirt, saw the answering chord of passion in the way he looked down at her, and all rational thought fled.

It will be all right now, she thought in silent triumph, I have him where I want him. We'll make love and he'll forgive me and we'll forget this stupid quarrel. She sighed contentedly, let her body grow limp, and moistened her lips in anticipation of his kiss.

But instead of ardent kisses and capitulation, instead of worshiping her with his body, the moment she relaxed beneath him, he placed his hands on the bed and pushed himself away from her.

"Not this time, Gabrielle," he muttered grimly. "What happened is too serious to sweep away in the heat of passion. Too many times we've substituted passion for discussion."

Disconcerted, she whispered, "What do you want to discuss?"

"'Have you broken your marriage vows? Have you committed adultery with your cousin?"

"How dare you . . . oh, you're impossible, evil-minded—how can you suggest such a thing?" Even to her own ears, she was blustering.

For a split second Hugo's features were contorted by anguish and anger. Her heart sank. He knew she was lying. Striding to his armoire, he pulled out a jacket and put it on.

She watched disbelievingly. "Hugo, what are you doing? Where are you going?"

He barely glanced in her direction. "Away from here, Gabrielle. Away from you."

She sat up, pulling her dressing down together and holding it with one hand. Her heart was hammering painfully, but she drew a deep breath, forcing herself to speak calmly. "Are you leaving me? If that's your intention, then you'd better hear what I have to say about the woman and the baby you've been supporting in Natchez."

His back was turned to her, but she thought she saw his shoulders stiffen. He turned slowly. She could see a pulse beat in his temple, but his face was a mask.

He pulled a chair away from his desk and turned it to face her. Seated, he assumed an attitude she recognized, that of the hardheaded businessman capable of dealing ruthlessly with insurrection or opposition.

She felt herself cringe inwardly, but she knew she must brazenly defend her position. If he detected weakness or reticence now, she would be lost.

He said briskly, "I am not going to discuss Mrs. Nesbitt and her child with you, and I warn you that I will tolerate no accusations or suppositions from you. What I am going to do is propose an arrangement between us that will be mutually acceptable."

She met his gaze levelly. "And that is?"

"We will no longer continue this pretense of a marriage—no! Hear me out. I will visit you here frequently enough to dispell any rumors or gossip, and you, my sweet, will be as discreet as a nun. You will see Alain Marchand only in the company of others. I will pay all of your bills and continue to support your family. In other words, the world in general and our families in particular will believe all is well. But from this day forward we will each go our separate ways.

Gabrielle jumped to her feet. "No! You can't do this—not now! Alain is dying—we don't make love, I swear it. Hugo, please—" she broke off, appalled that she was begging him to stay. Oh, dear heaven, she thought, at least let me preserve my dignity. Gabrielle Marchand never groveled to any man.

He stood staring at her for a moment and seemed to be waiting for her to say something, to make some statement that perhaps could wipe out all the misunderstandings. But she knew if she said another word, she would be conceding defeat. Her pride was too important to her to allow him to believe he had won. At least he wasn't suggesting divorce.

What did she care if he went his separate way, as long as her comfort and that of her family were assured?

But in a blinding flash of enlightenment, she realized at that moment that she cared a great deal. Hugo had managed to inveigle himself into her very being, and she suddenly saw a bleak and empty future without him. He couldn't leave now, not when Alain was lost to her, too.

But he had already turned away from her and was walking through the door, which closed with awful finality behind him.

Chapter 19

*

DELIA

*Hugo is everything a man should be, strong, brave, compassion-
ate toward those weaker than he. How that vixen of a wife caught
him is a mystery. She would have made a better partner for Julian,
who is just as devious and conniving.*

"My God, what have you done to your hair?" Julian entered Delia's hotel room, as usual without knocking, and
found her seated at her dressing table.

Her pale blond hair had been cut almost as short as a
man's. Julian was too furious to notice what everyone else
had pointed out to her: that the clipped hair and men's clothing emphasized her femininity rather than concealing it, a fact
that she had not anticipated and which pleased her not all!

"I go away for a few days, and you do something stupid
like this. I can't believe it!"

Delia ran her hand through her shorn locks and turned to
face him. "I'm going out to dinner. If you've come to tell me
about your trip south, do it quickly."

"When did you cut your hair? You haven't been on stage
like that? This is Sunday ... perhaps we can have a wig
made."

"Read the theater gossip articles, Julian. I had my hair cut
several performances ago. As usual, everyone was shocked
and appalled and utterly fascinated. The more outrageously I
behave, the better audiences like it."

"One of these days you're going to go too far, Delia. Do
you realize there have been rumors that you are a transvestite,
and worse, that you prefer women to men?"

She shrugged. "Perhaps the rumors are true, who knows?"

"Don't talk like that. You know how I hate it. Where are
you going for dinner? I'll go with you."

She smiled sweetly. "No, you won't. I am having a private dinner with a friend."

"Who?"

"An admirer, of course."

He raised an eyebrow. "Male or female?"

She gave him a pitying glance, refusing to be baited.

Julian frowned. "I was going to tell you about the investments I made for you. I bought shares in an oil drilling enterprise in Los Angeles and some land outside the city limits."

"Why? Aren't we going back to Louisiana soon? Won't it be difficult to manage investments from that distance?"

"Let me worry about that. I'm going to make you rich, Delia."

"What makes you think that's what I want, Julian? No, don't bother to answer. I'm not really interested."

"Then perhaps you'll be interested to hear I've also bought a house, here in San Francisco. I for one am tired of hotel living."

That stopped her short. "But if we're going home to New Orleans . . ." She paused, realization dawning. "But we're not leaving, are we? You've extended my booking here."

"There's nothing for you in New Orleans yet. Not until we have enough money to restore Courtland Hall. I've decided not to accept Hugo's offer of financing. We'll do it on our own, so we never have to be obligated to him. Why not stay and enjoy your success here? Besides, you might find that your flamboyant style is not as well received back home as it is here on the Barbary Coast."

She didn't argue with him. Even if the contract she had signed with him were not still in effect, her success in San Francisco had made her realize that she needed Julian to manage her career, her money, and, not least, to protect her from the reporters who were determined to uncover every detail of her past. Although her own instincts proved best regarding her performances, she could never have dealt with the business end of her bookings, nor kept the reporters at bay. She stood up and removed her peignoir. "Make yourself useful, Julian. You can button my dress."

"Don't tell me you're actually going to dress as a woman?" His gaze was mocking. "When you dine with me, you insist upon masquerading as a man. Your dinner companion must be someone you want to impress."

She picked up a dress that had been laid out on her bed, and his expression changed to one of surprise. The gown was a drab mud brown, looked well-worn, like nothing he had ever seen in her wardrobe. A cheaply made coat and an out-of-style hat completed her outfit.

Julian grinned. "I must correct my original thought. What happened? Did your admirer request that you don female attire and to discourage future requests you ransacked someone's ragbag? I doubt he'll be so foolish in the future. You look like someone's destitute relative."

On her way out of the room, he called after her, "Get into the restaurant as quickly as you can, I could see fog across the bay."

She was glad of the mist that swirled around her as she alighted from a cable car half an hour later. It was becoming increasingly difficult for her to travel about the city without being recognized, even on the odd occasion she wore a dress, which was why she had borrowed the drab brown outfit from a hotel maid. The clothes would not make her stand out in this part of town.

The address she was seeking proved to be a modest house with a weathered wooden shingle that read JOSEPH SIMMINGTON, M.D.

She lifted a brass doorknocker, and almost instantly the door was opened, leading her to surmise that Dr. Simmington had been watching for her arrival.

The man who came to the door was probably in his mid-thirties, with sandy hair and mild hazel eyes encircled by gold-rimmed spectacles. Although his clothes were dated and a little shabby, there was a scrubbed-clean look about him that appealed to her. That and the fact that he had only recently arrived in San Francisco, so probably had not heard about her, or, if he had, had not yet been subjected to all of the gossip she continued to generate.

Only one item seemed out of place. She glanced toward his shingle. "For a brand-new doctor just starting his practice, your shingle seems a little weather-beaten."

He smiled apologetically. "It belonged to my father. I

brought it with me from the East Coast. Won't you come in, Miss . . . Jones."

"Thank you for seeing me on a Sunday evening." Delia followed him into the front room of the small house, which was furnished simply: a desk, two chairs, and an examining table, with cupboards lining the walls. The room was evidently both his surgery and his office.

He pulled out a chair for her. "Apart from the fact that I desperately need patients, I would have got up in the middle of the night to see you had I known Miss Jones was actually the great Cordelia. You see, I was fortunate enough to hear you sing—indeed, I waited among the throng of stage-door johnnies to catch a closer glimpse of you as you left the Opera House—my seat, you see, was a long way from the stage."

Delia sighed. She had sent the hotel maid to make the appointment for "a friend named Miss Jones," but the ruse had obviously been futile. She rose to leave.

"Please, don't go," the doctor said quickly. "I can assure you of my complete discretion. Nothing that transpires of a medical nature will ever be divulged by me to anyone else."

She regarded him silently for a moment. "I've had little reason to trust members of your profession, Doctor. But I must have an answer to a question."

He waited expectantly for her to continue.

She had remained standing and now took off her coat. Bending quickly, she lifted her skirt and petticoats to her waist, revealing cotton pantalettes, although she was well aware that few doctors examined female patients without their clothes.

"I had a baby—almost a year ago. I have not yet resumed my monthly cycle and . . ."

Pushing down the cotton pantalettes, she added, "I have a scar . . . here."

Dr. Simmington hesitated for a second, then came around to her side of his desk and looked more closely at the scar, which with the passing months had faded to a silvery welt on the pale skin of her abdomen.

He raised his eyes to hers. "You don't recall having an operation? Perhaps at the same time you gave birth?"

She shook her head and began to rearrange her clothes. "A

midwife delivered my baby. I . . . had a fall shortly afterward. Could I have injured myself then?"

"Sit down, Miss . . . let's dispense with the pseudonym, shall we?" He returned to his chair behind the desk, as though needing to keep a barricade between them. "Cordelia, your scar is the result of an incision, made by a doctor. I can't believe you were, or are, ignorant of what was done to you."

Her mouth was suddenly very dry. "*What* was done to me?"

He looked away from her searching gaze. "I really should refer you to the doctor who performed the operation."

Delia placed her hands on his desk and leaned toward him, her expression composed. "I was unconscious for a time and, I'm told, delirious. I don't remember much about the week after I had the baby. The doctor who treated me said I had toxemia and a high fever. If an operation was performed on me, it was without my consent or knowledge. I do remember being very weak for months afterward and . . . I had trouble going to the toilet."

Something else occurred to her. "There was a binder around my abdomen, and the nurse insisted it be kept tightly in place. She said it was so that I would regain my figure, and I do remember my mother used to wear one after she had her babies. But, well, the day I left the nursing home, I'm sure I was given something that put me to sleep for a while, although the nurse just said I'd dozed off again. But this was mid-morning and I'd slept well the night before. If I'd been operated on, they could have removed any sutures then, and I wouldn't have known. I saw the scar later, of course, but thought I'd done it when I fell."

The doctor's expression was now very grave. "These are very serious charges, Cordelia."

"If I swear on a Bible that I will take no action against that doctor—will you please tell me what he did to me?"

"Your delivery was perhaps difficult? You hemorrhaged?"

"The baby was in a breech position, but the midwife was able to turn her."

"I've never known a midwife capable of that. Are you sure she didn't injure you?"

"I can't be absolutely sure, but I felt all right the next day, just sore and tired."

"That was the day you had the accident?"

"Accident?"

"You said you fell."

"Oh, yes."

The doctor cleared his throat and a faint flush stained his cheeks. "Is it possible that the physician consulted your husband in regard to your condition?"

"I don't have a husband."

If the doctor was shocked, he didn't show it. But he hesitated an unbearably long minute before saying, "Cordelia—I believe you were sterilized."

She stared at him blankly.

"If I'm correct, you will never have another child."

She sank slowly back into her chair. "But you're not sure?"

"Only an internal examination could absolutely confirm my assumption, and I realize that few women—or for that matter, few doctors, consider such examinations proper."

White-lipped, Delia was on her feet in an instant. "I want to know for certain, Doctor."

He nodded. "Very well. If you will remove your lower garments and then lie on the examining table. Cover yourself with the sheet. I will endeavor to spare you as much embarrassment as I can. Excuse me for a moment, while I go to wash my hands."

Delia undressed quickly and climbed onto the leather-covered examining table. She pulled the thin sheet up and let out her breath slowly.

In the quiet left in the wake of the doctor's departure, city sounds crept into the room: the clop of hooves and rumble of wheels, passing voices, a foghorn's mournful warning. It seemed that the thundering of her heart competed with the other sounds.

Drawing a deep breath, she willed herself to think of the songs she would sing at her next performance. Filling her mind with music was a trick she had learned from Marcus Van Courtland long ago. But instead the doctor's voice intruded, repeating, over and over again, *sterilized . . . you will never have another child.*

Then, somewhere in the mist-muted din of the city, she thought she heard a piano playing. Perhaps it was only her imagination, an echo of a memory. Still, all at once she was a fourteen-year-old girl again, spending a few days at the Willows.

The haunting nocturnal notes had called her from sleep once again. Marcus was playing a heartbreakingly beautiful sonata.

Moonlight spilled into Delia's room, and a faint breeze from the bayou stirred the curtains at her open window. Her room was directly above the terrace, and the French doors leading from the drawing room where he played the grand piano must have been open, as the music seemed close enough to seep into her body.

The melody was a refrain she'd heard him play before, and was so beautiful she wanted to capture it and examine it to learn all the secret yearnings it expressed.

Almost without thinking, she slipped out of bed and pulled her dress on over her nightgown. Moments later she was tiptoeing down the stairs.

Everyone had warned her never to approach Marcus during his nocturnal concerts, and she really had no intention of doing so. It was the siren song of his music that impelled her down the stairs and out onto the terrace to crouch in the shadows. She felt drawn to the piano as if pulled by puppet strings, wishing to be close to the source of the magical sound, needing to hear every note, every significant pause, every nuance, wanting to be consumed by it.

So enraptured was she that she didn't realize she was perilously close to a row of flowerpots arranged along the terrace until her bare foot connected with one. She cried out, the pot crashed over, and almost instantly Marcus appeared at the French doors.

"Who's there? Show yourself, dammit."

Shaking, Delia stepped forward into the pool of amber light.

Marcus said, "Oh, it's you." He didn't sound surprised that she would have the temerity to spy on him. "I thought you were still away at school."

That was a lie, Delia knew, as she'd seen him at his window watching her arrival that afternoon. Besides, it was Good Friday, or had been before midnight, so he surely knew she would not be at school. "I'm sorry I interrupted you. I didn't mean to."

"Nonsense. Of course you did."

"No, really. I just wanted to get closer to the music. The piece you were playing ... was so beautiful."

"*Everything* I play is beautiful."

Since he had not turned into a raving monster as she had expected, she couldn't resist asking, "Why do you play the piano in the middle of the night?"

His response was unhesitating. "To kill the silence. The silence of the night is a curse, an abomination, it chips at my soul, piece by piece, bit by bit."

"Oh, no!" she exclaimed. "The silence is a friend. Nothing comes out of the quiet to bother you, no voices screaming at you, no babies crying because they're hungry."

"If you're so fond of the silence, why do you sing? Surely that shatters your precious silence."

"I don't sing in the middle of the night. I mostly just sleep. Don't you sleep?"

"If I sleep at night I am savaged by dreams."

She said thoughtfully, "Sometimes I have nightmares, too, but I can't stay awake."

"If you awaken from a nightmare, you may come and sit beside the piano and listen to me play," he said in an offhand tone that did little to diminish the incredible invitation. Then he abruptly closed the French doors in her face and went back inside.

Delia crept back to her room. Marcus didn't play again that night.

That Easter weekend Delia had another secret. She was hoping, sometime after the sunrise mass on Easter Sunday, to slip away to meet Thad.

He was now her only connection to Daddy Lou and Mignon and Eulie, since she had been forbidden to visit them. Once, the first summer after she went away to school, she had defied Julian and made her way to the old house where she had been so happy.

Daddy Lou had been alone and in one of his cantankerous moods. He was not pleased to see her and told her in no uncertain language that she was never to go there again. She was not one of them and had a new life to lead.

"And doan y'all go looking for Mignon, neither," Daddy Lou had added darkly. "She ain't working at the Cajun Club no more. Y'all git back to the Van Courtlands and be real careful how y'all choose your friends from now on."

Baffled and hurt, Delia had slunk away like a whipped hound.

But what Daddy Lou didn't know was that Eulie's son, Thad, while on his grand tour of the United States, had sent a message to her Philadelphia school that he was in town visiting friends of his father who were having a musical evening, and would Delia care to go. Delia attended the event, and although neither she nor Thad performed, they did huddle together in a corner and talk. How they talked!

From then on, after Thad returned to Paris, they wrote to each other regularly. Perhaps it was the safety of sharing confidences at such distances, the feeling of anonymity in writing private thoughts rather than giving them voice, but whatever the reason they each poured out their hearts to the other.

Delia knew she had never been closer to another human being in her entire life, nor so separated by distance. Their pen friendship became her pillar of strength, enabling her to deal with school and the Van Courtlands and, not least, memories that still gave her nightmares.

Now Thad was back in New Orleans, and she was at the Willows, and they had vowed, one way or another, to meet. Throughout the Easter Sunday sunrise service she rehearsed several excuses to use in order to slip away to meet him. She was ill—a headache? upset stomach?—and must lie down. No, Julian or his mother would see right through that. The family was returning to the Willows to spend the day, and Julian would accuse her of trying to get out of singing for them, despite the fact that she had to sing in the choir that morning.

Then, just as she was to sing the opening verse of the hymn, "He Is Risen," Delia remembered the fateful day Eulie had been unable to sing because she had the quinsies.

Clutching her throat dramatically, Delia pointed to her mouth and shook her head. The choir director quickly signaled for everyone to sing.

Julian came to her as they were leaving the church. "What's the matter? Why didn't you sing your solo?"

She repeated her charade, mouthing the words, "Lost my voice."

His hand promptly went to her forehead. "You don't seem to have a fever."

She mouthed, "Sore throat."

"Well, I doubt we can get the doctor to look at you today. You'd better rest and I'll take you into New Orleans to a throat specialist tomorrow."

Delia looked away quickly, to hide her elation.

She was allowed to go straight to her room, and a lunch tray was sent up to her. She waited until everyone had gathered in the dining room, then arranged a bolster in her bed and covered it with a sheet. Placing her lunch tray outside her door, to indicate to the maid she did not wish to be disturbed, she ran quickly down the stairs.

The main entry hall, she decided, was her safest route, as the servants would be busy serving lunch and would enter the dining room from the corridor leading to the kitchen and servants' quarters.

Thad was waiting for her, perched on the huge gnarled root of a cypress at the edge of the bayou. He was skimming pebbles over the still water, watching them bounce.

As she came running toward him he jumped down from the cypress, his face breaking into a welcoming smile. He seemed to have grown a great deal since their last meeting.

"Delia! How pretty you look—how grown-up!" His slightly accented English was such a joy to hear. She had often imitated it, in private.

"You've grown so tall, Thad. You must be at least six feet."

He grinned. "And one inch. Now, if I could add a few pounds."

"I brought you some cold beef and stuff from my lunch tray." She handed him a napkin-wrapped bundle, and he grimaced. "I never should have told you in my letters that I'm too thin."

"Eat," she ordered. "Then tell me all about Oxford."

He had written that he had been accepted at the great English university and hoped to read law, having finally convinced his father that he was not interested in the sciences and that it made more sense to study English law than French, since eventually he wanted to settle in the United States, despite his father's misgivings.

Thad's eyes lit up. "I am ... enthralled with English Common Law. There are insufficient hours in the day for all I wish to absorb. And I like England, especially Oxford—such serenity! How can I describe listening to the bells of Christ Church College tolling as they have since the seventeenth century? The sense of antiquity and continuity is somehow comforting." He shrugged self-consciously. "Of course, the English climate is atrocious and the pater is not happy with me."

He paused. "Why are you grinning?"

"You're picking up an English accent," Delia replied. "Now you have a blend of English and French accents and a touch of the Caribbean and a dash of Louisiana, and it's absolutely wonderful."

"You speak differently, too. I'm not sure I prefer it yet, but we'll see," he replied between mouthfuls of bread and beef. "At least neither of us have an accent when we write."

"You were saying your father isn't happy," Delia prompted.

Thad nodded. "He says if I must become a lawyer, then at least I should be one in France—or even, if I must, in England. My plan to come to the United States fills him with dread. He says it is not even my country, since I was born in Martinique. But my mother has spent most of her life here, and I am fascinated by this country, by its people—by the sense of vastness and unlimited opportunity and ... newness, I suppose. You know, I wanted to come here to study law, but he wouldn't hear of it. I was fortunate he allowed me to go to England—and that I was accepted at Oxford."

"It would be wonderful if you could go to school in Philadelphia," Delia said. "We could be real friends then."

"We *are* real friends, Delia."

"Penfriends, really."

"But you know you can always count on me, for anything, any time."

"I just wish you lived here. I can't seem to make friends at school."

"That's because they are jealous of you."

"I think it's because I don't have a pedigree."

They laughed conspiritorially. They had already decided that their somewhat cloudy family backgrounds was one of the reasons they were drawn to each other.

"How did you manage to talk your father into letting you come to America this time?"

His eyes clouded. "I didn't want to tell you in my letter, because I was afraid you'd go to her and I know you've been forbidden. My mother is ill. Daddy Lou wrote asking me to come."

"Oh, I'm so sorry, Thad. What's wrong with Eulie?"

"It's her throat again, but far worse than quinsies this time."

Delia thought of Eulie's magnificent singing voice and was deeply saddened. She squeezed Thad's arm. "How awful for her—and for you. What's wrong with her throat?"

"Well, that's the strange part. The doctors have not been able to find anything wrong, but my mother can't speak above a whisper and she can't sing at all. She's convinced someone has put a hex on her. The doctors aren't helping at all. Mignon brought in a voodoo woman."

"Mignon? But I thought Daddy Lou said she had left?"

Thad looked blank. "No, she is still living with them."

Delia sighed. "I wish I knew why Daddy Lou hates me so much he tells me lies to keep me away from them all."

"He doesn't hate you, Delia. He's so proud of you. He often says he hopes he lives long enough to hear you sing in concert. Why, he was even talking about those new phonographs and saying one day you'll make a . . . what do they call it?—a record—and then your voice will live forever and people not yet born will be able to hear you sing."

Delia digested this information for a moment and then asked, "Then why won't he let me visit?"

Thad spread his hands helplessly. "I don't know."

"Will you ask him if I can come to visit your mother and Mignon? I'm going back to Philadelphia tomorrow, but I'll be here for the summer—"

She shrieked as suddenly she was seized from behind by hands that held her powerless in a viselike grip. Thad leaped forward, as if to rescue her, but faltered as Julian's voice slashed between them. "Take another step, boy, and I'll have you arrested for kidnapping this child."

"Please, sir, don't hurt her—"

"Julian, he's my friend," Delia sobbed.

"You are never to come near her again, do you understand?"

Thad said quietly, "I can't promise that. One day she will be old enough to make such decisions for herself."

"Stay away from her, or you won't live to see her grow up."

With that, Delia was dragged away. Thad called after her, "I'll write to you, Delia."

Julian didn't speak to her on the way back to the Willows. Upon arrival he grabbed her arm and propelled her into the drawing room, seized her shoulders, and shook her until her teeth rattled.

"You are never to see him again, do you understand? If you aren't concerned about your reputation, then be concerned for his life."

"But he's my friend—"

"He can't be your friend. He's *colored*. Nothing else matters—not his fancy clothes or his French accent or even his light skin. He's still colored, and you're white, and that's all there is to it. You'll get him killed if anybody finds out you've been alone with him."

"But he was staying with white people in Philadelphia, and they treated him just like their own people," Delia blurted before she stopped to think.

Julian's eyes narrowed to slits. "You *saw* him in Philadelphia?"

"There was a musical evening. I wasn't alone with him."

"His so-called friends should have known better, but some Northerners have strange ideas about how to treat Negroes; although I don't notice any of them relishing the idea that their daughters might marry one. Look, Delia, you can't judge what's proper by the way Thaddeous was treated in the North, or in New Orleans for that matter, because the city tends to be somewhat color-blind, due to the various nationalities and cultures that settled there and often intermixed. But you travel away from New Orleans, especially out here in the county, and it's a vastly different story."

"Could I write to him?"

"No! Dammit, Delia, have you forgotten our agreement? You were supposed to sever all ties to those people."

"You said I wasn't to see Daddy Lou and Mignon, or go to their house. But Thad lives in France—"

"And turned up in Philadelphia and is here now. This so-called friendship is over, Delia."

Julian released her and strode from the room. She sank down onto the floor and buried her face in her hands.

Until this moment she had not realized how much her friendship with Thad meant to her. She had not made any friends among the girls of the exclusive private school in Philadelphia, perhaps because she didn't have a home to which she could invite them, although her music teacher had warned her that her spectacular singing voice might cause some jealousy among less talented students. Nor could she take her questions and concerns about life and approaching womanhood to Mignon or Eulie, as she had when she lived with them. She also missed Daddy Lou's simple wisdom. Thad, through the medium of the mails, had filled so many empty places in her life.

"What my brother was trying to tell you," a voice drawled, "is that if anyone else sees you with your colored friend, they'll probably lynch him."

She jumped. Marcus lounged against the door.

"Where did you come from?" Delia demanded indignantly. "Why, you're a . . . an eavesdropper."

"I was merely passing by on my way to my room. How did I know Julian had dragged you in here to berate you? You were supposed to be sick in bed. Who is this colored boy he was talking about? Thaddeous, wasn't it?"

Delia sank to the floor and buried her face in her hands. "He's my friend and Julian is going to kill him and I don't know why."

For the second time that day Delia was seized by hands that this time yanked her to her feet. Marcus's expression was harsh. "Don't do that! Don't ever wallow in fear and defeat. Learn to grow a steel shell. No matter what you are thinking, what you are feeling, remember that only what you say and do is observed by others. If you believe you might be about to give in to such a display, then fill your mind with music.

Think only of your music. After all, nothing else, no one else, matters anyway."

Delia remembered his admonition as she lay on the cold leather examining table in the doctor's office in San Francisco waiting for confirmation of the unthinkable. That she would never be a mother.

Would she be able to face the truth? Lies could be so persuasive, so comforting. The worst kind were the ones perpetrated in the belief they were somehow preferable to the truth, because they were so easy to believe. Gazing down the long corridor of memory, Delia realized that Daddy Lou had never intended for her to know the truth. She thought of the last time she had seen him, that same Easter weekend.

Chapter 20

*

I never understood why Daddy Lou never told me the truth, even when he was on his deathbed. He told no one, for if Eulie or Mignon had known, they surely would have taken great pleasure in informing me. And it would be years before Thad uncovered the old man's secret.

There was a brooding sense of foreboding abroad at the Willows that Easter Sunday night. Delia tossed restlessly in her bed thinking of the events of the day. Branches rattled against her window in a rising wind, and the old plantation house creaked and groaned like a timbered galleon tossed upon forbidding seas. A spring storm was moving up the river.

Unable to sleep, she arose and went to the window to watch scudding clouds blot out the moon. Spanish moss blew from the trees like the long gray hair of ancient hags. Thunder rumbled in the distance, and in a sudden flash of lightning Delia thought she saw a familiar figure standing on the lawn near the terrace, staring up at her room.

Surely it was only a shadow? After Julian's threats earlier, Thad wouldn't dare come to the Willows, would he?

Another lightning flash illuminated a tall, lanky figure bending to scoop up a handful of pebbles, and she flung open the window without stopping to think that the pebbles might come flying toward her. She waved her hand and called, "I'm coming down."

Racing through the house as the thunder moved closer, she skidded to a stop when another sound made itself heard.

Marcus was playing the piano.

Would Thad be able to hear the piano out on the terrace?

He mustn't be caught here! She didn't dare imagine what Julian would do.

Rain bathed her face in a soft spray as she ran outside, and she wished fleetingly that she had put on a coat instead of her flimsy dressing gown. But it was imperative that she get Thad away from the house quickly.

The French doors leading from the drawing room where Marcus played the grand piano were closed, but lights spilled across the terrace. Delia ran down the steps to the lawn and in the intermittent flashes of lightning saw that Thad was no longer standing beside the terrace. She paused, looking around, and a moment later he came running toward her.

Seizing her arm, he pointed toward the river, and she found herself running beside him, feeling the urgency of a mission not yet explained. As they reached the riverbank, she saw he had come by canoe.

"What happened, Thad?" she asked breathlessly. "Where are we going? Is it your mother?"

He helped her into the canoe. "No. It's Daddy Lou. He's dying, Delia, and he's asking for you. Mignon told me how I could find your room—I didn't want to wake up any of the Van Courtlands and cause trouble. I'll have you back before morning, so they shouldn't miss you."

Delia settled into the boat, shivering as the rain soaked her and scarcely aware of Thad removing his own coat to put around her shoulders. *Daddy Lou was dying.*

As Thad dipped the paddle into the dark water and the canoe slipped away from the bank and caught the main current, Delia pushed aside the memory of her last meeting with the old man, when he had brusquely ordered her to stay away from him and make new friends. Instead she remembered a happier occasion.

Mardi Gras . . . that first year when she lived with the exotic inhabitants of Daddy Lou's household. On Fat Tuesday—which she knew as Shrove Tuesday—he had marched in the parade, blowing his trumpet and outshining every other musician. Eulie, magnificent as Cleopatra, was carried in a wicker sedan chair by splendid black warriors, while Mignon, striking in a brilliant yellow silk costume, rode in a flower-bedecked carriage pulled by satin-draped horses. Delia was equally fascinated by a grottolike float, from which red-clad,

ferociously leering devils tossed beads and trinkets and dou-
bloons to the crowds filling the narrow streets of the French
Quarter.

What an exciting night that was! What a polished gem of
a memory! The Quarter had been the heartbeat of the ancient
city, throbbing with music and laughter. She had danced
alongside the mummers, dodged a clown atop ten-foot stilts,
chased a huge red-feathered turkey bird, and all the while
Daddy Lou's horn had filled the night with magic.

Now he was dying.

She didn't ask the how and why of it as Thad paddled
swiftly downriver, then negotiated the shallow waters of the
bayous that would take them to him. Daddy Lou was, after
all, a very old man. Besides, the rain was now heavy, and she
pulled Thad's coat over her head, making conversation impossible. Nor did she worry about getting back to the Willows before anyone missed her. She did worry that Daddy
Lou would have passed over before they arrived.

His house seemed already to be mourning him. The shutters were tightly closed, lamps were turned low. Mignon was
sobbing quietly in a corner of the living room, and the rest of
his family and boarders milled about in bewildered disorder,
making a low moaning sound like a distressed river flowing
over inhospitable terrain.

Eulie, gaunt now where formerly she had been statuesque,
stood like a silent sentinel beside Daddy Lou's bed, which
had been brought downstairs. No one spoke as Thad ushered
Delia into the room and led her to the bedside.

Delia's heart sank as she looked into the gray and oddly
shrunken features of Daddy Lou. His eyes were closed and
only a faint wheezing emitting from his slack mouth indicated that he was still breathing.

Thad bent close to the old man's ear and said, "Delia's
here, Daddy Lou."

She saw Daddy Lou's lips move, and Thad had to lean
closer to hear what he said, then Thad straightened up and
said to her, "He wants you to sing for him, Delia."

"I can't," Delia said, biting back tears, "I . . . can't."

Someone pinched her arm viciously and shoved her closer
to the bed. She looked up into the fierce gaze of Eulie, who

did not speak, but her message was clear. Delia was to sing, or else.

Biting her lip, Delia cleared her throat.

The mournful murmuring in the room stopped as she began to sing the only words that seemed appropriate: *"Swing low, sweet chariot, coming for to carry me home. . . ."*

She had barely sung the opening bars when Daddy Lou feebly raised his arm and beckoned for her to move closer to hear what he had to say.

"Sing something cheerful, chile. Doan be depressin' all these folks with funeral songs. 'Sides, I want to take the sound of your voice on to glory with me."

She sang with tears streaming down her face, sang with all her heart and soul, ignoring the claps of thunder and the sound of Mignon weeping in the background, and every time she came to the end of a song, Daddy Lou's weak gesture signaled for another encore.

Then at last he beckoned that he wished to speak to her, and she again bent over his ravaged face. "Ain't never been a voice lak' yours on this earth before, Delia, ain't never gwine be another."

"Why didn't you let me know you were sick, Daddy Lou? Why were you so mean to me, that day I came to visit? What did I do?"

"Why, Sugar, y'all didn't do nothing. It was jes' the way it had to be, for a whole mess of reasons. Someday you'll understand."

"No, I won't. I won't ever understand why you couldn't at least let me visit."

"Hush yo' mouth and listen now. I ain't got much time. Always remember this, chile, nobody owns you. *Nobody.* You is free. Say it, Delia."

"I am free," Delia said solemnly. "Nobody owns me." The old man was surely delirious. Perhaps he was recalling that he had once been a slave and had forgotten that slavery no longer existed anywhere in the country, and in fact, never had for white people.

"Try mighty hard to make good choices, Delia. Y'all has a good mind, use it, y'heah? The Good Lord done gave you the voice of an angel. Don't never squander His gift."

"I won't, Daddy Lou, I promise," Delia whispered.

"I is weary now, sugar. Tell Eulie to bury my horn with me and promise me you won't come to the cemetery."

She nodded, too overcome to speak.

Daddy Lou sighed in an almost contented way. Mignon crept close to the bedside and picked up his hand, cradling it to her cheek.

Then Thad began to play his clarinet softly. The music did not quite mask the death rattle in the old man's throat.

Mignon's wail of anguish startled Delia, but almost instantly Thad put down his clarinet and said urgently, "Come on, Delia, I must get you back before you're missed."

They didn't say much on the return journey, but Delia did remark, "Mignon seemed more distraught than anyone."

"She was the old man's great-granddaughter, his only living relative. Didn't you know?"

Delia shook her head.

"He hated what she did—you know, working at the Cajun Club. But he always let her come home."

The capricious spring storm had moved on, ending almost at the moment of Daddy Lou's death, and Delia remembered her mother used to say that if it rained when someone died, they were glad to go. She hoped it was true of Daddy Lou.

The first streaks of dawn were gilding the eastern sky by the time they reached the Van Courtland boathouse.

Thad helped her ashore. "I'll leave you here, Delia. No sense in riling everybody."

"I didn't get a chance to speak to your mother, Thad. Tell her I hope she feels better soon. She looked very thin, quite haggard."

"She claims her throat has closed up and she can't swallow, so she's getting by on thin gruel and broth and not much of that. She can't talk, can't sing. Can't make a sound, in fact. I'm trying to persuade her to come back to Europe with me, to see a doctor I've read about who believes the mind can cause physical illness. But she trusts the mambo."

"Mambo?"

"Voodoo priestess. She has my mother convinced she is under a black magic spell and only the right juju can cure her."

Delia would have liked to hear more, but it was growing

lighter every second, and so she bade Thad a hasty goodbye and hurried back to the house.

She slipped in through the tradesmen's entrance, hoping that several young housemaids who were beginning the day's chores would not report her arrival to anyone.

There was no one in the main hall. She crossed the burnished oak floor quickly and ran up the staircase.

She didn't see Marcus until she reached the bend in the stairs. He stood on the landing, watching her implacably.

Delia stopped in front of him. She looked up at him defiantly. "I don't care if you do tell on me. Daddy Lou died last night and I had to go to him."

"What makes you think I'd tell anyone about your nocturnal excursion? I'm a creature of the night myself."

She hesitated a moment, then darted around him and went to her room.

Two weeks after she returned to her school in Philadelphia she received a letter from Thad, postmarked New Orleans:

Dear Friend:

Our reunion was not quite what we expected, was it? I shall be returning to England within days and wanted to let you know what transpired here.

Daddy Lou's funeral parade was one of the largest the Vieux Carre has ever witnessed, I'm sure. The old man would have been proud. Every jazz musician in town, and half of those from the paddle wheelers on the river, must have been there; it was a concert to reverberate around heaven. We buried him with his horn, and my mother and Mignon decorated his tomb with brass and copper wires they had fashioned into the shape of a trumpet and musical notes.

Someone from the church choir sang. My mother still can't speak. I fear she is falling more and more under the power of the mambo woman.

I had urged Daddy Lou to make a will before he died, and this he did. To my surprise, however, he left the house and all of his possessions—there was little or nothing in the way of cash—to my mother. I argued, begged, and pleaded with him to at least include Mignon, but he refused. Still, I expect things will go along pretty much as they have in the past.

I shall never forget your singing for Daddy Lou. Your voice is magnificent, Delia. Do you save all of your passions, all of your emotions, for your singing? You are transformed when you sing.

Write soon.

Thad

"Delia—did you fall asleep?"

She started, the doctor's spartan office coming back into focus. She was in San Francisco, and Dr. Simmington was bending over her. "Shall I proceed?"

"Yes," she whispered.

Chapter 21

*

Delia pounded on Julian's door in the San Francisco hotel, oblivious of the lateness of the hour and the protests of several other guests at having their sleep disturbed. When the door yielded at last, she stumbled into his room.

"Good God, Delia, what is it?" Julian fumbled with a lamp.

"You bastard. You unmitigated swine. Why didn't you tell me?" She was breathless from her mad dash across town from the doctor's office and her furious assault on his door, and the words came in short bursts.

"What are you talking about?"

"A doctor examined me this evening. Tell me about that other doctor, Julian. The one in the New York nursing home where you took me. Who gave him permission to operate on me?"

Julian swore under his breath. "You fool! You saw a doctor here? Do you realize what will happen if it gets out that you had a child out of wedlock?"

"Never mind that. I was *sterilized*, Julian. You had my womb cut out of my body, and I'll never have another child."

"It was necessary. I had to make a decision for you. You were bleeding to death. The doctor couldn't stop the hemorrhaging, and he warned me that even if by some miracle he did, a future childbirth would surely kill you. He advised an immediate operation. Delia, I thought you knew. I thought the nurse had explained to you before we left the nursing home."

Her legs had turned to rubber. She sat down on his bed. "No one told me anything. You didn't even tell me my baby was dead until we were almost in San Francisco."

"I thought it was better to wait until you were feeling stronger." He walked over to the dressing table, opened a drawer, and pulled out a small bottle. "You're shivering with the cold and your clothes are damp. Drink this brandy and then let's get you into bed."

"I don't want to go to bed. I want to talk about this, Julian, and I want to talk about the death of my baby. Now that I know I'll never have another child—" Her voice broke, and to her complete astonishment she began to weep uncontrollably.

Julian was not a man who was moved by feminine tears, and heaven knew she was not looking for sympathy; rather she wanted an outlet for her anger. But the news she had received from Dr. Simmington had released the cork on emotions long held in check.

After handing her a handkerchief, Julian sat down, apparently unconcerned, and waited until her tears were spent. Then he pressed a glass of brandy into her hand. She gulped it down, feeling the fiery warmth wend its way through her chilled body.

"Accept the fact that you are not an ordinary woman, Delia." He poured more brandy into her glass. "Your destiny has never been to be a brood mare. Now you will never have to worry about another unplanned pregnancy interrupting your career."

She flung the brandy in his face.

He calmly reached for a towel and mopped his face.

When she had recovered sufficiently to speak, she asked, "Did you arrange a funeral for my baby? I never asked."

Was there a slight hesitation before he answered? "I assume the nursing home did. Their bill was certainly high enough."

"I left almost all the money I earned from the performances in Europe with the midwife. She must have been surprised at how well paid she was for delivering the baby. I intended to ask her to find someone to take care of the baby, and the money was to pay for her care for several months— until I could send some more. I never intended to keep the baby with me, I knew I couldn't. I didn't even dare hold her, you know, in case I grew attached to her. Oh, God, Julian I feel such guilt."

"You weren't responsible for the baby's death. Lots of babies die in the first days, you know that."

"That's not what I feel guilt about—don't you understand? I didn't *want* the baby, I hated the whole idea of the baby. How many times I wished I'd miscarry. God forgive me, I even tried to end my pregnancy, but that baby was determined to be born . . . that's why her dying so soon after birth seems so . . . ironic."

Julian listened in silence, and when she paused for breath he said, "Do you really expect me to believe that? You wanted that child, Delia, because you were in love with its father. You would have thrown your career to the winds if he'd asked you to."

She propped her head against her palm, feeling exhausted, drained, but needing the release that only the truth would bring. "If Hugo had been the father, yes, that might have been true. But Hugo was not the father."

"If not Hugo, then . . ." Julian's mouth clamped shut, and she knew his immediate conclusion was that Thad had fathered her baby.

"Let's be honest with each other at last, Julian," she said. "No more secrets. Tell me where Thad is."

Julian was on his feet, pacing about the room. "If you had come to me the minute you realized you were with child, I could have taken you to a doctor to take care of the situation. Why didn't you tell me? You surely didn't want to give birth to a colored child?"

"My baby wasn't colored, Julian."

"Just because a child is born with fair skin doesn't mean the colored blood isn't there. Do you want me to tell you how many white parents suddenly produce a colored child because somewhere back in their ancestry there was a darky? Dammit, I should have let them lynch him when they had him."

She raised her head and stared at him. "We made a bargain, Julian. I signed your damned contract, agreed to everything you asked. Did you keep your part of the bargain, or did you just let me believe you had?"

They stared at each other in silence for a moment, remembering the occasion, and the bargain.

Delia's sixteenth birthday had been the happiest day of her life. She was at last leaving the Philadelphia school, and Julian was taking her to Italy for a tour of the great opera

houses, and then he would select a maestro under whom she
would begin serious voice training. Perhaps she could persuade him to allow her to study in Paris instead, so that she
could see Thad. But in any event, Italy seemed much closer
to France and therefore to Thad. He was more than a pen
friend, he was almost family. Sometimes she pretended when
she wrote to him that he was her wise older brother.

Thad had been forced to give up his studies at Oxford the
year before, due to the death of his father. He had returned to
Paris to take care of his father's business affairs, and his
widow. Delia had often wondered about a woman who would
take into her household her husband's love child, especially
one of mixed blood, and decided that Parisiennes must be
very sophisticated.

Julian had been working in New York with a theatrical
agency and couldn't leave for at least two weeks, so he instructed her to go to the Willows and wait there until he sent
for her. They would sail to Italy from New York.

Then, two days before graduation, she received a cablegram from Paris. Thad was coming to America.

She traveled to Louisiana in a state of high excitement. Not
only was she finished with school, but she would see Thad
again, and Julian would not be dogging their footsteps.

Thad sent word that he would travel by skiff and wait for
her near the Van Courtlands' boathouse around four o'clock
on the first Saturday they would both be in Louisiana. She
was at the boathouse long before he was due, eager to ask
questions and receive immediate answers, instead of having
to wait ages for a reply to cross the Atlantic.

But when the skiff pulled into the bank, Delia saw at once
that Thad had changed during the two years since she saw
him on the sad occasion of Daddy Lou's death. Thad's formerly thin frame had filled out, and he seemed more manly,
more sure of himself. There was something else different, she
wasn't sure what; perhaps it was the way he looked at her,
with the eyes of a stranger.

For the first time they regarded each other shyly, ill at ease
with the new grown-up versions of their long-time penfriends.

Delia was aware that she had also changed considerably.
She was still slender, but her breasts were now softly
rounded, and her features, although still dominated by her

large blue-lavender eyes, had lost the pinched look of an undernourished child and acquired the sculpted cheekbones and
full lips of a woman of extraordinary sensual allure. She had
been assured of this fact by Julian, along with his customary
warnings to beware of would-be seducers. But until she saw
the way Thad looked at her with a mixture of awe and discomfort, she had not concerned herself with her looks, and
certainly didn't consider herself to be beautiful.

"Why, Delia . . ." Thad said, keeping his distance, "you
have grown up, haven't you?"

"I put up my hair," she said awkwardly, her hand straying
to her pale gold chignon.

He smiled. "It's a little more than that."

"You look . . . very well."

"Thank you."

"How is your mother?"

His smile faded. "Not very well, I'm afraid. That's why
I'm here."

"Her old trouble?"

"Not exactly. I'd tried to get her to come to Paris, you
know. Especially after my father died. But she wouldn't leave
that damned woman—oh, excuse me, Delia. I get so angry
when I think about the web of superstition and deceit she has
my mother trapped in."

"Which woman? Not Mignon?"

"No, no—as far as I know Mignon is living in the Vieux
Carre nowadays. There's no one at the house except my
mother and Abebe." He paused. "She's the mambo woman."

"You mother's still involved with voodoo?"

Thad glanced about uneasily. "Let's get away from here,
shall we? Before someone sees us."

"You seem very jumpy," Delia said. "You're not under a
voodoo spell, too, are you?" She stepped into the skiff.

"We shouldn't be alone together, Delia." He pushed the
skiff away from the bank and jumped in with her. "You're not
a child anymore, and I . . . well, I've come to realize my father was right. There's no place for me here."

"Something happened. What happened, Thad?"

He paddled rapidly downriver as he spoke. "I lost some of
my youthful idealism, I suppose, and recognized the world in

general and American society in particular for what it really is—at least as far as people of color are concerned."

"I'm beginning to feel guilty and don't know what I've done," Delia said.

"I'm sorry. I've been trying to deal with white officials and lawyers in New Orleans and getting nowhere. You see, Abebe has somehow acquired Daddy Lou's house and everything he left to my mother—who is now completely in her power. She's given up her church, her friends, everything. Her former pastor was so worried about her that he wrote to me."

"Eulie was so devout, I can't believe she would give up her own religion for voodoo."

"You don't understand the power of the old ways, the hold they have on my mother's people. How could you?"

"Thad ... I just had a funny feeling that you were going to ask how could I because I'm white."

"I wasn't, but it's true you've never seen a voodoo ritual, or the effects it has. People have died, Delia, because of a voodoo spell—otherwise healthy, young people have died. My mother came originally from Martinique, and the Caribbean islanders' culture is so thoroughly enmeshed in voodoo, it's a wonder she gave it up in the first place."

"But she was a Baptist, singing in the church choir, when I knew her, and seemed very secure in her faith."

"I believe the repeated throat abscesses she suffered and the fact that the doctors couldn't cure her sent her back to the old ways."

"And this mambo woman, Abebe, has cured her?"

"Apparently, yes. But my mother lives in fear that an enemy will stick another pin in the throat of a voodoo doll."

"What probably happened is that a throat abscess burst— and it had nothing to do with Abebe or her spells."

"Perhaps. But you'll never convince my mother of that. She's completely under the influence of that woman, she can't even think for herself. I'm trying to track down the transfer of title on the house from my mother to Abebe. If, as Abebe says, she now owns the place, then I can't very well throw her out. But nobody in authority seems to care about a passel of no-account darkies and their squabbles."

Delia was so shocked by his tone she didn't know what to say.

Thad went on: "The clerks simply ignored me—left me waiting around until the Hall of Records closed."

She said awkwardly, "Perhaps I could go into town and check for you?"

"No!" the word came out like a small explosion. "Delia, I was uneasy about this meeting, and now we're together I know my instincts were correct. We can't see each other alone again."

He guided the skiff to an island of cypress, separated from the bank by a narrow stretch of shallow water. "Let's stop here. I don't want to take you too far from the Willows."

"Thad, what's happening here? I was so looking forward to seeing you again and you're acting so strangely. Aren't we going to be friends in the future? What have I done? Why are you so cold?"

Thad held up his hand suddenly to silence her. "Listen! Do you hear something?"

All she could hear was the buzzing of insects, and an occasional soft splash in the water. Then, a moment later, she heard the sound of voices and boots crashing through the dense growth of pine saplings on the bank.

"Hunters," Thad whispered. "We'd better move around to the other side of this island and try to get out of sight."

"Why? We're not doing anything."

"Hush!"

He paddled swiftly around the small island, and as the skiff came to rest the voices on the bank were closer, more distinct.

"You hear something, Jeb? Thought I heard a splash."

"'Gator, maybe?"

"I think it was over by that island. Shall we go look-see?"

"Hell, no. I ain't figuring to get a leg gnawed off by no 'gator."

"Shoot at that cypress over there, then. Flush it out."

Delia's mouth opened in fear. If the men on the bank had a shotgun . . .

Thad clapped his hand over her mouth to silence her, then lifted her from the skiff. On the far side of the tiny island there was a mossy clearing, and he pushed her down into a tangle of vines and creepers. Except for a pair of mature cypress, the marsh grasses, vines, and a few saplings offered little protection from gunfire, and Delia struggled against Thad's restraining hands, convinced it would be better to show themselves.

"Ain't no 'gator, Jeb. Lookee there—ain't that the stern of a boat sticking out behind that cypress? Somebody's over on that island. Hey, who's there? What y'all hiding for?"

Hearing the menace in the man's tone, Delia froze.

"Cover me, Jeb. I'm going over there."

A moment later they heard him splash into the shallow water.

Thad released her. With a cautionery finger to his lips to warn her to keep quiet, he rose to his feet. "It's just me, boss. Doing some fishing."

Delia was aghast at Thad's ingratiating tone and his calling the unknown hunter "boss." Both sounded odd on his lips, especially spoken with his distinctly European accent.

"Who you got with you, boy?" the voice asked suspiciously.

"Nobody here but me, boss."

Delia held her breath. There was a moment's silence, and then, terrifying, the snapping of twigs and rustling of vines as the hunter came through the undergrowth in their direction.

Seconds later he stepped into the clearing. He gave one startled glance at Delia, then yelled, "Jeb, there's a nigger here with a white woman—"

Instantly Thad sprang at him. Delia watched in fascinated horror as the two men grappled in the confined space. She rolled away from their crashing feet, then crawled up on the kneelike cypress root and covered her ears with her hands to shut out the sickening sound of bone striking flesh.

It was instantly evident that the hunter was no match for Thad, who was both taller and heavier. The man screamed for his companion to come and help him just before Thad's fist connected with his jaw.

The man fell backward, his head striking the root just below where Delia crouched. His eyes rolled upward and a trickle of blood dribbled from his slack mouth.

Delia looked from the unconscious man to Thad standing over him. There was a triumphant look on Thad's face, and bloodlust in his eyes.

Before either of them had time to react, there were splashing sounds, curses, and a gunshot exploded, sending birds shrieking aloft.

Thad spun around, blood spurting from his shoulder. He went down on one knee as a second gunshot rang out.

Heedless of the flying bullets, Delia scrambled down from the cypress root to help him. She had barely reached his side when the second man burst onto the island, a rifle in his hand.

"Get out of the way, missy, I'm going to save you!" he yelled, and she was close enough to see the red gleam of hatred in his eyes.

Thad pushed her aside and, incredibly, hurled himself toward the man with the gun.

Grabbing the barrel of the rifle, Thad twisted it, forcing the stock backward and upward. Taken by surprise, the hunter offered little resistance, and the wooden stock struck him squarely on the chin. He fell sideways, beside his unconscious friend.

"Get in the skiff," Thad ordered, his voice weak and pain registering in his eyes.

"But—"

"Don't . . . argue . . . got to—get you home."

Delia jumped into the skiff, and he almost fell in beside her. She picked up the paddle, and he didn't protest until she pushed off. "Not that way, Delia . . . back to the Willows."

"You need a doctor," she said, paddling desperately. "You've been shot, Thad."

"No, please!" Sweat beaded on his forehead now. "You can't—please . . . take me to my mother if you must. . . ." He slumped to the bottom of the boat, his eyes glazing in shock.

Delia didn't dare stop until she was certain there was enough distance between them and the two hunters, who no doubt would quickly recover consciousness and come after them. When she was sure they had a good head start, she pulled into the bank and took the time to tear her petticoat into strips and bind up Thad's shoulder as tightly as she could to slow the bleeding. Then, hoping she could recall the shortcut through the bayous to Eulie's house, she set off again.

Thad groaned several times, and once muttered something in French, but didn't respond when she asked for directions.

Time was passing, and the makeshift bandage around his shoulder was soaked with blood.

The afternoon was waning by the time the old house came into view, but she didn't give any thought to the fact that a hue and cry might be raised for her if she didn't return to the Willows soon.

Dragging the skiff up onto the bank, she yelled, "Eulie! Come quick—it's Thad. He's hurt."

Eulie and a black woman Delia had never seen before appeared on the porch. Exhausted, Delia waited until they came to her aid, then helped them carry Thad into the house.

"He's been shot," she said breathlessly, "and he's lost a lot of blood. You must fetch a doctor."

"I reckon I know what I must do for my son." Eulie spoke in a hoarse whisper, so unlike her formerly mellifluous tones that Delia wondered if the voodoo woman's cure had not left Eulie worse off. She was able to talk again, but she sounded like a frail old man.

They carried Thad into the living room, and Eulie's companion said, "Put him on the table."

For the first time Delia looked at the woman called Abebe. Like Eulie, she was a tall, impressive figure. Darker of skin, and younger than Eulie, she appeared to Delia to be a warrior woman, strong, lithe, powerful. The gold necklaces she wore gleamed against her smooth dark throat, an almost defiant symbol of wealth not enjoyed by many, black or white, in bayou country. She regarded their unexpected visitor with undisguised hostility.

"You go now, missy," Abebe hissed. "We have work to do."

Delia glanced from Thad's inert form to his mother's lowered eyes and attitude of subservience, then back at the mambo woman.

"Oh, no, you don't," Delia said between clenched teeth. "There'll be no voodoo mumbo-jumbo here today. You're not going to go into a trance and call on your spirits to heal him. He's got a bullet in his shoulder, and it has to come out. Either you get a real doctor or I will, even if I have to bring the law here to do it."

Eulie and Abebe exchanged glances, then Eulie whispered,

"We'll take out the bullet, Delia. Go now. If they catch you here, it will be worse for him."

"If who catches me here?"

"Why, sugar," Abebe said in a deceptively soft voice, "the men who shot him, of course. They's probably tracking you right now." She turned to Eulie. "Boil up the kettle, girl, and get my bag." Her fingers were busy with the blood-soaked bandage.

Delia stood back as Eulie hurried to obey. Watching Thad's mother, Delia was struck by the contrast between this shuffling, hunched-shouldered woman and the Eulie of old. She recalled the magnificence of Eulie, dressed as Cleopatra, riding in the Fat Tuesday parade, and, even more poignantly, her inspiring voice leading the church choir.

Thad's eyes flickered. He whispered, "Delia?"

"Yes, I'm here."

"Do as she says."

She hesitated, unwilling to leave him to the uncertain ministrations of this black woman with her fierce eyes.

The decision was taken out of her hands a moment later when someone pounded on the front door.

Eulie grabbed Delia and shoved her toward the back porch. "Go on—git. They find a white girl and a black man with a bullet in him, and we's all in deep trouble. You ain't seen nothing, remember."

Reluctantly Delia made her way back to the skiff. Twilight had fallen, and blue-green wisps of vapor rose from the bayou. It would be completely dark by the time she reached the Willows.

Her thoughts in turmoil, she whispered a hasty prayer for Thad's recovery and, as an afterthought, asked for guidance in finding her way home.

The latter prayer, at least, was answered. She reached the Van Courtland boathouse as a crescent moon was rising. She was about to step ashore when a lantern suddenly flared to life and Marcus stepped out of the shadows.

Caught in the glare of light, Delia froze.

"Good God," Marcus said. "Look at you."

It was then that she realized her summer frock was spattered with blood from bodice to hem.

"Oh, it's you," Delia said as nonchalantly as she could. "I'm all right. It's not my blood."

Marcus gave an evil smile. "Then it must belong to a darky who got himself shot this afternoon. Or to the two hunters he attacked in a mad frenzy when they caught him raping a white woman."

Delia answered without thinking, "That's not true. We were just talking."

"Ah," Marcus murmured, "she admits she was with her colored friend, just as the two hunters who came crawling here for help described. He's done for now, Delia. They'll lynch him for sure. They've been searching for you for hours, and when they see that torn and bloody dress . . ."

As he spoke he extinguished the lantern. The return to darkness gave her hope that he might listen to reason.

Delia thought quickly. "Marcus, please, you've got to help me. Would you go back to the house and get me another dress? I'll go to Fontenay and ask Monique to say I was visiting her. She always seems so kind, not like Gabrielle. If I explain what happened, Monique will understand, I'm sure."

"No need to involve the in-laws, Delia. I shall be your alibi. I'll say you've been with me all afternoon."

"But they'll know that isn't true—you've been here."

"Here in the boathouse, ever since you left with your colored friend, waiting for you to come back. I'd have followed you if I didn't harbor a profound revulsion for the water."

"Then how—?"

"I hid in the old pirogue when the search party left—heard them talking about the two men who got beaten up. I knew sooner or later you'd come back this way."

"Would you really say I was with you?"

"Sure. I'll enjoy the drama of it all. Life has been dull lately, with Julian gone and Hugo and his bride keeping to themselves in N'Orleans. Stay here—if someone comes, get into the pirogue. I'll be back shortly."

She waited, shivering with fear, for Thad, for herself, jumping at every sound. Then, above the murmur of the river and the shrill song of crickets and frogs, she heard Marcus whistling softly as he approached. She knew it was Marcus because he was whistling one of his own compositions.

He had brought a dress, a petticoat, a pair of shoes, and a

shawl. She dressed quickly, and they hid her bloodstained gown in a corner of the boathouse.

They made their way toward the house, and as they reached the terrace Marcus offered his arm. "Head high, now, no apologetic murmurs. Act offended that anyone dares question you, but let me do the talking."

Inside the house they were surrounded by family, servants, searchers, and besieged by angry questions. Fleur was a quivering reed of rage, her face livid. "Where did you find her, Marc? Oh, you wicked, wicked girl—"

Marcus cut short her tirade. "Mother, I didn't *find* Delia—she's been with me all afternoon."

There was a stunned silence. Fleur said, "Please—all of you, go about your business. Marc, I'll speak with you in private. Delia, go to your room. I'll deal with you later."

"Divide and conquer, Mother? I think not. Delia has been assisting me with the operetta I'm writing. We were so engrossed, we didn't realize we'd missed dinner."

"How could you possibly not have heard the commotion? Where were you?"

"In the old summer house."

Listening, Delia decided that Marcus must have planned what he was going to say. The old summer house was a considerable distance from the main house, almost engulfed by magnolias and dogwoods, and rarely used.

Fleur regarded her son suspiciously. "There's no piano in the old summer house."

"One doesn't need a piano in order to write a score. My penmanship is so atrocious, I had Delia translate it into legible form. Naturally I had to remain with her in order to answer any questions. Mother, what is this uproar all about?"

"There was an incident this afternoon, involving a Negro and a white girl we believed was Delia. Evidently we were wrong."

"Good Lord!" Marcus exclaimed, sounding, to Delia's ears, sarcastic.

Fleur glared malevolently at Delia. "Fortunately the man involved has already been caught."

Delia felt as if the ceiling had descended on her head. Before she could respond, she felt Marcus's fingernails dig painfully into her arm, which was still slipped through his.

He said in an offhand tone, "Good. Now will you excuse us, Mother, we're going to have something to eat and then get back to work."

Somehow Delia managed to walk away, feeling Fleur's eyes burn into her back. Marcus led her to the drawing room, rang the bell to summon a servant, and then turned to Delia. "Sit down at the piano. I'm going to have sandwiches and coffee brought to us. We're going to work on an operetta."

Every nerve in her body was twitching. "Didn't you hear what your mother said? They've caught Thad. Oh, dear God, he was shot and bleeding ... I must go and tell them what happened."

"You're going to stay right here," Marcus said, a dangerous edge to his voice. "Nothing's going to happen to him tonight. Besides, where would you go? Who would you talk to? You have no idea where they're holding him. Tomorrow I'll find out and decide what should be done."

"You're enjoying this, aren't you? What did you say—that you like the drama?" Delia said tearfully, although it was a relief to have someone take charge of the situation. But she knew from past experience that Marcus could just as abruptly change his mind, going off on some completely unrelated tangent. She couldn't trust him.

A servant appeared and he ordered a tray of food. Delia sat down at the piano. "Could we send word to Hugo in New Orleans? He'll know what to do."

"No." Marcus smiled his peculiarly evil smile. "We couldn't. Hugo is in Europe. But if you do exactly as I say, I'll send a wire to Julian in New York. He's due home soon anyway. He might be able to save your friend's black hide."

They worked long past midnight, and Marcus did indeed compose the first act of an operetta. He seemed imbued with superhuman energy and a wildly elevated sense of his own genius, convinced that what he was creating was above and beyond anything ever written by any other composer. Delia could barely keep up with him as she scribbled notes onto the sheets of music. The pace was so frantic that she didn't have time to worry about Thad.

Marcus was still dancing maniacally about the room, occasionally pausing to pound out a phrase on the piano to illustrate what she was to write, when she slumped to the floor in a dead faint brought on by exhaustion.

He must have carried her to her room, for she awoke to find the sun high in the sky. After dressing quickly, she went downstairs. The sound of Marcus playing his operetta reverberated throughout the house. She went directly to the drawing room.

He looked up as she entered the room. "This is the best thing I've ever done. I'm ready for you to copy the second act."

"You promised to find out what happened to Thad."

"No time. I must capture the music in my head before it escapes. I did wire Julian, however, and he's leaving New York on the first train. Sit down, I've much for you to copy."

"I haven't eaten yet," Delia muttered and fled.

Fearing another fainting spell if she left without breakfast, she hurried down to the kitchen and asked Cook to give her a sandwich wrapped in a napkin.

Delia was about to slip down to the boathouse, with the intention of going immediately to Eulie, when she was confronted by Fleur and two housemaids.

"And where, pray tell, do you think you're going?" Fleur demanded.

"I . . . just thought . . . I'd go for a walk."

"You just thought you'd go running to that Negro, didn't you? Oh, I know it was you who was with him yesterday. If you think you are going to drag this family down into the mire, you are gravely mistaken."

Fleur nodded to the two maids, who seized Delia's arms and propelled her back up to her room. The door was locked, and no amount of pounding or screaming brought anyone to free her. Since there was a sheer drop to the terrace from the window, she could not escape that way.

She was left alone, except for the arrival of a dinner tray, until the next day. She awakened from an exhausted slumber as the key turned in her lock and Julian, looking as red-eyed and haggard as she felt, walked into the room.

Delia was still fully dressed, and she struggled up from the bed to face him.

"Don't say a word," Julian warned. "I'm in no mood for

excuses or arguments." He brandished a sheet of paper as he spoke. "Read this."

"What is it, a confession?" Delia asked, trying to come fully awake. Her head throbbed and her mouth felt as though it were filled with cotton. "I haven't done anything and neither has Thad. Please, Julian, we've got to go to him."

"That is a contract, authorizing me to represent you for a period of five years following your first concert in America. There are various other clauses. That you will not marry, for instance. These are the oral agreements we made long ago—but now, in return for my saving Thaddeous Bouchet's neck, I want a legal contract with you."

Alert now, Delia asked eagerly, "You've seen Thad? He's all right? Was he arrested? Honestly, Julian, he only struck those men in self-defense."

"I will take care of everything, providing you sign that contract—no, don't do it now, we need witnesses."

Delia faced Julian in his hotel room in San Francisco and said, "I didn't see Thad again until we met in Paris, nearly two years later. Nor did I receive any letters from him. I thought it was because he wanted to end our friendship—but I always suspected you might have intercepted his letters."

Julian regarded her enigmatically. "What is the point of treading this old ground?"

"I tried to get Thad to tell me how he escaped from jail—how he managed to get out of the country. He just said he had help."

"So? I told you I'd taken care of everything."

"And let me believe you had engineered his escape."

"How do you know I didn't? Besides, even if he did manage to break out on his own, who do you suppose kept the hounds from baying at his heels until he managed to get aboard a ship?"

"You were furious when you found out I'd seen Thad in Paris. It was ironic, really, because he wasn't pleased to see me, and, in fact, sent me packing."

She paused, then looked him straight in the eye. "If I swear to you now that Thad is not the father of my child, will you tell me what happened to him?"

Julian was silent for a moment. "It has to be Thad. Who

else could it be? I know I'm not the father, and you've already sworn Hugo isn't."

"I'll tell you—if you tell me where Thad is."

Julian chewed his lower lip. "I tried to find out. I even hired a Pinkerton to trace him. He did come to America—I presumed because you wrote and told him you were carrying his child. Then he just dropped out of sight. He didn't return to Paris; we even checked to see if he'd gone to his mother's relatives in Martinique. The truth is, I don't know what happened to him. But I have a pretty good idea. I hope to God I'm wrong."

Chapter 22

*

MARCUS

Delia and I were kindred spirits, I knew that from the start, but she was too blind to see that no one understood her as I did. She believed I hated her. The truth was, I hated myself.

Sometimes, at the moment he forced himself back from fitful slumber, he felt he had returned to a reality that was even more terrible than the nightmares. Especially on the day Hugo smashed down the bedroom door and forced him to read those damned San Francisco newspapers.

"This has gone on long enough, Marcus," Hugo had said, standing amid the wreckage. "Your mother is making herself ill worrying about you. What purpose is being served by you locking yourself up in here, refusing food, spending endless hours in darkness?"

As he spoke, Hugo kicked aside the accumulated debris of months of hermitage and made his way to the window, where he yanked the curtains so roughly they tumbled to the floor in a shower of dust.

Marcus cried out as daylight struck his eyes like a steel whip. He rose drunkenly to his feet, waves of dizziness engulfing him.

He gasped as a gaunt scarecrow of a man loomed in front of him, then realized he was seeing his own reflection in the mirror. He staggered over to the dresser and stared at the emaciated figure, who looked back at him with hollow eyes like empty black holes. There were silver streaks in his formerly dark hair, which was now long and unkempt, and the skin on his face was gray and creased above a straggly beard. Raising one hand to the mirror to be sure this apparition was indeed himself, he was startled to hear his fingernails, inches long, screech against the glass.

"Take a good look at yourself, Marc," Hugo said. "You are committing slow suicide. Look at this room—it's a chamber in hell."

"Get out and leave me alone," Marcus muttered. "What I do to myself is my business."

"This is my house, Marc. I will not allow you to kill yourself in it. Get dressed, pack your things, and get out."

Marcus stared at his half brother uncomprehendingly. "What . . . do you mean?"

"Exactly what I say. Go and kill yourself somewhere else."

"I haven't anywhere else to go, you know that."

"Then take a bath, shave, put on clean clothes, and get out of this room so that I can have it fumigated."

"You don't understand—"

"I understand that we've all catered to you long enough. Look at the fireplace—overflowing with soot and burned paper . . . You could have burned the entire house down."

"I had to burn the operetta Delia committed to paper for me, and the letters she wrote me from Europe, you do realize that, don't you? I had to get rid of everything she had touched."

"Marc, do you want to tell me why you're blaming Delia for this bout of madness? God knows you've withdrawn from the world many times before, although not for this long."

"She bewitched you, just as she did Julian. You know her power, I don't have to tell you. She destroyed your marriage, didn't she?"

"Gabrielle and I share the blame for our troubled union. Delia had nothing to do with it. Tell me what you think Delia did to you, Marc."

"I don't want to talk about her."

"So be it. But you might be interested to hear she's a tremendous success—the toast of San Francisco, apparently. When you're presentable again, you can go downstairs and read the reviews and articles Julian sent about her."

Hugo stepped over the splintered door. "Be downstairs in fifteen minutes, Marc, or I'll be back to carry you down."

He meant it, Marcus knew. Hugo did not make idle threats. As his brother disappeared from view, Marcus's valet came hesitantly into the room.

In a way, it was a relief to emerge from the darkness of his soul. He'd wished a thousand times that he could find the courage to kill himself swiftly, cleanly. But although the idea of death was appealing, he couldn't face the moment of dying.

"Draw a bath for me," Marcus said to his valet. "And you'd better cut my hair."

It took considerably longer than fifteen minutes to restore his appearance to anything close to presentability, but after checking to be sure the ablutions were progressing satisfactorily, Hugo left him alone.

When at length Marcus left the room that had been his sanctuary and own private hell these past months, his clothes hung loosely and his head felt curiously exposed without the matted hair and beard.

He paused at the top of the stairs, watching the steps writhe serpentlike before his blurred vision. Blinking the stairs back into focus, he grasped the banister rail and took a cautious step.

Downstairs his mother fluttered about the hall like a little silver moth. She ran to meet him, but he waved her away. "Not now, Mother. I must read the newspapers."

"Yes, darling, of course. They're in the breakfast room, and I've ordered a nice hot meal for you."

"I'll eat alone," he warned.

"Yes, dear. Perhaps we could take a walk later?"

He didn't respond, as he had to concentrate upon reaching the breakfast room before his knees buckled.

A blank-faced servant waited for him with enough thickly sliced ham, biscuits swimming in milk gravy, and hot coffee to feed an army. Marcus collapsed into a chair, rifled through the newspapers laid out, and snapped, "Hugo said he had some San Francisco papers."

The man fled, returning minutes later with the papers.

Marcus read every one of them, every word, and then sat back and stared at a photograph of Delia. She was dressed in a man's suit, and her hair had been hacked off.

"Penance, Delia?" Marcus asked under his breath. "Did you do this to yourself, or did Julian decide to punish you? Either way, you deserve to be marked as a dangerous woman. Other men need to be warned off, before you destroy them."

He hadn't realized he'd spoken aloud until the servant asked, "Beg yo' pardon, suh, can I get you something else?" "No. Get out of here and leave me alone."

Delia's image regarded him mockingly from the printed page. She wore an expression he remembered well, the slightly parted lips, the half-closed eyes, the incline of the head. The deliberately alluring invitation of the temptress, which had not been diminished by the attempt to masculinize her.

Oh, yes. He had recognized her for what she was, the very first time he saw her. Yet he had also recognized her incredible gift. That magnificent voice. How he envied her the ability to bring forth the music from within herself, needing no instrument to transmit the glorious sound. He had even— magnanimously, he thought—put aside the certain knowledge that the Van Courtlands were doomed from the day she set foot among them, in order to develop her talent.

Hadn't he allowed her to creep into the drawing room in the small hours of the morning to listen to him compose his music? Hadn't he been the first to teach her how to read music? Hadn't he introduced her to a world of music she hadn't dreamed existed, explaining the strengths and weaknesses of the classic composers, going so far as to confide in her the agony and elation of creating a new kind of music that owed no allegiance to the past masters?

And what about the time she and that mulatto had been caught in *flagrant delicto* by a pair of hunters? Who had saved her from the wrath of the county by giving her an alibi? Hadn't he at least deserved her gratitude? But no, Julian came charging in and whisked her off to Italy, taking all the credit for averting a scandal.

Somehow Thaddeous Bouchet had escaped, bullet wound notwithstanding, thereby depriving a number of people, Marcus included, of delivering well-justified punishment for his crime. The maddening thing was, Marcus had been prepared to forgive Delia, or at least to give her the benefit of the doubt. The hunters believed Bouchet was in the act of raping Delia, but she claimed it was simply a meeting of penfriends. Marcus wanted to believe this, because he was sure she was drawing closer to him. Her crush on Hugo, he thought, was a thing of the past; of necessity, since Hugo spent most of his time traipsing off on business trips and she rarely saw him.

To be fair, Delia had written him from Italy. Her letters had been burned along with the operetta in his fireplace, on the day she had run away for the last time. But he could still remember every word she had written. . . .

Marcus, I sat in a plush velvet seat in the Teatro dell'Opera in Rome, cheering "Bravà, brava!" with a thousand other voices screaming their homage as the great diva took her bows at the conclusion of Puccini's La Bohème. *She walked to the edge of the curving stage, bathed in the glow of the footlights, and was showered with flowers.*

The audience seemed to move toward her, like a great mythic beast arousing itself from slumber. They pressed against the orchestra pit, hung precariously from the boxes and balconies, spilled down the aisles toward the stage. Oh, Marcus, to be able to command such adoration! To hold a thousand people in thrall!

How can I describe the wonder of it all—the high frescoed ceiling, our gilded box seats—in the palco di platea, which is the first level of boxes—how I love the soothing melody of the Italian language . . . I am picking up many phrases and am determined to learn to speak Italian now that I have mastered French and German.

Someday I shall stand alone on a great stage and sing and I shall touch the hearts of the audience and they will never forget me. This is my dream, my passion, and my life.

But, Marcus—I am writing to you to say what I never dared tell you in person (thousands of miles between us gives me courage), and that is, you are not only being selfish in denying the world of your own music, but I fear may cause the God who gave you your priceless gift to punish you for not sharing it.

Marcus supposed he remembered that particular letter because it was the first she ever wrote to him and because she had finally expressed her admiration of him—surely her superstitious threats about the wrath of God descending upon his head proved that?

Delia had gone on to thank him for helping her, and he knew she referred to the many nights she had sat on the floor beside the piano and he had shared his musical knowledge with her, for he was surely her mentor—not Julian—who saw in her only his own passport to fame. Hadn't he, Marcus, given freely without thought of reciprocation? But she had not thanked him for saving her skin over the Thaddeous business, and that irked him.

She had written several letters from Italy, mostly about the various opera houses—in Venice and Bologna, Naples and Florence. He did not reply.

Apparently Delia enjoyed writing letters. She also sent stilted little notes to his mother, perhaps at Julian's urging, since Julian never wrote anyone. The best they could hope for from him was an occasional newspaper clipping or theater program with a comment scribbled across it. Delia sent picture postcards addressed to both Hugo and Gabrielle, and letters to Gabrielle's ailing younger sister, Monique.

Then one day Delia had made the classic, clichéd error of the prolific letter writer. She had carelessly written two letters and put them in the wrong envelopes. Marcus often wondered what was in the letter to him that had been inadvertently sent to Thaddeous Bouchet in Paris. Apparently Thad never told her of her mistake, and neither had he.

The letter Marcus had received, intended for Thaddeous, was revealing.

My dearest friend, oh, Thad, how could you write so coldly to me?

I waited ages for you to respond to my anxious pleas for news of you, and you finally respond by stating only that you have recovered from your wound, with no details of your escape and return to France. Then you tell me you don't want to hear any more of my—your words—fawning descriptions of bejeweled society ladies with whom I share opera boxes. You say I have moved into an arena you loathe and detest and that if I lose touch with the common people I will forfeit much of my appeal as an artist.

Thad—there is no possibility that I will ever forget where I came from. You know we were a poor immigrant family, but do you know what that meant?

My parents were part of the flood of immigrants who came from Ellis Island to a six-story tenement building on the Lower East Side. We paid ten dollars a month—when my stepfather hadn't spent all the money at the local tavern—for three rooms with no running water, no indoor toilets. There was a wood-burning stove in the kitchen, for which I had to steal wood to keep it going most of the time. When we could, we took showers at the public bath house on Allen Street. There was an old man who had a pushcart who liked to hear me sing, and he'd give us the overripe fruit and faded vegetables sometimes, but we were always hungry. My mother didn't make enough milk for the babies, and they cried all the time. My real father was killed in a street brawl, and my stepfather beat us constantly.

I still wake up in the small hours of the morning, clammy with the sweat of fear, worrying that I'll never be warm and safe and get enough to eat ... terrified that my stepfather will come bursting into the room in a drunken rage. So don't accuse me of losing touch with my origins, Thad. I wasn't born on a balmy Caribbean island with a wealthy father to provide for me.

Apart from the insight into Delia's humble origins, the letter indicated that Delia had not learned her lesson following the near-tragedy of her encounter with Bouchet and the hunters. She still maintained an association with the mulatto. Some day, Marcus decided, something would have to be done to end that perilous connection. It was, in a way, akin to Gabrielle's poisonous attachment to her consumptive cousin.

Marcus, who never left the Willows, sometimes felt like Zeus, sitting atop Mount Olympus, since he was privy to all of the drama of the lives of lesser mortals without being a part of them. At least, that was the way things were when Delia sailed off to Italy with his brother. It was when they returned that they—she—broke through the barricade and forced him to face the fact that he was also a mere man.

Chapter 23

*

Marcus was disappointed that after their prolonged tour of the Italian opera houses, Julian and Delia went to France, where Julian had secured the services of a renowned voice trainer. There was no time for a visit home, Delia wrote.

He missed his brother and the little waif, more than he cared to admit, even to himself. Delia had been an intrusion into their orderly life at first, and he'd resented Julian's pre-occupation with her, but after she began to join him in those post-midnight hours, Marcus realized that, whether he liked it or not, she was a kindred spirit. He could speak to her of the great oratorios and symphonies inside his head, and she alone understood.

His mother, also missing Julian, went into a frenzy of entertaining, filling the house with guests and musicians and begging Marcus to join them. He had to shut his ears to the sound of his beloved piano being assaulted by some oaf who used such phrases as "tickling the ivories" and played ragtime.

Even when he slipped down to the moonlit drawing room late at night to play, he found the solitary recitals had lost their appeal because he kept waiting for Delia to come creeping into the room to curl up beside the piano.

The realization that she was half a world away preyed on his mind to the point that he was completely blocked, unable to compose a note, hardly able even to play old familiar pieces. This made him angry. Obviously, Delia had insinuated herself into his consciousness, casting a spell over him that paralyzed him.

He approached Hugo, on one of his infrequent visits to the Willows, and demanded that he bring Julian home. He was careful not to say "Julian and Delia."

Hugo regarded him in that infuriatingly patronizing way that everyone did, with the exception of Julian and Delia. "What makes you think I can do that, Marc?"

"You must be footing the bill, Hugo. Father left you all his money, didn't he? Cut off Julian's funds, and he'll come home damn quick."

"Ah, but you're wrong about that. Julian worked like a Trojan in New York while Delia was in school. He saved every penny in order to finance their tour of Italy and pay for her voice training in Paris. Not only that, but Delia has already given several paid performances. They are self-supporting, Marc. I've contributed nothing."

"But you paid for her education?"

Hugo shook his head. "Not a dime. Julian managed that, too. Look, Marc, I know you miss your brother, but you'd do well to realize that he's probably never going to come back to live at the Willows. You need to get out and find other friends, other interests. Moping about the house all day is the worst thing you can do."

Marcus didn't hear anything Hugo said after his prophecy that Julian and Delia were lost to him forever. For days prior to this conversation Marcus had known that he was in for what his mother called "one of his spells." The flashing aura of light behind his eyes, the lurking threat of hammer blows of pain that would soon begin to pound his brain, the maddening whispers in his mind that made no sense yet he suspected were the answers to urgent questions he must have answered if he was to survive. In his delirium of agony he would slam his forehead against walls to try to blunt the internal pain, smash furniture, even strike servants in the hope that they might fight back and perhaps end his suffering. Hugo and Julian, if they were present, always put a stop to such behavior. These episodes usually ended in a complete blackout, when he remembered nothing. He suspected his mother probably slipped something into his food to cause these lapses of awareness.

He had just emerged from such a period when Julian's cable arrived. They were coming home!

*   *   *

Marcus watched from his bedroom window as Julian stepped down from the carriage, then offered his hand to Delia.

Once, when he was a small boy, Marcus had fallen from a tree, landing flat on his face. The impact of his first sight of Delia after her European sojurn reminded him of that fall. All the wind was knocked out of him, he felt dazed, there was a knifelike pain in his chest, and his head throbbed.

Watching as Delia came toward the house, he felt an inexplicable sense of panic, of wanting to run and hide. He stared down at the tall, slender woman dressed in the latest Paris fashions, who ignored the offer of Julian's arm and walked with a confident step, and a terrible premonition gripped him. Dizzy with anxiety, Marcus reeled backward, away from the window, away from the approaching disaster.

That evening Marcus joined the rest of the family for dinner, feeling like a mariner being drawn to the fatal rocks by the song of the irresistible siren. Since he had remained in his room all day, it was his first meeting with Julian and Delia. He ignored Julian's outstretched hand and Delia's cool smile, muttered a brief greeting, and took his usual place.

Julian pulled out a chair for their mother, and she gushed, "Oh, Julian, how we've missed you. How wonderful it is to have you home again. I do hope you intend to stay for a long visit." She glanced in Delia's direction. "Your gown is lovely, Delia, although that shade of lavender perhaps makes you look older."

"Ah, but look what it does to her eyes, Mother," Julian said.

"As you might have guessed," Delia said, "Julian selected this gown. I find it a little fussy for my taste."

Fleur blinked, and Marcus knew that she was as much taken aback by how Delia sounded as by what she said. Gone were the earlier speech patterns and grating accent, and gone, too, was the hesitancy that formerly caused her to sound apologetic. Her speaking voice was now a pleasant contralto, devoid of any accent that he could detect. One would be hard put to determine where she hailed from, he decided. Furthermore, she spoke in a way that suggested she had always been accustomed to dining in a beautifully appointed room, with servants to wait on her. Marcus thought of the letter she'd written to Thad, telling of the tenement in the Lower East

Side and the rotten fruit and vegetables she'd received as a reward for singing for her supper.

Observing Delia throughout the meal, Marcus saw that Julian had been right to take her to Europe. The pretty but somewhat shy and awkward girl had been polished in the way a master jeweler hones a gemstone, and had emerged as a woman who was exciting yet unattainable. A goddess to be worshiped but left untouched. If her stage presence generated the same magnetism that she exuded in that small gathering, then Julian had created a star to glitter more brightly than any other in the cosmos.

If Delia had one flaw, Marcus decided, it was her lack of gratitude. Just as she'd never properly thanked him for saving her from scandal in the incident with Thad, she now treated Julian with indifference, for the most part ignoring him. Her attitude toward his brother began to grate on Marcus's nerves. Fleur obviously felt the same way and glared at Delia, causing Julian to apologize for her.

"The journey from New York, after the sea voyage, was tiring. Delia and I are both a little out of sorts."

Although Delia did not respond, she turned those huge lavender-blue eyes questioningly in Julian's direction, and he added, somewhat lamely, "Delia wanted to stay in Paris, but it was time to come home."

"Why didn't you leave her there, then"—Marcus spoke for the first time since the meal started—"and come home without her?" Then he astonished himself by adding, "If you want to manage somebody's musical career, you can take care of mine."

He was gratified by the way they all turned to look at him in amazed wonder.

"Marc! Do you mean it?" Julian exclaimed. "Will you let me arrange a concert for you?"

Fleur closed her eyes and whispered, "Thank you, Lord."

Delia smiled encouragingly at him and nodded her approval, despite the fact that he'd just said she should have been left in Paris.

Marcus shrugged, as though he couldn't understand what all the fuss was about. "I've finished my operetta. I'd like to see it produced. I don't want to *perform*, Julian. I'll leave that to the exhibitionists of the world."

"Dammit, Marc, that was uncalled for," Julian snapped.

Dismayed at losing his adored brother's approval so abruptly, Marcus said quickly, "I wasn't referring to Delia, but to composers who insist upon playing their own work."

Even as he spoke, he felt his old animosity toward Delia return. He had resented her when Julian first brought her home because she deprived him of his brother's company and attention. Then he had found a niche in his own life for Delia, and some of his antagonism had faded. Now that they were both home again, he had expected that somehow the three of them would form some new and wonderful alliance. Yet here was Julian attacking him on her behalf, while she, ingrate that she was, treated Julian like some sort of lackey.

Marcus felt a familiar buzzing begin in his ears, drowning out whatever it was Julian was telling him so earnestly. He could see his brother's lips moving, but the buzzing in his head was joined by those tormenting whispers that occasionally plagued him, usually accompanied by one of his fierce headaches.

He rose to his feet, knowing he must get away quickly. Sometimes, if he could get to the piano in time, he could drive away the demons with his music. "I'll play the first act of my operetta for you."

Fleur was speaking, but he ignored her and stumbled from the dining room. By the time he reached the drawing room, the voices in his head were shouting. Why did they keep repeating her name?

With trembling fingers he raised the lid of the piano, lowered himself to the bench, and clutched the keys like a drowning man reaching for a straw.

He was panting, as if at the end of a long race, and he felt sweat bead on his brow. He raised his hands and brought them crashing down on the keys in a bruising chord.

A second later Julian slid onto the piano bench beside him. Julian's comforting hand gripped his shoulder. "It's all right, Marc. I'm here. I want to hear your operetta. Why don't you play it for me."

Slowly, painstakingly, Marcus groped for the right notes. Even if the sheets of music Delia had written for him had been on the stand, he could not have read them, because he could see only a shadow-filled red haze where the piano should have been. But it didn't matter, because the music was in his head, it was just a question of finding it in the babble of voices.

Then all at once, as Julian gently massaged his shoulder, the music flowed from his mind to his fingertips and the voices faded away.

Marcus had seen Delia slip into the solarium just after his mother and brother retired for the night, and he followed her. In the three days since their return from Europe, Marcus had been in a state of turmoil, observing Delia's coldness toward Julian, angered by her treatment of his brother, but at the same time mesmerized by her. Did he hate her, or love her? That was the question that had to be answered, or else Marcus knew he would surely lose his mind.

The solarium was filled with the earthy scent of the orchids, which always made him think of the grave. His father had brought the orchids from a South American rain forest because they were becoming popular among wealthy Europeans at the time, and it was a challenge to make them grow where they had never flourished before. The orchids were only one of his father's eccentricities, but in Marcus's mind were perhaps the most sinister. Usually he avoided the solarium, but he overcame his distaste of the exotic blooms in order to confront Delia without fear of interruption.

Delia was sitting on a bench, the amber light from a nearby lantern gilding her fair hair. She was lovelier than any orchid. He blinked, hoping to see her in the proper perspective, as a mere mortal woman, with no supernatural powers. But she just sat there quietly, and her stillness was more compelling than Salome's dance.

He asked harshly, "Why are you treating Julian so badly?"

She jumped. "Marcus! You startled me."

"Do you feel no gratitude for all he's done for you?"

"Of course I do. But he denied me my chance to sing with the Paris Opera Company. I was offered a part—as an understudy—but the diva's health is frail; I might very well have sung at least one performance. But no, Julian insists upon dragging me back here. I am not to be allowed to fulfill my dream of an operatic career; he says I am to be some new sort of American performing artist."

"I'm sure Julian has a very good reason for his decisions. He is far wiser than you in such matters. Perhaps your range is not of operatic quality."

She gave him a contemptuous glance, as if such a possibility was out of the question, and said coolly, "I will sing opera, one day. No one can stop me."

"Without Julian, you'll be nothing."

"I am not simply the creation of one man, Marcus. There are others to whom I owe a great deal."

She meant those damned darkies, of course. How often he'd had to banish her from his post-midnight recitals when she'd start talking about Daddy Lou's horn, or Eulie's singing of the spirituals.

"Marcus, will you excuse me? I don't feel like talking just now. I came in here to be alone."

"You used to come in here every chance you got to talk to Hugo. I know, because I saw you. You were never cold toward Hugo. Yet he has never done anything for you."

She sighed almost imperceptibly, and her voice was softer when she answered, "Hugo was kind to me. A woman never forgets a man's kindness."

"But you owe a debt of gratitude to Julian."

Delia rose to her feet. "Which I will repay. But he doesn't own me, Marcus. Nobody does." She swept past him, without so much as saying good night, leaving only a hint of a subtle fragrance in her wake that was quickly overwhelmed by the earthy scent of the orchids.

The following day Marcus saw Julian and Delia go into the study, wearing grim expressions that indicated an important discussion was about to take place. Marcus raced outside, making his way around the house to the study window, which, as he expected, was open to catch any breath of air from the river. He crouched below the window and listened to the conversation taking place inside.

"We have to end this impasse," Julian was saying. "What if I agree to delay your first American concert for another year? What if I go to England and see if I can arrange a concert for you there?"

Delia answered at once. "Find me an opera and I'll go. I don't care how small the part is."

"I can't make any promises. But I'll see what I can do."

"When can we leave for England?"

"Not we. I'll go alone. You won't be leaving until I've made the arrangements. I don't want you to be only a few miles across the channel from temptation in Paris while I'm busy. You'll remain here until I send for you. If I can put something together quickly, then it will only be for a few weeks."

There was a slight pause, then Delia's voice, sounding less enthusiastic. "I don't want to stay here. Your mother can't stand me, and if Gabrielle happens to visit, it will be a nightmare."

"You can put up with them for a few weeks. I can't afford to put you into a hotel. We're short of funds right now. It will be a pinch to scrape up enough cash for my passage to England. I shall have to find some financial angels to help as it is."

"If we'd stayed in Paris—"

"So you could have an affair with the maestro?"

"That's nonsense and you know it."

"Shall we discuss Bouchet, then?"

"Oh, go to England alone. Nothing I say is going to convince you that I'm not sleeping with every man I meet."

"While I'm gone you must rehearse daily . . ."

Desolate, Marcus crept away. A dull throbbing began in his temple. A distance voice warned that he was about to lose his beloved Julian again. It was all her fault. *Delia*, the voice whispered. *Delia*.

So Julian departed, almost before Marcus had time to get used to him being home. There was a brief, illuminating conversation before he left.

Julian, looking distracted, said, "Marc, I have to return to Europe. I'm going to send your operetta to a friend in New York. It's good, Marc—excellent, in fact. He will make all the arrangements for you and—"

"No!" Marcus had thundered. "You won't give it to anyone."

"Perhaps when I get back . . ." Julian had responded vaguely, his eyes already searching for Delia.

Marcus stormed about the house, terrifying the servants and reducing his mother to a quivering bundle of nerves.

Delia ignored his rampage and disappeared whenever he came on the scene. Since the evening he had followed her into the solarium, she no longer used it as a refuge, and he suspected that she went out to the old summer house. She appeared only for meals.

Delia made several trips to New Orleans. Marcus was curious about her destination. Julian's conversation had indicated that Thad Bouchet was in Paris, but steamships were crossing the Atlantic at ever-increasing speeds, and he could have sailed shortly after Julian and Delia and be here now.

Marcus had not left the Willows since his father's last disastrous attempt to enroll him in school, an experience that still haunted his nightmares, and did not even consider following Delia to see where she went. He had no intention of ever leaving the sanctuary of the old plantation house. The world beyond the bayous was filled with people who would surely try to destroy him.

As the days passed, he grew more and more angry that Delia avoided him. No one ever heard her singing, despite the fact that Julian had instructed her to practice daily. There was no piano in the summer house, so she could not accompany herself, and any fool knew that a singer must rehearse with musical accompaniment. Had she asked, he might even have accompanied her himself. But she was too stubborn, too arrogant, to ask him to play for her.

Then Hugo and Gabrielle made one of their infrequent visits, the occasion being Fleur's birthday, and suddenly Delia was very much in evidence, wearing her prettiest gowns, smiling her most seductive smiles, and plainly infuriating Gabrielle. She was also wreaking havoc with Marcus's emotions.

The dining room was crowded for Fleur's birthday dinner, the chandeliers glittering like ice palaces above the snowy-white damask-covered table with its enormous centerpiece of white orchids and settings of silver cutlery so pure that no polishing was ever needed.

Marcus sat beside his mother, proud of her feminine charm, and the ease with which she presided over a gathering that included a senator, two congressmen, a highly decorated former general, and, in fact, the crème de la crème of county society. Fleur wore a pale blue gown that set off her magnolia skin and silver hair to perfection and Marcus decided that, since it was her birthday, he would be on his best behavior. This decision was made easier by the fact that Monique Marchand was not present, due to her lingering illness, and therefore his mother would not be shoving her down his throat as a prospective bride.

Hugo sat on his mother's left, Gabrielle opposite to him, while Fleur had wisely placed Delia at the far end of the table.

Marcus spent the first courses comparing Hugo's wife to Delia. What a contrast they were! Gabrielle so petite and dark, with her flashing green eyes, mischievous dimples, and lively attitude, and Delia so regally tall, with her smooth fair hair, her mysterious blue-lavender eyes and her remote, touch-me-not demeanor that paradoxically turned every man present into a hunter. Gabrielle wore a perilously low-cut scarlet satin gown, while Delia was clad in virginal white and looked more than ever like a goddess or some other mythical creature.

Somewhere at the back of Marcus's mind the first notes of a musical definition of each of the two women began to form.

Gabrielle was enchanting the men seated on either side of her, giggling coyly and flattering them with her eyes, but constantly glancing at her husband, as if to reassure herself that Hugo also found her irresistible. Her cousin Alain was not present, although his consumption seemed to be in remission. Marcus had noticed that Alain never attended any affair to which Hugo had been invited. Coincidence, perhaps, but an interesting one.

Delia was responding to questions from guests in her vicinity with cool aplomb, and Marcus marveled again at her transformation. How far the little beggar had come since Julian found her beneath the wrought-iron balcony of the Cajun Club! What would those fawning table companions think if they knew her origins?

Marcus felt his mother's sharp elbow against his arm. "Hugo was speaking to you, Marc."

Hugo smiled kindly. How Marcus would have loved to wipe that benevolent smile right off his half brother's face.

"I just said I hoped you'd play for us this evening, Marc," Hugo said. "I hear you have a new composition."

"Oh? From whom did you hear that?"

"From Delia. She tells me you've written an operetta."

Down at the other end of the table Delia immediately looked at Hugo. Over the hum of conversation and tinkle of glasses and shuffling of chairs, could she really have heard her name on Hugo's lips? Or did some sixth sense tell her when she was on his mind? Marcus knew very well that her sudden emergence from the solitude of the summer house was solely because Hugo was here. Damn her, she never exhibited such empathy with Julian, who had quite literally saved her from the streets.

Marcus was so angered on behalf of his absent brother that he wasn't aware at first that an awkward silence had fallen at the head of the table and nearby guests were either watching him covertly or pretending to concentrate on their food while obviously waiting for him to speak.

Damn, what had Hugo asked? Marcus couldn't remember. His collar suddenly felt tight, and the whiteness of the tablecloth blinded him. He blurted out, "Julian could have waited for mother's birthday. He didn't have to leave just a couple of weeks before her birthday."

As always, Hugo bridged the gap. "Yes, it's too bad he missed her party, but I understand he had urgent business in England. Now, as I was saying, we're all hoping you'll play for us later, Marc. Perhaps something from your operetta?"

"It's not finished," Marcus muttered. "Besides, why would you want to listen to me when I'm sure Delia will be only too pleased to entertain you."

"Darling, of course we want to hear you play," Fleur protested. She glanced around the table and added brightly, "Many of us *prefer* the soothing melodies of the pianoforte, do we not?"

"Indeed, yes," Gabrielle chimed in. "One can carry on a conversation while a piano is played, but a singer stops a party dead."

"Perhaps some of us feel a little envious of talent, or resent having to share the limelight?" Hugo suggested, a sharp edge to his voice that caused Gabrielle's lips to compress into a tight line.

Fleur's cheeks turned slightly pink, and she quickly signaled the butler to serve the next course.

After the meal ended, the guests adjourned to the east drawing room, which was the largest of the entertaining rooms, where the carpets had been rolled up ready for the dancing. The French doors were open, and tables and chairs had been placed on the terrace to accommodate the overflow of guests who did not wish to dance. A trio of musicians had been hired, and one of them was already seated at Marcus's beloved grand piano.

Marcus went out on the terrace and found a shadowed spot that afforded a view of the revelers inside. Unfortunately he could still hear the badly played music. Torches had been placed along the edge of the lawn, both to light the terrace and in the hope that the curling wisps of smoke the torches emitted would drive away any marauding insects.

The Louisiana night was hot and humid, heady with the scent of magnolias and jasmine, and every instinct warned Marcus that he should not stay and witness the ritual of the party. But if he went to his room and if he fell asleep and if the nightmares returned, then he would be unable to come down to the piano, because the party would surely go on all night. A tightness made itself felt in his chest. He flagged down a passing servant and ordered him to bring a bottle of whiskey and a glass.

In the drawing room Hugo had danced the obligatory first waltz with Fleur, then the reel with his wife. Delia was surrounded by men, but allowed no one to lead her out onto the floor. Marcus never took his eyes off her, knowing that sooner or later she would dance with Hugo, and then her perfidy would be obvious to everyone.

A short time later Hugo did approach Delia, and there was a brief conversation. But instead of leading her out onto the dance floor, he took her to the grand piano, murmured something to the pianist, and then announced that Delia would sing.

She sang an aria from *Tosca* with such fire and passion that, as Gabrielle had predicted, a complete hush fell over the party, not because of reticence on the part of the guests to converse, but for the simple reason the assembled guests were spellbound.

Leaving the piano as she sang, Delia moved about the room as though on the stage, acting out the part of the desperate Fioria Tosca, making her audience believe she would indeed sacrifice everything for her doomed lover.

Marcus felt awed, intimidated, humbled. Surely there had never been a voice like Delia's before, nor would be again. He who had never considered a singer to be in the same class as an instrumental musician, certainly not to be compared with a composer, now realized that such a voice eclipsed all of their efforts. He felt tears spring to his eyes, a lump formed in his throat, and his chest was tighter than ever. He gulped a nearly full glass of whiskey, feeling it ignite in his veins and send molten lava rushing about his body as Delia's voice reached, without strain, the finale of the aria.

The marvelous sound echoed around his head even after the last note faded and the drawing room reverberated with applause and bravos. Marcus raised his glass in a silent toast to her accomplishment. To his surprise, he saw the whiskey bottle was now half empty. Shrugging, he filled his glass again and drank deeply. His vision blurred, he leaned back in his chair, breathing heavily.

Occasionally time played tricks with him, passing unaware, especially after such a soul-wrenching experience, and he thought he had lost several minutes when the drawing room again came into focus, because Delia no longer stood in front of the piano, and the musicians were again playing a waltz. He searched for her, and, lo and behold, she was being whirled around the floor in Hugo's arms.

Marcus rose to his feet, took several unsteady steps across the French doors, and might have gone storming inside had not his mother suddenly appeared in his path.

"There you are, Marc. I wondered where you were hiding. I suppose you heard her sing? That minx has a lot to thank Julian for."

He wanted to say something, but the lump was still in his throat and the terrace had begun to revolve slowly before his gaze. He made a strangled sound and turned and stumbled across the lawn. He would detour to the rear entrance and get to his room that way. His mother called something after him, but he ignored her.

Reaching the sanctuary of his room, he crawled into bed and pulled the covers over his head, then pressed his hands to his ears. Squeezing his eyes shut, he fought to make his mind a blank, knowing that his last thoughts before falling asleep would determine the quality of his dreams.

But the nightmares that night were his worst ever. They began innocuously enough. He was in a large deserted ballroom, whirling around the floor in a fast Viennese waltz. At first he couldn't see the woman he held in his arms, he knew only that she was light, ethereal, matching her steps to his so perfectly that soon they were both floating above the floor.

Then all at once her tiny hand in his grew claws that pierced his flesh. He tried to let go of her, but he was impaled on those talons. Now the music roared in his ears, faster and faster and he had to dance like a madman to keep up with her. It was a dance of death, because he couldn't keep up and he couldn't let go, and she would not let him stop.

He was panting, dying, screaming the silent screams of sleep, begging for mercy. He still couldn't see the face of his partner, but he heard her mocking laughter. Delia. Of course. Who else would it be?

Marcus sat bolt upright in bed, soaked in sweat, fighting his way to back to consciousness.

Casting aside the clutching covers, he scrambled out of bed and lurched toward his dresser. He kept a flask of brandy concealed beneath his socks for nighttime emergency use. This night it took the entire flask to calm him enough to pull on his shirt and trousers. Then he stumbled out onto the landing.

The house was quiet and still. The party must have ended early, or perhaps he'd been in the grip of the nightmares most of the night.

A sense of urgency impelled him as he moved cautiously toward the staircase. His heart was pounding, voices were clamoring inside his head. The memory of Delia in Hugo's arms, smiling up at him seductively, refused to fade.

Waves of nausea and weakness washed over him. Recalling how much whiskey he'd consumed earlier, he wished he hadn't had the brandy.

If he could just get to the piano . . .

As he reached the foot of the stairs, there was a flutter of white on the periphery of his vision. Turning, he saw the front door close softly. Someone had just gone outside.

He hesitated, then, as if drawn by an invisible thread, went to the door and opened it.

She was walking slowly across the lawn, heading in the direction of the summer house. Delia, in her white frock, a wraith that might vanish into the night, leaving havoc in her wake.

The voices in Marcus's head began to chant, *stop her, stop her* ...

Chapter 24

*

Following Delia, Marcus moved cautiously through the shadows of the live oaks and willows, keeping out of sight. She went into the summer house and closed the door.

By the time Marcus reached the porch, a lamp had been lit inside the house, and through the uncurtained windows he could see that Delia was seated on the sofa facing the fireplace, gazing up at a portrait that hung over the mantelpiece.

The portrait was an early picture of his father and had been relegated to the summer house by Fleur, who preferred portraits of her late husband in his maturity. For the first time Marcus saw that the man in the portrait, had he not been dressed in old-fashioned clothes, could very well have been Hugo. Marcus had not realized before how much Hugo resembled the old man in his youth.

The drums in Marcus's ears began to pound again. So that was why Delia came here. To stare at the picture. Worshiping it with her eyes.

Marcus wished he had never taken her to the old summer house that day when she'd needed an alibi because she'd been caught with Thad Bouchet. She had obviously turned the place into a shrine for worshiping Hugo.

How dare she take so much from Julian, not to mention himself, yet give all her love and homage to Hugo?

Marcus heard the growl of rage rumble up from deep inside him at the moment he kicked open the summer house door and burst into the room.

Delia gave one startled glance over her shoulder, then jumped to her feet. "Marcus! What—"

"You are never to come in here again. I forbid it."

She looked bewildered, but unafraid. "Why? I am doing no harm."

"You used to slip into the solarium and wait for him there, didn't you? But he hardly ever visits the Willows when you're here nowadays, so you come here instead and stare at the portrait."

Enlightenment swept over her exquisite features then. "Ah, we're talking about Hugo. But the portrait is of your father, Marcus, and I wasn't consciously staring at it."

"You're a liar."

She shrugged, still unconcerned. Couldn't she sense his growing fury? It was a phantom warrior, occupying the room with them, and he would not be able to contain it much longer unless she recognized the folly of her ways.

"Julian has done more for you than anyone else. Yet you treat him like a dog. Why are women so fickle, so ungrateful? Why do they always fawn all over the men who don't give a damn about them?"

"Why don't you go back to your piano, Marcus? I'm in no mood to discuss your brothers with you. You have a false perception of my association with both of them. Oddly enough, I was always better able to understand you than either of them. When I first came here I was awed by your talent and longed to be your friend. I even dreamed of somehow coaxing you out of that cocoon you wrap around yourself to escape from the world."

"Oh, you're such a glib liar. You used me, just as you used Julian. You twisted us around your little finger. The only time you felt like being my friend was when you needed an alibi so the whole county wouldn't find out you'd been with a Negro. I should have told Julian—yes, and Hugo—the truth about that sorry little episode. But I didn't want Julian to be hurt. Were you grateful? No, not for a minute."

"That's not true. I was extremely grateful—didn't I write you all those letters from Italy? Why would I do that if I didn't look upon you as a friend?"

"You wanted to gloat, that's why. To remind me that Julian preferred to gallivant all over Europe with you rather than stay here with me."

Blue fire flashed in her eyes then. "You're being ridiculous now, Marcus. Why do you say such idiotic things? Why do you act like a spoiled child? I know you aren't stupid, and I don't believe you're insane either, you are simply the most self-indulgent, peevish, antisocial—"

He didn't give her a chance to finish her diatribe. How could he let her speak to him so? He had to make her stop. He flung himself at her as Hugo's eyes watched from the portrait of their father.

The impact of his charge across the room sent them both lurching back toward the fireplace, and he held her tightly to keep her from crashing into the marble mantelpiece. For a moment, as he tried to regain his balance, they spun around in a grotesque *pas de deux*, and he was reminded, frighteningly, of his nightmare.

He wanted to shake her, to make her admit she was ungrateful and faithless. He wanted to hear her beg for forgiveness and express everlasting thanks for all they had done for her. He wanted to make her apologize for speaking to him the way she had. He wanted to tame her, to humble her, to humiliate her.

But she showed no fear, only a faint expression of surprise that quickly changed to contempt. "Take your damned hands off me, Marcus."

His fury erupted in a molten flood. He slapped her, hard, across her cheek. She gave no sign she had even felt the blow, and promptly slapped him back.

Pinpricks of light exploded in his eyes, and he uttered a low guttural sound as he flung her down onto the floor and crashed on top of her.

She fought like a tiger, with claws and teeth. She attempted to bring her knee up to his groin, but he pinned her with the weight of his body and twisted her wrists up above her head.

Her hair came loose and was tossed between them like a silken web. As they struggled, her gown slipped from her shoulders. He tore her shift away from her breasts and caught his breath at the perfection of twin alabaster globes with their pale pink areolas.

In that instant she managed to free one arm and raked his face with her fingernails.

Recapturing her hand, he pulled her arm under her, forcing those delicious breasts upward so that he could feel the pliant flesh through his shirt.

Their eyes met for an instant, hers filled with hatred and

defiance, despite the fact that she was well aware of his superior strength and of his manhood surging against her.

This was what she wanted, of course. She'd tempted both of his brothers and even the mulatto. Hadn't Julian hinted that he'd brought her home because she wouldn't stop seducing every man she met in Europe? She wanted all men to desire her, it was a compulsion with her. Conquer and then torment. Well, she wouldn't cast her spell on him. He'd show her. He'd tame her.

He seized her hair and smashed her head down on the floor, and as she looked up at him with dazed, defiant eyes, he drove his knee between her legs, ripped aside her undergarments, and opened his trousers.

A great symphony burst forth in his head as he probed her warm flesh and then, in a blinding moment of triumph, thrust himself inside her.

Had it all been a dream? Or had the events of the previous night really taken place? Marcus splashed cold water into his face and stared at his reflection in the mirror.

There were deep, oozing scratches on his face. A tuft of hair was missing from just above his temple. His lip was raw and swollen.

It had not been a nightmare, then. His mirror offered ample evidence that he had tangled with a wildcat.

Vague memories flickered into his mind, of Delia's fingernails raking his face, of her sharp teeth tearing at his mouth as he attempted to kiss her after he reached his zenith.

He recalled looking down at her lying at his feet, her white gown torn and bloodied, her matted hair silvered by the moonlight. She looked so fragile, so . . . broken, like a blossom crippled by the wind.

His attempted kiss had been a gesture of reconciliation, an acknowledgment that he had forced her to submit to him, and a plea for forgiveness. But she had responded with viciousness, giving him a look of such utter hatred that the memory of the loathing in her eyes made him recoil in horror at the realization of the enormity of the crime he had committed against her.

Why had he not felt this remorse, this sudden tenderness toward her, *before* he raped her? Why had the act that was now so abhorrent to him seemed justified at the time it occurred? Not only justified, but necessary? Hadn't he merely administered the classic punishment the temptress deserved?

Marcus searched his memory frantically, seeking explanations for the unexplainable. The actual sequence of events was blurred in his mind, he remembered only the rage he'd felt, and the need to humble her. She had goaded him, was that it? Vague recollections of her worshiping the portrait of Hugo returned.

He blinked. What portrait of Hugo? The only portrait in the summer house was of their father as a young man.

Why did everything seem so inevitable last night and so shocking this morning? The pounding in his head, the bile in his throat, his churning stomach, and shrieking nerves sent him crawling back into bed. He'd have to consider the consequences of his actions later, when his physical woes subsided.

Marcus locked his door and refused to leave his room. After all, how could he face her? How could he face anyone? Apart from the guilt that weighed like a shroud, there was the need to wait until his scars faded.

Since there had been other periods when he retreated from the family, and as neither Julian nor Hugo were in residence, remaining in his room was not a problem. A tentative knock on his door in the morning indicated that hot water for his ablutions had arrived, and later a second knock heralded the arrival of his breakfast tray. Lunch and dinner were also placed on the landing outside his bedroom door. The servants who delivered the meals knew better than to be there when he unlocked the door. At least once a day his mother came and spoke to him through the door. Sometimes he responded. She offered no information about Delia, and of course assumed he was having "one of his spells."

He dared not ask his mother about Delia. He could only hope she had recovered from her ordeal. He worried about the blood on her gown. He did not recall striking her, he'd thought he had held her down and made her submit to him, but the images in his mind were fragmented and became more so with the passing of time.

Could she have been a virgin, after all? Would the penetration of a maidenhead create so much blood? Perhaps it was his own blood? There had been blood on his pillow when he awakened the following morning, and he *was* subject to nose-bleeds. Then there were the scratches on his face and his bitten lip. He felt a brief but almost sensual thrill to consider that perhaps their blood had blended.

Days passed. Perhaps weeks. He lost track of time. Then one morning instead of the tentative knock on his door to announce the arrival of his shaving water he awakened to the sound of his mother's voice.

"Marcus, please open the door. I must speak with you."

He burrowed more deeply under the covers.

"Marcus!" his mother's voice said sharply. "You must come out. Julian is on his way home."

He sat up. "When will he arrive?"

"Open the door."

Between the bed and the door he paused at his dresser mirror. There were no longer any scars on his cheeks, and his hair had started to sprout again in the bare patch. He pulled on a dressing gown and unlocked the door.

His mother's delicate nostrils clenched slightly, and she didn't step into his room. "You've been in here for weeks, Marc. We must change the bed linen at once."

"When will Julian arrive?"

"He left London over a week ago."

"Is Delia still here?"

There was a slight pause before she replied. "Yes. She's . . . well, she had an accident. Nothing serious, but she took to her bed and claimed she was sick. I had to write and tell Julian, of course. That's why he's coming home."

"What sort of an accident?"

"She said she fell down the stairs one night, after we'd all gone to bed. No one saw her."

"You sound as though you don't belive her."

"Oh, she was bruised and shaken, but she was very evasive. I think she'd left the house that night to meet a man who treated her roughly."

Marcus fixed his gaze on the wall opposite to his room. "A man? What man?"

"I suppose that mulatto, Bouchet. I understand he's been visiting his mother in New Orleans. And as for Delia's illness, Marc, I think she's been emulating you. You took to your room and so did she. But she refuses to eat. We must get things back on an even keel before Julian arrives. If you get back to normal, perhaps she will, too."

Marcus digested this news silently for a moment and then asked, "Have you told Delia he's on his way home?"

"Not yet. I only received his cablegram today."

"Go and tell her. I'll be downstairs shortly."

"Marc, you need to bathe, dear . . ."

"Order breakfast for two in an hour."

Marcus was beginning to think he might have to go and batter down Delia's door when she suddenly appeared in the breakfast room.

He was shocked by her appearance. She looked like a wraith, ghostly pale, thin as a stick, her eyes dull and glazed, with none of their former iridescent lavender sparkle.

But despite her obvious malaise, she took the initiative immediately. "So you're at last ready to face me? What a coward you are, Marcus. What a miserable, misbegotten wretch you proved to be. You are an inhuman beast and I hate you with a passion that will sustain me through this ordeal. I shall turn my hatred of you into my strength to endure. Just as you took your hatred of me to its utmost limits. But I'll rise above your assault on my body and climb to heights beyond your reach. Then, you pitiful excuse for a human being, I shall look down and see that you are nothing more than an earthworm, crawling in the muck of your worthless life."

He cleared his throat. "You goaded me, Delia. I didn't know what I was doing."

She approached the table and leaned into his face. "*Goaded* you?"

"Tempted me." His voice sounded hollow.

"I am responsible for your attack, is that it?"

He wanted her to shut up, to stop talking about it. He felt his head begin to throb. He said conversationally, "Julian's coming home."

"You will rot in hell, Marcus. You do realize that, don't you? You are not getting off scot-free. Oh, I shan't tell your brothers—one of them would surely kill you if I did. I thought of killing you myself, you know. But I decided you aren't worth it."

"It will be all right when Julian arrives," he said, desperate to end the harangue.

"I shall be gone by then."

"You can't leave. You have an agreement to live up to."

She gave a short mirthless laugh and ran from the room.

Sometime that day, she either left the Willows of her own volition or was spirited away.

When he went down to dinner that evening, his mother told him of Delia's departure.

Marcus promptly went back to his room and locked himself in, where he remained until Hugo broke down the door months later.

Chapter 25

*

MAGGIE

I was living in a dreamworld, pretending that outside our precious little circle no one else existed. But beyond that little island of serenity lurked those who were merely biding their time, waiting to attack our fragile cocoon.

Patience looked up from her reading primer as the whirr of her mother's sewing machine stopped abruptly. "Mama?"

Her mouth full of pins, Maggie couldn't answer immediately. She pointed toward the window, and the little girl jumped up and ran to look out. "He's here!" she exclaimed excitedly. She raced from the room. "Jemmie! Jemmie, Uncle Hugo is here."

Maggie transferred the pins from her mouth to the pincushion and, standing up, smoothed her dress over waist and hips, wishing she had worn the becoming blue rather than the tasteful but somewhat drab mauve. After all, she had expected Hugo to come for Patience's sixth birthday, and it was, after all, New Year's Day. She patted her hair into place as she went out into the hall.

As always, her heart turned over at the sight of Hugo's tall, broad-shouldered frame almost filling the tiny entry hall of the house rented a year earlier when their living quarters over the shop became too cramped for her growing business. He had picked up Patience, and she was hugging him as Jemmie attempted to relieve him of his hat and gloves.

Both Jemmie and the little girl were bombarding Hugo with questions. "How long can you stay?" "Where have you been on your travels?" "What did you bring for me?"

The last question caused Maggie, who was hovering in the background, to interrupt, "Patience! That was very impolite."

"But it's my birthday and Uncle Hugo promised—"

Hugo's eyes met Maggie's over the pale silken hair of the child and he smiled. "A birthday gift. I most certainly did. Am I in time for the cake?

"Oh, yessuh," Jemmie responded, beaming. "And for supper. We done waited for you."

"I'm sorry I couldn't get here sooner, or let you know I was coming."

"I knew you would come," Patience said sagely. "Mama wasn't so sure, 'cause she didn't dress up for you like she usually does."

Maggie felt herself blush and was thankful for the dimly lit hall. "You know I had to finish up a ball gown."

"It was finished ages ago," Patience informed Hugo in a stage whisper. "Mama just went on sewing and made me study even though it's New Year's Day, just so we wouldn't worry that you might not come."

Hugo chuckled and Maggie decided for the hundredth time that Patience was far too perceptive for a six year old. She chattered on, "I can read my first storybook now, Uncle Hugo. Did you know that *Y* is sometimes a vowel?"

"The English language is tricky, isn't it?" he replied. "I'm proud of you, Patience. I don't believe I could read at your age."

"Mama's been helping."

"Did you have a nice Christmas?" Hugo asked as they went into the front room, where Jemmie had set a festive table and the little fir tree, although dropping needles profusely, brightened a corner with its candles and decorations.

"Santa brought me a doll and a doll house," Patience said. "And Mama made clothes for my doll, and Jemmie made furniture for the house."

"You're a lucky little girl to have two such talented ladies at your beck and call," Hugo said. "You must have been very good, for Santa to bring you such nice gifts."

"I'm fixin' to serve right away," Jemmie announced, "on account it's way past somebody's bedtime."

"Oh, I should think a little leeway could be granted," Hugo said. "After all, it's a double celebration. A birthday and a brand-new year."

Jemmie brought out the baked ham, and Maggie carried in steaming dishes of yams and black-eyed peas, along with biscuits piping hot from the oven. Hugo had brought champagne to toast the New Year and sarsaparilla for Patience.

When the food was assembled, they took their places at the table. Jemmie and Maggie had long ago given up any pretense that they were mistress and servant, and so Jemmie always ate with them.

Patience had never had a hearty appetite and she remained, in Maggie's eyes, far too thin. But on this night she valiantly struggled through the heavy meal in order to hasten the time for cutting the cake and opening her presents.

She blew out the six candles, closed her eyes to make a wish that Maggie knew was always the same, that Uncle Hugo would stay with them forever. Then with squeals of delight the wrapping paper was torn from the doll carriage that Hugo had brought for her, and from the storybooks and set of watercolors that were Maggie's gift.

Jemmie then handed the little girl a small package. Opening it, Patience looked puzzled. She turned the short sticklike object over in her hand.

"Blow gently into the hole, sugar," Jemmie said, her old eyes gleaming. "It's a flute. I done made it for you, jes' lak' I made one for another chile, long time ago."

Maggie, seated at the table, saw Hugo's shoulders stiffen. He looked at Jemmie, who returned his stare defiantly. Maggie wasn't sure what had passed between the two of them, but she wasn't surprised that Jemmie was eager to learn if Patience had any musical inclinations. After all, Delia was now as famous as Jenny Lind. During the preceding four years Delia had made a triumphant European tour, performing before most of the crowned heads, and had also been wildly acclaimed in New York, Boston, and Philadelphia. But she had never returned to New Orleans, and she continued to make her home in San Francisco.

Patience blew tentatively into the mouthpiece of the flute. The single sweet note she created brought a look of wonder to her eyes. A little while later she said she'd like to go to bed, and Maggie noted that the flute went with her.

Maggie helped clear away the dishes, and Jemmie said her old bones were tired and she was off to bed.

Left alone with Hugo, Maggie expected they would share a companiable but brief conversation before he departed, as was their custom. She had years ago ceased to harbor any hope that he came to see anyone but Delia's daughter, because although he was friendly toward her and expressed interest in her business, he maintained strict decorum during his infrequent visits.

But instead of making a quick departure, this evening Hugo said, "Let's sit down and talk, Maggie."

Her heart fluttered again, although she knew the subject of conversation would surely be Patience.

"Your shop is doing well now that you've employed a saleswoman?" Hugo inquired.

She nodded, and he went on, "Perhaps you're ready to expand to a larger market?"

"Leave Natchez?" Maggie asked, surprised.

"You could hire a manager to run the business here and move to New Orleans. Patience is ready to move on from nursery school, and this would be a good time to make a change, for both of you. I'll be honest, Maggie, if you were to move to New Orleans, I'd be able to see Patience more often. Besides, it would be good for you, too. You work far too hard, Maggie. You're a talented seamstress, but you're throwing away your talent as a designer. You should hire women to do the sewing for you and spend your time designing. The ladies of Natchez have enjoyed your services as both a designer and a seamstress long enough."

"Well . . ." Maggie said slowly, "we've been very comfortable and happy here. But I must confess I've thought about expanding the business, and I'd love to spend my time sketching instead of sewing. But New Orleans . . ."

"You're afraid Delia might return? After six years? It's not likely. She and Julian have made San Francisco their home. I thought after her European tour they might come back here, but they went directly out to the West Coast."

He paused. "When Julian came home just before his mother died, I asked if Delia would ever sing in New Orleans, and he said he didn't think so because she had unhappy memories here."

"If Delia were ever to see Patience . . . she'd know."

"Yes. But would she care?"

Maggie stared into the leaping flames of the fire and tried to imagine a woman who could deny her own flesh and blood. Perhaps if such a creature existed, it would be Delia. "I don't know, Hugo—it seems so risky, what with Julian being her manager. If he brought her with him to visit you or Marcus—"

"He and Marcus have been estranged for years. I doubt Julian will ever visit the Willows again—and as for myself, well, he always resented the fact that Father left everything to me. I tried to make amends—signed most of my father's extravagances over to him, the private railroad car, the racehorses—Julian's response was to rent out the railroad car and send me the proceeds; then hire the best trainers for the horses, win several races, and send the purses to me. Julian, you see, decided after a somewhat misspent youth, to settle down and become twice the businessman either my father or I ever was."

Recalling her brief meeting with his half brother, Maggie commented, "Perhaps you and your father weren't ruthless enough."

"Oh, I believe we acquired more than our fair share of ill-gotten gains. Speaking of which, one of the things that prompted this suggestion was that I acquired several pieces of property recently, including a small house in the Garden District and two adjacent storefronts in the Quarter that could be converted to a workroom and a showroom for your designs."

Hugo paused, his deep blue eyes twinkling. "Naturally you will pay exorbitant rents. I learned my lesson regarding your precious independence when you walked out of the Palmetto Street cottage. Well, Maggie, what do you say? Are you ready for the big city?"

Would she have gone to the ends of the earth if he'd asked? She had to stifle a twinge of apprehension that someone in New Orleans who had known Delia as a child might recognize that Patience was her daughter.

Maggie and Jemmie were so busy, finishing up orders and packing to get ready for their move to New Orleans, that Patience was left to her own devices. She ignored her new Christmas and birthday toys for the most part and spent hours playing the flute Jemmie had made for her.

Maggie was disappointed that the child did not use her watercolors, as she'd hoped it might encourage any latent artistic inclinations. Patience's fascination with the flute became almost irritating. Was the reason for this, Maggie wondered, that she believed if she could inspire her own love of sketching and painting in Patience, there might be more of a connection between them? At least, Maggie reasoned, the little girl so far had shown no interest in singing.

There was one incident that gave her pause. They had wrapped all of their china and breakables in newspapers, and as they unpacked the boxes at their new home, newspapers were scattered everywhere. Jemmie put Patience to work gathering up the discarded papers, and one morning Maggie came upon her sitting crosslegged on the floor smoothing the creases from one of the newspapers.

Maggie paused at the door, smiling. The child looked so serious, poring over newsprint she surely could not yet read, as she was still mastering the easy words of her first primer. Then Patience sensed her presence and turned her head. "Why is this lady in the paper?" She pointed to a photograph.

Maggie walked slowly through the drifts of crumpled paper and looked down at the page Patience had spread out. And her heart lurched.

Patience was sounding out the letters in the caption beneath the photograph. "*Co*—no, that's *or* . . ."

"Cordelia," Maggie finished for her. "She's a singer."

"Why is she dressed like a man?"

"Perhaps to get her picture in the paper." Maggie looked down at the perfection of Delia's features that were repeated, heart-wrenchingly, in the child.

"If she didn't have that ugly suit on, she'd look like a princess."

No, Maggie thought, she'd look like an older, cynical, world-weary version of you. But surely Delia had never been blessed with the pure innocence and wonder that lit Patience's features with such an inner glow that strangers on the street would stop to admire the little girl.

"Mama? Why are you frowning?"

"I'm not frowning at you, my precious. I was just thinking we must get rid of all this paper."

Patience looked at Delia's picture again and said slowly, "Her eyes won't let me look away from her."

Maggie scooped up the page and crumpled it. "There. She's gone."

But, of course, Delia would never be gone. She would always hover in the background, a lurking threat to Maggie's happiness with her daughter. Patience *was* her daughter, after all. She was only Delia's child by the accident of birth.

Maggie was pleased with the window display she and Jemmie had created. They had taken one of Maggie's gowns and pinned it to a plain backboard, along with several pieces of Jemmie's handmade jewelry and a long feather boa, giving the illusion that an invisible woman was gliding by, with a breeze catching her skirts and sending the ends of the boa flying.

"One day we'll have a mannequin to put our clothes on," Maggie said. "But in the meantime I think this will do nicely."

With Mardi Gras fast approaching, they were soon inundated with orders for both ball gowns and costumes. The latter proved to be especially challenging and fun, but obviously far more work than the two women could handle. A card taped in a corner of the shop window advertising a need for seamstresses brought more applicants than Maggie expected. She hired two full-time seamstresses and sent piecework home with several women who were glad to earn a little extra while caring for young children.

The hours flew by, made even more pleasant by the fact that Hugo was now a frequent visitor.

"I'm so happy we came to New Orleans," Maggie confided to Jemmie. "But sometimes I worry about how well we're doing. Everything is going so perfectly I'm afraid it won't last."

"Doan' say that! That's the wust kind of bad luck thing to say," Jemmie warned, but Maggie laughed at the old woman's fears, because that very day a horse and cart had delivered two large boxes bearing shipping marks that indicated their point of origin was Cherbourg, France. Upon unpacking the boxes, they discovered to their delight bolts of fabric and patterns of the latest Paris fashions, consigned to them by Hugo.

That evening when Maggie saw his carriage draw to a halt

in front of their house, she went flying downstairs as Jemmie opened the front door, wondering how she could possibly thank him for taking the time and trouble to order and ship the fabric to her.

"Oh, you wonderful, wonderful man—" she called as Jemmie stepped aside to admit him.

But it was not Hugo who entered the house. Gabrielle, his wife, placed her dainty feet firmly inside the hall and regarded Maggie with an implacable stare.

Chapter 26

*

"Yes, my husband *is* a wonderful man, is he not?" Gabrielle said in a dangerously level voice.

"What can I do for you, Mrs. Van Courtland?" Maggie asked in as civil a tone as she could muster.

Gabrielle's green eyes flickered in Jemmie's direction. "Perhaps we could speak in private?"

"I don't confer with clients in my home. You could visit my place of business tomorrow."

"Oh, I'm not here to order one of your little gowns." Her tone matched the chill of her narrowed gaze.

"I'll jes' go see to—"

"Stay where you are, Jemmie," Maggie snapped.

Gabrielle's full lips curved slightly. "Very well. I'll be brief. Several bales of expensive fabric were delivered to you today. I trust you did not believe these were sent as gifts?"

There had been only a bill of lading, showing the shipment was prepaid, with the delivery. Maggie fully intended to pay for the fabric promptly, whether or not Hugo intended it as a gift, but she was not going to give Gabrielle the satisfaction of saying so.

"As I just said, this is my home. Not my place of business. If there's nothing else?" Maggie opened the front door again.

Gabrielle's eyes were now as veiled as a cat's. "You made a mistake by moving to New Orleans. One I believe you will live to regret."

"Mama—did Uncle Hugo come?" Patience's voice came from the top of the stairs.

"No, honey. Go back to bed," Maggie said quickly.

Gabrielle glanced up at the child and then back to Maggie, and now her expression was one of satisfaction, as though she had just seen the solution to her problem. "A *terrible* mistake."

Maggie was tempted to slam the door after her but restrained herself. She turned to face Jemmie.

The older woman's face was creased with worry. "She *knows*, Maggie."

"Perhaps she guesses," Maggie said. "But she doesn't know." She looked up to be sure that Patience had gone back to bed and then added, "Besides, what can she do to hurt us?"

"Ah doan' know, Maggie, but ah does know that you and Mr. Hugo both set too much store by that chile and she ain't your'n."

"Surely Gabrielle was threatening me and my business? You don't really think she would try to harm Patience?"

"Maggie, ah doan think you understand a woman like Gabrielle. She doan play by no rules you 'bide by. She's afeared that now y'all done come here, to her own backyard, you might steal Mr. Hugo away from her."

Maggie felt herself flush. "That's ridiculous."

"She doan know that."

Maggie was inexplicably annoyed. "You don't have to make it sound as if it would be impossible for a man to be attracted to me. If you recall, Mr. Lucas Stone, a fine and upstanding young lawyer in Natchez, pursued me quite relentlessly."

Jemmie's old eyes gleamed mischievously. "Ah didn't say it was ridiculous—y'all did. But ah reckon if Mr. Hugo was gwine stray, he'd have strayed afore now."

"Implying that I would consider it?"

"Honey, ah knows how you feel about Mr. Hugo. And how he feels about you. Only what we got here is two people who'd rather cut out their hearts than break the rules."

Maggie reflected upon the truth of that statement as she went upstairs to say good night to Patience.

Maggie was assisting one of her seamstresses to pin a paper pattern to a length of velveteen when the bell over the shop door tinkled. She turned, expecting to greet a prospective customer, or perhaps a salesman hoping to sell her something. Instead a slender man clad in a shabby overcoat, a slouch hat pulled low over his forehead, leaned heavily upon a cane and politely waited for her to notice him. There was something about him, a certain aristocratic demeanor, that suggested impoverished gentility.

He removed his hat. "Mrs. Nesbitt?" His almost effeminately handsome features were marred by dark circles under his eyes, and the waxen pallor of his skin told its own story.

Maggie's first impulse, to tell him she wasn't in need of any goods, faded before the pleading sincerity of his dark eyes.

"May I help you?"

"I must speak with you privately, Mrs. Nesbitt."

"We can go into the back room," Maggie said. "This way."

The room was both a storeroom and an office, and she had to move several spools of thread from a chair in order to offer it to him.

He sank into the chair gratefully. "Thank you, you're most kind." He cleared his throat, patting a linen handkerchief to his lips as he did so. "I have come to you—and please be aware that no one sent me—to ask you to end your association with Hugo Van Courtland."

For a moment Maggie was too surprised to react. When she recovered her senses, she asked stiffly, "Who are you and how dare you come in here and speak to me of such personal matters?"

"I am Mrs. Van Courtland's cousin, Alain Marchand. I thought perhaps I could appeal to your better nature if I explained to you that, despite what you may believe, Hugo and Gabrielle do care—very deeply—for each other. The troubles between them are compounded by the presence of yourself and the child in his life and, I regret to say, by my clinging to life when I should have left behind this mortal coil long ago."

"You have me at a disadvantage, Mr. Marchand. You obviously know a great deal more about the Van Courtlands than I do. I will say only that I am acquainted with Mr. Van Courtland and am offended by your implying that there is something improper about my knowing him."

"You have a child, do you not? A child in whom Mr. Van Courtland shows extraordinary interest. You strike me as being a straightforward woman, not one given to coyness in such matters, so please allow me to be frank. While you and the child remained in another city, Mr. Van Courtland's visits to you were of necessity few and far between. It will undoubtedly be a different matter now that you have a house and a business so close to his. The Van Courtlands are well known in this city, and people are bound to talk. The rift between Hugo and Gabrielle will grow, perhaps to the point where their estrangement becomes irreconcilable. As a woman of honor, I'm sure you would not want that to happen."

Maggie knew she should act with outrage, protest her innocence, and demand that he leave, but something about this frail sad-eyed man stopped her.

"I would like you to know, Mrs. Nesbitt," he continued, his voice a tortured whisper, "that I have not been a threat to their happiness for many years—indeed if ever I was. But you and the little girl . . . you could easily destroy my beloved cousin's marriage. I am begging you to let him go. To end the affair."

"I am not having an affair, Mr. Marchand. You should not judge others by your own lack of morals. It sounds very much as though you are—or were—far more than a cousin to Mrs. Van Courtland. Do you believe that gives you the right to march in here and accuse me of the same conduct—or to insist that my daughter and I leave town?"

"Let's not pretend. I know she is not your daughter."

"You know nothing of the sort," Maggie snapped, rising to her feet. "I'll ask you to leave my premises now, and please don't return."

He also rose, somewhat unsteadily, to his feet. "Please think about what I've said. If you do I'm sure you'll do the right thing and avoid a great deal of heartbreak for all concerned. Good day to you, Mrs. Nesbitt."

His walking stick clicked across the wooden floor. He paused at the door to put on his hat, bowed in a courtly gesture that had a curiously calming effect on her anger, and left. She moved to the window and watched him walk away, relying heavily on the support of his cane. There was something gallant and unforgettable about him, and the memory of his visit stayed with her all day, because far from being outraged by his plea on behalf of his cousin, Maggie felt troubled and guilty.

Were there degrees of betrayal? Had she complacently assured herself that since they had not committed adultery,
everything else about her association with Hugo was acceptable? Hadn't she done everything in her power, yes, even using the child, to make sure he kept coming back to spend
time with them, and wasn't every second of that time stolen
from his lawfully wedded wife?

After Patience had gone to bed that evening, Maggie went
into the kitchen, where Jemmie was seated at the table, folding clothes from a basket of laundry. There were few secrets
Maggie had not shared with the old woman, and she had
come to rely on her wisdom, if not always to follow her advice.

"Gabrielle's cousin came to the shop today. He practically
demanded that I leave town and take Patience with me."

"Why, that trashy, low-down scalawag!" Jemmie exclaimed indignantly. "He's a fine one to be settin' in judgment over other folks."

"You never mentioned him to me when we talked about
the Van Courtlands."

"No," Jemmie agreed darkly, "I reckon if'n I tole you how
Miz Gabrielle done carried on with her cousin you might
think . . . mebbe you—" She broke off, clearly embarrassed.

"That I would take it as a license to carry on with Mr.
Hugo?" Maggie finished for her.

Distractedly, Jemmie dropped a folded towel back into the
jumbled laundry basket. "Her cousin, he's got the consumption. Been at death's door for years. Funny how some of 'em
linger on in misery—lak' they's being punished for their
sins."

"Oh, I don't think God punishes sinners like that, Jemmie.
Maybe Mr. Marchand has the will to live and hope for a
cure."

"Ain't no cure for the wasting disease."

"Then perhaps he feels compelled to accomplish something before he dies—from what he said to me, that could
very well be a reconciliation between Hugo and Gabrielle.
You know, I always knew there was something very wrong in
their marriage, but until Mr. Marchand came to see me today,
I never really saw the whole picture."

"Ah done tole you we should've stayed in Natchez."

"I don't think that was the answer, either. I believe we were destined to come here and be part of a more complex scheme of things."

The old woman's brow wrinkled as she strove to understand. "What you tryin' to tell old Jemmie?"

Maggie smiled. "I'm not sure myself. I just know that Mr. Marchand's rather restrained pleas unsettled me far more than Gabrielle's accusations and threats."

"Doan do nothing hasty, Maggie. We's heah now and there ain't no gwine back."

"No," Maggie agreed thoughtfully. "We can never go back and undo what's done."

Uncle Hugo had given Patience a fine new hoop, and she bowled it along the street in front of her house, her pale gold braids flying after her as she darted around the caged trees set in the pavement and swerved to avoid colliding with strolling neighbors.

The morning was new and bright with sunshine, and Patience only intended to go a little way from her garden gate, because neither her mother nor Jemmie had actually given permission for her to be out on the street by herself. But breakfast wasn't ready yet, and the two women were deep in conversation in the kitchen as they stirred grits and fried ham, and Patience simply wanted to try out the new hoop. She certainly couldn't bowl it around the tiny courtyard of their house, which was filled with flowerpots and a big old gnarly tree.

There were few people about so early, and not much traffic on the street, so Patience was startled when a lady suddenly appeared in her path and caught the rolling hoop neatly in her tiny gloved hand.

The lady was very pretty, with two corkscrews of glossy dark hair hanging from beneath a frothy confection of a hat. She had bright, glittery green eyes, and she dimpled enchantingly as she smiled. When she spoke, her voice seemed to drip into the ears like warm honey. "Why, hello there, Patience. Where are you off to all by yourself?"

Patience squinted in the bright sunshine, studying the lady curiously, from her slanty black eyebrows to her dainty high-arched feet, trying to remember where she had seen her before. "Ma'am? How did you know my name?"

"We have a mutual acquaintance. Mr. Hugo Van Courtland."

"Uncle Hugo?" Patience wasn't sure what "mutual acquaintance" meant, but she now remembered where she had seen the pretty lady before. She had called on Mama only days earlier, but hadn't stayed long.

The lady was now frowning. "*Uncle* Hugo—is that what you call him? I suppose you see him often?"

Patience was beginning to feel uneasy. She tugged at the hoop, but the lady held it firm. Reluctant to return home without the hoop, Patience stammered, "N-no—not often."

"But now that you have moved to New Orleans, I'm sure that will change. Uncle Hugo will be coming to your house regularly in the future."

"I've got to go now, my mama will be looking for me."

"Your *mama*? You mean Mrs. Nesbitt?"

"Yes. She's my mama."

The black brows arched upward, as if in surprise. Then the lady bent lower so that her face was only inches away. Patience wanted to back away, but they were still connected by the hoop.

"Darling, Uncle Hugo and Mrs. Nesbitt have been lying to you. Now listen closely, you must never tell them I spoke with you, because if you do, I shall never be able to help you. And I do so want to help you. You won't understand this now, but it's true. I have a plan that will prove to you that I am your friend. Don't tell anyone we met this morning, but the next time Uncle Hugo comes to visit I want you to tell him you had a dream about a lady with very fair hair, just like yours, who was wearing a man's suit, and she was singing to you."

Patience was startled. She had seen the lady singer's photograph in the paper, so she was real, not a dream.

The dark-haired lady added, "Watch your uncle carefully when you say this. He will be quite surprised. Perhaps he will even tell you about that lady singer. You see, Patience, she is someone who is very important to you. But Uncle Hugo and Mrs. Nesbitt are keeping you from her."

Patience wished she would not keep calling her mother

Mrs. Nesbitt. It sounded threatening, somehow. "Please let me have my hoop now. I must go home."

"I've waited for days hoping to catch you alone, Patience. You may wish to see me again after you've spoken with Uncle Hugo. If you do, tie a ribbon to one of the branches of the dogwood in your front garden. When the ribbon disappears you'll know I have received your message, and the next morning I shall meet you here. Do you understand?"

Patience nodded, desperate now to escape. She could not imagine ever wanting to see this lady again. The moment the hoop was released from the tiny gloved hand, Patience sped off down the street, carrying the hoop rather than bowling it.

Chapter 27

*

Maggie laid down her pen and stared unseeingly at the sketch she was working on, still undecided whether to tell Hugo of the visits of both his wife and her cousin.

If she told him, he would be angry, and there would undoubtedly be confrontations and repercussions. Perhaps Jemmie was right, it would have been better to stay in Natchez.

It was early evening, and Hugo had taken Patience for a drive in his new horseless carriage. Maggie had excused herself from accompanying them on the pretext that she must finish a design for her seamstresses to begin sewing the following morning. The real reason for not going was that she was afraid they might be seen.

In the kitchen Jemmie was preparing dinner, and Maggie decided she had better go and help as the older woman tended to work herself into a state of exhaustion when her beloved Mr. Hugo was eating with them.

As she made her way downstairs, Maggie considered the fact that women of all ages adored Hugo. He treated all women with Old-World courtliness and obviously revered them, while having the reputation of being tough and hardheaded in his dealings with men. Perhaps that contrast was what made him so attractive, since women sensed his strength and felt protected by it rather than threatened.

Before she reached the kitchen she heard the horseless carriage arrive and reminded herself she was supposed to call it a motorcar. She went to open the front door and smiled as she saw Hugo helping the little girl to the sidewalk and opening the garden gate for her. How he idolized the child. Surely no flesh-and-blood father could have loved her more. Over the past six years there had been many times when Maggie allowed herself the fantasy that they might one day be a family, a real one, husband and wife and daughter and later on, more children. But she had not indulged in that particular daydream since Alain Marchand's visit.

"Mama, Mama! We drove to the levee and watched the riverboats leaving and there was colored steam just like rainbows and Uncle Hugo said he'll take me on a boat and let me play the calliope next week and he bought me pralines."

"Goodness, I hope you didn't spoil your appetite. Jemmie is cooking your favorite jambalaya, and she baked a pecan pie."

As she helped Patience remove her bonnet and coat, Maggie suddenly became aware the Hugo seemed unnaturally quiet and withdrawn. His mood matched her own. Several times during dinner she thought, *This is wrong, we shouldn't be dining together like this. We aren't his family.*

They had, of course, dined together many times in Natchez, but there he was visiting from out of town. It was different here in New Orleans, where he had his own home and a wife—was Gabrielle eating a lonely meal at this very moment?

By the time the meal was cleared away and Hugo had read a story to Patience before she went to bed, Maggie had worked herself up into a state of great anxiety and guilt.

"I'd like to speak with before you leave," she told Hugo as he came downstairs after the story hour.

He nodded. "And I with you. We have a serious problem to discuss."

Her heart sank. Why, oh, why had she agreed to come here? Everything had been so perfect in Natchez, and now not only would she lose Hugo's friendship, but she would also deprive Patience of the only father figure she had ever known.

They went into the front parlor, and Hugo closed the door and turned to face her, his expression grave. "Patience told me of a dream she had. . . . Maggie, have you—or Jemmie— ever mentioned Delia to the child?"

Maggie caught her breath. Of all the things she had expected him to bring up, Delia had been nowhere on the list.

"No, never. I'm certain of it . . . well, wait, there was one incident." She told him of Patience finding the photograph of her mother in the newspaper and being strangely fascinated by it.

"Perhaps that precipitated the dream, then," Hugo said, clearly relieved. "She said she dreamed that a woman with light hair like her own had been singing to her. I don't know what I thought—that perhaps she sensed some bonding with the woman in her dream—you know how a guilty conscience can weave an intricate tapestry of reasons to explain the most innocent of incidents. But still, all the way back here I have been feeling profound remorse about our deception. Yet I am not sure it would be in Patience's best interests to reveal the truth to her."

Maggie felt a chill that was soul-deep at the mere possibility she would have to tell Patience she was not her mother. For a moment she couldn't speak.

Unexpectedly Hugo reached out and laid his hand on her shoulder. She shivered as the warmth of his touch seeped through an icy veil that seemed to have descended upon her emotions.

"Maggie, you're pale as a ghost. Come and sit down. I didn't mean to upset you, but we must make some decisions about this."

He led her to the sofa and sat down beside her, withdrawing his hand from her shoulder as he did so. She felt the loss of his touch acutely.

"I can't give her up, Hugo," Maggie whispered. "I can't."

"Did I suggest it would come to that? As I said earlier, we have to consider what is best for Patience. She has the right to know who her parents are, but when do we tell her? Would any purpose be served in telling her now, or would that be harmful?"

"To her? To us? Oh, Hugo—I don't ever want to tell her. I want to go on being her mother in every sense of the word. Why must we tell her? Delia abandoned her—she doesn't deserve her."

"And what about Patience's father? Have you considered him?"

Maggie's head snapped toward him. "Are you saying—"

"No, I am not her father."

"But you know who is?"

"I've no proof, but I've suspected for some time that Marcus, the younger of my half brothers, is her father."

Maggie digested this surprising news silently.

Hugo went on: "Delia and Marcus were drawn to each other from the start, because of their mutual love of music. She was the only person alive, to my knowledge, that he ever allowed near him when he was composing, or playing the piano for his own pleasure—which, incidentally, he did in the middle of the night. All this despite the fact that, when anyone else was present, he was extremely hostile toward her. I suppose we should have recognized the volatility of a love-hate relationship and taken appropriate precautions."

Maggie listened with growing alarm. She had heard snatches of gossip about Marcus, and although Jemmie refused to confirm any of the whispers about his "strangeness" or his "mad spells," neither did she deny them. Had Patience inherited any of those traits? The child had not demonstrated any such peculiarities, but she did like to be alone, and since Jemmie had given her the flute, she spent hours playing it. There was a fairy-tale quality to the sound of the flute, making Maggie think of toadstool rings and pixies and stolen children and changelings. She had wished a thousand times that Jemmie had never made the flute, or that she could close her ears to the eerie sound of it.

At length she said, "But you're not sure Marcus is her father? I mean, he hasn't admitted it, has he?"

"No. But I believe Julian also thinks so. You see, I wired Julian to come home when his mother was taken ill; however, the crisis came while he was still traveling across the country and she died before he reached the Willows. What with the funeral arrangements and friends and relatives arriving, I was so busy that at first I didn't notice that Julian and Marcus were at odds, or if I did I put it down to their grief over losing their mother. But then, immediately after the funeral, Julian left without so much as a goodbye to anyone. When I questioned Marcus, his response was to curse the day Delia had come into our lives."

"But I thought Julian continued to insist that Delia never had a child?"

"He did and does. But there was an angry confrontation between Julian and Marcus before the funeral. I don't know what it was about, but I suspect Julian accused Marcus of getting Delia in the family way. They were up in Marcus's room, but we could hear them bellowing at each other, although couldn't make out what they were saying. My main concern is that if Julian ever returns, he might find out about you, Maggie. I doubt he imagines that you kept Delia's baby—he probably believes you took her to an orphanage. But if he ever returned to New Orleans . . ."

"We shouldn't have come here. We should have stayed in Natchez."

"You can't live your life in hiding. Besides, he could run into you in Natchez, too. The chance that someday he or Delia will discover that you have her child makes me wonder if Patience should be told the truth now."

"Whose truth, Hugo? Do any of us know the whole truth?"

He sighed heavily. "Delia does, I guess."

Maggie wasn't sure what prompted her next question, whether it was her sense of impending doom or merely hearing the man she loved sigh over Delia. But in one impulsive moment the question was out and couldn't be retrieved. "Were you in love with Delia, too, Hugo?"

He swiveled his head and fixed her with an unreadable stare, one black eyebrow slightly arched.

Maggie felt herself flush. "Well, it seems that your half brothers were both besotted by her, and I just wondered . . . I mean, well, everybody is so fascinated by her."

"You've never heard her sing, have you?"

"She sang a little—while she was in labor."

"If she was in pain, I'm not sure you could feel the full impact of her voice. To answer your question, I was moved by her singing, and always felt protective toward her. She was such a gallant little waif, so stoic, so resilient—courageous, in view of the hard knocks life threw at her. I admired her, was awed by her talent, but was I in love with her? No. She was a child when I knew her. I prefer mature women."

"I'm sorry," Maggie said quietly. "I had no right to ask such a question."

"A mature woman such as yourself," Hugo added in a tone

that made Maggie's nerves tingle. "If, of course, I were free to harbor such thoughts."

"Oh, Hugo," Maggie breathed. "Your wife is so beautiful and I—"

His hand cupped her cheek and turned her face toward him. They were so close she felt the heat that radiated from his body. Hugo said, "Do you know how many times I've longed to take you in my arms and hold you close to my heart? Or the nights I've left your house to walk the streets until I was exhausted enough to sleep? With you and Patience I feel I can shed all my cares for a little while and pretend we are a family, loyal and true to one another and living happily ever after. I've tried to stay away from you, yet I always come back, knowing I'm playing with fire."

Maggie felt herself lean forward slightly, her lips parted, her heart hammering. Surely now she could find the courage to tell him that she loved him.

Before she could speak, he abruptly drew away and rose to his feet. "Don't say anything now, Maggie. Let me paint a picture for you. There is no greater scandal than divorce, and it affects every aspect of a man's life—his family, his friends, his business. Divorce has ruined more than one man. But as bad as it is for a man, it is even worse for the woman who is perceived to have come between a husband and wife. You would, literally and figuratively, be tarred and feathered. Forget about your thriving business; no woman would patronize you. Patience would be affected, too, taunted and reviled and called bastard. When I insisted that you file a birth certificate naming yourself as her mother, I did not foresee how dear you would both become to me, or realize the ramifications of you passing yourself off as her mother. In short, for me to divorce Gabrielle and marry you would be tantamount to my admitting you were my mistress and she was our love-child. This would cause untold heartache for you and Patience. But there is—for you—an even greater impediment, and that is my uncertainty. Am I in love with the idea of you and Patience and I living in perfect harmony—which, of course, is impossible for any human beings—or do I love Maggie Nesbitt, completely and wholly, and convention be damned? You see before you, my dear Maggie, a man who has been charred in the flames of failed matrimony and who is now more than a little cautious about taking such a risk again."

"Hugo, let me tell you how I feel—" Maggie began, but again he interrupted.

"No, don't say a word. If you offer one word of encouragement, we shall both be lost. Let me tell you this. I have not touched my wife for some time. We maintain only a brittle facade of a marriage. But neither have I lived the life of a priest. I have given in to my primal urges with other women. They were, without exception, women who understood that they would never mean more to me than they did for a passing moment. I would never ask you to place yourself in such a position. You have too much integrity for that, and I respect you too much to ask. Maggie, I've said a great deal more than I intended, but perhaps it was time to get it out into the open. I pretended to myself that I wanted you to come to New Orleans so that I could see Patience more often and so that your business could expand and grow ... but I see now my motives were less honorable than that, and I am ashamed of them. Good night, Maggie. Think about all we've discussed this evening, and when I return from New York we'll talk again."

She wanted to cry out, *No, don't go, please don't leave! Stay and hold me, make love to me.* But the words stuck in her throat and her feet had taken root, for she could not move.

As the door closed behind him, Maggie slumped back against the sofa, feeling drained. Several minutes passed before she remembered that she had not told him about her visits from Gabrielle and her cousin.

She remained sitting before the long-dead fire until the mantelpiece clock chimed midnight, then went up the stairs and as was her custom, paused at Patience's door. She stood there for a moment, watching as a moonbeam played across the sweetly curved form of the child. Patience had brought Hugo and herself together, and he was right, if there was any justice in the world they should be living together, they should be a family. But, of course, there was no justice in the scheme of things.

As she was about to close the bedroom door, the little girl suddenly sat up and saw her. She rubbed her eyes sleepily.

Maggie went to the bed and bent to kiss her. "Back to dreamland for you, sweetheart. Good night, sleep tight."

"Mama ..." The child's voice was drowsy. "Why are we here? I mean, why did God put us on earth?"

Maggie stroked her hair. "To love one another, my darling."

Chapter 28

*

DELIA

How could it be that what I was so sure was true turned out to be false, and what I never suspected as even a remote possibility was a fact of my life?

"Who is this Oscar Latimer?" Delia demanded. "How dare he write this? I want you to sue him for libel."

Julian looked up from his morning coffee, mildly interested.

She thrust the newspaper under his nose.

He read the key phrase aloud. " 'Sexual ambiguity . . .' " then silently skimmed the rest. The journalist commented on her male attire and shorn locks, speculating that there might have been a vicious male in Delia's past who had caused her to be confused about her gender.

After a minute Julian asked, "Did you read the entire article?"

"No," Delia answered. "I can't believe the editors let him use the word *sexual*."

"If I were you, I'd worry more about *ambiguity*," Julian said dryly. "But before you challenge him to pistols at dawn, you should read all that he wrote. He goes on to say that there has never been a more commanding presence onstage than you, nor a more versatile performer. He saw you in *Tosca* during your European tour and writes that you transformed yourself into a fiery Fioria Tosca, filled with rage and despair that—he felt—owed more to your own tethered passion than to Puccini's music or the libretto. He feels you display an icy facade to hide that passion . . . obviously he doesn't know you."

"Nor do you, Julian. Even though you believe you do."

"Latimer also writes that whatever you sing mesmerizes

audiences, and when you are onstage no one can take his eyes off you. In other words, no matter if there is a hint of sexual ambiguity in your offstage appearance and manner— and yes, occasionally onstage, too—you can still present yourself as a passionate woman when the role demands it."

"Dammit, Julian, he's saying that I am neither a man nor a woman."

"He's undoubtedly a student of that doctor in Vienna, what's his name—Freud? This article reeks of the so-called new science. Forget about it, Delia. You'll only give him more ammunition if you acknowledge you've even read it."

"How I hate the press. Why can't they judge my performance and leave my character out of it?"

"Because their readers are interested in everything you do, my sweet. At this very moment there could be a reporter lurking outside, wondering about this early morning visit."

"You're my business manager. Why shouldn't I visit you any time I please?"

He folded up his newspaper and looked at her with hooded eyes. "Well, now, if they didn't see you arrive but observe you leaving, it might suggest an overnight tryst." He paused, contemplative. "Of course, in view of that hint about your sexual ambiguity, that might be a good thing."

"I've been seen in the company of plenty of men."

He raised a black eyebrow. "A dinner here, a play there, a carriage ride now and then; never seeing the same man more than twice . . . You behave like the ingenue you never were as a young girl. You know, this article could precipitate others. Why not put all the speculation to rest and marry me?"

Delia gave an exasperated sigh. "Oh, don't start that nonsense again."

He looked pained but his tone was mocking. "*Nonsense?* I am very serious in my intentions. Who knows you better than I do? I'm already managing your career and all your investments and sometimes we even manage to get along without quarreling for five or ten minutes."

"I'd rather deal with that journalist's poison pen. Besides, I wouldn't want to join your harem." She snatched up the offending article and left.

As she walked back up Nob Hill to her own house, it occurred to her that Julian was right, he *was* privy to all of her secrets.

There had been a subtle change in their relationship after she confessed that Marcus had fathered her child. She had not told Julian that his brother had raped her. She wasn't sure why she had left out that important detail, but thought it might have been a hope that her sense of shame would be lessened if she pretended she had been a willing partner.

Julian had been at first incredulous, then angry, and finally resigned. He asked only one question: "Did you refuse to marry him because I'd insisted that you not marry for five years?" and she had replied, "He never asked me to marry him."

After that day he never mentioned returning to New Orleans, or reopening Courtland Hall, or even visiting the Willows. Only when Hugo wired that Fleur was seriously ill did Julian at last go home. He never confided what, if anything, had transpired between himself and Marcus.

As she went up the steps to her front door, the glass panels rattled suddenly and the trees fluttered although there was no wind. Delia felt a moment's dizziness and gripped the handrail for support. Another earth tremor. There had been several lately. She gave the shaking earth only passing acknowledgment and went back to thinking about the journalist who had insulted her.

Perhaps Julian was right, a husband was the answer. But where would she find a man who would agree to a marriage in name only? For the truth was, Delia was terrified of the thought of allowing a man the physical intimacies that Marcus had so brutally inflicted upon her.

Delia prowled restlessly around the office of Dr. Joseph Simmington as she spoke: "I suppose you read the article accusing me of being sexually ambiguous."

"Yes. You seem upset by it."

"Not really."

The doctor waited patiently for her to continue. He had prospered over the years and now owned a house on Telegraph Hill and rented a clinic downtown where occasionally Delia consulted him. On her second visit shortly after his bombshell about her hysterectomy, after prescribing a soothing elixir for her tonsilitis, he had shyly asked if she would have dinner with him.

At the time she declined, but fearing he might disclose her medical history, she had sent him tickets to her next performance. And so a friendship of sorts was formed.

Delia thought sometimes that they were like a pair of polar bears sharing a glacier, each acknowledging the presence of the other but never invading each other's territory. If Delia needed an escort on short notice, she knew Dr. Joe was always ready and willing. In return, she provided theater tickets and, more infrequently, had a late supper with him.

"Joe . . ."

"Yes?"

"There . . . isn't any way that journalist could know that I . . . am not a whole woman?"

The doctor was on his feet instantly. He closed the distance between them in three steps and took her hands in his. "Oh, my dear, is that what's troubling you? You are a lovely, desirable woman and every man in town is in love with you. How many proposals do you receive every week nowadays?"

"But I can never have another child."

"The orphanages are filled to capacity. There's no shortage of infants and children needing homes."

"But doesn't a man want his own issue? Blood of his blood?"

"Some do, perhaps. But many more would forgo fatherhood in order to claim you as his own." Joe paused then added softly, "And you can count me among them."

"Do you mean that? Or are you giving me the benefit of your best bedside manner?"

His eyes twinkled. "I should be delighted to show you a bedside manner far superior to what I bestow on anyone else—in or out of my office."

"Why, Dr. Joe, are you flirting with me?"

He flushed slightly. "I've flirted with you many times, Delia, but you always pretended not to notice. Are you noticing now because that article worries you? Surely you must have realized when you cut your hair and dressed as a man you would sooner or later cause such speculation?"

"I thought I was demanding the respect that men get, and the autonomy, and asking to be judged by my talent rather than my clothes and appearance. I never expected . . ." Her voice trailed away. The words *sexual ambiguity* echoed in her mind, but she did not utter them.

She forced a smile. "Would you like to take me out to supper tonight?"

"Have I ever been known to refuse?"

Julian came backstage after her performance that evening. He shooed everyone out of her dressing room and then said, "There's someone asking to see you."

"Send him away, I'm having a late supper with Dr. Joe."

"Not a him, Delia—a her. Or should I say a she? Someone from your past whom I believe we should see and decide what to do about . . . since she knows a lot about your origins that we'd rather keep buried."

Delia was wiping kohl from her eyelids and glanced up at his reflection in her mirror. "Who is she?"

"Mignon Chamond."

Delia jumped to her feet. "Mignon! Let her in, you fool—"

Julian intercepted her before she reached the dressing room door. "Wait a minute. Stop and think about what she was doing for a living when you knew her. You do recall the Cajun Club, don't you? I'm fairly sure she's been working in one of the bordellos here, and the years haven't been kind to her. I think she's down on her luck."

"Then I'll take care of her. Just as she once took care of me. Let go of me, I want to see her."

She opened the door and looked out into the narrow passageway. There was no one there.

"Dammit, Julian, she's gone. What did you say to her?"

"I told her to wait until I got rid of the crowd in here."

"Did you at least find out where she's living?"

"No, but she won't be hard to find. I know most of the owners of the sporting houses."

"I'm sure you do." Delia gave him a withering glance. "Find her for me, Julian."

The restaurant was packed with after-theater diners, but as usual the maître d' attempted to lead Delia and Dr. Joe to one of the best tables. Delia said quickly, "We'd like some privacy tonight, please. Is the banquet room in use?"

"For the great Cordelia, even if it were, we would order everyone out," the maître d' responded gallantly. "But perhaps you and the doctor would be more comfortable in the owner's private dining room? He is not here this evening, but I know this is what he would suggest."

Dr. Joe looked mystified as they were seated in a small but comfortably appointed room a few minutes later. "Delia, this is an unexpected pleasure. I shan't have to compete with hordes of autograph seekers and slavering stage-door johnnies. Not to mention journalists."

Delia smiled enigmatically, but didn't explain her need for privacy until they had placed their order, a chilled bottle of wine had been delivered, and they were left alone.

"I mentioned the journalists who interrupt our meals deliberately, you know, Delia," Joe said then. "I presume you're still fretting about that Oscar Latimer article and want more reassurance that I have told no one of your medical history."

"I know you haven't, Joe," Delia said quietly. "No, I wanted to be alone with you to pursue something you said to me earlier. You said some men would not care if I could not give them a child and that you were one of them."

Joe leaned forward. "I said it and I meant it. Delia, you must know that I worship you—"

She had to cut that line of thinking off immediately and so interrupted, "Please, hear me out before you say anything further." She twisted her napkin into a knot and then plunged on: "You know that I gave birth to an illegitimate child. That child was conceived ... I was not a willing partner ... I mean—" She fumbled for the words.

Joe caught his breath. His hand slid across the table and found hers. "You were raped?"

She nodded. "I've not been with a man since, and, well, I never want to have intimate relations again."

Joe swallowed. "That's understandable."

"But I do want to get married," Delia went on. "I need a husband to dispell all the rumors about me. I'd like to find a man I respect, one who would be ... who is—a good friend. But he would have to understand it would be a marriage in name only."

Joe gave her a sad smile. "Are you proposing to me, Delia?"

She bit her lip. "I suppose I am."

Chapter 29

*

Delia insisted upon waiting until Julian was in Southern California checking on their investments before allowing Dr. Joe Simmington to make arrangements for their wedding. No one was told in advance of their plans. A justice of the peace pronounced them to be man and wife at ten o'clock one morning, and she did not miss a single performance. She did, however, have her dresser call all the newspapers, with an especially detailed report to Oscar Latimer's paper.

The headline CORDELIA ELOPES brought Julian rushing back to San Francisco. He burst into her house, pushed aside her maid, and confronted her in her bedroom where she was resting before the evening's performance.

"What the hell do you think you're doing, Delia? Have you lost your mind? You let that hack reporter goad you into turning yourself into a *doctor's wife*! What was the point? You've destroyed all of your mystery and allure. Simmington is a dull oaf who will bore you and everybody else to tears. If you had to marry somebody, why couldn't you have married me?"

She was tempted to retort, *because you would have expected me to consummate the marriage.* Instead she pushed her black satin eye mask up over her forehead and said, "Didn't my maid tell you I was resting?"

Julian's narrowed eyes swept the room. "I don't see any evidence that a man shares this room. Just what sort of a marriage do you and old Joe have?"

She knew better than to let him goad her into defending her actions, since the resulting argument might disclose more than she wanted him to know. She answered coolly. "My marriage is my business. Just as your harem of whores is your business. Get out and let me rest."

A slow grin crept across his face. His eyes flickered over the length of her body, outlined beneath a satin bedspread. "So that's it."

"I have no idea what you're inferring. Nor do I care to find out." She pulled the eye mask down again and lay back on her pillow.

The next second she felt Julian's lips against her mouth, his breath warm, his tongue probing her teeth. For a moment she was too surprised to react, and he pressed that advantage, kissing her with a persistence that suggested he was not going to stop with a mere kiss. His hungry devouring of her mouth was more than a preliminary to seduction, it was an inexorable force.

Behind the mask Delia experienced a sensation of melting, of her limbs becoming heavy and her body light. She had a sense of his power over her, but felt no real fear, only an overwhelming curiosity about what would happen next. It was almost as if, since her vision was blocked by the mask, what she was experiencing was something between a dream and a fantasy, and the lips claiming hers could have belonged to a phantom lover she had conjured out of her own imagination. As the thought formed, the image of Hugo's face flashed into her mind.

Did she sigh, or move, or did Julian somehow read her mind? He withdrew his lips from hers, at the same time snatching off her mask. His face was close to hers, his breath still warm against her lips. "He's not man enough for you, Delia. Some day you'll realize who is. I can wait."

Was he referring to Hugo—or to her husband?

Julian turned and strode from the room, and for a moment she lay still, breathing raggedly, unsure what had just happened. Julian had kissed her before and in the past she had responded by slapping his face, or at least berating him with angry words. But there was something different about this kiss. Perhaps the concealing mask had somehow absolved her of responsibility for what had almost been an act of love in itself.

She realized then that Julian had not touched her, or kissed her, since the day she told him that his brother had fathered her child. Had her new status as a married woman, in his mind, given him permission to resume his relentless pursuit of her? Or was it that he had at last forgiven his brother for impregnating her? In either case, this could signal a disturbing change in their relationship.

She did not give any thought to her own response to the kiss, since she was convinced that she loathed the idea of physical contact with a man. Any man. Even her beloved Hugo, whom she had not seen for over six years, but still loved with an aching sadness.

Mignon had not tried again to see Delia, but Delia always scanned the faces at the stage door, hoping she would return. Julian claimed he had been unable to find her.

One evening as Delia came offstage just before intermission, she heard a soft footfall behind her in the dimly lit wings and stopped to looked around, wondering if her old friend had returned. But except for a stagehand carrying a cardboard tree, she saw no one. Still, as she made her way to her dressing room, she had a feeling she was being followed.

Deliberately leaving her door ajar, she sat at her dressing table, where the mirror afforded a clear view of the open door. A moment later a pale face peered into the room.

Delia slid her stool backward, pretending to bend over to untie her shoe, then skidded all the way to the door, leaped to her feet, and seized a pair of scrawny shoulders.

A boy of about eight or nine struggled to free himself from her grip. "Please, miss, don't send me to jail. I didn't mean no harm. I just wanted to see you up close."

He was painfully thin, there seemed to be no flesh at all on his delicate bones. Glancing down at him, she saw he was barefoot, and his clothes were threadbare. A quick vision of herself at his age flitted into her mind. She relaxed her grip. "How did you get in here?"

"With the cleaners at noon."

"You stayed all day?"

"I wanted to hear you sing. Hid under a seat on the balcony. 'Course, I couldn't see you, I could only hear you. I didn't mean to scare you, honest."

"You didn't scare me. How old are you? What's your name?"

"Danny. I'm ten."

Undersized for his age, probably because he was undernourished, she decided. "So you like music, Danny?"

He nodded, his glance still wary and his body poised for flight.

She had never dealt with children and wasn't sure what to do with him. "Well, I'm flattered that you want to hear me sing, but you shouldn't have sneaked into the theater. If one of the stagehands had caught you ... I'd better take you out to the stage door. I have to go back onstage shortly, and I don't think I'd better leave you here."

"I wouldn't steal nothing."

"Did I suggest you might? I'm sure someone is wondering where you are. You should go home." She knew by the quick downcast glance and the way his jaw clenched that he had no home. She had, after all, been in exactly the same situation and recognized all the defenses. She went to her dressing table and found her purse. "Next time you want to hear me sing, you can buy a ticket."

He eyed the five-dollar bill she offered longingly but shook his head. "I ain't no beggar."

She hesitated, remembering how she sang on street corners, a battered hat upturned on the pavement in front of her. Had she been a beggar? Thad had said no, she had been part of a long tradition of street performers that dated back to the time of the Romans. But then, Thad always knew what to say to make her feel better about herself. How she missed hearing from him and, perhaps even more, writing to him. Writing to Thad had been a catharsis. She could pack up her troubles and concerns and send them far away.

"Well, Danny, perhaps you'd like to earn the price of a ticket. Wouldn't you like to sit in a seat, rather than under one, to hear me sing?"

He eyed her suspiciously. "What would I have to do?"

"Odds and ends. Run errands for me, for instance. Right now I'd love one of those meat pies they sell at the café across the street, but I can't go over there myself. You could go and get one for me. Come on, I'll introduce you to the doorman so you can get back in."

She stood at the stage door and watched the barefoot boy dart across the street.

The doorman gave her a cynical sidelong glance. "You'll never see that five bucks again."

"No," Delia answered, "I'll see a meat pie and the exact change."

She was right. Danny returned within minutes. She offered to share the steaming pie with him, but he politely declined, despite the fact that his eyes were fixed hungrily on the food.

Delia nibbled a few bites, then said he'd have to leave as she had to change. "I'm not going to finish that pie. Why don't you take it home with you? It's a pity to let it go to waste."

Danny hesitated, as though considering whether or not to humor her by accepting, then said, "I guess I could take it if you're sure you don't want it."

She assured him she didn't, then added, "Come back tomorrow night. I may need you again. Ezra, the doorman, will let you in."

The boy reported faithfully each evening, eager to do whatever she requested.

Her dresser, currently a dour middle-aged woman named Mrs. Voss, wrinkled her nose each time Danny appeared.

"Is that boy coming tonight?" Mrs. Voss asked before the Saturday evening show.

"Danny? Yes, he is."

"He smells bads."

"He's living on the streets," Delia replied.

"How do you know?"

Delia shrugged. "As soon as he trusts me, I'll take him home for a bath and a change of clothes."

"As soon as *he* trusts *you*?" the dresser repeated incredulously. "Why, he could be a thief. I'm afraid to leave my purse lying about, and Lord knows what diseases we might pick up from him."

"If you feel uncomfortable, Mrs. Voss, I certainly don't expect you to stay."

The woman sniffed, her lips compressing. "Then I'll take my leave. I don't know why you need a dresser anyway. You wear britches more than a dress, and your hair's too short to style."

"I'm certainly not a worthy object for your attentions, Mrs. Voss. So please, don't stay another minute. Julian will give you your wages—tell him I said he's to pay you until the end of the month."

It was a bleak and bone-chillingly damp night in the middle of January, and Danny was shivering with the cold when he arrived. Delia immediately became concerned that she would have to send him back out onto the streets again when she left the theater, especially since she would not return until Monday evening. But he was a nervous fawn, only half out of the forest, and she knew from personal experience that if she made any false moves he would bolt.

She gave him her shoes to shine, and he sat cross-legged on the floor of her dressing room polishing the leather to a fine sheen. His shaggy brown hair had fallen across his brow, and she felt a passing impulse to gently stroke the errant locks back out of his eyes.

Instead she ran her fingers through her own hair and wondered, since he'd now appeared for three consecutive evenings, if he trusted her enough to go home with her.

A curt rap on the door announced Julian's arrival. He entered without waiting for her to respond. Neither of them had mentioned the incident in her bedroom, and Julian had resumed his former businesslike attitude toward her.

"I just ran into Mrs. Voss on her way out. So you've fired another dresser," he said. "We've probably exhausted the supply of experienced women."

"I don't need a dresser."

"Nobody needs one more, but that's another story." He glanced at the boy. "So this is the object of the dissent. Mrs. Voss is right. He does smell bad."

"Julian . . ." Delia warned, seeing Danny bristle with wounded pride.

"All right, we'll discuss it later. Are you ready? You're on in two minutes."

"Hand me my shoes, Danny," Delia said, pointing Julian toward the door.

The boy held them at arm's length to pass to her, keeping as much distance between them as possible. The comment about his body odor had obviously found its mark.

"Danny, I'm afraid they're right. But you know that, don't you? Would you come home with me tonight?"

"I got my own home to go to."

"No, you don't."

"How do you know?"

"Because there was a time in my life when I didn't have one either, and I recognize all the signs."

His gray eyes widened. "You? But they say you're royalty."

She shook her head. "Not true. Look, I've got to run. Tonight you'll come home with me. I have a lot of chores for you to do there, too."

As she anticipated, her husband merely gave her a quizzical smile when she presented him with a barefoot ragamuffin. Joe was as comfortable to be around as any old shoe. Sometimes when she found him waiting up for her, she would blink in astonishment, wondering what he was doing in her house. She had persuaded him to move into her Nob Hill mansion, which was larger and more luxurious than his house on Telegraph Hill, but when he wasn't there, she simply didn't think about him. He spent some evenings watching her perform, but frequently his ever-increasing practice required him to be on call.

At her insistence they had installed telephones at the house and in the clinic, but Joe was reluctant to let go of the old ways and refused to buy a motor car, which Delia felt would have transported him about town in grand style, albeit not always as reliably as a horse-drawn carriage.

"I'm not your business manager," Joe chided good-humoredly. "Julian seems to need to acquire every newfangled gadget that comes along. From what you've told me, he has a fierce rivalry with his half brother, so probably feels compelled to display his wealth. Delia, my dear, I have neither wealth nor a half brother to compete with."

"But I would buy a car for you—"

He cut her off instantly. "Please don't ever suggest such a thing again. I've moved into your house, but I will not allow a woman to support me."

She responded impatiently, "Joe, I earn a lot of money, and Julian has invested it so well that I honestly don't know what to do with it all. I don't see that you can compare a few gifts with living the life of a gigolo."

He winced at her use of the word. "No more gifts, Delia. I have a wardrobe full of clothes that are not of my choosing and are far too flashy for my profession, and my surgery and office are full of gadgets I shall never use." He paused. "There's no need for you to compensate me for not sharing my bed, you know. I knew what I was getting into."

It was the first time he had brought up their bargain, and she dropped the subject immediately. Since Joe never gave her the hungry glances she received from other men, she had assumed he was asexual and needed nothing more from her than the haphazard companionship she offered. The great love of Dr. Joe's life was undoubtedly his profession. Or at least that's what she told herself whenever she felt a twinge of guilt about him.

On the night she brought Danny home, Joe suggested that after the boy was scrubbed and fed, a medical examination would be in order. "I'll do it here, if you think he'd be frightened by the clinic."

"Not yet, Joe," Delia said. "Perhaps in a few days."

"Is he going to be staying here in the house?"

"Yes. The servants' quarters are full, but I thought he could sleep in that little storeroom next to the pantry."

"Then I'll examine him tomorrow," Joe said firmly. "He could be carrying tuberculosis. He's very thin and I've seen that particular pallor on TB patients in the past."

"I haven't heard him cough. Please, let's not scare him."

"Tomorrow," Joe repeated. He could be unyielding when he chose, and so she didn't argue.

Danny submitted to the indignity of being forced into a steaming bath tub by Delia's housekeeper, then dressed in a hastily cropped nightshirt. He devoured several cold beef sandwiches and pickles. When shown to his sleeping quarters, however, the boy planted himself squarely in front of Delia and announced, "I ain't going to bed till I've earned my supper. You said you had chores for me to do."

"Time enough in the morning, Danny. It's very late."

"Tell me what you want me to do then, and I'll get up early and do it."

Delia looked at her housekeeper, a sturdy Irishwoman named Mrs. Delaney. "Do you have any chores for him?"

"Oi'll be after foinding the lad something to do. Now off to bed with ye, boyo, so we can all get some sleep."

Delia never arose before noon, and when she went downstairs the following day she had temporarily forgotten about bringing Danny home. She was drinking her first cup of coffee when she remembered and asked Mrs. Delaney to send the boy to her.

"He's gone, missus. Left right after he finished the chores. Worked like a little Trojan, he did, then off he went. The doctor inquired about him, too, but the lad was gone by then."

Delia wasn't surprised. No doubt if they'd given the boy some work to do the previous night, he would have left as soon as he felt he'd earned his supper. She understood his need to control his own destiny and felt a little envious of his resolve. But independence had always been easier for a boy than for a girl.

"I'll fetch some of me own lad's clothes he's outgrown when I go home this afternoon," Mrs. Delaney added, "if you think Danny will be back?"

"Thank you, that's kind of you," Delia said. "I expect we'll see Danny again at the theater."

When Danny appeared at her dressing room door that evening, he made no mention of his abrupt departure from her house and simply asked if he should begin by shining her shoes.

She decided not to interrogate him, although she did wonder if he'd overheard Joe suggesting a medical examination and that had caused him to shy away. In any case, it was important to allow the boy to preserve his pride, for he had nothing else.

As usual, she sent him to bring a hot pie during intermission. When he returned he said, "A woman stopped me on the street and told me to tell you Min . . . Minnie something wanted to see you."

"Minnie? I don't know . . ." The boy's fumbling with the name brought realization then. "Oh! Mignon! Did she say her name was Mignon?"

"Yeah, that's it. What kinda name is that?"

Delia was already halfway through the door. "It's French. I'll be back in a moment. Eat the pie, Danny. I don't want it."

Chapter 30

*

The woman waiting in the shadows still bore some slight resemblance to the Mignon of old, but Delia was shocked to see her old friend clad in flashy clothes that were none too clean, and her features had acquired a hard look that was emphasized by face paint. Bright red lips being the badge of the prostitute, it seemed that Julian had been correct in his assumption that Mignon was still following the oldest profession. But to Delia there was a vast difference between the high-class girls of the Cajun Club and the pathetic creature that shyly whispered, "Thanks for seeing me, sugar. I was sceered you wouldn't."

Delia embraced her briefly but was glad when Mignon pulled away, as she reeked of cheap toilet water. "Let's go inside, Mignon, out of the cold. I have to go back on stage soon, but afterward we're going to have supper and talk all night long."

Mignon gave a mirthless chuckle. "Honey, I can't go in there with you. What would folks think?"

"I don't give a damn what people think. If I did, would I be wearing britches and a frock coat?"

They laughed together then, the ice broken, and Delia led Mignon past the wide-eyed doorman and into her dressing room.

Danny eyed Mignon knowingly, and Delia decided he was too worldly for his years. She said, "Mrs. Delaney has some chores for you at my house, Danny. Do you think you can find your way there?"

"Sure."

"Wait there until I get home. Don't leave, understand?"

"That doctor ain't gonna examine me," Danny said flatly.

"That doctor is my husband. Dr. Simmington to you. And

nobody is going to do anything to you without your permission. Now run along so I can talk to my friend."

After he left, Mignon sank wearily into a chair. "You collecting strays now, honey?"

"Like you used to do, you mean?"

"Why, sugar, you sure done come a long way since I found you on the balcony of the Club."

"The crossroads of my life, Mignon. But you know that. Tell me about yourself—where have you been? When did you come here? Why did you drop out of sight without letting me know where you were going?"

Mignon sighed. "Reckon after he passed over, Daddy Lou's nagging started to make sense. He used to say folks come together for different reasons—some of us are meant to stay and some are just passing through. He said we had to let you go, on account of you needed other people for the next stage of your life."

"The Van Courtlands," Delia said, frowning.

"Mr. Julian, he's still with you, ain't he?"

"Yes."

"Reckon if Daddy Lou was still here, he'd have told you to move on from him, too?"

"Yes, I suppose he would. From all of the Van Courtlands, as soon as I was able. But Julian handles all my business affairs nowadays, and besides, I do owe him a great deal."

Mignon was silent for a moment, and it seemed to Delia she was considering what to say next, or perhaps *if* to say anything else on the subject of the Van Courtlands. At length Mignon whispered, as if afraid she would be overheard, "He never told you the truth then, about who paid for your schooling and voice training?"

"He didn't have to. I always knew it was Hugo. When I first met Julian, he had only a small trust fund that barely covered his tailor's bills. Later, after he began to work in New York, he had a little money, but not enough to pay my expenses, too. Certainly not enough to take me to Europe."

Mignon was staring at her oddly, but at that moment there was a knock on the dressing room door and a voice called, "Two minutes, Cordelia."

"I have to go on. Do you want to wait here or come up front?"

"I'll wait here."

"Promise?"

Mignon nodded.

Delia almost collided with Julian as she left the dressing room.

"You'd better hurry. You'll miss your cue."

"Mignon's in there," Delia whispered. "Don't go in."

He muttered a curse.

"Julian, if she's gone when I come back, I swear I'll never speak to you again as long as I live."

"Don't believe a word she says."

What was he afraid that Mignon would tell her? Delia wondered as she stepped out into the glare of the footlights to thunderous applause.

Mignon was still waiting when Delia returned to her dressing room, but Julian was in the room with her, and Delia knew at once that he had been bullying her friend. Mignon seemed to have clenched her entire body into a defensive arc, huddling in the chair with a sequined purse clutched in front of her as if to ward off an attack. Delia knew only too well how Julian could reduce the strongest adversary to a quivering mass of nerves. She was surprised Mignon had not fled.

Julian said easily, "Here she is, Delia. I made sure she'd be waiting, just as you instructed."

Delia looked at Mignon. "What has he been telling you?"

Mignon's eyes darted past her to the door. "Nuthin', sugar. We was just talking 'bout how famous you are."

Delia whirled on Julian. "Damn you, I know what you've been up to. Get out. Go on, leave us."

Julian regarded her with a hooded gaze. "Take my advice and don't take her home to Dr. Joe. He might put up with a stray puppy following you home, but an alley cat? Never."

Delia raised her hand to slap his face, but he was too quick for her. He caught her wrist and held it. "You know better than to try that." Dropping her arm, he gave Mignon a penetrating glance before departing.

"I shouldn'ta come," Mignon said miserably.

"Yes, you should. Don't pay any attention to him. Come on, let's go."

*   *   *

Delia had forgotten that she asked Danny to wait at the house until Mrs. Delaney, her mouth agape at the sight of Mignon, told her, "The boyo worked so hard I feared he'd drop. I've run out of chores for him, missus."

"Put him to bed in the storeroom again," Delia said absently, eager to be alone with Mignon.

"Oh, he's gone. Left as soon as he finished the work."

Delia sighed. "Prepare the guest room, would you? Miss Chamond will be staying the night. And we'll have some tea and sandwiches in my sitting room."

"You shouldn'ta done that," Mignon whispered as she followed Delia up the stairs. "I can't stay here. Your husband—"

"This is my house, Mignon. I do as I please. Besides, Joe doesn't choose my friends for me any more than Julian does. Come on, let's sit by the fire."

Mignon perched on the edge of a chair, obviously having second thoughts about her visit.

"Forget whatever Julian told you, and I know he probably said something, because I'm so glad to see you again," Delia said. "We're going to send for your things, and you're going to stay with me as long as you like."

Mignon burst into tears.

Delia, who onstage could act out a variety of emotions ranging from hysteria to inconsolable grief, never knew how to respond to genuine distress. She felt uncomfortable in the presence of those who were unable to conceal their feelings since she herself rarely lost control, and then gave in only to anger, never to sadness. Only once had she allowed sadness to overwhelm her, and that had been when she learned her child was dead. She had replaced her grief with anger toward Julian and, finding anger easier to deal with than sadness, vowed to continue the practice.

To try to distract Mignon, she handed her a handkerchief and asked, "Where are you working?"

Mignon sniffed and murmured the name of a well-known bordello. " 'Leastwise, I was working there. They kicked me out. I reckon some folks decided I should leave town."

"Julian, you mean? Mignon, if he threatened you, I swear—"

"No, honey, don't say nuthin' to him. He's right to protect you. Jes' like Daddy Lou done told him."

"Your great-grandfather was a wonderful man, Mignon. You must miss him. Did he really tell Julian to protect me? From what?"

"Why, from folks findin' out about him—'bout Daddy Lou. He knew if any rumors started that y'all had colored blood, it would ruin things for you, and it wouldn't make no never mind that you're fair as a magnolia blossom, 'cos folks speckerlate about throwbacks and all, and if'n anybody found out that he was paying for your education, they'da been convinced you was kin, no matter what you said."

Delia felt as though for an instant everything she remembered, all that had gone before, had rushed away, and when it returned the pieces of her life had assumed subtly different shapes. In one blinding instant of revelation she saw what should have been clear to her all along.

Gripping the arms of her chair, she whispered, "*Daddy Lou* paid for the school in Philadelphia. Not the Van Courtlands?"

Mignon snorted indelicately. "Daddy Lou paid for *everything* you got, honey. Your clothes and train fares—everything. All them Van Courtlands ever done was to have you over to the Willows once in a while, so's that fancy school would think that was where you'd come from."

Delia leaned back in her chair, feeling weighted down by the sudden knowledge, still unsure what it all meant, either to her past or her future. "But how—why—"

"You wasn't supposed to know, honey. Nobody was. I didn't find out myself until after Daddy Lou passed over. Well, I didn't exactly find out. Thad did."

"Thad knew—and you knew—and neither of you told me." Delia felt a stab of hurt that, for the moment, was easier to deal with than all the unanswered questions.

"Sugar, until this very minute, I ain't seen you since I found out. And maybe I wouldn't be tellin' you now if'n Julian hadn't got himself in such an uproar about it. I figured if he was so all-fire determined you never know who your sponsor really was, then maybe he was still making you pay him back. I didn't see no reason for you to go on being beholdin' to the Van Courtlands all of your life. I reckoned he shoulda told you the truth by now and let you off the hook."

Mrs. Delaney arrived with a tray, but Mignon shook her head when Delia offered her a plate of sandwiches. "I'd rather have a drink."

Since Mignon looked tense and possibly on the verge of maudlin tears, Delia decided sherry wine would be less likely than anything stronger to ruin their conversation. She poured two glasses and handed one to Mignon, which she promptly drained.

"What a sacrifice Daddy Lou made," Delia mused. "How could he afford it? And what about you, surely he must have deprived you to help me. How did it all come about, Mignon?"

Mignon bit her lip. "You mustn't blame yourself for things not going right between the old man and me, honey. We was at odds long afore you came along. He didn't like me working at the Cajun Club and I was too stubborn and foolish to listen to him. There was a man—ain't there always? He got me into the life, and I was too dumb to realize he didn't care about me. Oh, he was long gone by the time I met you, but me and Daddy Lou, we just couldn't see eye to eye ever again. I never knew he had money put away—saved up from the days he played his horn on the gamblin' boats—so I never counted on no inheritance."

"Mignon, I feel like a thief. I stole what belonged to you. How can I ever make it up to you?"

"Don't talk like that! I didn't come to tell you this because I want anything from you, Delia. Lordy, don't think that, please! I just don't want them Van Courtlands sucking the life blood out of you. When I read about Julian being your manager, I knew I had to get me to 'Frisco and tell you the truth. Then when I came to the theater and he was here, lookin' at me with those Van Courtland eyes that go right through you—I lost my nerve. But when he went to the madam at the house and had her throw me out of the house . . . leastways I figure it was him . . . I knew I had to come back and tell you before I left town. And tonight, while you was onstage, he walks into your dressing room and looks me straight in the eye and says, 'You know, don't you?' and I was too scared to say anything, and he says, 'You'd better keep your mouth shut, or you could wind up in an unmarked grave, too.' "

Delia's mouth was dry. "What did he mean?"

Mignon's eyes were wide and frightened. "Have you seen or heard from Thad in all these years?"

Delia's hand crept to her throat. "No. But Julian swore to me he didn't know what had become of Thad. He said he'd hired a Pinkerton to try to find him. Besides—I can't believe even Julian is capable of murder—and surely the stakes weren't high enough."

"Honey, all I know is what I heard."

"Tell me everything you remember, Mignon. When did you first find out Daddy Lou was paying my way?"

"It was when Thad came back from Europe because the pastor at Eulie's church had written him 'bout that voodoo woman, Abebe, moving into the house."

"I often wondered why you moved out—you left even before your great-grandfather died. I know because I went to see you, and Daddy Lou said you'd gone. I didn't know you were living in the Quarter—I only found that out from Thad later."

"We had a falling-out, the old man and me. Same old quarrel 'bout me working at the Cajun Club. He said he was going to give the house to Eulie when he died, so I never went back, not until he was on his deathbed. Thad came back after the voodoo woman moved in with his ma, and he asked me if there'd been a proper will and a deed—'cause he was trying to find out how Abebe came to be there. I didn't know, so Thad started poking 'round looking. That was when he found all the bills for your schooling and clothes and traveling that Julian Van Courtland sent to Daddy Lou and he paid. Thad said he showed the bills to Eulie and asked her if she knew about them, and she said she'd overhead Daddy Lou and Julian Van Courtland strike a bargain."

Delia listened silently as Mignon related the story, and filtered as it was through Eulie to Thad and then to Mignon, Delia could see how it all came about.

Daddy Lou had been convinced Delia saved his life—first by preventing the cottonmouth from biting him, then by going for help when he was trapped under the icebox during the hurricane. After the funeral of the Van Courtlands' butler, Julian had gone to Daddy Lou to invite Delia to sing at the Willows. When it was apparent Julian was interested in helping Delia but did not have the means to do so, Daddy Lou saw a way to repay her for saving his life. Eulie overheard the old man make Julian promise to protect Delia, to see to it that she received the proper education and voice training, and to make certain no one ever learned that an old black jazz musician was her actual benefactor. Afterward, Eulie had confronted Daddy Lou, and to buy her silence, also, he promised that when he died she would inherit his house.

Mignon finished, "Thad came to tell me what he'd found out. He asked me if I wanted to try to get the house away from his mother and Abebe, because he hadn't found any will, or any transfer of deed. I said I'd have to think about it. Tell you the truth, I was scared of what that ole voodoo woman might do to me if I crossed her. Then I asked Thad what he was going to do, and he said he didn't know yet. That was the last time I saw him."

"I went to see Eulie a couple of times," Delia said. "The last time she didn't know me. She was muttering and mumbling and made no sense."

Mignon nodded. "She was out of her head for a couple of years before she died."

"I didn't know she had died. If Thad didn't go to her funeral, I suppose he must be dead, too. God, I wish I knew what happened to him. I still can't believe Julian would go that far."

"Honey, it weren't just a case of you being friendly with darkies—everybody knew Thad loved you, and you know what kind of a sin that is. More'n enough reason to lynch him, that's what Julian and his kind would think."

"Thad and I were just friends. Penfriends, actually. Why does everyone find that so hard to believe?"

Mignon shrugged. "Whatever you say, honey."

Delia stood up and walked around the room. "Everything has changed, and nothing has changed. What shall I do now? Fire Julian and try to find another business manager? I'd be cutting off my nose to spite my face. Besides, the financial backing notwithstanding, Julian is, after all, the one person who prodded and urged and bullied me and yes, stood by me every minute, and I doubt I'd be where I am today without him. I guess his only real crime is that he never told me the truth about Daddy Lou."

Mignon looked at her dubiously. "If'n he didn't do nothing to Thad you mean."

"Yes," Delia agreed, biting her lip.

"Honey, I'd best be leaving. Y'all can sleep on it and decide what you want to do in the morning."

"You're staying the night," Delia said firmly. "No arguments. Come on, I'll show you your room."

Delia awoke earlier than usual the following morning, and when she went downstairs her husband was still sitting at the breakfast table, reading the newspaper.

Joe lowered the paper and said, "Good morning. You're up early." He paused, his eyes alert behind his gold-rimmed spectacles. "I didn't disturb you when I came home last night because Mrs. Delaney said you had a visitor."

"Mignon Chamond—she's an old friend." Delia poured herself a cup of coffee and sat down.

"Our housekeeper seemed to think you'd brought home a lady of the evening."

"She was quite correct. Mignon was recently kicked out of one of the finest bordellos in town. She's still an old friend."

"Delia, far be it for me to censure you, but first the boy and now this. I hope this isn't going to become a habit. I really can't condone you bringing such a person into our home. I trust she'll be leaving forthwith?"

"Mignon took me in when I was all alone in the world, and no, dammit, she will not be leaving forthwith. In fact, I'm thinking of asking her to be my dresser. Mrs. Voss quit because of Danny."

"Do you think that's wise? It's been my experience that women who tread the primrose path rarely reform."

Delia was no longer listening. She had picked up a section of the newspaper and now said, "Caruso is coming to San Francisco. He'll lead the Metropolitan Opera Company in a tour across the country and perform at the Grand Opera House here."

Joe, an opera lover, caught his breath. "Delia, if only you could sing a duet with the great Caruso! My Lord, what an occasion that would be!"

"Apart from the fact that Julian canceled my booking with the Grand Opera House somewhat abruptly when he opened his Music Theater and we're persona non grata there, I've heard that the great tenor is impossibly temperamental."

"Ah, but what a voice!"

"I'll ask Julian to get tickets for opening night for us. I can't see myself competing with Enrico Caruso for an audience that night." She paused. "Besides, I'm thinking of leaving on another tour."

"When did you make that decision? Or is Julian angry about our marriage and wants to separate us so you can reconsider? He must know it would be impossible for me to leave just now. He's aware that I'm in the middle of a battle with the Board of Health."

"He is? When did you talk to him? And what battle is that? You never mentioned it to me."

"Julian owns some property in Chinatown that would be affected by the plans I'm hoping the board will implement."

Delia looked away. They were both aware of the rumors that Julian had an Asian mistress. She had asked him about his property in Chinatown, and he'd said offhandedly that he'd invested in a couple of lodging houses. She said lightly, "I expect he's afraid that whatever your plans are, they will affect his pocketbook."

Joe's brows knitted. "I wish you'd talk to him about the suggestions I made for the work that needs to be done on his property—indeed, on most of Chinatown."

"What work? And what has it to do with the Board of Health or, for that matter, you?"

"I don't want to worry you—"

"Joe!" Delia warned in a tone not to be deterred.

"I treated a case of plague a few weeks ago," he answered heavily, "and I suspect it wasn't an isolated case."

"My God! Not bubonic plague?"

He nodded. "The mayor and city council have gone to extraordinary lengths to cover it up, or pass it off as what they call an Oriental or rice-eater's disease—that is, confined to Chinatown, but the case I saw was a white clerk living near Telegraph Hill."

"How bad is it?"

"I believe our worst problem is convincing people of the threat. A Federal health inspector was arrested and the mayor even tried to remove two Board of Health members from office for stating we had the plague in the state, so you can see what we're up against. But we must act soon or we'll have an epidemic on our hands."

"But how did it get here?"

"From what I've learned, it was first seen in Chinatown in 1900—probably brought in by rats on the ships coming from either Canton or Hong Kong, where a pandemic had killed more than a hundred thousand people."

"Joe, you'd better be careful in your dealings with City Hall. Julian says the graft and corruption in this city are unbelievable."

"Nevertheless, I must warn them we are all in the gravest danger. We must trap and poison the rats and destroy the places that harbor them. We must get the landlords—like Julian—to pave basements and fill the spaces under the tumbledown shacks with concrete, or even tear down the structures if the problem can't be solved any other way. If Julian wants to take you on tour, he might be hoping I'll go with you, but I simply can't leave now."

"Actually he doesn't even know of my plans yet, I haven't talked to him, and as far as you are concerned, I certainly don't expect you to accompany me. I'm going home to Louisiana and frankly would prefer to go without you."

He considered this silently for a moment. "I take it the arrival of your friend Mignon had something to do with that decision?"

"Yes." Delia saw no reason to elaborate. She put down the paper and picked up the coffeepot and a cup. "I'm going upstairs to see if Mignon's awake. I'll see you this evening."

Her husband's cheek, beneath her perfunctory kiss, felt as though he were clenching his jaw.

Mignon was awake, and when Delia explained about her need for a dresser and offered her the job, Mignon hesitated, obviously reluctant to accept.

"I'm planning a trip to New Orleans, Mignon. You could come with me. See all your old friends . . . make a new start."

A tear welled up in Mignon's dark eyes. "Oh, sugar, I gits so homesick sometimes. But . . . y'all didn't jes' decide to go on account of what I told you last night, did you, honey?"

"No," Delia lied. "I've been planning a tour for some time. You'll find all the clothes you need in my closet. I hardly ever wear dresses, so just help yourself." There was no need to point out that the clothes Mignon had worn in a bordello should be left behind. "You can stay here until you find a place."

"Oh, I'll move on out today," Mignon said hastily.

"In that case, here's an advance on your salary." Ignoring Mignon's protests, Delia opened her purse and placed several bills on the dresser. "I've got to go now, Mignon. I have a bone to pick with my manager."

Delia walked into Julian's office on the second floor of the Music Theater. He had bought the theater with several partners a year earlier and transformed it into a glittering palace that in opulence rivaled the newly refurbished Grand Opera House.

He was dictating a letter to his secretary, a nervous young man who jumped to his feet the moment Delia appeared, then tripped in his haste to leave the room.

Julian regarded her quizzically. "You seem to be making a habit of getting up early."

She leaned on his desk, palms flat. "I have a great urge to strike you, Julian."

His black eyebrows arched slightly. "So? You frequently have such urges."

"Why didn't you tell me it was Daddy Lou who paid my way through school?"

Julian rarely showed any reaction to any abrupt announcement, and he didn't now. He answered in a disinterested tone, "Apart from the fact that he didn't want you to know who your benefactor was, we agreed—he and I—that it was not in the best interests of your career to be open about the arrangement."

"But after he died—after I was no longer receiving his financial support—why didn't you tell me then? Dammit, Julian, you kept me in . . . in"—she fumbled for a word—"involuntary servitude."

He laughed. "Oh, come on. I guided your musical training and got your career off on the right track. I also managed all of your affairs, sparing you the mundane details of all the negotiations, and making sure that your earnings were invested wisely for your old age. You are a wealthy woman, thanks to me, and you've never had to deal with the sharks and charlatans of either the theatrical or the business world."

"You should have told me."

"And if I had, you'd have gone off on some tangent. I suppose Mignon told you? I knew I should have got rid of her when she first showed up on our doorstep."

"Like you got rid of Thad, you mean?"

His eyes narrowed. "What the hell do you mean by that?"

"Didn't you ask Mignon if she wanted to end up in an unmarked grave, too?"

Julian stood up and walked to the door. He glanced up and down the corridor outside his office, then closed the door. "I wish you'd be more careful about your conversation here. Couldn't this have waited for a more private place?"

"No, it couldn't. What about Thad? Is he dead? Did you have him killed?"

"Don't be a fool, Delia. Why would any sane man do such a thing? What would I have gained? But I do think there's a good possibility that somebody decided to remove an uppity nigger."

The telephone on his desk rang shrilly and Delia jumped. Julian picked up the receiver and said, "I'll call you back."

Delia lowered herself carefully into a chair, her mind racing. Julian had said *no sane man would do such a thing*. Her eyes met Julian's, and what she saw there caused her stomach to lurch. "What are you implying, Julian?"

"Did you tell Thad you were expecting a child?"

"No. Of course not."

"Somebody did. He went to the Willows—during the time you were hiding in New York, the last three months before you gave birth."

Delia's throat was dry. "Marcus . . . he saw Marcus?"

"I can't be sure. My mother swore Marcus had locked himself in his room at the time, but she would have lied to protect him. If Thad made a scene at the Willows—accusing one of us of impregnating you—it's entirely possible that Marcus, in the heat of the moment, would have shut his mouth permanently." Julian paused, then added grimly, "I might have done the same thing myself had I been there."

Delia straightened up. "I'm going to New Orleans. Make arrangements to end my run here, and as soon as I can break free, I'm leaving. You can say I'm going on another tour if you wish."

Julian was silent for a moment. "If you intend to confront Marcus, I'd better go with you."

She was about to retort that she didn't need him, but the steely resolve in his eyes warned her it would be useless. He added, "Leave the good doctor at home, Delia. He bores me."

"With his concerns about your rat-infested properties in Chinatown, you mean?"

"Ah, so he told you. Your husband sees himself as some sort of latter-day Pied Piper. Still, for your information, I believe he's right about the threat of bubonic plague. In fact, I'm in the process of selling the Chinatown properties."

"Oh? That will be make it difficult for you to visit your Chinese mistress, won't it?"

"Do I detect a note of jealousy?"

"Don't be a fool."

"Delia, oh, Delia," he murmured mockingly. "What a hypocrite you are. You're filled with outrage that I would associate with an Oriental woman, even as you make plans to go looking for your Negro—"

But Delia was already on her way out.

Chapter 31

*

The day had been unseasonably hot for April, and Delia was not particularly looking forward to the going-away party planned in her honor at the Palace Hotel that night, especially since the great tenor Enrico Caruso was staying at the hotel but had refused an invitation to attend the party.

"I didn't expect him to come," Julian remarked. "He's opening tonight in *Carmen*, and certainly expects his own celebration afterward."

"I heard he was angry at the manners of the audience at the Opera House last night and stalked out before the final curtain."

"From all accounts *The Queen of Sheba* was a spiritless performance. Most people feel the Metropolitan Opera Company's season really begins tonight. But apart from Caruso's feelings about ill-mannered San Franciscans, he's worried about the eruption of Mount Vesuvius. Apparently he was born in its shadow."

Delia fanned herself with a theater program. "I read that two thousand have died, thousands are homeless, and the lava flow is threatening Naples. Have we contributed to the relief fund?"

"Of course. Caruso has offered to give a charity performance to aid the relief effort. He told one reporter that a volcano is the most frightening experience of all, and the reporter asked if it was worse than an earthquake. Caruso said he'd never been in an earthquake, but he doubted it held more terror than an erupting volcano."

"If he stays here for any length of time he'll certainly be able to compare the two. By the way, I don't intend to stay long at the party tonight."

Julian shrugged. "Suit yourself, but then, you always do. I

hear you booked a Pullman for Mignon tomorrow, so I take
it she is going with us? I'm surprised you aren't taking the
boy, too."

"No one takes Danny anywhere, but Mrs. Delaney has
promised to keep an eye on him."

To her surprise, the party proved to be more enjoyable than
Delia had anticipated. The Palace Hotel was not only luxurious, but had been built with the two great natural hazards native to San Francisco in mind. To guard against earthquakes
the hotel was built on pillar foundations twelve feet deep, and
the walls were reinforced with iron bands. Fire precautions
were also thorough, since in the city's short history there had
been numerous disastrous blazes. If the city's reservoirs ran
dry, the Palace had its own tanks in the basement and on the
roof, high pressure pumps, piping, fire detectors in each
room, and a team of patrolling watchmen helped reassure
even the most nervous guests, especially Caruso, who was
not convinced of his safety in what he felt was the Wild
West. It was said that if the Palace ever burned down, the city
itself would be lost.

With champagne flowing freely, music, dancing and sparkling conversation whirling around her, and everyone lament-
ing her departure, Delia suddenly realized that she was going
to miss San Francisco. Not that she was leaving for good, but
her plans for the future were vague, depending upon what she
learned in Louisiana.

Somewhere in the back of her mind lurked the thought that
if she learned Thad had indeed been killed by or on the instructions of Marcus Van Courtland, then she would see justice was done, no matter how long it took. Although Julian
had announced to the press that she was going on tour, no
bookings for any performances had been made. She suspected
that Julian, like herself, was going to wait and see what happened.

Delia had decided to dress for the occasion, and she felt
admiring eyes follow her as she swept out onto the dance
floor in her white chiffon gown with its tight waist and floating panels that whispered about her slim figure like drifting
clouds. Mignon had even managed to weave tiny white daisies into Delia's short hair and persuaded her to wear the di-

amond necklace that Julian had insisted upon giving her after her first performance at his Music Theater.

Only Julian seemed oblivious to her charms as he circulated among the guests, paying particular attention to the most influential men in the city, especially those who could further his various enterprises. Since Julian now owned a great deal of property in San Francisco, he felt it behooved him to cultivate the goodwill of politicians and city officials.

Delia's husband, although he was exhausted from a long day, was also clearly dazzled by her, and his eyes followed her every second. About two o'clock, however, Joe tapped her on the arm and said, "I'm afraid if I don't retire soon I shall disgrace myself by falling asleep on my feet. Would you mind if I went home? Perhaps Julian could bring you along later?"

Delia smiled at him fondly. Joe would never suggest that she should leave with him, and for the thousandth time she reminded herself how glad she was that she had such an understanding husband. "Good night, Joe. I'll see you before I leave tomorrow."

She watched him make his way through the crowd, his shoulders slightly drooping, his steps weary, and she felt a pang of guilt as she realized she had danced with him only once and would be leaving him the following day for an indefinite period. She was about to follow him to at least give him a good night kiss, when a tall, thin man with hawklike features stepped into her path. He asked, "Do I dare assume you don't have a partner for the next waltz, and if so, may I make so bold?"

He was unfamiliar to her. Probably one of Julian's business acquaintances, she decided.

As if reading her mind, he bowed slightly and said, "Latimer. Oscar Latimer. We haven't been formally introduced."

The name sounded vaguely familiar. "I'll have to check my dance card," Delia began, then remembered where she had seen the name Latimer before. She glared at him. "How did you get in here? I thought the doorman had strict instructions to keep out vermin and reporters."

He grinned. "I see you read my piece. Do I dare assume that my criticism of your mode of dress influenced your appearance tonight? You look stunning in that gown, Cordelia.

Why would a woman with your looks ever don men's clothes?"

"Will you leave of your own volition, or shall I call for a doorman?"

"Come on, Cordelia, at least give me a hint about what this so-called tour of yours is all about. I've checked, you aren't booked to appear *anywhere*."

Delia looked around, but Julian had already seen Latimer and was making his way rapidly toward her. The reporter, evidently deciding that discretion was the better part of valor, hastily retreated. Julian, clearly angry, followed him.

When Julian returned a few minutes later, he said, "I don't know how the hell Latimer got in, but he's gone now. What did he say to you?"

"He'd checked and learned I'm not booked to perform anywhere."

"I doubt he'll follow us across the country." Julian took her arm and slipped it through his. "Come on, they're playing my favorite waltz, and I see your husband has deserted you. Past his bedtime, I expect."

"Joe puts in a day's work before you even get out of bed in the morning," Delia retorted, but allowed herself to be led onto the floor.

Julian was an accomplished dancer, and she relaxed in his arms, enjoying the exhilarating movement and the familiar strains of *The Blue Danube*. When the waltz ended, Julian guided her to a chair and asked if she would like a glass of champagne.

She shook her head, feeling an inexplicable wave of sadness. He looked at her sharply. "What is it? Did Latimer say anything else?"

"No. I don't know what ails me tonight. Everyone is being so sweet to me, and I really am enjoying the party, but . . . I feel vaguely apprehensive. I can't get rid of a disturbing premonition that everything is coming to an end."

"Then let's cancel the trip to New Orleans. It isn't too late. Delia, think about it carefully, do you really want to know what happened back there six years ago? Perhaps it would be better to let sleeping dogs lie."

"No . . ." she said slowly. "I need to know the truth. But, well, if I were superstitious I'd really be on edge. I had a nightmare last night that I was enveloped in a great billowing black cloud and I couldn't see a thing—"

"Probably had a blanket wrapped over your face."

Ignoring him, Delia went on, "But I could hear people crying and horses screaming and dogs barking. Then on the way over here this evening . . ."

"I suppose the good doctor brought you in his carriage? When is he going to move into the twentieth century and buy a car?"

Delia wasn't listening to him. "Just as we left the house, one of our horses screamed, for no apparent reason, and Joe had a terrible time coaxing it to move. I don't know if it was the horse's cry, but instantly it seemed that dozens of dogs began to bark and howl. It was all very eerie."

"You definitely need more champagne. I'll get you some. If you have a monumental hangover tomorrow, you can sleep all day on the train."

Several times during the following three hours Delia considered asking Julian to take her home, but she was reluctant to break up the party. A disturbing premonition persisted that when the last goodbyes were uttered, the fairy tale would end.

The guests had dwindled to a handful, and yawning waiters and musicians eyed her hopefully as dawn approached.

She had just asked Julian the time, and he pulled out his pocket watch and answered, "Twelve minutes past five," when a faraway rumble, growing louder like an approaching freight train, caused everyone to stop what they were doing and look around, seeking its source.

In less than a second the great roar thundered across the Bay from the north and obliterated every other sound in the city.

Overhead the chandeliers swayed and rattled, pictures crashed from walls, and furniture skittered across the floor. Guests reeled drunkenly, clutching at one another to try to keep their balance.

Delia felt the floor heave under her feet. The polished parquet writhed horizontally, as if in the jaws of some mythic beast determined to shake the hotel from its foundations.

Then the floor seemed to slip away, and the next second she was flat on her face, glued to the parquet by an unseen vacuum. The deafening sound continued, and she felt Julian's hand scrabble toward her and seize her wrist as he attempted to crawl on his hands and knees to where she lay.

The giant temblor lasted some thirty seconds, and then, as suddenly as it had hit, quieted itself. An eerie silence gripped the now still hotel.

Julian leaped to his feet, dragging her with him. She broke free of his grasp and ran. Julian followed, steps behind her.

He caught her as she reached the lobby, stopping her just before she plunged out into the street. At that moment the second temblor, equally ferocious, hit.

Julian pulled her under the doorway and wrapped his arms around her as the earth heaved again. Panting, Delia clung to him as the cobblestone street outside undulated in three-foot waves.

She screamed, "Julian, we've got to get out! We'll be buried alive." She struggled, but he held her tightly.

"We're safer here," Julian hissed in her ear. "The Palace is built like a fortress. Out there we could be hit by falling bricks or caught under a collapsing wall."

Terrified, she buried her face in his chest, amazed that he somehow had braced his back against the doorway and remained standing as the earth continued its mad dance of destruction and the deafening roar assaulted their senses.

Then the frenzied shaking began to subside and the roaring gradually faded. There were several spasmodic twists as the final fury of the earthquake was spent, then the spring morning was quiet.

The silver light of the rising sun, filtered through rolling clouds of dust, crept along the ravaged city streets. A moment later the silence was broken by the babble of voices, excited, terrified, some crying out in pain, others calling for loved ones. Worst of all were the thin cries for help, from those buried under the rubble of collapsed buildings.

Stunned, Delia stared up at Julian. "I must get to my house."

"You can't go wandering about the city. I doubt many buildings are still standing, and the streets will be filled with debris. You'll be safer here at the Palace. I'll go and find out if the trains are still running."

"We can't just leave," Delia protested.

"Why not? We can buy whatever we need en route. Look, Delia, a quake that strong is going to generate numerous aftershocks, and with buckled roads and fallen buildings and God knows what else this city is going to have to contend with—martial law probably—life here is going to be unbearable. We have to get out any way we can."

"But there are people I care about—I must know they are all right. Joe, and Mignon and Danny, and—perhaps we could call my house and then the theater?"

Julian's mouth twisted into a grin. "You don't really think the phones are still working, do you? And nobody's going to be at the theater at this time of the morning. Look, you wait here, I'll try to get to Nob Hill and see how the doc is doing, then come back for you."

"I'm going, too. Don't try to stop me."

He sighed. "Very well. I'll try to find your wrap."

"No time for that, come on."

Frightened people were now spilling out onto the street, many clad in nightclothes, and, joining them, Delia was appalled by the havoc wreaked by the earthquake, which she estimated had lasted only seventy seconds or so, including the ten-second lull.

Fighting their way through the crowd, Julian cursed her foolishness for not staying in the well-built and practically fireproof Palace Hotel, as already spires of smoke were rising above the ruined skyline and the hiss of escaping gas warned that fire might be a greater danger than the earthquake.

There was no sign of his new four cylinder Oldsmobile, which was either buried in the rubble or had already been appropriated by someone else, so they set off on foot, detouring around piles of bricks and the splintered glass of broken storefronts, stepping over fallen lampposts.

Everywhere there were tumbled walls and grotesquely leaning buildings. It seemed every chimney in the city had toppled. There were great fissures in some of the buckled streets, and the cable-car rails were twisted and useless.

The City Hall, which had taken twenty years to complete, had been destroyed in seconds. They looked up to see its dome suspended on a skeletal frame of girders.

Their progress was slow through the hundreds of people

clogging the streets. They had to duck under sagging electric lines and walk carefully over split cobblestones.

A fire engine, pulled by two white horses, came flying toward them, and Delia saw that clouds of black smoke were blotting out the rising sun.

Several torturous blocks later they came upon a group of firemen beating out the flames of a ground-floor building with blankets and jackets, their hoses lying useless on the ground because the water mains were broken.

Julian watched the spreading smoke with growing concern. "This is a waste of time. We're hardly making any progress at all. We'd be better off going to the Ferry Building. I expect the ferries are still running. The smoke and dust are bad for your throat. Let's get out of the city while we still can."

"No. I won't leave until I know Joe is all right. You do as you please, I'm going to my house."

At the next corner a man was harnessing a horse to a dilapidated cart. Julian walked up to him. "I'll give you a thousand dollars for your horse and cart."

The man didn't hesitate. "Done."

Delia watched in silent amazement as Julian whipped out his wallet and a checkbook. "Two hundred dollars cash and a check drawn on Wells Fargo Bank for the rest." The man nodded, accepted the payment, and handed Julian the reins.

As he helped her climb onto the cart, she reflected briefly that, despite all his other faults, Julian was resourceful and cool-headed in a crisis. She was glad he was at her side.

The ride to Nob Hill was a hair-raising journey through crowds of refugees, past buildings either demolished or knocked askew, turning back when streets were impassable. Julian drove the sweating horse relentlessly, and Delia could only hang on to the splintered cart and pray as she had not prayed since she was a child.

At the crest of the hill Julian reined the horse and Delia jumped out. She looked down at the tumbled walls of the downtown district spread below. Surely only the Palace Hotel remained unscathed, its flag still flying bravely.

Julian gripped her arm and pointed to an ominous column of black smoke rising to the southeast. "Look at that—and see, there are smaller plumes of smoke everywhere. The fire brigade can't possibly contain so many blazes with the water mains knocked out, and when they join up, the entire city is going to burn. Let's get your husband and get the hell out of here. There's no time to lose."

Delia ran to her house, which from the outside appeared to have sustained little damage. But the front door was jammed in a twisted frame, and Julian had to put his shoulder to it. Inside a crystal chandelier had crashed to the marble entry hall, shattering into a million pieces. Several pieces of furniture were overturned or out of place, and ceiling plaster coated everything.

"Joe!" Delia called, picking up her skirts to step over the broken crystal. "Joe, are you here?"

Mrs. Delaney peered out from beneath the staircase. "Is it over? Holy Mother, I thought the world had come to an end. The doctor told me I'd be safe under the stairs, and I was afeared to come out."

"Where is he, Mrs. Delaney?"

"Why, he went downtown. Soon as the earth stopped shaking, he picks up his black bag and climbs into the buggy and off he goes without so much as a bite to eat. He says there'll be hurt people needing help. A saint that man is, I tell you."

"Did he leave a message for me?"

"He said you was with Mr. Julian and planned to leave today, so no doubt the two of you would be on your way. He said you'd be safe enough at the Palace Hotel and Mr. Julian would get you out of the city all right."

"You see?" Julian said. "We could have saved ourselves a futile trip. Now we're going to have to fight our way back through those clogged streets with fires spreading in every direction."

"It's after worrying I am about me husband and boy," her housekeeper said. "I'd no sooner got here than the earthquake struck. The doctor wanted to take me along with him, but I was sure me husband would come for me, only he didn't."

"I'll go and change clothes," Delia said, "and then we'll take you home."

"Mrs. Delaney, why don't you go and pack us some sandwiches while you're waiting?" Julian said. "And see if you can find any bottles for water to carry with us."

"Shall I make you some ham and eggs, sir?" Mrs. Delaney asked, ever the conscientious servant.

"No. I'm going to turn off the gas at the main, just in case."

Delia ran up to her room and changed into trousers and a shirt. She slipped on socks and boots, then picked up a jacket and, as an afterthought, jammed a hat over the wilting daisies in her hair. Into the pockets of her jacket she stuffed a change of underwear, a handkerchief, toothbrush, comb, and—she wasn't sure why—a small bottle of eau de cologne.

Downstairs, Julian was carrying bottles of water out to the cart. Mrs. Delaney, looking more relaxed now that she had something to do, came from the kitchen carrying a formidable package of sandwiches, a wedge of cheese, and a fruitcake. The two women followed Julian outside. The horse was nibbling daintily on the privet hedge. Julian filled a bucket with water and the animal drank thirstily.

By the time they set off down the hill, they could hear explosions in the city below, and Julian said, "They're dynamiting buildings to try to stop the fires from spreading."

When they reached the street where Mrs. Delaney lived, she gave a cry of fear as she saw that the row of wooden houses were tilted at crazy angles and several had collapsed. A fire hydrant had snapped and shot water forty feet into the air. Julian tossed the reins to Delia, jumped from the cart, and turned off the valve.

The street was filled with people, many of the men digging in the rubble while the women wandered about carrying prized possessions or attempting to comfort frightened children. Near where Julian had reined the horse, some men were frantically tossing aside planks from a completely destroyed house. A child was crying piteously beneath the debris. Julian ran to help, picking up a formidably heavy door and heaving it aside.

Delia watched for only a split second as Mrs. Delaney clutched her arm and pointed. "Oh, Holy Mother of God, look at me house!" It, too, was a pile of rubble.

"Come on," Delia said, helping her housekeeper out of the cart. "Your husband and son are probably here somewhere." She hoped her voice carried more conviction than she felt.

The two women were quickly swallowed by the milling crowd of bewildered and frightened people.

Mrs. Delaney ran to one after another of her neighbors to

inquire if they'd seen her husband and son. When they reached the ruins of her house, she screamed, "Sure and they're dead and buried in the rubble, oh, dear God!"

Before Delia could stop her, Mrs. Delaney scrambled into the debris, which was shifting precariously, calling for her husband and son. Delia plunged after her, grabbed her arm, and pulled her back. "Wait—don't disturb anything until we get help."

Something touched Delia's leg, and she looked down to see a bedraggled and dusty puppy trying to climb onto her shoe. She bent and picked up the little dog. Almost simultaneously two dust-covered figures materialized out of the dust cloaking the street, calling to Mrs. Delaney that they were safe.

Anxious to find her own husband, Delia watched the Delaneys' tearful reunion impatiently. At length she said, "We can all get into the cart. We can either take you to my house, or if you want to get out of the city, you can come with us. But I must warn you that we're going downtown to my husband's clinic first."

They made their way back to the corner of the street, arriving just in time to see Julian lift a small child from the rubble and hand her to a weeping woman.

Catching sight of Delia, he made his way to her. "Where is the horse and cart?"

Delia looked around with growing dismay. There was no sign of the horse or the cart. "Oh, no! I should have stayed with it. I'm sorry, Julian, I didn't think." She turned to her housekeeper. "I guess we can't give you a ride after all."

"We'll be all right," Mrs. Delaney said. "We're alive, that's the main thing."

"Are you still determined to find your husband?" Julian asked.

"Yes, of course. His clinic isn't that far from here. I can walk. You don't have to come."

"Put down the pup, Delia, and let's go. We'll be lucky to make it before all of the downtown area burns to the ground."

She put the squirming puppy into the arms of Mrs. Delaney's son, who immediately forgot the devastation around him and began to play with his new friend. Delia looked at Mrs. Delaney. "Are you sure you'll be all right? If you need anything—"

"Go on, be off with you, go find your husband."

Once again they set off on foot through the swarming refugees.

Firemen raced from building to building, attempting to head off the approaching fires, or clear threatened buildings of rescue workers. They used any available weapon against the blazes, emptying cisterns, pumping sewage through their hoses, even dumping wine on the flames. They cursed the useless hydrants and stared helplessly as three different fires linked together and a wall of flames roared unchecked through the downtown streets.

Soldiers were on the scene now, and with the police they attempted to guide the hordes of fleeing citizens toward safety.

"We're going against the tide," Julian said. "We're never going to get through."

Delia ignored him, plodding resolutely on through the smoky confusion.

Just before they reached the clinic, they saw a man come out of a store, laden with merchandise.

"Damn looters." Julian had hardly got the words out of his mouth than a shot rang out and the man fell, spilling his goods in the street. Nearby a soldier lowered his rifle.

Delia was too numbed by the horror of the day to react, but later it occurred to her that the man possibly could have been the owner of the store attempting to salvage his own goods.

As they approached the clinic, she saw that the doors gaped open and there was no sign of anyone inside. A fireman came running down the street, yelling, "I thought I told you to get out—the street behind us is on fire."

At that moment the flames roared up over the roof, and Julian grabbed her and pulled her back. They ran with the fireman as the fire exploded across the street behind them and sparks flew all around. When they reached the corner Delia clutched the fireman's arm and asked hoarsely, "The doctor—Dr. Joe—do you know where he went?"

"To the hospital," was the curt reply before the man dashed off.

"But we passed the Emergency Hospital on our way to Nob Hill," Delia said to Julian. "It was in ruins."

"Are you ready to give up now? Joe thinks you're on your way out of the city. What's the point of searching for him?"

Delia looked around wildly as the crush of terrified people caught them and they were carried along with the crowd.

Then all at once, she wasn't sure how they got there, they were in front of the smashed hospital. Makeshift operating tables had been set up on the street and injured people clustered about them. Some lay on the ground or wandered about in shock. Cars and buggies were disgorging still more injured. Bodies had been placed to one side and covered with tarpaulins. A small band of doctors and nurses worked frantically, but their task was impossible.

Thick smoke now rolled from the buildings on either side, and the air was stifling. Windblown cinders landed on the roof and started small fires. Instantly orders to evacuate were shouted, and volunteers picked up stretchers while nurses grabbed children in their arms.

Nearby a policeman was ordering a man to get into his car with as many of the injured as possible, but the man babbled that it wasn't his car and he didn't know how to drive.

In the confusion Delia did not see one of the blood-spattered doctors approach until Joe suddenly appeared before her. "What are you doing here?" Fear for her sharpened his tone. "I thought you'd be safely out of the city by now."

"Joe—thank God you're all right."

"Of course I'm all right," Joe said shortly, his red-rimmed eyes flickering over her briefly. "Wait!" He grabbed the arm of the policeman who was trying to force the reluctant man to drive the car. "Here's your driver, Officer. Julian, take care of her, will you?"

Delia found herself pushed into the front seat while three frightened children, a baby, and her mother were squeezed into the back seat. Someone put a second baby into Delia's arms. Julian took the wheel, and even before the car started to move Joe had returned to his patient. The last glimpse Delia had of him he was tying a tourniquet around the arm of an elderly woman.

Letting her breath out in what sounded like a moan, Delia realized she had not even had time to say goodbye.

Julian drove to the Palace Hotel, stopped the car, and said, "Get out, Delia. No arguments. You'll be safe here. As soon

as I've taken care of my other passengers, I'll try to get back
to you. But if I'm not back before noon, you'd better get out
of the city. The hotel will no doubt be arranging transporta-
tion for their guests."

Seeing the look on Julian's smoke-streaked face, Delia silently handed the baby to one of the older children and got
out of the car.

The Palace Hotel staff were attending to their duties
calmly, apparently secure in the knowledge that their hotel,
which had withstood the earthquake, was impervious to the
flames consuming lesser structures. They spoke in quiet,
courteous tones as they carried guests' luggage down to the
lobby, then raced away to store delicate lamps and linens in
the basement. They dragged hoses along the corridors to wet
down overheated walls and windows with water from the hotel's basement and roof cisterns.

But in the lobby there was chaos. Baggage was piled high,
and frightened guests huddled together, jumping as dynamite
explosions thundered, while harried clerks and bellboys
helped others bargain with carriage drivers and draymen to
haul them and their baggage to safety. Enrico Caruso sat amid
his suitcases, clutching an autographed photograph of Teddy
Roosevelt like a talisman and telling anyone who would listen that he'd trade San Francisco any day for Vesuvius and if
he got out alive he'd never come back.

Delia walked into the dining room, where white-coated
waiters were serving breakfast to a few unperturbed guests
who appeared to be oblivious to the panicked exodus from
room to lobby and to the yellow smoke filling the street outside.

She was shown to a table, ordered coffee and, realizing she
was ravenously hungry, scrambled eggs and toast.

By the time she finished eating, the heat was stifling and
she was choking on the smoke that now filled the hotel. Most
of the others in the dining room had left. She looked up to
see a tall, gaunt figure approaching and recognized Oscar
Latimer.

Uninvited, the reporter took a chair opposite to her. "The
Metropolitan Opera Company managed to hire a wagon for
its players—they're loading them now, including Caruso.
Maybe you should join them. I'm sure they'd make room."

"I'm waiting for a friend."

He leaned forward. "Unless there's a miracle and they're able to divert the flames, they're not going to be able to save the Palace. The fires are closing in on all sides and the water in the cisterns is running low. The bartenders know the hotel is going to go up in flames. They're giving expensive bottles of wine and liquor to all the departing guests."

"Then perhaps you'd better go and get some free liquor," Delia suggested. "I'm not ready to leave yet."

Latimer regarded her with amazement. "Are you really as cool and collected as you appear to be? Or is it that you don't realize the peril you're in?"

"I've been outside on the streets, I'm well aware of the danger. What about you, Mr. Latimer? Aren't reporters supposed to cover the news?"

"I just got back here. I have my story. Within twenty minutes of the quake more than fifty fires were reported in the downtown area, but the Fire Department's central alarm system was out. The first shock broke nearly all of the wet-cell batteries that operate the system. Federal troops are on their way. They're shooting looters. Refugees are clogging every street. Chinatown is burning like a tinderbox, and hundreds of rats are running from the flames."

At the mention of the rats Delia looked up, recalling her husband's fear of the plague-carrying rats moving out of Chinatown into other parts of the city. But somehow the prospect of succumbing to disease seemed a distant threat beside the more imminent prospect of suffocating on smoke, burning to death, or being buried alive by one of the aftershocks that continued to rock the city.

Latimer pointed to a leather case he had placed on the table. "I have photos of the destruction. Unfortunately I've run out of film, or I'd get a picture of the great Cordelia, dressed in her signature male clothing, calmly sipping coffee while Rome burns."

"I wish I knew if Danny was safe," Delia murmured, speaking to herself rather than to him.

"The street urchin you befriended?"

"How did you know about him?"

"I've made it my business to learn all I can about you. You might say you've almost become an obsession with me. The boy, incidentally, came from the Barbary Coast, which, like Chinatown, is riddled with a private network of tunnels and cellars. He'll be all right."

"If you know so much about me and my friends, perhaps you can offer an opinion about Mignon—my dresser? She lives south of the Slot."

His expression didn't change, but he hesitated before he answered. "You'd better hope she's long gone from there. That area is a pyromaniac's dream. It burned down three times between 1849 and 1851, and still they rebuilt clapboard shacks and crammed them all together next to warehouses and factories."

A waiter, coughing and attempting to breathe through a napkin, came to their table. "Excuse me, but we're evacuating the hotel. You must leave immediately. We have a carriage waiting."

To Delia's annoyance she was forced to leave with Latimer. As she made her way through the smoke-filled lobby, it occurred to her that she was leaving town with a man she despised, while her husband was caring for strangers and heaven knew what Julian was doing.

Out on the street firemen, policemen, and soldiers were anxiously scanning the roof in the brief intervals the yellow-black clouds of smoke parted. Then there was a hoarse cry that the fire was in the back of the hotel, and the remaining employees rushed outside.

Delia recalled that it was said if the Palace ever burned, the city would also be gutted. Her last glimpse of the hotel was to see it engulfed in flame. Black smoke closed around the flag that had flown bravely from the roof all morning.

The eastern-bound crowds were heading for Market Street and from there would converge on either the Ferry Building or the Southern Pacific Station.

"I heard the Metropolitan Opera Company has chartered a launch to take their people across the bay," Latimer told her. "Do you want to go to the East Bay towns, or take a train to Los Angeles? Southern Pacific has been running trains south since dawn."

"I'll take the train. I'd intended to leave today anyway," Delia answered.

Down Sixth Street she could see smoke-grimed soldiers sitting on the Mint steps, rifles across their laps. A crowd surrounded the Post Office, no doubt desperate to get word out to family and friends that they were safe.

Smoke poured from the Call Building, and the Chronicle building was being consumed by fire. The marquee of the Columbia Theater was a twisted mass of black metal. Julian's pride and joy, his Music Theater, was a blackened shell.

"And have you made arrangements to rendezvous somewhere with Julian Van Courtland?" Latimer asked.

Delia wasn't listening. She was gazing in stupefied horror at the smoking ruins of her beloved San Francisco.

Chapter 32

*

JULIAN

Delia believed I saw her only as a commodity to be marketed to the highest bidder, of course, and I admit I fostered that misconception, because I knew that if I revealed my true feelings, I would lose her completely. She'll never know what it cost me to part from her as the city burned.

The narrow streets of Chinatown were filled with the babble of fear, punctuated by crashing temple gongs and wailing moon fiddles, and backed by the dull thud of dynamite explosions.

Julian pushed through the throngs of merchants, coolies, crib girls, and terrified children, traveling a serpentine route past tong rooms, joss houses, brothels, opium dens, tenements, and banner-hung bazaars.

He had arrived back at the Palace Hotel to find it engulfed in flame and learned that Delia had been evacuated with the other guests. At that instant he heard a fireman yell that Chinatown was on fire. He hesitated for only a second before heading in that direction, on foot since the car he'd driven had been confiscated by a Federal officer.

He passed a gang of prisoners from the city jail who were digging shallow graves to bury the dead, and stopped once when he heard a man's voice yelling for help from beneath a pile of rubble. The cries were filled with agony and fear, and Julian tossed aside chunks of concrete and bricks, but the cries stopped before he reached the man and discovered his rescue had come too late. When he realized how much time he had spent on his futile efforts, he raced to Chinatown, hoping against hope he wouldn't be too late there, also.

The lodging house Julian was seeking was less than a block away when a new, even sharper cry of fear filled the street. A huge bull, screaming in rage and terror, lumbered through the crowd, pursued by knife-wielding men who shouted, "Go back beneath the earth, bull, your brothers need you."

Julian paused to observe the spectacle, wondering if he were hallucinating. He knew, having studied the Chinese, that they believed the world was supported on the backs of four bulls. Undoubtedly they thought this was one of them and that since he had deserted his post he had caused the earth to tremble.

As Julian watched, a young Chinese buried a machete into the animal's side. Sickened by the sight of spurting blood on a day filled with horrors, Julian turned away. The bull, head lowered, charged past him, followed by the screaming horde.

Julian fought his way down the street, detouring around crates of bamboo shoots and *gaichoy* stacked outside grocery shops, leaping over boxes of dried sea slugs, shark's fin, and seaweed. The broken window of a general store spilled a jumble of back-scratchers, artificial flowers, and lichee nuts out onto the sidewalk.

Reaching the lodging house at last, he noted as he went inside that since he had sold the property, the front door had been enameled bright red and emblazoned with white Chinese symbols. No doubt the new owner had plans for a business other than renting rooms to newly arrived Asian immigrants.

Most of the occupants of the house had already joined the panicked throngs in the streets, leaving behind a trail of discarded possessions. Julian made his way to the rear of the house and knocked on a door that opened instantly.

Meng Li's black hair was sprinkled with ceiling plaster shaken loose by the temblor, giving her a curiously aged look. Coal-black eyes, dull with shock, regarded him as if he were an apparition. She clutched a delicate Ming vase, a gift from him, that had somehow escaped damage.

His hands gripped her narrow shoulders, slid down silk-covered arms. "Are you all right, Meng Li? You're not hurt?"

She shook her head, but she was trembling.

"Come on, grab some clothes. You have to get out of here, the fires are headed this way and nothing can stop them."

With her free hand she clung to him, her face buried in his chest, and he had to peel her away in order to gather some of her clothes and trinkets. She watched helplessly, still clutching the vase.

He found a valise and stuffed a pair of black silk pajamas and an embroidered mandarin jacket into it. A fleeting image flickered in the back of his mind, of the first time he had undressed her. He had never been intimate with an Oriental woman before, knowing that hidden beneath the kimonos and face powder of the crib and parlor girls were frail and frightened children. But Meng Li was a full-grown woman, daughter of a merchant who had died, leaving her to run his store. Scorned by customers unwilling to patronize a lowly female, she had been forced to sell the business, then her house, in order to survive. Julian had met her when she moved into the lodging house, which was part of a block of buildings in Chinatown he owned. When Joe Simmington and several other doctors and Board of Health people began to raise the specter of bubonic plague if the owners didn't spend a fortune on rat-proofing, he put up his buildings for sale and offered to buy her a house. She refused. Later he learned the manager of the lodging house had been spending more time in her room than his own. That the manager was also the new owner of the lodging house had perhaps influenced her decision.

Still, Julian felt a responsibility to see Meng Li was out of danger. She had been on his mind from the moment the earthquake struck, despite the fact that he had not seen her for months. Since she appeared to be the last resident remaining in the house, he was glad he had come.

Hastily closing the valise, he took her hand and led her from the room.

In the dimly lit corridor she paused. "Must lock door."

Julian shook his head in disbelief, but waited as she fumbled with a key.

He didn't hear the approach of stealthy feet, muffled by the continuing sounds of the mass exodus out on the street. At the last second he turned his head and caught a glimpse of the livid face of Meng Li's lover. Then something smashed into his skull, and he slumped to the ground as oblivion took him.

The blankness gave way to confused dreams. Once or twice he struggled close to the surface of consciousness, but the lure of sleep was too great and he drifted off again.

Dreams came then. He and Marcus roughhousing. How did Marcus get here? No, wait, they were on the lawn at the Willows, laughing together in the carefree days of their youth. Then all at once Marcus's eyes clouded over in that abrupt way they did when he plunged into his netherworld of solitude and depression.

Julian had punched more than one unwary observer who pronounced his brother "crazy." Marcus wasn't crazy. No one was as astute and intelligent, certainly few were as gifted and creative. Julian always reasoned that Marcus's black moods of despair were probably the price he paid for his extraordinary talents. Wasn't it logical that a mind that could reach such heights might also occasionally be required to plumb the depths?

In the wordless realm of his dream, Julian attempted to coax Marcus out of his mood. Then all at once they were fighting. Not roughhousing now, but going at each other with blood in their eyes.

Julian's eyelids flickered open. The sienna afternoon in the doomed city had given way to a red darkness. He coughed, trying to remember where he was.

Pulling himself into a sitting position, he saw pieces of shattered pottery, a joss stick, and an ebony cane lying beside him. His head ached abominably, and his throat was dry. Opposite to where he had fallen, Meng Li's door yawned open. Her room was empty.

He climbed to his feet, supporting himself with one hand against the wall, and lurched toward the front door. Out on the deserted street several rats were gnawing on the carcass of the bull, which mercifully had been shot dead.

Orange flames formed a solid wall at the end of the street, and he stumbled in the opposite direction, gasping smoke into his protesting lungs as he moved on unsteady legs, accompanied by squadrons of scurrying gray shadows.

Tens of thousands of rats were the last to leave Chinatown, carrying with them the menace of plague. Some of the rodents darted toward a large cupola that had fallen intact to the street. He saw that when the cupola fell, it had crushed at least two people. Protruding stumps of limbs were being gnawed by the rats. Sickened, he broke into a run.

* * *

As the evening shadows gathered, the glow of the conflagration deepened, rising two hundred feet in the air and
crowned by a dense pall of smoke. The flames crept inexora-
bly along street after street, preceded by showers of red-hot
cinders.

By eight that evening the fire covered a three-mile
crescent-shaped front and continued to advance. There was
no water and now the dynamite was running out. Julian
paused to rest at the corner of Market and Kearney. Two
mounted cavalrymen were silhouetted against the approaching blaze, watching impassively. There was no one else in
sight.

They've given up, Julian thought. The city is lost. He plod-
ded on to Union Square, where a makeshift refugee camp was
being established. Tents were being pitched and meals were
being cooked, but some were urging refugees to go to the
Presidio and Golden Gate Park as their safety couldn't be assured with flames only blocks away.

Someone tugged at Julian's elbow. "Sir? Is she all right?
Did she get out all right?"

He looked down into the anxious, grimy face of Danny.
The boy's eyes reflected the red glow of the night, and his
ragged shirt was smoke-blackened. He was barefoot.

Julian, who still battled the grandfather of all headaches,
and whose mental capacities seemed to have slowed to a
crawl, at first didn't realize that the boy was referring to
Delia, as his mind was still on Meng Li.

"I went to her house, but she was gone," Danny added, a
panicked edge to his voice. "Then I went to the theater, but
it had burned."

"Oh," Julian said, comprehending, "Delia. Yes, she's safe.
Out of the city by now, I'm sure."

Danny's relief was touching to see. Impulsively Julian said,
"You shouldn't stay here. The fires are coming this way.
Come on, let's go to the Presidio."

The boy hesitated. "You're *sure* Miss Cordelia is all
right?"

"I'm sure." Julian clamped his hand on Danny's shoulder
and propelled him forward.

At the Presidio thousands of refugees were camped between rows of Army huts and tents. Danny stayed close by

his side, casting wide-eyed glances at the huddled evacuees, no doubt amazed to see wealthy San Franciscans now reduced to circumstances akin to his own.

Some of the women were hysterical, and some of the men laughed like maniacs in some sort of mad enjoyment of the terror, while others had tears coursing down smoke-grimed cheeks. Mothers searched frantically for missing children, toddlers wailed at the loss of familiar surroundings and routines, and dazed people of every age wandered in aimless confusion.

Then all at once within the circle of the flickering light of a campfire they heard the age-old words of comfort as a sweet-voiced woman led several children in reciting, *"Yea . . . though I walk through the valley of the shadow of death . . . "*

Suddenly weary, Julian slumped into a sitting position on the grass to listen. Danny looked at him. "Your hair is all matted with blood."

Julian lay back and closed his eyes, not wanting to deal with either his bloodied skull or the boy.

Danny curled up beside him and instantly fell asleep.

After a few minutes Julian sat up, pulled off his jacket, and put it over the boy. The dull sounds of agony filling the night pounded on his already aching head, and the events of the day crowded his mind.

Midnight came and, having examined all his actions that day and decided he probably would have done everything in the same way had he been given the choice, he thought of Delia, who would arrive in New Orleans before he did. An old nagging fear returned then.

So many times, since the day she had admitted that Marcus was the father of her child, Julian had pondered the irony of his being convinced Delia loved Hugo. Yet in the end she had given herself to Marcus.

What would happen when the two of them met again?

Julian recalled his last meeting with Marcus, on the occasion of their mother's funeral, and as sleep eluded him, he went over that last meeting carefully, seeking a hint as to the true relationship between his brother and the woman they both loved.

Chapter 33

*

Hugo's wire to Julian that his mother was terminally ill had arrived at the worst possible time. He had been in the midst of negotiating to buy more oil wells in the southern part of the state, Delia had again decided she wanted to join an opera company and tour Europe, and he had recently met a man in Los Angeles who wanted Delia to appear in a film he was producing.

Julian had protested that Delia was a singer and would be wasted in a medium without sound. The film producer's response was that she was also a born actress. He'd seen her in *Tosca* and had been amazed by the way she could convey intense emotions by her expressions and poses, which was exactly what silent films demanded.

How that damned *Tosca* performance came back to haunt him! It seemed everybody on earth had seen in it. She had toured Europe, giving single performances in most of the capitals. In San Francisco he dissuaded her from appearing in grand opera, because he did not want her to be part of an ensemble; he felt Delia's star shone more brightly when she sang alone, without the distraction of lesser voices.

The film offer had come with the promise of an astronomical salary and might be preferable to her gallivanting off all over Europe again. Julian had been on the point of discussing the offer again when Hugo's wire arrived. Julian immediately boarded a train for New Orleans.

He felt guilty that he had not returned to see his mother for so long. But since the day Delia confessed that Marcus had fathered her child, Julian had not trusted himself to return to the Willows. He loved his mother and his brother, despite being well aware of their shortcomings, but his anger toward

Marcus for impregnating Delia and then withdrawing rather
than taking care of the situation knew no bounds.

Julian had offered to send the private railroad car, which he
never used himself nowadays, to bring his mother to San
Francisco. She had refused to come, pleading social obligations, or sick friends, or her own poor health and aversion to
travel. The real reason, of course, was Delia.

After the cool climate of San Francisco he felt the humid
heat of the Louisiana summer acutely. It was late afternoon
when he reached the Willows, and the instant he stepped into
the house he felt the oppressive atmosphere of death in the
uneasy silence and knew, even before Hugo came down the
stairs to meet him, that his mother was gone.

"I'm sorry, Julian," Hugo said in that low tone people use
in the presence of death, as though the departed might somehow be awakened or disturbed by a normal voice. "Fleur
tried valiantly to wait for your arrival, but she slipped away
last night. The doctor said the end was peaceful."

Julian dropped his suitcase, and the dull thud of its landing
seemed magnified by the silence. He asked, "Is she still in
her room?"

Hugo nodded.

"Is Marcus with her?"

"No. I told him early this morning she was gone, but he
says he doesn't wish to view her. He prefers to remember her
in life."

"I'll go up now."

Julian started up the stairs and Hugo called after him, still
in that sepulchral tone, "I'll take care of all of the arrangements if you want me to, Julian."

"Yes, I'd appreciate that. I shan't be staying long." Julian's
reply, tossed over his shoulders, reverberated about the shadowed hall.

Marcus remained in his room and Julian did not go to him.
He and Hugo had a quiet dinner together that evening, discussed the funeral arrangements that Hugo had made, and
then Hugo said, "Before you leave we must decided what to
do about Marcus."

Julian shrugged indifferently. "Why should we do anything

about him? He's free, white, and over twenty-one. He's his own man, responsible for himself and his own actions."

Hugo glanced at him sharply. "You surprise me, Julian. You were always so protective of him. What changed? You've stayed away from him for a long time and, to my knowledge, have made no attempt to see him since you arrived this afternoon."

"Oh, I'll see him before I leave," Julian replied grimly. "Look, Hugo, now my mother's gone I'm sure you'll want to sell this old white elephant of a house. The cost of maintenance alone must be a tremendous burden. Do you want me to tell Marcus to move out?"

"No," Hugo said quickly. "Marcus is reasonably content here. Father bought this place to give him a safe haven, and I'm not going to uproot him."

"Lord, you're so altruistic it turns my stomach."

"People have different ways of dealing with grief, Julian. I'm sure your grief is speaking now."

Julian rose, tossing his napkin on his untouched plate. "Don't expect me to contribute to my brother's keep."

Hugo merely gave him one of his infuriatingly understanding looks and said in his sympathetic murmur, "The funeral will be the day after tomorrow. It will be a rush, but . . . well, Fleur left instructions that she did not wish to be embalmed." He added quickly, "Most of Fleur's family and friends are close enough to get here in time."

His mother's relatives began to arrive at the Willows the following morning, and Julian tired quickly of responding to expressions of sympathy. He escaped from the house before noon, took a skiff from the boathouse, and set off downriver.

Out of sight of the house he drifted for a while, watching the iridescent flash of dragonflies over the surface of the water, listening to songbirds in the dense interweaving of branches overhead, thinking about his mother. Strange how death erased all of a person's faults. All he could remember now was the faint scent of verbena and the softness of her arms when he and Marcus were small boys; her soothing voice as she read to them, her infinite patience, especially with Marcus. Julian also recalled, with a rueful smile, how his mother could turn into a tigress if their father's discipline became too harsh.

Julian felt intense regret that he had not seen his mother during her last years. Damn Marcus, it was his fault. Julian simply hadn't trusted himself to be in the same room with his brother.

After a while the memories became too painful, and he forced himself to think of other matters.

He wasn't sure when he decided to go to the old house on the bayou, which Daddy Lou had apparently left to Eulie. Perhaps it had been his intended destination all along. Eulie was, after all, Thad Bouchet's mother, and hadn't Delia hounded him about Thad for years? Surely if anyone knew where he was, she would.

Glimpsing the gracious columns of Fontenay through the tree-lined banks of the river, it occurred to Julian to wonder about Gabrielle's absence at the Willows. After all, she was not only Hugo's wife, but purportedly a close friend of Fleur.

As he drew closer to New Orleans, the sights and sounds along the riverbanks began to change, and he found he had forgotten the landmarks that would direct him to the bayou where the house was located. At length, after several exasperating detours due to the constantly changing course of the river, he pulled over to the levee where several Negroes were preparing to launch a fishing boat.

"I'm looking for the house where Daddy Lou used to live—he was a horn player on the riverboats in the old days. I believe only Eulie lives there now. I've never tried to get there by boat before, and I seem to have lost my way."

Was it his imagination, or did the men glance fearfully at each other before one of them said hesitantly, "Miz Eulie, she done passed away, suh."

"Damn," Julian muttered without thinking. "Who lives there now? Any of the others who used to share the house with Daddy Lou?"

"No, suh, they's all gone. Jes' Miz Abebe."

"Who is she? Did she buy the place?"

"Ah reckon."

Julian turned the skiff around and headed back to the Willows.

The house was filled with weeping relatives, but Marcus still had not put in an appearance.

Julian retired early. Marcus would have to show himself for the funeral.

Julian remained in his room the following morning until it was time to leave for the funeral service. When he went downstairs, all of the mourners had departed, and only Hugo, now with his wife at his side, remained.

Gabrielle was as lovely as ever, Julian thought, and decided she was probably the only woman in the world, besides Delia, who could wear stark, unrelieved black and still be breathtakingly beautiful.

There was no sign of Marcus.

"He hasn't come down," Hugo said, noting Julian's searching gaze. "I'd better go up—"

"No. I'll go." Julian turned and ran back up the staircase before Hugo could argue.

Marcus didn't respond to his first knock, and so Julian pounded with his fist. "Marcus, open this damn door or I'll break it down."

Before Julian could put his shoulder to the door, he heard the key turn in the lock.

He shoved Marcus back into the room. "Get dressed. You're going to your mother's funeral. You will show her respect, Marcus, if I have to beat it into you."

Marcus's hollow-eyed stare and shaking hands, the way he stumbled as he moved, and, not least, the empty bottles on his bed table told their own story.

"Respect, Julian? What kind of respect did you show these last few years? You never came near her, and all she talked about was what a big man you were, how successful you were, and how soon you'd be coming home. . . . She looked for you every day of her life, but you never came."

"You know damn well why I never came. To see her, I'd have to see you, and to see you might have meant I'd commit fratricide. I didn't want to kill you while Mother was still alive."

A flicker of derision appeared in his brother's gaze. "Do it now, then, Julian, and we can bury me at the same time as Mother and save our dear half brother the bother of two funerals."

Julian grabbed him by the soiled nightshirt he wore and

shoved him toward his dressing room. Marcus offered no resistance, but the instant Julian released him, he spun round and faced him defiantly. "Go ahead, Julian, beat me into submission. You're bigger and stronger than I, it won't be much of a contest, but it sure as hell will make you feel better."

"For God's sake, Marcus, why are you behaving like this on the day of her funeral?"

"She's gone, Julian. Dead and gone. Do you think she cares about all this ritualistic nonsense?"

"Some of us feel the need for rituals, Marc. We like the order and comfort of them, they show respect."

"There's that word again—"

Julian struck him then and instantly regretted it when Marcus fingered the red mark on his jaw and smiled triumphantly. "There now, doesn't that feel better? Do it again, Julian. We both know it's long overdue. You're not angry about my so-called lack of respect for Mother. The reason you want to kill me is because I showed no respect for your songbird."

All at once Julian felt his rage dissipate. "For the love of God, Marc, why didn't you marry her?"

His brother laughed so hard that Julian had to restrain himself from hitting him again.

"Stop it. Shut up, Marc, or by God I'll—"

"Trying to think of something worse to do to me than kill me? Let me help you out—it's worse to go on living. Far worse. But I see you were serious about my marrying Delia. I thought you were joking. I suppose you've come to accuse me of getting her in the family way—just like that damned mulatto accused me."

Warning bells clanged, somewhere in the back of Julian's mind. He asked cautiously, "Thad Bouchet? When did you see him?"

"He came here—can you imagine the gall of the man? Demanding to know where she was. Now I ask you, how did he know she was pregnant?"

"You can't blame it on him, Marc. Delia herself told me you were the father."

"I'm not denying that I was with her. But so apparently was Bouchet. Otherwise why would he suspect that she'd run off to have a child? By God, Julian, I've never felt such fury."

Julian looked at the white-hot rage in his brother's eyes, still burning brightly after all this time, and decided he didn't want to know what had happened to Thad Bouchet. Nor, all of a sudden, did he want to know about his brother's affair with Delia.

He said, "I'm going to say my final goodbye to Mother. You can do as you please. Rot in here forever, for all I care."

"Julian—did she have the child?"

"Hugo didn't tell you?"

Marcus shook his head.

"No, she didn't. It was a false alarm."

Downstairs again Julian told Hugo, "He's in no condition to come. He's evidently been drinking since she died. We'd better go, they'll be waiting for us."

"They can wait," Hugo said grimly. "Marcus won't be able to live with himself if he doesn't come. I'll get him."

To Julian's surprise and chagrin, Hugo did indeed persuade Marcus to dress and accompany them to the service.

Immediately after the funeral Julian left for San Francisco.

Chapter 34

*

Julian awakened in San Francisco on April 19, 1906, unaware that a sunny spring morning gilded the hills outside the city, which lay under a dense pall of billowing smoke that soared two miles into the air. His head pounded and his throat was raw. The stench of burned and dynamited buildings seemed to have permeated his very bones.

He looked down to see the boy Danny, still sleeping beside him on the grass, and memories of the horror of the previous twenty-four hours flooded back.

Carefully moving away from the boy, he stood up, stretching cramped limbs. Instantly Danny awoke and leaped to his feet.

"Come on," Julian said, "let's see if we can find something to eat."

Rubbing his eyes, Danny wordlessly glued himself to Julian's side, and they made their way through the refugees filling the grounds of the Presidio.

Julian wasn't sure why he felt responsible for Delia's waif. Was it that he remembered Delia as he'd first seen her, a beggar child?

They found a relief tent and were given water and some sort of gruel by a harried volunteer. Danny ate hungrily while Julian questioned an exhausted fireman resting nearby.

No, the fires were nowhere near containment and not likely to be, not with the wind rising.

"We've got over two hundred thousand homeless people," the fireman went on, his voice hoarse. "And another fifty thousand have been driven up into the hills outside the city. The Barbary Coast is gutted. Southern Pacific Hospital was destroyed only minutes after the patients were brought here by wagon. The mansions on the crown of Nob Hill all burned during the night. I tell you, it's an inferno, worst I've ever seen."

The news that both his house and Delia's were lost, not to mention his theater, seemed of little consequence in view of the more basic needs of the citizens. Julian asked, "What's being done to bring in drinking water and food? How about tents, blankets?"

The fireman shook his head. "All I know is that there's no more dynamite and no water to put out the fires. City's going to burn to the ground, mister, you'd best get yourself and your boy out as soon as you can."

Julian glanced in Danny's direction. It seemed he was saddled with the boy whether he liked it or not. "What do you suggest, the ferries?"

"Ferry Building is a madhouse. You could try. Or I hear Southern Pacific Railroad's running trains south to Los Angeles."

Julian walked back over to Danny. "We're going to put you on a train, Danny. I know some people in Los Angeles who'll help you. I'll give you a note to take to them."

"You going, too?"

"No. I'm staying here."

"Why?"

Julian gave a short laugh. "Damned if I know, boy. Some sort of newfound civic responsibility, I guess."

Danny looked at him blankly.

Julian translated: "I'm going to stay and do what I can to help."

Danny watched with a suspicious glint in his gray eyes as Julian scribbled a note to the film producer who was interested in Delia. He wrote:

Danny is a protégé of Cordelia's. He's an orphan. Take care of him for her, and she'll be grateful. I'll transfer funds to cover his keep from my bank as soon as I find out if it's still operating.

"Sir, they won't take me in. Maybe I'll stay here. I won't know my way around Los Angeles."

"Listen, boy, the man I'm sending you to wants Cordelia to be in a show. I've told him you are a friend of hers. He's going to take care of you so that she'll be in his show. Understand?"

Danny flushed with pleasure. "Did she say I was her friend?"

"You are, aren't you?"

"I'd do anything for her," Danny breathed fervently.

"Then let's get you on a train south." Julian fished in his pocket and found a couple of bills, regretting now that he'd given most of his available cash to the owner of the horse and cart. "Here, this will pay for a cab from the station to Hollywood."

All day the flames advanced, up the sides of Russian Hill and toward Telegraph Hill, roaring up one street after another, borne on fierce winds. Julian found himself caught up in a band of beleaguered firemen, soldiers, and civilians—often conscripted at gunpoint, to fight the blazes.

They fought furiously, using every means available: water from private tanks, mud, sacks of flour, bare hands. Fight and fall back, make another stand.

There was never any time to pause and assess the hopelessness of the situation. Julian's anger that they were losing the struggle drove him to lengths he would later scarcely believe. He was not accustomed to being defeated and several times was only driven back at the last second as flames were about to engulf him. He lost count of the people he pulled from beneath the wreckage or helped out of the path of the flames. He no longer thought about evacuating, or about how Delia was faring, or considered the enormous property losses he had suffered. He was engaged in a battle to the death with a monster that was destroying his beloved adopted city.

A wall of heat preceded the fires, so intense that paper lying on the street a block away spontaneously burst into flame. Occasionally he stopped to help carry priceless paintings or other works of art from doomed buildings, or help fleeing refugees load their possessions into or onto anything that could carry them, from automobiles to a ladder held at each end by the owners.

Shortly after midday he stared at the advancing wall of flame and saw the hopelessness on the faces of the firefighters. There was simply no water, nothing with which to fight the conflagration. Overworked fire engines lined the boulevard, and exhausted firemen collapsed where they stood, on the curb, in the gutter, pulling their helmets down over their eyes and immediately falling asleep. They were caked with mud and ash, and many had bloodstains on their clothes.

Julian slid into a sitting position, his back to the wheel of an engine. Looking down, he saw that his hands were blistered. He was regarding his blisters with vague interest, as though they belonged to someone else, when a voice spoke over his head.

"Well, well, Mr. Music Theater Van Courtland, as I live and try to breathe."

He looked up to see the mayor regarding him with red-rimmed eyes. Eugene Schmitz was a man Julian, like many San Franciscans, neither liked nor trusted. He knew the feeling was mutual.

"I'd have thought you'd have been on the first train south, Julian. Your theater was one of the first casualties, and your house went up in flames last night. But I heard Cordelia got out, along with Caruso. Your songbird may have escaped you at last."

The formerly dapper mayor's clothes were rumpled and stained, his shoes mud-caked, and his hands trembled. Realizing that Schmitz must not have slept for over thirty hours, Julian bit back a barbed retort and said only, "You look like hell. What are you doing about this disaster, Mayor?"

"You mean, apart from organizing volunteers to bring in food, tents, disinfectant? Why, Mr. Van Courtland, I'll tell you what I'm going to do. Yesterday we ordered the army to dynamite only those structures alongside the fires. I knew it was a mistake, but I was afraid of the wrath of the city if I ordered distant breaks and the flames burned themselves out before reaching them. Now I intend to dynamite the biggest and best damned firebreak possible, regardless of the cost."

"Van Ness Avenue," Julian said.

The mayor nodded, his bloodshot eyes boring into Julian's with fierce resolve. "How would you like to do something more useful than searching for underground cisterns or hauling paintings out of mansions? I'm going to commandeer a boat to bring dynamite from across the Bay, and I need men to bring it in wagons to Van Ness."

"Drive a wagon loaded with dynamite over ruined streets into an inferno?" Julian inquired mockingly, "Why, Mr. Mayor, I'd be delighted."

The mayor seemed astonished by his response, and Julian himself was mildly surprised that he would volunteer for such hazardous duty. The mayor was called away, and Julian made his way to the dock at the northern tip of Van Ness to await the expected shipment of dynamite.

But as the long afternoon dragged on with no sign of the desperately needed dynamite, all coordinated action disintegrated in the face of leaping flames and mass confusion, smoke, and noise. Julian encountered a woman frantically searching for her husband and child, hysterically attempting to enter a burning building.

Grabbing her, he found himself fending off talonlike fingernails. "My husband and baby!" she screamed.

"There's nobody left in there. Where do you live? Where is your home?"

"Russian Hill."

"Come on, I'll take you home."

On the slopes of Russian Hill he delivered the woman to her family without ever learning how she became separated from them. Minutes later he ran into a contractor he recognized as one who had worked on the building of the Music Theater. "What the hell is the mayor planning to do?" the man asked.

Julian told him of the dynamite that was supposed to create a huge firebreak at Van Ness but which still had not arrived.

"There's a launch loaded with dynamite from Contra Costa County lying at Meiggs Wharf right now."

"What the hell are we waiting for?" Julian asked.

"Something to haul it in?" the contractor suggested, but he didn't hesitate to join Julian as he set off for the wharf on Powell Street. Minutes later a car came creeping down the hill on its wheel rims. Recognizing one of his millionaire theater patrons, Julian waved him to a halt. The man listened to his explanation of the situation and agreed to unload his personal possessions from the car.

"I'll go alone," Julian said. "I need all the room I can get for the dynamite."

"You don't think I'm going to let you drive my car?" the

owner inquired, apparently oblivious to the condition of the vehicle.

"You can ride shotgun," Julian said shortly, getting behind the wheel.

At Meiggs Wharf two pairs of formerly manicured hands packed dynamite into every available inch of space, and the car's owner found himself holding the detonators in his lap as Julian drove through the dense smoke over buckled streets.

Before they reached Van Ness, they were almost run off the road by a fire engine retreating from a new blaze.

Julian stopped the car. "Hell, we'll let the mayor and the army take care of Van Ness. We'll blow a firebreak here. Are you game?"

The owner of the car blinked uncertainly. Julian explained, "We'll dynamite a strip the advancing fire can't cross."

He found an electric battery and cut loose wires from a telephone pole, galvanizing his companion into action. They laid the dynamite and strung the wires.

"Ready?" Julian called to a man who had never soiled his hands or lifted a finger to help himself or anyone else in his entire life.

"Send 'em up," came the response.

They worked their way down the street, blowing up houses, schools, churches. Julian began to feel an exhilarating satisfaction at denying the flames their fuel.

When the dynamite was gone, he returned to Van Ness to see if the supply ordered by the mayor had arrived. It had not, although he learned it was now on its way. The last evacuees were ordered out of the fine houses and apartments on the east side of Van Ness in preparation for the dynamiting.

Drained now, every nerve twitching with fatigue, Julian paused to watch the departure of those stubborn millionaires who had remained in their mansions until the last possible moment. They went gallantly, heads up, without a murmur of complaint, leaving behind their treasures without a backward glance.

By three in the afternoon the dynamite still had not arrived, and determined to raze a strip the fire could not cross, it was decided to set fire to the houses. Soldiers began to enter the mansions carrying inflammable material, breaking windows to create drafts to speed the flames. Half an hour later all the houses from Bush to Washington were on fire.

Julian turned away in despair. He began to wander aimlessly, disoriented by exhaustion, blinded by smoke. The entire side of Nob Hill was a solid sheet of flame, and the fire roared along Polk, a block from Van Ness.

The nightmare afternoon faded into evening and became a kaleidoscope of images, smells, sounds, snatches of conversation. Priests carrying axes ascending the steep steps of St. Mary's Cathedral, flames licking at the steeple. A long procession of exhausted Chinese women who had walked miles—now barely moving past the Presidio, inching along, in such agony they couldn't talk, making their way to Golden Gate Park. He searched their faces for Meng Li, but she was not among them.

Near midnight the inferno leaped Van Ness, breaching the last line of defense. Word swept the city that General Funston had just telegraphed Washington: FIRE CROSSED VAN NESS AVENUE TO THE WEST. ALMOST CERTAIN NOW ENTIRE CITY WILL BE DESTROYED.

Julian slumped wearily to the ground, surrounded by a forlorn mass of humanity, dirty, bedraggled, hungry, barefoot, half-dead from lack of sleep. Before he closed his eyes, the thought crossed his mind that even Delia would be hard put to recognize him—or identify his body if it came to that. A mixture of dried blood and mortar ash coated his head, his face and hands were blackened and blistered. His clothes were filthy and in shreds.

Tomorrow, he thought, surely tomorrow we can lick this monster.

But two more days would pass before the flames would diminish, smoldering throughout Saturday. That night it began to rain.

As Julian stood in the midst of the ruins feeling the blessed relief of raindrops bathing his blistered face, a woman obviously in the last stages of pregnancy approached him and asked wearily if he knew where she might find shelter. Her house had collapsed in the last aftershock. Her husband had been killed on Wednesday morning.

He directed her to Golden Gate Park and offered to take her there, but she shook her head. Watching her plod along the ravaged street, he wondered if her child would be born in the park as the young mother grieved for her husband.

Julian was well aware that he had come close to being killed himself, more than once during the past three days. Was it that sense of his own mortality, or the ghastly images of those days, that now generated feelings he had never experienced previously, or at least had never acknowledged. Compassion, empathy, regret.

He had bullied and lied to the woman he loved, justifying his actions in his own mind by pretending he was, after all, acting in her best interests. But the truth was he had always acted in his own best interests.

The pregnant woman was almost out of sight. Unbidden, the question posed itself: What if Delia's infant had survived? She would never be able to conceive another child. Did she harbor any maternal yearnings? Would it be too cruel to tell her now that the fact was, he didn't know what had become of the baby, who could well be growing up in an orphanage somewhere? He had seen plenty of orphans these past days, and the thought of Delia's child out there alone in the world was almost too much to bear.

Feeling like a phoenix rising from the ashes, he vowed that when they met again, Delia would find that the old ruthless, heartless Julian had indeed vanished with the San Francisco that used to be.

Chapter 35

*

MAGGIE

I had long ago ceased to think of her as Delia's daughter. She was my child and no blood tie could have created a closer bond between us. Perhaps that's why I was unprepared for the unthinkable, and failed to recognize that as the city of San Francisco was shaken from its foundations, so, too, was my world crumbling.

Jemmie brought their breakfast to the table and began to butter the grits as Maggie read aloud from the newspaper: "It says seventeen babies were born, at least one on the grass in Golden Gate Park. Three hundred thousand people homeless. Twenty-eight thousand buildings gone, and three thousand acres burned."

"My land, it must have been terrible for them folks in Californy," Jemmie said. "Is there anything about . . . you know?"

Maggie scanned the rest of the front page account of the San Francisco earthquake and resulting fires. "Yes—Caruso and . . . another famous singer were evacuated safely. Her whereabouts are presently unknown."

"You're talking about Cordelia," Patience said.

Maggie and Jemmie exchanged startled glances. "Yes, we are," Maggie said faintly. "How did you know?"

"My friend told me about her."

"Which friend is that, honey?"

The little girl knitted her brows. "Well, she keeps telling me she's my friend, but she's really too old. She says some day Cordelia will come here and I'll get to meet her 'cos she's somebody 'portant to me."

Maggie felt a tight knot close around her heart, but she tried to keep her tone light. "Patience, is this an imaginary friend you're talking about? You know, I had one when I was a little girl—"

"No! She's real, and she's a grown-up lady."

"What is her name?"

"I don't know."

"Where do you see her?"

"If I want to talk to her, I tie a hair ribbon on the dogwood, and when the ribbon is gone, I know she'll be waiting for me the next morning. I wasn't going to do that—you know, tie the ribbon on the tree—but everybody was talking about the earthquake and I was afraid the singing lady might be hurt when all the houses fell down."

Maggie cleared her throat. She would have to be very careful not to frighten the little girl. "But if you were so interested in the singing lady, why didn't you ask me or Jemmie about her?"

Patience bit her lip, looking perplexed. "I don't know."

"Yes, you do, dear. You can tell us."

The child fidgeted in her chair, her eyes downcast.

"Let her be," Jemmie said gruffly. "Let the chile eat her grits, or she'll be late for school."

"I'm not hungry," Patience whispered, her lavender-blue eyes brimming.

Maggie dropped the newspaper and attempted to gather the little girl into her arms to comfort her, but Patience resisted, her thin body stiffening.

Releasing her, Maggie felt a wave of irrational fear. "Patience, if you've been secretly meeting someone we don't know, then this a very serious matter."

"You *do* know her. She came to see you."

"Maggie!" Jemmie warned. The old woman grabbed the child's hand. "Come on, sugar. We's got to get your hair brushed."

Patience was holding back sobs. "I didn't mean to make you mad, Mama. My friend tells me about Cordelia, but you and Jemmie always stop talking about her if I come in. I only put the ribbon out one time, honestly. I tried to ask you about Cordelia. I showed you pictures of her in the paper . . ."

"Who is the woman who's been telling you about her?" Maggie demanded.

Jemmie cradled Patience to her bosom and glared at

Maggie over the child's silky pale hair. "I never figured y'all for a fool, Maggie. It's Gabrielle, of course."

Maggie felt her mouth drop open. She sat limply in her chair as Jemmie ushered Patience from the room. A little while later the front door opened and closed. Maggie remained at the breakfast table until Jemmie returned after walking Patience to school, although her calendar was packed with appointments.

When Jemmie reappeared, Maggie was brusque. "Did you know Gabrielle was sneaking around seeing Patience?"

"No, ma'am, not till jes' now. I done figured it out soon as the chile said her friend had been talking 'bout Delia. I done tole you Gabrielle was cunning."

"What is she trying to do?" Maggie whispered.

"Find out if the chile is Delia's, I reckon."

"I could forbid Patience to see her—but it sounds as if the damage has already been done." Maggie played distractedly with the edge of the tablecloth. "I believe Hugo is in New York, so I can't ask him for advice."

Jemmie was silent, no doubt thinking that they had not heard from Hugo, nor had he visited them recently.

"The paper says Delia's present whereabouts are unknown. I don't suppose she'd come here, would she?"

"Honey, sooner or later she's bound to come heah."

"For a short visit maybe. She wouldn't stay. She's too big a star nowadays. If she leaves San Francisco, she'd be more likely to go to New York. That was her home originally."

Jemmie began to clear the breakfast dishes, muttering under her breath about folks who keep their heads in the sand.

Maggie's business was thriving, and recently she had acquired a new outlet for her designs. She had been approached by a traveling theatrical company whose costumes had been lost on the road with a request to replace their entire wardrobe, practically overnight. With only a vague description of the costumes to go by, Maggie had not only met the deadline but to the delight of the actors had provided far superior designs than those that had been lost. Word had quickly spread, and she was soon contacted by a repertory company who felt that the costumes rented from a central agency were tired, overused, and expensive.

Since she was already fully booked with orders for her gowns, she was forced to hire more seamstresses, promote the most reliable woman to run the workroom, and concentrate on her designs. It was clear she would soon also need larger premises.

During the days following Patience's revelation about her friend, although Maggie promised herself she would have a long conversation with the child and get to the bottom of the matter, it seemed that one business crisis after another kept her from spending more than scant minutes with her daughter.

Then one evening she returned home to find Jemmie bursting with news. "She's coming . . . I heard it today at the fish market. She's coming to N'Orleans."

All the breath left Maggie's body. She glanced around. "Where is Patience?"

Jemmie rolled her eyes upward, and at that moment the sweet-sad strains of Patience's flute floated on the warm still air. Maggie didn't know a great deal about music, and it was astonishing to her that the child played recognizable tunes, since she'd never had a lesson and played by ear. Not that Maggie knew most of the tunes; they just sounded right. She assumed Patience had heard them at school, where the children had a half hour "musical appreciation" lesson each week.

Maggie asked, "Does she know?"

Jemmie shrugged. "Mebbe she heard at school. She didn't say nothing, but she's been up in her room practicing ever since she got home."

Maggie unpinned her hat. "I wonder how the Van Courtlands are dealing with the news."

"Well . . . I done heard something else today. Seems lak' Miz Gabrielle's cousin . . . he's dying."

Maggie thought of the frail, hollow-eyed man who had come to her to beg her not to see Hugo again, and sympathy mixed with apprehension about what these developing events might mean.

Jemmie went on: "Reckon if Miz Gabrielle loses Mr. Alain, she'll be bound and determined to get Mr. Hugo back.

Between her and Delia, we's gwine have our hands full and that's a fact."

Patience sat at her school desk wishing she had the courage to ask Miss Wilson to teach the class how to read the musical notes, for wouldn't it be easier to "appreciate" the music if the students understood how it came to be?

But Miss Wilson propped the sheet music on the piano, turned on the metronome, and played the piece. Afterward she talked about three-four time and four-four time and had the class tap out the rhythms with pencils on their desktops.

Later they would sing a ballad and talk about the words of the song. Why didn't Miss Wilson explain how to read the musical notes printed with the words, which surely were the main part of the ballad?

Fanny LeBeau, who lived next door and who was two years older than Patience, took piano lessons from an old maiden lady who lived down the street. Fanny hated the lessons and having to practice the scales almost as much as Patience longed for them. But she dared not broach the subject of piano lessons to Mama, who sometimes got a funny, tight look on her face when Patience played her flute. Oh, Mama always complimented her on her playing, but somehow the words didn't quite match that worried frown she wore, and Patience had learned to limit playing the flute when her mother was around. But Mama was gone so much nowadays attending to her business that this was no longer a problem.

Perhaps, Patience thought as she dutifully picked up her pencil to tap out waltz time, Fanny LeBeau would tell her why some of the stems of the written notes went up and others went down and what a dot beside a note meant.

When they finished tapping out the waltz, instead of selecting a ballad for the class to sing, Miss Wilson said, "Now today, children, we are going to talk about a very famous singer who is coming to New Orleans. Does anyone know the name of the singer? You may have heard your parents speak of her. She is very talented, for she not only sings grand opera but also popular ballads, showboat songs, and sometimes even Negro spirituals. Her voice has what we call tremendous range. Who knows her name?"

It's Cordelia, Patience thought, but she didn't raise her

hand to give the answer, just in case Miss Wilson told Mama she was the only student in the class who knew of the great singer. For if Mama's expression grew tight when she heard the flute, it became frozen if anybody ever mentioned Cordelia.

So the great Cordelia was coming to New Orleans, just as the dark-haired lady had said she would. Patience's grown-up friend had appeared as promised when Patience tied a ribbon to the dogwood, and she had blurted out her fears for the singing lady.

"I heard Mama and Jemmie and their grown-up friends all talking about a terrible earthquake and fire and somebody said the world might have lost two great singers and I heard them say Cordelia's name and I thought she might be dead and then she wouldn't come to meet me like you said she would."

"Cordelia is safe, never fear," her mysterious friend responded. "And she will come. I would have written and asked her to come myself, for I am very well acquainted with her, but you see someone very dear to me has been gravely ill, and I haven't left his side. In fact, had I not instructed one of your neighbors to watch out for your signal on the dogwood, I might not have received your message today."

"You told me . . . last time . . ." Patience fumbled to recall exactly what the lady had said. She thought it might have been a hint that the great singer and herself shared some secret, even though Patience knew she had never met Cordelia.

"I told you that she was someone important in your life. I'll tell you now that I believe she is more than that. I believe you two are closely related to each other. What do you think about that?"

Patience struggled to try to understand. Related? She was related to Mama, and once she'd asked if she had cousins, like Fanny, and Mama said no, she had no other relations. Not even Uncle Hugo? Patience had asked and Mama said, "Well, yes, I suppose you could count Uncle Hugo."

Sometimes it was very hard to make any sense of what grown-ups said.

"Has your Mama talked to you about Cordelia? Did you bring up the subject as I suggested?" the dark-haired lady had asked.

Patience shook her head.

"What about your uncle Hugo? Did you ask him?"

"He hasn't been to see us for a long time."

The lady seemed very pleased to hear this.

So now the great Cordelia was coming here, and Patience felt both excited and afraid. The other morning when Mama had read in the paper about the earthquake and the famous singers who had escaped, Patience had believed it was a good opportunity to bring up the subject of Cordelia. But Mama had become upset, and Jemmie whisked her away and brushed her hair so hard it felt like bees were stinging her scalp.

How she wished Uncle Hugo would come. Patience missed him so much and, except for a picture postcard from New York City, had not seen or heard from him for ages. Funny thing was, the last time he was here, Patience had peeked through the banister rail and seen Uncle Hugo and Mama standing very close together, and he had raised his hand and touched Mama's cheek and it looked like he was wiping away a tear. Then abruptly he took his leave. Patience caught a glimpse of his face in the instant before he reached the front door, and he looked so sad it broke her heart.

Why, why didn't Uncle Hugo stay with her and Mama? He loved them both, that much Patience knew for certain.

Chapter 36

*

The workroom was quiet and still, the air clammy with the threat of an approaching storm. Paper patterns curled in the humidity, and Maggie's blouse clung to her back. Tendrils of her upswept hair had escaped and lay damply on the nape of her neck.

The last of her seamstresses had departed, but she lingered, going over invoices without really seeing the figures, her mind occupied with thoughts of flight.

Delia's presence so close by was simply too much of a threat. Maggie hated the prospect of giving up everything she had built in New Orleans, but it had been a mistake to come here, and surely she could start again somewhere else. Someplace where she and Patience would be safe. But how long would it take to make arrangements to move? Where to begin? And why had she waited until the last minute to decide what to do if Delia arrived on the scene? But regrets were pointless.

The bell over the showroom door tinkled, and she gave an exasperated sigh. The last thing she needed just now was yet another client.

But as she walked into the showroom and saw the tall, broad-shouldered man standing in the reception area, her heart quickened and her hand made an involuntary movement to smooth her hair.

"I thought we'd better talk," Hugo said, removing his hat.

"About Delia, of course."

He nodded.

"I knew you'd come hurrying back as soon as you heard she was here." Maggie knew there was a hint of censure in her tone but didn't care. He had stayed away from them for so long.

Hugo studied her expression for a moment, then turned and locked the door. "Let's go into your office, shall we?"

Maggie knew he was afraid they would be seen from the street, and her resentment built still further as she turned to lead the way to her small office. She sat at her desk, keeping a barrier between them.

"Maggie, do you have any idea how difficult it has been for me to stay away from you and Patience these past months?"

"You don't owe me any explanations, Hugo. But I wish you'd stop by the house and talk to Patience—try to make her understand that she didn't do anything to offend you."

His jaw moved slightly, but for a moment he didn't speak. He took the chair in front of her desk and stared morosely at a stack of swatches. Maggie waited, unwilling to break the silence.

At length he said heavily, "You know, Maggie, we none of us can be privy to all the bits and pieces of someone else's life. Don't judge me too harshly."

She was not about to give him absolution. His withdrawal from her was one thing, but Patience had looked for him in vain for so long now, and the child's hurt was more than she could bear. Maggie said coldly, "You came to discuss Delia, I believe?"

"I'm afraid my wife may inform Delia you are here and that you have her daughter. I felt you should be forewarned. Gabrielle has gone to Delia's hotel this evening, ostensibly to welcome her back to New Orleans, but . . ."

Maggie felt a hammer begin to pound against her brain. Had she waited too long? "I think your wife has been talking to Patience, too. I was going to tell you as soon as I got a chance."

Anger sparked in his gaze. "What did she tell the child?"

"Apparently she foretold that Cordelia would be coming to New Orleans—some time ago, before the earthquake—and said that Patience would meet her. She said that Cordelia was someone important to her."

Hugo cursed under his breath. "So that's why Gabrielle wired me to come home. Her wire arrived before I read that Delia had returned to New Orleans."

"In view of the San Francisco earthquake and fires, it

didn't take a fortune-teller to surmise that Delia might come home. But if your wife wired you, then it looks as if she's put two and two together regarding Patience and me."

"Patience is growing to look more like her mother every day," Hugo said. "Gabrielle couldn't help but see that."

"Your wife must know that it would break my heart to lose Patience. Why does she hate me so? Surely she doesn't still think you and I—that we are—"

Hugo looked at her with a mixture of sadness and longing etched deeply into his handsome features, and for an instant she was tempted to fly into his arms. But she felt suspended in the hot, humid air, like a swimmer trapped below the surface of a bottomless lake, caught in a mysterious current that paralyzed her. For a moment they stared at each other, feeling the unspoken yearning, and Maggie had never imagined that she could feel such pain and joy at the same time. He loved her, she knew it beyond a shadow of a doubt. But it was a hopeless love, that, too, was written in his eyes. She had to fight to retain her composure.

At length Hugo said, "Gabrielle is a paradox, I believe even to herself. She married me to save her family from financial ruin and didn't give a damn about me until I no longer wanted her. I think perhaps I then became a challenge to her. If I were to again become the pursuer, I have no doubt she would lose interest in me. But for now she is enjoying the conflict. I am some sort of prize to be won, and she sees you as a rival to be defeated, just as she once felt Delia threatened her."

Maggie shivered. "And she has found a weapon to use against both Delia and me . . . Patience."

"Not that I'm excusing my wife's behavior, but she is quite overwrought at present. You see Alain—her cousin—passed away." Hugo paused, contemplative, then added, "They were—very close. I fear in her own hurt she may be lashing out at others, wanting company in her misery."

"Dammit, must you always try to see the other side of any situation? Can't you react like a normal human being occasionally and rage at the world like the rest of us do?" Maggie burst out.

"Oh, I rage at the world, Maggie, believe me. But I recognize true grief when I see it, and I know it affects different people in different ways. Frankly, I would have found some way to stop Gabrielle from going to Delia's hotel if I'd known of her intention. But I didn't until her maid informed me—after she'd already left. I went straight to your house, and when Jemmie told me you were still working I came here."

"What can we do, Hugo?"

"We have to tell the child."

"No! Please—I've been thinking about it ever since I read that Delia was coming to town. I could take Patience and leave New Orleans—go somewhere where Delia wouldn't find us."

"Maggie, you're not thinking clearly. You have a thriving business here—would you give it up?"

"Yes," Maggie declared fiercely. "In a minute I would. But I'll never give up my daughter."

"Think back, Maggie. You volunteered to take care of a child not your own. She is still not yours. You have no right to her—neither by blood ties nor legal adoption. Now, I accept my share of the blame for this situation, but we can't go on lying—either to the child or to ourselves. Patience must be told."

"I have her birth certificate, and it lists me as her mother and Will Nesbitt, my lawful husband, as her father," Maggie said desperately. "I daresay it might stand up in a court of law."

Hugo regarded her with compassion tinged with dismay. "Maggie, you can't mean that you'd perjure yourself."

"There's nothing I wouldn't do to keep Patience. Hugo, would you really want me to turn her over to Delia?"

"We don't know that Delia would want to take her. I doubt very much that she will. But Delia and the child have a right to know each other, and we have to recognize that there'll never be any peace of mind for any of us until the truth is out. I'm not going to argue the point with you. I must warn you, however, that it would be foolish for you to take the child and run. That will create more problems than it will solve."

Maggie stood up. "I'd better go home. Jemmie and Patience will be worrying about me."

"Tell her, Maggie," Hugo urged. "Tell Patience right away."

Jemmie folded her arms over her chest and regarded Maggie defiantly. "No, ma'am, I ain't gwine take that chile no place. Mr. Hugo, he says we's got to stay right heah and tell the chile the truth."

"Jemmie, I'd take her myself if I could. But I can't just walk out on my business—too many people are relying on me. But I promise as soon as I put everything in order here I'll come to you."

Maggie felt panic plucking at every nerve in her body. She should have had a plan in place before now, but Jemmie had been right, in typical Maggie fashion she had kept her head in the sand and hoped it would never come to a confrontation. If it hadn't been for that damned earthquake . . . "Jemmie, I thought you were my friend. I thought you loved Patience."

"I is your friend and I do love that chile. That's why I ain't gwine take her away and hide her from her real mammy."

"Shh! Not so loud, she might hear us."

"I done sent her to play with Fanny LeBeau next door. I didn't want her to see you fussin' and packing her things."

Maggie continued to fold Patience's clothes and pack them into a suitcase. She had already telephoned a hotel in Baton Rouge, reserving rooms. The last obstacle she expected was that Jemmie would balk at the idea.

"Very well, if you won't take her, then I'll have to go myself. Will you take a note to my head seamstress for me? Perhaps she can take care of business until I get back. I shall have to find someone in Baton Rouge to take care of Patience for a while—I hate to turn her over to a stranger, but—"

Thunderclouds raced across Jemmie's eyes. "Doan' you dare give that li'l angel to no stranger! Why, I declare I—"

The doorbell rang shrilly, and both women jumped.

"That will be Mr. Hugo, he said he'd be back." Jemmie's relief that a stronger voice than her own would take up the cause was obvious as she lumbered down the stairs to open the door.

Maggie snapped the suitcase lid shut, then hurried into her own room to pack and write a note to her head seamstress.

Hugo could wait. He wasn't going to change her mind, no matter what he said. She was determined to get Patience out of New Orleans this evening.

She heard Jemmie climbing the stairs as she finished the note. The old woman was wheezing, and there was a look of fearful anticipation on her face when she reappeared. "Y'all best come on downstairs now. Somebody heah to see you."

"Hugo?"

Jemmie shook her head. "When I opened the door and saw her standing there, I didn't know what to do."

Maggie felt her spirits drop to the floor. "Oh, no, Jemmie! You didn't let her in, did you?"

But Jemmie had closed her eyes and was rocking back and forth on her feet. There would be no further communication, Maggie knew. She pushed a strand of her hair back from her brow and went downstairs.

An archway linked the living room to the entry hall, and from the bottom step of the staircase Maggie could see the woman who stood beside the window that overlooked the street. Even from the back, she looked regal, her presence radiating that elusive quality that Maggie remembered so well.

Delia's slim figure was clad in a beige linen suit, and Maggie's professional eye appreciated the simple clean lines of the cut and the fine weave of the material. When Delia turned toward her, she saw that beneath the suit she wore a white crepe blouse, and the effect was cool and elegant. She had removed a straw hat, and her pale hair shimmered in the lamplight.

Maggie realized with a start that it was almost completely dark outside, and Patience knew she must be home before dark. Maggie called up the stairs to Jemmie, "Perhaps you'd better go and tell Mrs. LeBeau that I shall be delayed here for a little while, Jemmie." She said a silent prayer that Jemmie would understand that she must keep the child out of the way while Delia was here.

The old woman came grumbling down the stairs as Maggie walked toward Delia, acutely aware of iridescent lavender eyes watching her approach.

"Maggie," Delia said, "I imagine you know why I'm here."

Maggie felt as if she no longer controlled her arms and

legs, and her voice, when she spoke, sounded like a stranger's. "I expect because Mrs. Hugo Van Courtland came to see you."

"Is it true?" Delia's cool facade seemed to have melted. She leaned forward, her hands raised as if in supplication, her lovely eyes pleading. When Maggie hesitated, Delia asked, "Is my daughter alive? Do you have her?"

For one stupefying second Maggie considered denying it, but then reason prevailed. It was too late for that. Delia caught her breath and clasped her hands together in a way that said she could see the truth written all over Maggie's face.

Delia swayed unsteadily on her feet. She seemed almost intoxicated with joy for a second, then her eyes focused on Maggie again with revulsion. "Why? Why did you keep her from me?"

"You abandoned her—you went away and left her. I thought you didn't want her."

"I believed she was dead. I was told that she died. But you—you knew the truth. Why didn't you at least write to me? Even if you didn't know where I was six years ago when I left New York, you must have known later I was in San Francisco."

A cold knot formed in Maggie's stomach, her throat constricted. Of all the reactions she might have expected from Delia, of all the explanations, these offered the least hope. If someone had lied to her about Patience being dead . . . if that joy in learning her daughter was still alive was not feigned . . . then she had indeed come to take Patience away from her.

"Where is she?" Delia asked, obviously struggling to keep her tone civil. "May I see her now, please?"

"She believes I'm her mother, Delia," Maggie said desperately. "Please don't disrupt her life and break my heart, please don't try to take her away from me."

"How dare you bargain with me! You're guilty of kidnapping, don't you realize that? If it were not for the fact that I don't want any publicity about this matter, I'd prosecute you. All I want is my daughter. I shan't leave without her."

Maggie squared her shoulders. "You're not her mother. You may have given her life, but you haven't given her love or cared for her day by day. You haven't laughed or wept over her, or made reckless bargains with God to keep her from harm. How can you say you're a mother?"

"I was never given a chance to be her mother. You stole my child—am I supposed to give her up permanently because you cared for her?"

Maggie stared at her, at the icy perfection that was Delia. Here was a woman who had the world at her feet, blessed not only with dazzling beauty, but with a God-given talent possessed by few mortals.

At length Maggie asked raggedly, "Do you have any idea of the tumult you cause in other people's lives? You think you can simply walk in, create a crisis, then walk out again when it suits you? Do you think I don't know of the havoc you wrought with the Van Courtland brothers? Well, I'm not going to let you walk into my daughter's life and then abandon her a second time."

Delia's lavender eyes widened slightly. "*Your* daughter?"

"Yes. Patience *is* my daughter. I'm the only mother she has ever known. To you she's nothing more than a possession you think was taken from you. What would you do with her? Drag her around the world with you? Leave her waiting in the wings while you're onstage?"

"And you, of course"—Delia's voice was lethally soft—"spend every waking moment with her? Or do you run a business that takes most of your time, and leave the raising of my daughter to an old black woman who is probably filling her head with bayou superstitions and voodoo spells?"

"That's not so! Jemmie doesn't . . ." Maggie's voice trailed away. She wasn't going to defend herself or Jemmie to this woman. "I'm going to ask you to leave now. This is my house and you're not welcome here."

Delia picked up her hat. "You can't keep me from her for long. My lawyer will be here with a writ first thing tomorrow."

Maggie led the way to the front door and opened it wordlessly. She watched Delia walk to a waiting cab, then sat on the stairs and wept.

Chapter 37

*

Patience couldn't sleep. She fingered her flute, but daren't play it because she was supposed to be in bed. She had come home after playing with Fanny LeBeau to find something very strange taking place.

There was a packed suitcase in her room. Mama's eyes were red and swollen, and Jemmie muttered and grumbled and wore what Patience privately called her "darkuns," a brow-knitted scowl that proclaimed she did not approve of what was going on.

Patience got out of bed and crept to her door. She could hear the muffled sound of voices, so Mama and Jemmie must still be up. Inching open the door, Patience slipped out onto the landing and crouched at the top of the stairs.

". . . that chile she knowed somethin' was wrong. Most likely she's worrying herself sick right this minute, 'magining all kinds of woe." That was Jemmie's voice, wise and all-knowing.

"All *right*!" Mama's tone was frighteningly shrill. "That's enough, Jemmie. I can't fight both you and Hugo."

Uncle Hugo was fighting with Mama? Was that why he hadn't come to see them for so long? Patience had missed her uncle terribly and had been afraid she had made him mad. It appeared that her worst fears were true. Somehow she had caused a big upset between the two people she loved most.

Mama was saying, "You think it's morally right to destroy the whole world of a little six year old, then be it on your heads and your consciences."

Patience just managed to get back into bed and pull up the covers before her mother opened the door and whispered, "Are you awake, angel?"

"Yes, Mama."

Her mother turned on the lamp on the dresser and came to the bed. Patience crawled into the shelter of her arms.

For what seemed like a very long time they just stayed like that, with her mother occasionally stroking her hair. At length she said softly, "I have something to tell you, Patience. I should have told you before now, but . . . I guess I was hoping I'd never have to tell you."

Patience held her breath, unable to imagine what horror was in store for her. Hadn't Mama said she was going to destroy the world? She had never heard Mama sound so sad. Not even that day when she asked where her daddy was, and Mama said he'd been lost at sea years ago. Patience often thought about him, vainly trying to find his way home and not knowing the way out of the vast ocean. How she longed to have a daddy of her very own, just like Fanny and all the other girls at school. When she asked how long it might be before he came home again, Mama had been a little impatient, perhaps because she had to rush off to make dresses, and she said, "Honey, I told you, your daddy's ship was lost. He won't ever be coming home again." Patience was perplexed, because once she'd been lost while shopping with Jemmie, but she found her way home. Surely her daddy could find his way home, too? When she asked Jemmie about him, she just muttered and put her darkuns on. Since it upset the two of them whenever she spoke of her missing daddy, Patience learned to keep her thoughts and yearnings for him to herself. But every night she knelt beside her bed and prayed to God to bring her daddy home to her.

"You see, when you were born . . ." Mama's voice sounded all husky and strange. "I was there, I helped to bring you into the world. But . . . angel, another woman gave birth to you. I was not your mother then. I didn't earn the right to call myself your mama until later."

Patience wasn't sure exactly what Mama was trying to tell her. A long time ago she'd asked where babies came from, and Mama said they came from a mama and a daddy loving each other, that they made a seed and the baby grew. So this new information was baffling. How could two women be involved in making the seed and growing the baby?

"Do you understand what I'm saying honey?"

Patience shook her head.

"I'm not your flesh-and-blood mother, angel. But I've taken care of you and loved you with all my heart, and I think of myself as your mother and always will."

Awful possibilities were now taking shape in Patience's head, and she shivered, afraid to say anything that might bring on even scarier revelations.

"Don't you want to know who your mama is, Patience?"

Scalding tears were pricking at the back of her eyes now, and all she could do was silently nod her head, because this seemed to be what Mama was expecting.

"It's Cordelia. The singer. Her name is Mrs. Simmington."

How could this be? Why, she had never in her whole life ever laid eyes on Cordelia. Why was Mama saying these terrible things to her? What had she done to deserve them?

"You see, I wanted you to be my little girl so much that I kept you with me, and I want you always to stay with me."

This was a little less frightening. Patience thought about the absent Cordelia for a moment, then asked, "Why did she give me to you? Why didn't she take care of me?"

"I don't know for sure, honey. She'll have to tell you herself. But she went away and left you with me, and you became my very own daughter, and I love you so very much."

"Didn't Cordelia love me?"

"Honey, I can't answer for her. But you'll be meeting her soon, and you can ask her anything you care to. I just want you to know that if I have anything to say in the matter, nothing is going to change. I'm going to do everything I can to make sure of that."

Patience was trying to keep her teeth from chattering with fear. "I wish my daddy would hurry up and find his way home. He's been lost at sea a very long time. He could tell us what to do."

"Oh, baby . . ." Mama held her so tightly she could hardly breathe. After a while Mama said in a choked-up voice, "My husband was lost at sea—he wasn't your daddy, any more than I'm your mother, except by reason of the love I have for you."

Patience began to sob. Now she was beginning to understand the enormity of what was happening to her. "Well, where *is* my daddy?"

"I'm not exactly sure, but I believe when Cordelia comes, she'll tell you all about him."

"You're going to give me away, aren't you, Mama?"

"No! Of course not. What makes you say such a thing?"

Patience silently pointed to the suitcase lying on the floor.

"Oh, no, baby. I was going to send you and Jemmie away on a little vacation and join you myself in a few days. But we've changed our plans. We're going to stay here. Would you like to help me unpack the clothes?"

Patience nodded and dutifully climbed out of bed to receive the folded garments her mother took from the suitcase, but she was not reassured. The suitcase could easily be repacked.

"Mama, why doesn't Uncle Hugo come to see us anymore? Was I a bad girl?"

"Oh, no, my angel! Your Uncle Hugo loves you very much. He's been busy . . . he travels for his business . . ." Her mother's voice trailed away. From the expression on her face, Patience knew that there was a great deal more to Uncle Hugo's absence than his need to take care of business. Mama's reluctance to tell her the truth surely meant that, as she feared, she had done something to drive Uncle Hugo away.

Placing her neatly folded underwear into her dresser drawer, Patience wished with all her heart that they were all living on Palmetto Street again where they'd been so happy and Uncle Hugo came all the time and Mama used to sing while she sat at her sewing machine and Jemmie hardly ever put on her darkuns. Maybe that was why her daddy hadn't found her yet. Maybe he thought they still lived in Natchez. Patience knew it was a long way from Natchez to New Orleans. But surely he would come soon?

Chapter 38

*

DELIA

I returned to New Orleans believing I was on a quest to learn the truth about what had happened to my friend Thad. Instead, I discovered my daughter was alive and well. For a little while I even allowed myself to hope that the most grievous loss of my life was about to be restored to me, and I would receive the greatest gift of all, a child of my own. But as usual fate had several surprises in store.

Delia returned to her hotel, where only hours earlier Gabrielle had informed her that her daughter was alive and being cared for by Hugo's mistress.

Still reeling from this revelation, Delia then had to cope with the identity of his mistress. Maggie Nesbitt.

What had she expected when she rushed to Maggie's house? A tearful reunion with her child? She had not expected that Maggie Nesbitt, former soft-spoken midwife and factory worker, would turn on her with the ferocity of a female wolf protecting her cub.

As Delia crossed the hotel lobby, passing guests stopped to gasp and stare, obviously recognizing her. She quickened her pace, anxious to reach her suite. How she wished it was not too late in the day to contact a lawyer.

How could she possibly sleep tonight, knowing that her child was out there somewhere? What would she be like? What would she think of her famous mother? What had she been told? Above all, how could Hugo have done this? And, somewhere in the darkest reaches of her mind, rage began to form that Maggie Nesbitt had not only stolen her child, but also the man she loved.

A woman blocked her path. "Excuse me, but aren't you—"

"No," Delia said quickly, "I'm not. I just look a little like her." She pushed past the woman into the elevator.

Alone in her suite, counting the hours until morning, Delia relived every second of the evening, from the moment Gabrielle had arrived at her hotel.

The desk clerk had called to ask if she would care to meet Mrs. Hugo Van Courtland in the lobby, and Delia, stinging from the stony silence of the Van Courtlands, especially Hugo, since her arrival in New Orleans, immediately invited her former nemesis to come up to her suite.

She was shocked by Gabrielle's appearance. She was in mourning, her black gown crumpled and not too clean, her glorious dark hair dusty and unkempt. Her face was pale and pinched, and there were dark smudges beneath her eyes.

After a perfunctory embrace, Delia led the way into her sitting room. "I could order some tea," Delia said.

"No ... nothing." Gabrielle's green eyes flickered over her. "You look very well—I guess I was expecting to see you dressed like a man."

Delia felt herself flush, knowing that she had been particularly careful about her appearance since her return to New Orleans, mainly because she hoped Hugo might come to welcome her. She murmured, "You're in mourning ... ?"

Tears glistened in Gabrielle's eyes. "I lost my cousin, Alain. He passed away a few days ago."

"I'm sorry."

Gabrielle seemed to be looking through her, into some frightening abyss. She wrapped her arms protectively about herself and shivered. "He ... he just wasted away. His skin was like brittle parchment stretched to breaking point. . . . He was a skeleton, too weak to move, racked with coughing—" She bit her lip and a tear coursed down her cheek.

Delia was surprised by the depth of Gabrielle's grief, although she couldn't stifle the cynical thought that perhaps what she was witnessing was Gabrielle's realization of her own mortality, and possibly fear that she might have contracted his disease herself. Gabrielle's visit was not turning out to be quite the welcome home Delia had hoped for. Had she come for sympathy over the loss of her cousin? Delia had only vague memories of Alain Marchand, and it seemed he had been frail and tubercular for a very long time prior to his death.

Perhaps Gabrielle had come to see her out of curiosity? To

find out what Julian's waif had become? Delia poured a glass of water and handed it to her.

Gabrielle took a sip and regarded her over the rim of the glass with what Delia suddenly realized was a malevolent stare.

Attempting to break the tension, Delia asked, "How is your family?"

"My mother died—hadn't you heard?"

"Yes, I'm sorry. I meant your father and sister and your husband?"

Gabrielle put the glass down. "My father and sister are well. Hugo is also quite well, I believe. He spends more time with his mistress than with me."

Delia swallowed. She made no comment, remembering the Gabrielle of old. She would never acknowledge that another woman had stolen her husband's affection unless she had a reason other than to shock. Delia began to feel increasingly uneasy.

Gabrielle suddenly pounced. "Was Hugo the father?"

Delia blinked. "I beg your pardon?"

"Did my husband father your child?"

All of the blood drained from Delia's face. "No."

"Then why on earth would he support the child?"

"I don't know what you're talking about. My baby died a few days after birth."

"Oh, don't lie to me. I don't care that you abandoned your bastard. All I care about is Hugo, and while he's involved with Maggie Nesbitt and your child—"

Delia's mind was reeling. *Maggie Nesbitt.* Dear God, was it possible?

". . . the Nesbitt woman has a dressmaking business, financed by Hugo, of course. He brought her and the baby from New York, bought the business and a nice house for them and has been blatantly carrying on with her. She passes the little girl off as her own—but I've seen the child—she looks exactly like you did when Julian first found you. I've spoken to her. I even told her a little about you. Naturally I didn't say you had abandoned her at birth, I couldn't be that cruel . . ."

That cruel . . . The words echoed in Delia's mind at midnight in the solitude of her hotel suite as she attempted to piece together the puzzle and make some sense of the lies and deceptions.

Julian had lied about her child's death. Hugo must have been searching for her in New York and found Maggie. Did he know Marcus was the baby's father? Was that why he cared for the child, because of her Van Courtland blood? Somehow the baby had brought Hugo and Maggie together, and she had become his mistress. Oh, how unfair it all was!

The real villain, of course, was Julian. Damn him, she'd see him in hell for this. She thought of Julian for the first time since he deserted her in San Francisco. Her thoughts also turned to her husband, and she wondered how Joe would react to being presented with a stepdaughter.

But of all the players in her life, the one Delia most wanted to see was Hugo. How she wished she could talk to him tonight. She would go to his office tomorrow morning, before she did anything else. Perhaps there would be no need for a lawyer when she told him that she had not willingly abandoned her child. Hugo had always been fair and just.

As the gray glow of dawn appeared beyond her window, she drifted off to sleep at last.

She awoke with a start to find the sun high in the sky and, disoriented, stumbled out of bed. It was almost noon. She had long been in the habit of staying up most of the night and sleeping all morning, but today of all days she needed to have made an early start.

A note had been slipped under her door and she picked it up. *We must talk right away. Call my office as soon as you can, and I'll come to you.* The initials HVC were followed by a telephone number.

Delia bathed and dressed, ordered tea and toast to be sent up to her room, then requested a cab, which she took to Hugo's office. She was not going to allow him to come to her hotel, as several reporters seemed to have taken up permanent sentry posts in the lobby, and Delia didn't want any hint of gossip about Hugo and herself to be printed. All at once it seemed prudent to establish that she was an upstanding citizen and perfectly capable of rearing her daughter.

A gawking bespectacled young man showed her into Hugo's private office, and she swept into the spacious room and stood far enough from Hugo's desk that he was able to

see all of her. She rested one hand on the top of her parasol
and inclined her head slightly. Delia had learned long ago
how to strike a pose that reduced an audience to a quivering
mass of anticipation.

Hugo came slowly to his feet. He looked tired, the lines of
strain and a sprinkling of gray at his temples making him appear older than she recalled. "Delia . . . I didn't expect you to
come here." He came around the desk to her, took her hand,
and kissed it. "Welcome home. You look . . . wonderful. Every inch the diva you are. Is Julian with you? I didn't read
anything about him—or about your husband accompanying
you."

"I'm alone," Delia said. She moved away from him, selected a chair, and sat down. "I suppose Julian was also part
of the plot to steal my daughter from me?"

"Ah, so my wife has done her mischief."

"Was Julian part of the plot?"

"No, he wasn't. The baby was left behind in Mrs. Nesbitt's
apartment when Julian whisked you away. But he didn't
know either that Mrs. Nesbitt kept her, or that she came to
me for help. By the time I entered the picture, you and Julian
were on the West Coast. Delia, I've spoken with Mrs. Nesbitt
this morning. It seems that there have been many false per-
ceptions, on our part as well as yours, about what happened
six years ago."

Mrs. Nesbitt, Delia thought. A formal title for your mistress. She said, "And for the last six years, Hugo, you
couldn't find it in your heart to let me know my daughter was
alive and in your care?"

"The child's welfare was our only concern—keep in mind
that we believed you had abandoned her. Delia, accusations
and recriminations at this point are useless. What we must
decide is what to do next. Mrs. Nesbitt tells me you want to
take Patience from her. I'm begging you to reconsider such a
decision. The child would be the one most hurt if she is removed from the only home she's ever known, and I'm sure
you don't want that."

Delia rose to her feet. "I hoped you would be fair, Hugo.
But I see that I am wasting my time here. After all, a mistress
can argue far more persuasively—"

"Mrs. Nesbitt is not my mistress," Hugo interrupted wearily. "Despite what my wife may have told you. Our only connection is that we share a great deal of affection for your child. Please believe me when I tell you that had I known you thought your baby had died, I would have told you the truth years ago. My heart goes out to you, Delia, and I can't begin to imagine how you've suffered. But I also know how much Mrs. Nesbitt loves the child, and my earnest hope is that we can find a solution that will be equitable for all concerned."

Delia looked into his eyes and saw that he was still the same man she had respected and admired and loved since she was only a child herself. Surely she could trust him to be fair, no matter what his relationship to Maggie was.

After a moment she said, "I want to see my daughter. I'd rather do so with Maggie's cooperation, but if I have to I'll bring in a lawyer."

"I'll take you to her. Maggie didn't send her to school today. It seems they were up most of the night talking about you."

Delia sat stiffly in Maggie's pleasant parlor, which was light and airy and filled with the scent of potpourri. Hugo stood in front of the fireplace. They both stared at the archway leading to the hall as footsteps descended the stairs. A moment later Maggie, holding the hand of the little girl tightly, led Patience into the room. It was immediately obvious that both of them had been crying.

Delia felt her heart lurch. She was looking at a replica of herself at that age. A pale, thin little girl with light gold hair who regarded her with lavender-blue eyes that were guarded and wary. Here was a child who sensed already that she was different in some way.

A rush of emotion that was difficult to contain swept over Delia. She wanted to hold the child close to her heart, to weep bitter tears over the lost years, to promise her the world. But reason prevailed. The last thing she wanted to do was to frighten the child and alienate both Maggie and Hugo.

"Hello, Patience." Delia arose and took a tentative step toward her daughter, who shrank back against Maggie. Delia could not have felt more wretched if the little girl had spit upon her. Taking a deep breath, Delia said carefully, "I'm very happy to see you again. What a beautiful little girl you are."

The child placed her small hand in Delia's for a split second, then snatched it away. Patience didn't speak, but glanced up at Maggie for reassurance, again twisting the knife in Delia's heart.

Maggie said, "Patience, this is Mrs. Simmington—the lady I told you about."

"Ma'am," Patience said in a barely audible whisper.

"I'm your mother, dear," Delia said quietly. "Your real mother. It's a very long story as to why we haven't been together before now. Someday you'll understand. And I promise I will make it all up to you if you'll give me a chance."

"Mama! Don't let her take me away!" Patience flung herself at Maggie, burying her face in her skirts and sobbing uncontrollably. Maggie dropped to her knees and wrapped her arms around the child. "She's not going to take you away, angel."

Hugo said sharply, "Let's all sit down and remain calm. Patience, listen to me. Nothing is going to change—" He held up his hand as Delia attempted to speak. "I repeat, *nothing* is going to change for the time being. You'll stay with your mama, but Delia would like to get to know you. Perhaps you two could visit each other."

Delia said desperately, "Patience, I know this is all very confusing for you. But please believe me when I tell you I would never do anything to hurt you."

Maggie edged the little girl over to the sofa, and they sat very close together, the child's shoulders still shaking with suppressed sobs as Maggie held her tightly.

Aching to comfort her daughter herself, Delia clenched her fists at her sides and willed herself to maintain her composure.

Hugo said, "Perhaps we're all a little too overwrought this morning. Delia, I believe it would be best if you waited a couple of days before you come to see the child again."

Patience's tear-drenched eyes peered over Maggie's arm. "I won't go with her. I don't want to leave my mama."

"Shhh, angel. It's going to be all right," Maggie whispered.

Delia was never sure how she managed to make a dignified exit. It seemed one minute she was on the point of breaking down, and the next Hugo's arm was through hers and they were making their way outside.

On the tree-shaded sidewalk she turned to him angrily. "That is my daughter in there, we all know it. You have to make Maggie Nesbitt give her up."

"Delia, we have to think about the child. You saw how upset she was. Such a demand is selfish and unreasonable on your part."

"How dare you castigate me? You and that woman stole my baby."

"We could accuse you of abandoning her. Perhaps when Julian gets here, he will corroborate your contention, but—"

"You just don't give a damn, do you, Hugo? I'm surprised you didn't suggest we cut Patience in half."

"As I recall, the real mother told King Solomon to give her child to the other woman. Look, Delia, let's not create a scene out here on the street. Get into the car."

"Eager to get rid of me, Hugo? You hardly said a word in there. In fact your whole attitude seems to be that you wish you were a thousand miles away."

"I must confess I do have other matters on my mind. My wife has recently been bereaved. She is grieving . . . her need for support and sympathy is equal to yours at the moment."

Delia sat rigidly beside him as he drove away. She stared out of the window, not seeing the city streets pass by, not seeing anything but her child's face.

They had gone only a few blocks when Hugo abruptly asked, "Would you prefer to go to the Willows?"

Delia sat bolt upright. "Why?"

"I just thought you might like to get away from the reporters·I saw hanging around your hotel. If they see that look of doom you're wearing, there's no telling what story they might concoct."

Was that the only reason, Delia wondered, or had Hugo guessed that Marcus was Patience's father? And if that were the case, did he now want to add yet another complication to an already impossible situation by bringing Marcus into it? She said, "I'd rather face the reporters than Marcus."

Hugo glanced sideways at her. "That seems to answer a question that's troubled me for years. I suppose we should have been more vigilant. We all knew that you used to slip downstairs to listen to him play the piano late at night. Looking back with the wisdom of hindsight, I can't imagine why we all assumed that Marcus was somehow impervious to your considerable allure. I suppose because at first he was so antagonistic toward you, and then the two of you appeared to become musical collaborators."

Delia's fingernails dug into the leather upholstery of her seat. She stared straight ahead, watching the cobbled street unfold beneath the wheels of the car. Like Julian, Hugo believed she had willingly given herself to Marcus. Should she tell Hugo the truth? Could she? Would he believe it?

"Take me back to my hotel, please. I don't want to see Marcus. Not now, not ever. Don't worry about my giving anything away to the reporters. I learned a long time ago how to hide my feelings."

Delia did not look at him. The men in her life were all at once unimportant, even Hugo, for whom she had pined for years. There was only one real and lasting connection, and no one, nothing was going to keep her child from her.

Chapter 39

*

Delia waited for an interminable minute while Jacob Lacey, attorney at law, scribbled something on a notepad on his desk. At length he raised his head and peered at her from beneath bushy white eyebrows. She privately wished she had selected a lawyer who was not quite so old. He had come highly recommended, but how could a man of such venerable years even remember what it was like to yearn for a child?

"Mrs. Simmington . . ." As usual, it took a moment for her married name to register.

"I fear, my dear lady, that this case is not quite as cut-and-dried as you believe. I have made discreet inquiries and learned that a birth certificate exists, naming the Nesbitts—Mrs. Margaret Nesbitt and her now deceased husband—as the parents of the child. There is also the fact that the child has been with Mrs. Nesbitt since birth, over six years."

"But I explained—"

Lacey held up his hand to silence her. "Apart from the fact that it appears—at first glance, you understand—that if indeed the child is the one you gave birth to six years ago and apparently only the woman who now claims to be the mother can testify to that—that you abandoned her, thereby relinquishing all claim to her. You must also consider, if we have to go to court, the perception of judges and juries that people in your profession are somewhat narcissistic and unstable, not to mention being vagabonds. I am, of course, only pointing out what opposing counsel may use as arguments against removing the child from a stable home and giving her to you."

"How can you say that Maggie Nesbitt, who is also a working woman, can provide a better home for my child than I can? She has no husband, and questionable morals. Whose side are you on, Mr. Lacey?"

"Yours, of course, Mrs. Simmington. Which is why I must play devil's advocate and point out what you're going to be up against. We must proceed very carefully. Very carefully, indeed."

"What do you suggest I do?"

"Well, you tell me Mrs. Nesbitt has allowed you to visit her and the child. I suggest you continue the visits."

"But I never see my daughter alone. That woman is always there."

"Still, the child is becoming accustomed to your visits? She's less afraid of you than she was initially?"

Delia nodded reluctantly. It was true. Patience had even shyly asked how it felt to sing for a large audience and confided that she had a flute she liked to play. Delia had eagerly asked if she would play for her, but Maggie had glared at the two of them, and Patience became confused and withdrawn.

Lacey said, "Be patient, my dear. I'll approach Mrs. Nesbitt's lawyer with the request that you be allowed to see the child alone."

"I didn't know she had a lawyer."

"A Mr. Lucas Stone. I believe he was originally employed by Mr. Van Courtland's law firm up in Natchez, but now has his own practice. He's apparently an old friend of Mrs. Nesbitt."

So Hugo had chosen sides, despite his carefully neutral and conciliatory attitude. Delia prepared to leave. "Please move as speedily as you can in regard to my seeing my daughter alone."

Delia had grown tired of the goldfish bowl of hotel living and had rented a house, only scant blocks from Maggie's house, since it appeared that her fight to regain custody of her daughter might drag on for a while.

A wire had arrived from Julian that he would be coming to New Orleans shortly, and she had written to her husband to give him the news about her daughter.

Her first letter from Dr. Joe was waiting for her after her visit to the lawyer's office.

My Dear Delia:
    Your news is, of course, both startling and joyous. But

Delia, do proceed carefully, and within the limits of the law. I look forward to meeting your daughter, but regret I cannot join you in New Orleans just now. The aftermath of the earthquake and fires are fearful. I am working twenty hours a day. As I anticipated, I have treated several cases of plague. It will be some time before the city is anything close to habitable again, although rebuilding has already begun.

As ever, Joe

She was disappointed that her husband had not seen fit to rush to her side to help her regain her daughter. Surely if he truly cared for her, he would have dropped everything and taken the first train? She decided to wire him with her other concerns: PLEASE LOCATE MIGNON CHAMOND AND DANNY STOP SEND THEM HERE STOP I NEED YOU STOP PLEASE COME ALL SPEED.

For the first time in years Delia was not performing, and the lack of structure to her days was troubling. She hired a housekeeper, had a telephone installed, then seemed to spend most of her time waiting. She sent for a seamstress to measure her for suits and gowns, since she had bought only a bare minimum of clothes in Los Angeles before boarding the eastbound train. But still the time passed excruciatingly slowly. She needed to work, but for so long Julian had handled all of her bookings that she felt adrift without him.

Hugo had kept his distance. Nor did he ever appear when she visited Maggie and the child. Delia felt some small satisfaction that apparently Maggie was currently being ignored while he comforted his wife in her bereavement.

Then late one morning Delia awoke to a commotion at her door and, slipping on a dressing gown, went to the top of the stairs. Her housekeeper, a sturdy Cajun woman named Ruby, was barring Julian's path up the stairs. "No, suh, you ain't going up there—she's sleeping."

"It's all right, Ruby," Delia called. "Show Mr. Van Courtland into the drawing room and make some coffee."

She didn't bother to dress, or even comb her hair. Julian didn't warrant such consideration.

"Did you come straight here?" she demanded of him, seconds later.

"Yes. I—"

"Tell me about the baby I bore six years ago, Julian. Tell me again how she died."

For once the old cynical and patronizing Julian didn't respond. He looked almost haggard. He gave a barely audible sigh, almost of resignation. "What happened? Something must have come up to make you think about her now. What?"

"Oh, no, you don't, Julian. This time you're not getting away with answering a question by asking one."

He dropped heavily into a chair and stared at her morosely. "Believe it or not, but I fully intended to tell you the truth about the child. I just didn't expect it to be the first thing we discussed."

"You've already talked to Hugo," she accused.

"I told you, I came straight here. I've spoken to no one."

"Tell me about my baby, Julian."

"Do you remember when I found you in New York? On New Year's Day? All I could get out of you was that you wanted me to take the baby to Hugo. My God, his name was like a red rag to a bull. I thought then, of course, that he was the father. I knew damn well I wasn't. Then you flew at me like a wildcat, raking my face with your fingernails, screaming at me. I tried to ward you off without hurting you, but you fell and struck your head. When I went to pick you up, I saw that the lower part of your nightgown was soaked with blood. I grabbed a blanket and wrapped you in it, then rushed you to the nursing home, which belonged to an old friend from my New York days."

"And my baby?"

He had the grace to look contrite. "I thought you were dying, Delia. I didn't even think about the baby until you were in the care of the doctor, then realized I'd left her at the midwife's apartment. I went back immediately. There was no one at the apartment, so I asked a neighbor where I might find the midwife. I was informed that she was at work—in a garment factory. I then asked if the neighbor knew where the baby she had delivered was being cared for, and she just gave me a pitying look that to me indicated that a midwife who also worked in a garment factory would probably have taken the infant to an orphanage."

Delia stared at him in horror. "But you told me my daughter had *died*."

"How can I explain my reasons? Although on the one hand I suspected Hugo was the father, I couldn't get rid of the nagging possibility that it might be Thad Bouchet's. That being the case, if it got out, your career would be ruined. We might have been able to cover up a love-child that was a Van Courtland, but a colored baby? Besides, I had no idea where the baby had been taken, or indeed if she had survived. My only concern at that time was you. Your health, your career. When we reached the West Coast, I decided it would be best to tell you she was dead. That way you could grieve, then get on with your career."

Delia couldn't speak. How could she have believed such a monstrous lie? Why hadn't she persisted in learning from the nursing home exactly what had become of her baby? At the time, of course, she had been weak and ill, but surely she must bear half the blame for trusting him. Hadn't she always known that to Julian she was only a voice, not a human being? Hadn't he lied and bullied and manipulated her in the past? Hadn't he been furious that she had borne an illegitimate child?

Julian ran his hand through his hair distractedly. "Delia, listening to these rationalizations now, and examining the events from the perspective of the years between, I, too, am appalled by my callousness. I was a different man then. Please believe that. If there was any way on God's earth I could make it up to you for what I did, I would. Anything."

"You can," Delia said coldly. "You can get my daughter back for me."

He stared at her. "You do realize that admitting to the world that you have an illegitimate daughter could be the end of your career?"

"I don't care. I want my child."

She waited for an argument that didn't come.

"I can't go on like this!" Delia cried. "I was allowed only fifteen minutes alone with Patience—oh, how I hate that name!—and I know Maggie Nesbitt was crouched outside the door. And do you know what my daughter's first question to me was? 'Where is my daddy? When is he coming?' You know Maggie must have put her up to that."

"What did you say?"

"I babbled something about her daddy being in San Francisco, but that she'd meet him soon."

"Dr. Joe isn't her father."

"He's my husband. He'll become her father. The child is confused enough without telling her who her real father is."

"You won't be able to avoid that issue forever, you know."

"For now all I want is to have my daughter with me. I'll worry about Marcus later. For God's sake, Julian, do something."

"Sit down and listen to me, Delia. Jacob Lacey and I have examined every aspect of the situation, considered every possibility. Now we're planning our strategy—not least of which is to anticipate what the other side might do or say. We can't go in half-cocked. If we do you'll surely lose."

"Then let's just spirit Patience out of the house and leave with her. That's what Maggie Nesbitt did."

"Don't be ridiculous. She has a powerful ally in Hugo. He has far more influence in this town than either you or I do. Look, part of your problem is that you have too much time on your hands to brood. How would you like to give a concert, here in New Orleans? It will probably be your last if we have to fight the Nesbitt woman in court, as then there'll be no way we can keep Patience a secret."

"I don't think so—"

"Hear me out. When you sing, you're magic, Delia. Onstage you're incomparable. Now imagine the effect you'd have on a six-and-a-half-year-old girl who already loves music. . . ."

"But I—" She broke off, a vision of Patience sitting in the orchestra stalls, wide-eyed with wonder, flitting tantalizingly through her mind. "I suppose I could give one performance."

"Good. I'll see to it." He paused. "I saw Hugo today, by the way, and made arrangements to buy Courtland Hall from him."

"The old concert hall? Hasn't it been shut down for ages?"

"Yes. I'm going to restore it. I have a feeling I'm going to be in New Orleans for a while, and I need something to do. When your career crumbles in ashes, you can come and sing there, just for me, since no God-fearing citizens will buy tickets when your past becomes public knowledge."

"But won't the cost of renovating that old white elephant be prohibitive? I mean, we lost everything in San Francisco."

He laughed and for an instant the old devil-may-care Julian, who had not been in evidence recently, was back. "Ah, you've been reading about the insurance companies who have gone under and the claims that are unpaid. But you see, I had the foresight to insure all of our properties with Lloyds of London, and they, my sweet, are paying all their claims."

"Good. Then I can also buy a house. I hate living in someone else's property. I wish Mignon would arrive—I shall need a dresser if I'm going back to work."

"Mignon? What makes you think she's coming here?"

"I asked Joe to find her and Danny and send them here."

"I don't know about Mignon, but Danny might not want to leave Los Angeles. Sorry, but in all the confusion about your daughter, I forgot to tell you I'd sent Danny to the Zimmermans—he's the producer who wanted you to make a film for him."

"How on earth did you persuade him to take Danny in?"

"By hinting you'd be grateful. Also by investing in his company. I offered to pay for the boy's keep, but it seems Danny has quite captivated them, and, in fact, they're giving him a small part in a movie."

"I'd better send word to Joe not to search for him then."

"While you're in touch with your husband, see if you can get him to come to New Orleans, at least until we settle the dispute over your daughter. Lacey thinks the presence of a husband might help our case. You'd be viewed in a more favorable light if you could offer Patience a stable family situation."

Delia was busy again, finding a house to buy, selecting furniture, replenishing her wardrobe, rehearsing for the upcoming performance, offering advice to Julian in regard to the renovation of Courtland Hall, and spending every minute Maggie would allow with the Patience.

As the days turned to weeks and spring slipped into a hot Louisiana summer of lazy days and warm humid nights, Delia realized that there had been no word from her husband. She sent a wire, stating her concern that he was working too hard and asking again that he come to her.

Julian seemed different, changed in some way that puzzled Delia. He was less apt to lose his temper, or run roughshod over people, and he actually seemed to listen to her views and concerns. He arranged a concert performance, supported by an accomplished pianist who would not only accompany her, but would also play several solos. There was also a tenor and a rising young violinist on the program. But it was the promised appearance of the great Cordelia that had the city wild with anticipation.

As the date of the concert approached, Delia casually mentioned as they were leaving the theater after rehearsal that she would be visiting her daughter that evening.

"You haven't met her, Julian. Why don't you come with me?"

He hesitated. "I don't know if that would be such a good idea."

"Why not? You're her uncle."

He held the door for her. "That's true."

Out on the street she asked, "Well? Will you come with me?"

"Delia . . . what about Marcus? Doesn't he have a right to meet his daughter? Has it occurred to you that not only could he be a valuable ally to prove your claim to her, but you're depriving the child of her natural father."

Delia compressed her lips, afraid to speak. In a blinding flash of insight she realized she could never tell anyone that Marcus had raped her, for if she did there would always be the possibility that Patience would learn the abhorrent circumstances of her birth. Delia knew she could never inflict such a terrible burden upon the little girl who daily grew more dear to her.

Julian went on: "Marcus never leaves the Willows, but maybe we could talk Mrs. Nesbitt into allowing us to take Patience out there. And if she balks, we could get Hugo to use his influence over her."

"I haven't told anyone but you that Marcus is her father," Delia said slowly. "I don't care if Hugo knows, but I don't believe I want to take Patience to the Willows. Marcus is . . . so unpredictable."

"Ninety percent of the time Marcus is perfectly rational," Julian said shortly. "He's subject to moods, I'll grant you, and doesn't always behave in a way the rest of us consider appropriate. But he's an extremely intelligent and creative man nonetheless and could perhaps add a great deal to your daughter's life. You said she plays the flute. Like it or not, Delia, Patience is the issue of two musical geniuses. She should be made aware of that fact and given the chance to meet her father."

"I'll think about it," Delia answered, knowing full well she would see Marcus in hell before she'd allow him near Patience.

"Good. Come on, let's go and meet her. What does she call Hugo?"

"Uncle Hugo."

"In that case I shall be Uncle Julian."

They were a little late in arriving at Maggie's house, and when Jemmie opened the door and saw Julian, her eyes widened. "Why, Mr. Julian, suh, I ain't seen you in a coon's age. Y'all sure look mighty fine. Come on in."

Although Maggie usually stayed out of the way during Delia's visits, the sound of a male voice brought her hurrying from the kitchen. Watching, Delia saw the look of anticipation on Maggie's face vanish. She had undoubtedly thought that Hugo had come.

"I'm Julian Van Courtland. I hope you don't mind my dropping in unexpectedly, Mrs. Nesbitt. I realize it's a tremendous imposition, but from what I've heard you are a gracious and understanding lady."

Julian offered his hand, and Maggie took it hesitantly. He smiled warmly. "As you probably know, I am Delia's friend and business manager and as such have a great desire to meet her daughter."

He looked around appreciatively. "You have a lovely home, Mrs. Nesbitt. Patience is fortunate indeed to live in such beautiful surroundings."

The old Van Courtland charm has felled many a less sophisticated woman, Delia thought, as Julian chatted smoothly with both Maggie and Jemmie, and somehow all of them moved into the drawing room, where Patience waited. Delia's pulse quickened as she saw that for the first time the little girl held her flute.

Delia was so filled with anticipation at the sight of the flute that she did not at first notice that Julian had stopped abruptly, obviously stunned by his first view of her daughter.

Before anyone could speak, Patience's eyes lit up, and she cried, "Daddy?"

There was an awkward pause before Maggie said, "Patience, this is Mr. Julian Van Courtland. He is Uncle Hugo's brother."

He gave the child a courtly bow and a friendly smile, but shock still lingered in his eyes. "I'd be honored if you'd call me Uncle Julian."

The disappointment in Patience's eyes at this announcement tugged at Delia's conscience. She salved her guilt by telling herself that when Joe arrived all would be well.

The little girl bobbed a curtsy, her pale face flushing in an agony of shyness.

Delia had had time to grow accustomed to the child's startling resemblance to herself, and it was reassuring to see how bowled over Julian was by it. Surely any judge and jury would see at a glance that she and Patience were mother and daughter.

"I hear you like to play the flute," Julian said. "Your mother has been eagerly looking forward to hearing you play."

Patience glanced at Maggie, whose expression was stony. Julian said quickly, "I mean Delia and I would love to hear you."

To Delia's astonishment, the child picked up the flute. She hesitated, blushing to the roots of her hair and visibly trembling. Julian smiled encouragingly, and Delia saw Patience relax slightly. He reminds her of Hugo, Delia thought, whom she obviously adores.

Then the hauntingly sweet notes of the flute filled the room, and they listened, spellbound, aware only of the music and not of the tensions and enmity between the adults.

When she lowered the flute and regarded them shyly, they burst into enthusiastic applause, and Patience lowered her eyes and smiled happily.

"What was that piece, honey?" Delia asked. "I didn't recognize it, but it was truly beautiful."

"I made it up," the little girl answered. " 'Specially for you, Delia."

Julian's eyes met Delia's, and she read his unspoken message clearly. *You see, she is a true child of my brother.*

At a loss for words Delia glanced in Maggie's direction and saw the tears coursing down her cheeks. Delia felt a wave of sympathy for the other woman, who seemed to be folding into herself. Did she realize now that she had lost the child? Surely she must see that Patience's destiny lay in her mother's world?

Maggie said in a choked voice, "Patience has homework to do. You were late getting here."

"My fault," Julian said quickly. "Come on, Delia, let's not wear out our welcome. Patience, thank you for playing for us. You are a very talented young lady. In your own way, you remind me of another little girl I once knew."

"Jemmie will show you out," Maggie said, turning away to try to hide the fact that she was crying.

Impulsively Delia bent and embraced her daughter. It was the first time she had dared to touch her, and feeling the silky hair against her cheek and the soft skin encasing delicate bones, Delia was overwhelmed with a powerful feeling of love and connection. Only when Julian coughed discreetly did Delia reluctantly release the child.

Patience was regarding her with eyes that were mirrors of her own. *She feels it, too,* Delia thought triumphantly.

It was difficult for her to say goodbye, and she was glad Julian was at her side, urging her out of the house, or she wasn't sure what might have happened.

As the front door closed behind them, Julian said quietly, "I don't believe you need fear the outcome of any legal dispute, Delia. No court in the world would question that she is your daughter."

How good it felt to be onstage again, the houselights dimmed, feeling the excitement of the audience out there in the darkness as the burst of applause that had greeted her appearance faded into an expectant hush. Then the spotlight found her, and the pianist played the first notes of her accompaniment.

Delia had selected a magnificent gown of white satin trimmed with seed pearls. No man's suit for this performance, not with her daughter sitting front row center. Delia wanted to be mother, star, fairy godmother, all rolled into one.

Julian had reserved the entire front row orchestra stalls for the family. To her surprise, Maggie had not only agreed to allow Patience to come, but accepted Julian's invitation to accompany her. Hugo had brought Gabrielle, her father, and her sister. Julian had remarked with satisfaction that this was Gabrielle's first public appearance since her cousin's death. She still wore deepest mourning, but in the moment before the houselights dimmed, Delia saw that Gabrielle's raven tresses were elaborately coiffed, and although she was very pale, she looked less haggard than at their first meeting. Delia wondered how Maggie felt, being seated so close to her lover's wife. Surely Maggie would not have come had she known Hugo would bring Gabrielle?

But, hearing her cue, Delia put aside all speculation and lost herself in her performance. Returning to her first and still most spectacular success, she did not just sing the part of Fioria Tosca, she became the passionate, enraged, fiery Fioria. Critics had said her rendition owed more to her own genius than to the libretto and this was never more true than now, for as she sang she was able to unleash all of the passion she kept so rigidly tethered in real life, which had never been more intense than during this battle to regain her child.

Her second selection was from *Madame Butterfly*, and again her interpretation was unique, for she refused to play the pathetic child-bride, Cio-Cio San, as a victim used and tossed aside, and instead transformed the character into a woman expressing her longing and loneliness. Delia sang directly to her daughter.

Only when the houselights came up and she scanned the orchestra stalls did she see that another man had joined the family on the front row.

He sat on the aisle, immobile as a statue, not rising with the rest of the audience, who were on their feet giving her a standing ovation. He sat with the Van Courtlands, yet seemed remote, alone, not a part of the family. Her smile froze on her face. *Marcus.* Julian must have invited him.

She was handed an enormous bouquet of roses, and dozens of single flowers were tossed onstage. She took her curtain calls automatically, acutely aware of Marcus only an arm's length away from her daughter. From his daughter.

Her dressing room was already filled with flowers and jammed with people when she reached it. She could see Julian, a head and shoulders taller than anyone else, but there was no sign of any other members of his party. She beckoned for Julian to come to her, but he rolled his eyes to indicate he was trapped and continued his conversation with one of the theater critics.

Delia said, "Excuse me," to the circle of well-wishers pressing close and inched her way to his side. Glancing down, he said casually that he'd arranged for a table at one of New Orleans' leading restaurants for a late supper.

"Is ... everyone coming?" Delia mouthed the words that would have been lost in the babble of congratulatory voices.

Julian shook his head.

Delia's usual post-performance euphoria had diminished considerably at the sight of Marcus, and she paid little attention to the accolades showered upon her. When at last they were able to escape from her dressing room, she kept silent until they were in Julian's car en route to the restaurant, then asked, "Why did you bring Marcus?"

"I didn't bring him," Julian snapped. "Nor did I invite him, or even tell him about the concert. When he came in just after the curtain went up, nobody was more surprised than I was. I suppose Hugo could have invited him, or perhaps Marcus read about the concert in the papers and simply decided on his own to come."

Delia digested this news silently for a moment, then asked, "Will Hugo be joining us at the restaurant?

"Gabrielle is in mourning, had you forgotten? And Hugo is playing the dutiful husband. It was quite a concession on her part to accept tickets for the concert. None of the others will be at your party; they all left immediately after the last curtain call."

Delia felt as if cold water had been thrown in her face. She said quietly, "I was hoping Maggie would bring Patience. I barely had a chance to speak to her—and they didn't come backstage."

"Rest assured, your daughter was duly impressed."

He sounded distant, his mind elsewhere.

She said, "Did Marcus . . . was he introduced?"

"To Mrs. Nesbitt and Patience? I don't know. As I said, he slipped in after the curtain went up and left without acknowledging any of us. But he saw the child when the houselights went on. And he could have spoken to Hugo and the others in the lobby as they were leaving. We were in your dressing room by then."

"Do you think he suspects?"

"That she's your daughter? How could he not? For all we know, Hugo's recruited him to their side. Why else would he bring him tonight, if indeed he did?"

"What can they do?"

"Well, Marcus has as much a claim to a blood tie as you do."

Delia felt a chill. She had never even considered Marcus might be an adversary to her regaining her child.

At the restaurant they were instantly surrounded by an adoring crowd of strangers, but for Delia the luster of the evening had faded.

When it was all over and she was alone in bed, she agonized over all of the possibilities. Surely Marcus would not stand in her way? But what if Julian was right, and Hugo planned to use Marcus in some way to ensure that Patience stayed with Maggie? She tried to reassure herself by remembering that Hugo didn't know that Patience was his half-brother's child.

Knowing she must think less of disturbing matters if she was to get to sleep, she forced herself to recall the rapturous applause after her performance. It was then, for the first time since meeting her daughter, Delia felt a pang of regret that the scandal of her illegitimacy would in all probability mean that she would never again experience the almost mystical bonding with an audience that occurred when she sang.

If only Maggie would give up Patience, quietly, without lawyers and publicity. There must be some way to convince her.

Joe will be here soon, Delia thought. When he arrives we will show everyone that we are a loving, devoted couple. I could give some charity performances, he can start another practice here. Compared to a single working woman conducting a back-street romance with a married man . . .

Delia fell asleep amid visions of domestic bliss and a continuing career.

She was awakened by Ruby urgently shaking her arm. "Miz Delia? Wake up."

Opening one eye Delia saw that it was barely eight o'clock. She groaned. "What is it, Ruby? I swear I only just fell asleep."

"Gentleman heah to see y'all. Sez he's got bad news, Miz Delia. I figured I'd best wake you."

"I'm not sure I want to hear bad news at this time of the morning. Who is it? Did he give his name?"

"Mr. Oscar Latimer."

The reporter who hounded her in San Francisco, Delia thought, and with whom she had left the devastated city. So he had followed her all the way to New Orleans. "Tell him to come back at a reasonable hour. I may consent to speak with him then."

"My news can't wait," Latimer's voice said from the bedroom door.

Delia sat up. "Damn you, how dare you burst into my house? Ruby, go and call the police."

"It's about your husband, Mrs. Simmington," Latimer said. "Better you hear it from me than read it in the papers. It's only a matter of time before somebody back in San Francisco realizes that he's married to you. I recognized the name immediately."

"Get *out!*"

"He's dead, Delia. Your husband is dead. He contracted bubonic plague."

Chapter 40

*

"You're feeling more guilt than grief," Julian said. "Why don't you admit it? Joe wasn't your husband, he was some sort of figurehead—a prince consort you felt you ought to have. Most of the time you were hardly aware of his existence."

For once Delia welcomed his taunts. She felt she deserved them. But Julian should be assigned his fair share of guilt. "Joe tried to get the city and the property owners to do something about rats. Including you, Julian. If anyone should feel guilt, it should be you."

"I owned one boardinghouse in Chinatown. You think if I'd eliminated the rats, my neighbors would have done the same? I listened to Joe's warning and heeded them in the only way I could—I sold the place and got out of the landlord business, as you very well know."

Delia paced distractedly around the cramped sitting room of her rented house. Her newly purchased house was much larger and would be ready to move into within days. She had planned to share it with her husband, creating a loving home for her daughter. But Joe wasn't coming, not now, not ever.

"Perhaps it's not true—perhaps it was another doctor?"

"It was Joe, Delia. I checked. He died the morning of the day Latimer boarded an eastbound train. With all the chaos of rebuilding San Francisco and taking care of the homeless, the newspapers have been concentrating only on major developments there. But even apart from that, I expect the politicians want to keep the outbreak of plague quiet. They probably brought pressure to bear to squash the story that a doctor and several of his patients had succumbed to plague."

"I should have stayed with him."

"Don't be ridiculous. What good would that have done?

You know, I'm surprised Latimer didn't break the news that you're a widow to the press, political pressure notwithstanding. He's up to something, coming here. Perhaps trying to win your confidence by pretending deference for your feelings."

"What about Mignon? He said she was one of Joe's patients."

Julian frowned. "She is dead, as he reported. But I don't know if it was plague, or from her injuries. She was trapped in a collapsed building for over forty-eight hours before they found her."

Delia placed the palm of her hand against her forehead, feeling her guilt intensify. If she hadn't been in San Francisco, Mignon never would have gone there, and would still be alive. "The funeral arrangements . . ." she began.

"Delia, they don't keep plague victims for days after death. He was cremated immediately."

She shivered. "What about Mignon?"

"Buried the day before Joe died. A state of emergency exists in San Francisco. Why, before I left they were unceremoniously burying corpses in shallow graves as quickly as they could, for obvious reasons. Look, Delia, that part of your life is over. There's no point in going back. The city is in ruins. What would you do? Try to hold some sort of memorial service for them? You can do that here. Besides, if you leave New Orleans now, you'll loose all the ground you've gained with your daughter."

Patience. Of course. She must think about her daughter now.

"Have you eaten anything today?"

"Ruby brought me a tray. Leave me now, will you, Julian? I have a headache."

He stared at her for a moment. "Are you going to be all right? You won't do anything foolish, will you? At least not without giving me a chance to talk you out of it."

"I just want to be alone for a little while."

"When are you scheduled for another visit with Patience?"

"We didn't make any arrangements. I expected to see Maggie after the concert."

"I'll come back this evening. We can have a quiet dinner and talk about it then."

After he left Delia found it impossible to sit down and relax. The lack of some ritual to perform in regard to her husband's passing troubled her greatly. Death should not be as distant and as vague as this. She wondered if Mignon still had friends or family here in New Orleans. They would want to know what had become of her.

Perhaps someone still lived in Daddy Lou's old house on the bayou. Someone who would know where to find mourners for Mignon.

"Ruby," Delia called to her housekeeper, "I'm going out. But first I'm going to bathe and change clothes. Would you make some tea for me, please?"

Delia stepped from the cloying scent of night jasmine into the musty long-dead odor of the house, and stood for a moment in twilight shadows.

Most of the living room furniture was gone; only the old sofa that had survived the hurricane's floodwaters remained, its colors faded into an indistinguishable blur, spilling stuffing from one arm as if it had been wounded.

For one disorienting instant echoes from long ago whispered in her mind. Eulie's full-throated contralto singing her praise of the Lord, Mignon's earthy giggle, the clear sweet notes of Daddy Lou's horn creating a new kind of music that was his alone.

But the music was long gone, and the only real sounds she could hear were the soft scurrying of mice and the chirp of crickets.

She walked slowly through the deserted rooms of the ground floor, remembering how Daddy Lou had once welcomed every vagabond and down-on-his-luck musician who knocked at the door. Now only the lonely echo of her own footsteps followed. The voodoo woman had driven them all away. How long had Abebe stayed after Eulie died? she wondered. Probably until there was nothing left to sell and the tax man was at the door.

In the kitchen the big old icebox still stood in the corner, a lonely sentinel that regarded her malevolently. "You ugly beast," Delia said softly. "You're still here, huh? You tried to kill the old man, but I didn't let you get away with it."

She wasn't sure why she reached out to open the icebox.

What had she been expecting to find? Some relic of the past? What could be inside except some mildewed cheese or a scrap of putrid meat?

Then the door came open, and she stared in astonishment at an array of fresh food. A quick check showed that the block of ice was only just beginning to melt and could not have been there long.

Spinning around, she looked at the dishes in the sink and then at the chair pulled up to the scrubbed wood table. Then she was running, out into the corridor, up the stairs, and into the first bedroom.

She was met with a veil of cobwebs and the stench of mouse droppings, and quickly retreated. The second bedroom was also empty and long-unused.

At the third door she hesitated, then slowly pushed it open.

The room beyond was filled with long shadows. The window was open, and the last light of the dying day picked a faint dust-flecked path through a jumble of boxes and broken chairs. A space had been cleared in front of the window, and a battered mattress lay on the floor, covered with a threadbare blanket. The last item her seeking gaze found lay on the window ledge.

She was staring at a clarinet, her mind reeling, when he said mockingly, "Welcome to my humble abode. How are you, Delia?"

A match flared, was touched to a candle, and he stood in the circle of amber light surrounded by shadows.

Only the voice was the same. That hypnotic mixture of French and British English, softened by a warm Caribbean lilt and lightly spiced with New Orleans patois. Had he not spoken, she doubted she would have recognized him in a crowd. Indeed would probably have looked away quickly from the dirty overalls hanging loosely on his gaunt frame. The skin of his face was stretched so tightly over the bones that only his eyes seemed to be living. She had seen pictures of starving people in distant parts of the world and recognized that he was severely malnourished. Yet there was plenty of food downstairs in the icebox.

"For God's sake, Thad, how long have you been living here?" she asked at last.

"Since my mother died."

"But why? *Why?*"

He shrugged skeletal shoulders. "I fought a long battle with Abebe to reclaim my mother's house. I thought I'd won when she at last moved out. But, as you can see, she was the final victor."

"Oh, for the love of heaven, you're not going to tell me she put a hex on you?"

He gave her a sad smile and shrugged again.

"Have you seen a doctor? Are you ill?"

"I am slowly dying, Delia. No one can stop it."

"That's ridiculous and you know it. Come on, let's go downstairs, and I'll make a meal for us."

"I can't eat."

"Can't—or won't? If you don't eat, why is there food in the icebox?"

"I put it there. The ice wagon comes, and there's a boy who goes to the market for me. But I can't eat. I try, but my throat closes up. She told me it would happen if I sent her away."

Frightened by the inevitability in his voice and the defeat in every line of his body, she snapped, "Thad, you're an educated, well-traveled man. You aren't some ignorant darky."

"Isn't it strange that I once thought so, too? But I was born on Martinique, and the old ways, the old powers, always had me in their grip. I just didn't want to accept it."

"You know damn good and well nobody has the power to will another person to starve themselves to death. *You are doing this to yourself.*"

"How beautiful you are," he said wonderingly. "So fair. My pale princess—that's what I used to call you, you know. What I felt for you was . . . a form of worship, I suppose."

"We were friends, Thad. You were the best friend I ever had. I didn't deserve to be cast aside like an old pair of shoes, without a word, or a hint of a goodbye. You must have known I would worry that you were dead, or hurt, or sick. Why, I even feared one of the Van Courtlands had lynched you."

He picked up the clarinet and held it to his lips, then lowered it to his side. "I went to the Willows when I heard you were expecting a child."

"How did you know? I told no one."

"The voodoo woman knew—all the darkies knew. There was only Marcus at the Willows, living in the old plantation house like some feudal lord. He was angry, threatened me. He acted as if I were the father."

"Thad, there's no point in going over this."

"But you just said I cast you aside. I want you to know that when I heard you were in trouble, I did go looking for you. I wanted to help you."

"But like everybody else, you were disappointed in me. I can hear it in your voice."

"As I said, I worshipped you. I felt you'd defiled yourself, I suppose. It's not rational, but it's the way men look at women—at least at the ones they care about."

"Marcus raped me." The words seemed to shudder from her.

The clarinet slid from Thad's fingers and crashed to the floor. He took a step toward her, his arms outstretched, and she allowed him to hold her for a moment, knowing he wanted to comfort her, but inwardly she recoiled from the proximity of his emaciated body and fragile bones. Perhaps she shivered involuntarily, for he released her at once.

"Delia, I'm sorry . . . I had no idea."

"I have a daughter," she said quickly. "It's a long story. And I have some bad news about Mignon."

"Where the hell have you been?" Julian demanded. "I've been out looking everywhere for you."

"I went out to the old house on the bayou where Daddy Lou and Mignon lived." She walked into the kitchen. "Did Ruby go home?"

"Hours ago. You might have told her where you were going."

"Where I go is nobody's business but my own. If you must know, I went to see if any of Mignon's friends or relatives still lived there."

"And did they?"

She hesitated. "No."

"Delia, I'm afraid we have a crisis on our hands."

"Patience? Is my daughter all right?" Panicked, she clutched his shirtfront.

"Maggie phoned, only minutes ago. I was just about to

leave to start another search. Don't worry, she can't have gone far."

"She ran away?" Delia felt her heart stop. "Do you think she might come to me? I told her I lived quite close, and even though she doesn't know the address, I told her there was a big old magnolia tree in front of the house and honeysuckle vines climbing all over the walls."

"You'd better wait here, just in case. I'll go to Maggie's house and start from there."

"But what did Maggie say? What happened? Patience seemed to enjoy the concert last night. Surely either Maggie or Jemmie must have seen this coming—couldn't they have stopped her? Oh, dear God, she's so little . . . I can't bear the thought of her being alone in the Quarter at this time of night."

"Delia, we'll agonize later. Let's find her first."

Chapter 41

*

HUGO

There were three women in my life, you see, and in a way I loved all of them.

"Calm down," Hugo said, "and tell me exactly what happened."

Maggie's russet-brown hair streamed wildly about her shoulders, and she had obviously dressed hurriedly as the buttons of her bodice were mismatched. Her arrival at his house in the early hours of the morning was reason enough for alarm without her almost incoherent recital of the events of the evening.

She drew a deep breath. "Patience is gone," she said again. "I went into her room to check on her, the way I always do before I go to bed. She wasn't there. I phoned Delia's house—I thought—I don't know—I just thought maybe Delia had come and got her, or at least persuaded her to sneak out to meet her. Patience was so entranced . . . seeing Delia on-stage."

"We must call the police and organize a search," Hugo said, reaching for the telephone.

"We've already done that. When I phoned Delia, she wasn't home, but your brother answered the phone."

"Julian?"

"Yes. He's out looking for Patience now. Delia is waiting at her house in case Patience goes there. Hugo, I'm sorry about waking you up, but I didn't know what your phone number here was, and the operator wouldn't give it to me."

"I don't have my home number listed in the directory. Maggie, think back to before Patience went to bed. Did she say anything? Was she unhappy, worried? Did she give you any hint of what might be troubling her?"

Maggie bit her lip. "She talked about Delia's singing all through dinner. I might have said something . . . maybe I was a bit short with her, you know, cut her off when she was going on about the concert. But not enough to cause her to run away. Oh, dear Lord, what if she's been kidnapped?"

"Let's not jump to any conclusions. Could you tell if she'd taken anything with her?"

"The only thing missing is her flute. She always slept with it on her bed table."

"I doubt a kidnapper would have picked it up. It sounds more like she ran away. Think, Maggie, something must have happened to precipitate this."

Maggie paced a small circle around his study, where he had hurriedly taken her after his butler awakened him, in the hope that Gabrielle would not hear them. "We've been under a strain ever since Delia arrived. It seems with every visit Patience gets more confused. You know it must have something to do with her finding out I'm not her mother. Oh, what shall I do? If any harm comes to my baby—" She dissolved into tears.

Hugo caught her and pulled her close to him. He wrapped his arms around her and stroked her hair back from her brow. He wasn't sure how long they stood there as he tried to calm her, but there was no passion in his embrace.

Gabrielle's voice slashed between them with the impact of a saber. "How dare you bring that woman into my house?"

They sprang apart guiltily. Gabrielle stood at the door.

"Mrs. Nesbitt's daughter is missing. Naturally she's distraught. Please go back to bed, Gabrielle. We'll talk in the morning."

Maggie said quickly, "I'll go, Hugo. I'm sorry . . ."

"Get in touch with all of her friends, talk to your neighbors," Hugo said. "Wake up the whole town if you have to. Somebody must have seen her. I'll come to your house as soon as I've made some inquiries of my own." He led the way to the door, and Gabrielle stood aside to allow them to pass, giving Maggie a venomous stare.

After seeing her out, Hugo ran up the stairs to his room to dress. Gabrielle followed and stood watching as he pulled on his trousers and reached for a shirt. "Please don't go chasing after her, Hugo."

"Don't you understand? The child has run away. She's only six. We have to find her."

"In all probability Delia has her. You saw how starstruck that little girl was when she saw her mother onstage. If, as you claim, the child is not yours, I wish you'd stay out of it."

"Patience is not mine, but that doesn't mean I don't care about her. I do. Besides, they've already established that she didn't go to Delia's."

"Hugo . . ." Gabrielle's voice was husky, seductive. "I thought we'd grown closer lately . . . you've been so kind to me since Alain died. Don't let that woman come between us now. I wouldn't be surprised if she hid the child away herself, just to get you back."

"That's unworthy of you, Gabrielle. But I suppose a childless woman could not imagine the torture a mother goes through in circumstances such as these."

"How cruel of you to remind me that I am barren, Hugo."

He stared at her for a moment, unreasonably angry with her for his own slip of the tongue. What he had said was unforgivable, and he knew it. Oh, Lord, was he still punishing her for Alain? Or perhaps for being the catalyst, by telling Delia about Patience, that precipitated this crisis. He muttered, "I'm sorry. But please try to understand that Maggie's whole world has been shattered. And this—this is the ultimate agony."

"No, it isn't, Hugo. The child will be found I'm sure—it won't be the ultimate agony unless she's dead, and I pray that won't come to pass," Gabrielle said quietly, all hint of seduction gone, replaced by that new maturity he had caught glimpses of recently and which had intrigued him, in spite of himself. Gabrielle was complex, unpredictable, and he never knew from one minute to the next what new facet of herself she would reveal. She added, "After you've found the little girl, we must talk about the future, Hugo. I'm beginning to see that there have been too many hurts, too many battles, just . . . too much in our past."

"What are you saying, Gabrielle? That you want a formal end to our marriage?"

"Perhaps." She stood facing him, with shoulders squared and chin high in her go-to-hell pose. She had faced him thus on the day he had been about to walk out on her, years ago when he learned of her perfidy. Perversely, it was her don't-give-a-damn attitude that made him stay, albeit on his own terms; which had turned their marriage into a sham that had punished him as much as her.

Without another word she turned and walked away. A moment later he head her bedroom door close.

Before dawn Hugo had assembled an army of searchers, police, Pinkertons, and a dozen of his own employees. Every house within a two-mile radius of Maggie's house was checked, every possibility investigated. But Patience seemed to have vanished without a trace. Hugo's heart was heavy as he walked up the garden path to Maggie's front door.

Jemmie opened the door before he reached it. She suddenly appeared very old and worn. He shook his head in response to her questioning look, and tears coursed down her wrinkled cheeks. Wordlessly he patted her shoulder and went into the kitchen, where Maggie sat slumped at the kitchen table, an untouched cup of coffee in front of her. The agony on her face as she looked up tore at his heart.

"I'm sorry, Maggie. No word yet. But don't despair. We'll find her soon." He spoke with more conviction than he felt, telling her of the organized search parties and how he had ordered his secretary to make telephone calls to city officials, sent his butler and menservants to put out the word to the street vendors and carriage drivers in the Quarter, and all of the business owners.

"Everyone in town is looking for her, Maggie. Why don't you try to get some rest?"

"If anything happens to her ... I don't know what I'll do. Oh, Hugo, my baby's whole world was thrown into turmoil, and I didn't help matters. I was so angry with Delia that I took it out on the child. Hugo, I remembered something Patience said yesterday. . . . I'd brought some designs home to work on after dinner, and one was a ball gown. Patience came to say good night while I was putting the finishing touches to it, and she said, 'Cordelia could wear that gown on the stage couldn't she?' "

Maggie dragged her hand through her tangled hair, raising reddened eyes to look at him. "I'm ashamed to say—I suppose I was jealous, and I thought, Patience doesn't see that

I've created a beautiful gown. All she sees is that Delia is a star to be worshiped and adored, and the rest of us are here only to serve her. I know it's too much to put on the back of a child, and I had no right to expect praise for my design. . . . After all, she'd heard Delia sing only the night before and she was magnificent."

Hugo stood beside her, wanting to comfort her but afraid to touch her. For the moment it seemed wise to merely allow her to talk.

She went on: "I don't remember exactly what I said—something to the effect that Delia would probably go back to wearing a man's suit before long, that she was just trying to impress the Van Courtlands the other night. Some mean, petty thing that I wish I hadn't even thought, much less said. And then Patience's eyes got huge, you know the way they do—that misty lavender glow they get that just breaks your heart . . . and she said, if I wasn't here you wouldn't be mad at Cordelia and Uncle Hugo wouldn't be mad at you and everybody would be happy."

Hugo felt a chill. "Why didn't you tell me this before? My God, you don't think . . ." *No, surely the child is too young to contemplate such a solution. But if she thinks she has caused the rift, she could well have hidden herself away where we might never find her in time.*

He dropped his hand to Maggie's shoulder. "Chances are, she hasn't run away at all. She has probably crawled into some hiding place, Maggie. Think—where might that be? She's a six year old who sees the adults acting crazy because of her and reasons that if she isn't here they'll all get along again. Perhaps she hid somewhere and became trapped. Do you have any trunks or cupboards or boxes? Anything she might be able to get into but can't get out of?"

Maggie jumped to her feet. "A steamer trunk—it has a heavy lid. It's in the attic. She sometimes goes up there to play her flute."

He raced ahead of her, shoving aside the thought that the child could already have suffocated, bypassing the nagging suspicion that if she went to the attic to play her flute, it might be because Maggie had tried to discourage her from any musical inclinations.

But the dust and cobwebs of the attic were undisturbed, the

steamer trunk empty. Patience had not been up here for some time. "Let's check all of the closets and cupboards again," Hugo said. "We'll do it room by room."

An hour later they completed their search of every inch of the house. There was no sign of the child.

They stood in the child's room, which had a curiously deserted appearance, despite the fact that the bedcovers were turned back, as though Patience had just got up.

Hugo looked at Maggie's ravaged face and felt helpless to comfort such agony. He said awkwardly, "I'd better go home—Gabrielle will be worried—"

Gabrielle would not be worried, of course. She concerned herself only with that which affected her personally. How he wished Gabrielle were more like Maggie, with her empathy and compassion. The thought startled him, for it seemed to hint that he had never really wanted Maggie after all, and he was not yet ready to admit even to himself that his feelings for his wife were still so strong.

The doorbell rang, shattering the silence. Hugo ran down the stairs and opened the door.

Julian stood outside. "Any word?"

Hugo shook his head.

Julian, who was as unshaven and disheveled as himself, said carefully, "I have an idea where she might be."

Chapter 42

*

Most of the journey had been made in tense silence. Hugo drove his car, although he knew the road ahead would be bumpy, possibly swampy, maybe impassable as they traveled deeper into bayou country. The automobile was a temperamental mode of transport, and as interwoven branches closed overhead, turning the dirt road into a dark tunnel, he began to regret not using the more reliable horse-drawn carriage. The humid heat of the afternoon was oppressive, and the lack of conversation grated on his nerves.

Julian sat beside him, staring straight ahead. They practically had to tie Maggie up to keep her from accompanying them, but managed to get out of the city without her by insisting that if Julian's assumption was correct, her presence would inflame the situation.

Hugo braked as he saw a fallen cypress blocking the road. Julian cursed. It was obvious they could not get around the dead tree, nor would they be able to move it.

Turning off the engine, Hugo said, "Fontenay is only a couple of miles away. We can get a skiff there and take the river the rest of the way."

They scrambled over the cypress and set off on foot. After a few minutes they both took off their jackets and loosened shirt collars.

"I hope this isn't a wild-goose chase," Hugo said. "You never said what makes you think the child is there."

"Process of elimination," Julian answered tersely.

Hugo waited for an elaboration, but none came.

Minutes later Julian suddenly asked, "When are you going to make up your mind about which woman you want, Hugo? Haven't you strung them all along for long enough?"

"What are you talking about?"

"Oh, don't play the fool with me. I'm talking about your wife versus your mistress and where Delia fits into the scheme of things."

Hugo wiped the sweat from his forehead with the back of his hand. "Not that it's any of your business, but Maggie isn't my mistress."

"And Gabrielle isn't your wife. Hasn't been for years. So who does that leave?"

"Ah, I see. Delia again. I don't know why you didn't marry her yourself years ago when you had the chance. But in any case, she's married to a doctor, isn't she?"

"Joe Simmington is dead. We just heard. She's a widow."

"And you think I might take that as a licence to pursue her? Julian, you're blinded by your own obsession with her. Oh, I'll grant you that she's beautiful, magnetic, and I'm sure every man who sees her lusts after her. For myself, I am awed by her talent, but I wouldn't want to spend my life with such a woman. Forever envied by other men, always in her shadow. I believe to play that role would take a different kind of man than myself."

"Someone who doesn't give a damn what people think?" Julian suggested.

"Such as yourself," Hugo agreed.

"What kind of woman does appeal to you, Hugo?" His half-brother sounded genuinely interested.

Hugo found himself facing the question honestly, although he didn't respond. He thought of Maggie and the fantasies of domestic bliss he had harbored. Had he really believed he could be happy with her? Like Delia, she gave most of her energy to a career. Would she be willing to give it up and devote herself to being a wife and mother? He had seen Maggie engrossed in one of her sketches, noted her pleasure when one of her designs captivated a client. Surely running his household could not compare in terms of personal satisfaction?

Gabrielle, on the other hand, gloried in her role as mistress of a fine house. It was what she had been raised for, groomed for, and performed to perfection. She loved to entertain, and invitations to her parties were keenly sought after. Hugo had relied on her to preside over gatherings of his friends and business associates, not to mention various and sundry politicians, even after for all intents and purposes their marriage had ended. She was vivacious, an interesting and well-read conversationalist, and knew how to flirt and flatter her male guests without either annoying their wives or crossing the line into indiscretion; skills Southern women of her class seemed to be born with.

He had not been madly in love with her when he married her, indeed believed romantic love was probably an invention of the poets, but he realized now that he had desired her more than any other woman. How ironic it was that the reluctant bridegroom had so quickly turned into the ardent husband, only to find that his bride loved another man. He had not admitted, even to himself, how Gabrielle's perfidy had devastated him. Perhaps that was why he had turned to Maggie, as a sanctuary from turbulence. The truth was, he still wanted Gabrielle, in spite of everything. But pride would not permit him to forgive her infidelity, nor even to attempt to understand it.

Lost in his own thoughts, Hugo was surprised when Julian spoke, seemingly reading his mind, "You know what I think, Hugo? I think what you really want is all three women— rolled into one. You'd like to combine Maggie's loyalty and motherly quality with Delia's stoicism and courage and wrap them up into a package with your wife's sophistication and physical desirability. At the same time, of course, dispensing with all of what you perceive to be their faults. In other words, you have unrealistic expectations of any woman."

"It's too damned hot and humid for such ruminations," Hugo muttered. "If we must talk, we should be discussing more pressing concerns."

Julian chose to ignore the remark. "It's interesting to note that not only has Delia been widowed, but so—in a sense— has Gabrielle."

"Oh, I'm still alive, Julian, and still married to her."

"I was referring to Cousin Alain's demise."

Hugo was silent for a moment. "How long have you known?"

"Since before you were married."

"Why didn't you tell me?"

"It was none of my business. Besides, I thought you knew. You two wouldn't be the first married couple with such an arrangement. I'm forever baffled by the need of people to keep things tidy, in spite of the misery their orderly lives cause."

"No one could ever accuse you of obeying the rules of society, Julian. But I hate to think what the world would be like if everybody indulged their every whim and propriety be damned."

Fontenay, with its gracious columns, magnolias in full bloom, and long driveway lined with moss-draped oaks, came into view.

Julian whistled. "Looks as if somebody did considerable restoration and renovation here. I wouldn't have recognized the place. I guess your wife found a way to amuse herself while you were on your travels and her cousin was on his deathbed."

It was true, Hugo thought, Gabrielle had transformed her family home. Seeing Fontenay through Julian's eyes, as a smartly dressed butler responded to the door and conducted them inside, Hugo noted that paintings and rugs had been cleaned and restored, fresh flowers decorated every table, and mirrors and brasses gleamed. His wife had spent her time, and his money, wisely and with considerable flare. She often entertained guests here, and, in fact, he had dropped in on several parties for appearances' sake. Since he had given the Willows to Marcus, Fontenay had become her country home, and the gracious old plantation house had been restored to the glory days of the past under her care.

Gabrielle's younger sister, Monique, who had become the official mistress of Fontenay upon their mother's death, came running down the stairs to greet them.

"Hugo! Julian! How lovely to see you both. Father is in town today. He'll be so sorry he missed you. Julian, I was just writing a note to you and Delia to thank you both for the most wonderful evening. We enjoyed the concert so much. We would have loved to join you for the party, but you know, we lost Alain and officially are in mourning—"

"Monique," Hugo interrupted. "We need to borrow a skiff. We have to get to the Willows right away."

Hearing his urgency, she caught her breath. "Is it Marcus? Is he ill?"

"No—but we need to talk to him. If there were any telephone lines out here, we could have simply called, but as that modern marvel hasn't reached you yet . . ."

Julian pulled the skiff up onto the bank. "The truth, remember. No more lies and deceptions."

"I don't want any shouting matches if Patience is here," Hugo warned. "And I'd still like to know what makes you think we'll find her here."

"He knows she's his daughter."

"*What?* Julian, you fool! How could you have let him find out about her? You know how he is. Couldn't you have foreseen something like this might happen?"

"Calm down, Hugo. How could I have known he'd come to the concert? You told me he never leaves the Willows nowadays. I certainly didn't invite him to the concert. I thought you did."

"I haven't even spoken to Marcus for months. How could he know about Patience, unless someone told him?"

"Use your imagination. Patience looks exactly like Delia—maybe a little younger than when we first saw her and certainly a hell of a lot more innocent. But he had to have recognized her—and why else would she be at the concert, sitting with the family? When I got through running all over town searching for her, I sat down and reasoned that a six year old wouldn't have got far if she ran away—ergo someone took her. But who? Who knew about her, or rather, about her relationship to Delia? There was no ransom demand, so the kidnapper wasn't motivated by profit. The only other possibility was Marcus."

"Let's get up to the house," Hugo said grimly. "If he has her, I may break his neck."

"At least wait until the child is out of harm's way."

As they made their way toward the house, the contrast between the Willows and Fontenay was immediately apparent. Here the grounds were overgrown with weeds, flowers had gone to seed, and the gravel driveway had all but disappeared under encroaching grasses and sprouting saplings.

Clouds had begun to gather and the clammy afternoon threatened to turn into a stormy evening. As they drew closer to the house, Julian murmured, "I used to get in and out without being seen by way of the solarium when I was a wild youth—through that outside door the gardeners use."

Hugo nodded, and they made their way to the solarium. Minutes later he looked with dismay at the withered remains of his father's orchid collection.

"What did you expect?" Julian muttered. "You insisted on giving him the place, remember?"

Hugo made no comment. The solarium smelled like the grave, and he was suddenly filled with dread. If Julian was right, and Marcus had kidnapped Patience . . . Hugo found himself praying as he'd never prayed before, *Please, don't let him have harmed her.*

They heard the music as soon as they opened the door to the hall. The two men stood still, listening to a blending of sounds that were wondrous to hear, caressing the senses, soothing the nerves, capable of transporting even the most musically illiterate to nirvana. The notes floated in the sultry air, bringing a sweet breath of spring, speaking of life and love and rebirth. They were listening to a magical duet for piano and flute.

Almost in a trance they walked in the direction of the music.

The door to the drawing room was open. Marcus sat at the grand piano, and Patience sat cross-legged on the floor beside him. She saw Hugo first and lowered her flute.

Smiling happily, she said, "My daddy found me."

Chapter 43

*

MAGGIE

I suppose it's a human weakness to yearn for the unattainable while overlooking what's there and available and might make us just as happy if we'd let it.

Maggie dozed fitfully in a rocking chair, pulled close to the front window so that she could watch the street. Her eyes flew open as the wrought-iron gate creaked open.

The man approaching her front door had already removed his hat, revealing russet-brown hair that almost matched her own. He wore gold-rimmed glasses now, behind which his pale blue eyes looked dreamy, an illusion that had caused opposing counsels to underestimate his abilities.

She had first met Lucas Stone when he was a young lawyer working for Walter Hepple in Natchez. He had asked her out several times, but she had always been too busy to accept. Still, he had continued to call on her occasionally, usually with some vague request for her advice as to a gift to buy for his mother, or help with planning a menu, always apologizing for his bachelor ineptness in such matters. In return he had handled the legal documents when she bought her house and advised her concerning her business. She had been surprised when he opened his own office in New Orleans shortly after she moved there, but put their simultaneous moves down to coincidence. She had turned to him for help when Delia demanded that she give up Patience, and so far he had managed to keep Delia and her lawyer at bay.

Maggie opened the door and said, "Ah, it's the man from Savannah." It was something that had started when she knew him in Natchez, as the first few times they ran into each other after their first meeting at the Hepples' party, Maggie always had to remind herself who he was. "Oh, yes, you're Mr.

Stone, you work for Mr. Hepple, and you're originally from Savannah," she used to say. Today the old joke sounded forced, and she sighed and gestured for him to come inside.

"I just heard about Patience, and I came right over." His brow was creased with concern. Always a thoughtful man, Maggie had often thought he was too transparently empathetic for his profession. Still, he appeared to be successful, perhaps because everyone instinctively trusted him. He added, "I was gone all morning, taking a deposition, or I'd have been here earlier. Is there no word yet?"

Maggie shook her head. Her knees were so weak from fatigue and tension that she sank back into the rocking chair. "I don't know what to do, Lucas. I feel responsible for this. I was selfish—I wanted so desperately to hold on to her—" Her voice broke and she buried her face in her hands.

His hand touched her shoulder tentatively. "Don't despair, Maggie. I'm sure she's safe and sound and will be found soon. And I do have some good news for you."

She raised her head hopefully.

"I spoke with Jacob Lacey—Cordelia's attorney—and he's proposed that there be a transition period while you and Cordelia share custody of the child. In return for this concession you must agree to settle out of court without any publicity."

"Share custody? You mean passing my daughter back and forth like a piece of baggage? You call that good news? How would you like to be little and helpless and be dragged from one household to another, never knowing where you belong, where to call home?"

He looked crestfallen. "Well, I believe it would be better than losing her completely. There was no mention of how long this transition period should last, and my hope was that it could go on indefinitely. With this type of arrangement Cordelia would be required to remain here in New Orleans, so you would not have to worry about her taking the child across the country, or across the world, for that matter. Cordelia might quickly tire of being a mother if her wings are clipped, as they will be if she's forced to provide a home for Patience here. Right now Cordelia feels she's involved in a fight—with you—that she must win. But has she looked into the future? Patience doesn't want to live with her—and you know how a child that age can be a trial to an adult unaccustomed to dealing with them. If we let Delia believe she's won, allowing Patience to spend a week with you, say, and one with her—as time goes on either Cordelia will grow tired of being tied down with a child, or Patience will become mature enough to recognize who her true mother is. Far better to keep this out of the courts, Maggie. We don't want accusations of kidnap on one side and abandonment on the other—that would be harmful to all of you, but especially so to Patience."

"I won't give her up, Lucas. I can't. And I won't share her. You must find a way for me to keep her. She's my child, I don't care who gave birth to her—I'm her mother."

"She's Delia's flesh and blood, Maggie," he reminded her gently. "If you refuse to compromise, I'm afraid you could lose her."

Maggie chewed her fist. "I can't think about this now, Lucas. Not until my baby is safely home with me."

"I understand. Perhaps I could—" he broke off abruptly. "Maggie, you have another visitor."

She turned to look out of the window and saw Delia alighting from a carriage.

"Let me send her away," Lucas murmured. "You two really shouldn't be in direct communication."

"She might have news of Patience!" Maggie cried, running to the door. "Oh, please, God . . ."

But Delia looked too haggard to be the bearer of good news. They spoke simultaneously, "Is there any word?"

Maggie shook her head. "You'd better come in." She looked at Lucas. "Will you excuse us, Lucas? I'll call you later."

He hesitated for a moment, clearly worried about the possible confrontation, but nodded to Delia and departed.

"Maggie, I'm so sorry," Delia whispered. "If I'd known this was going to happen . . ."

Maggie's pain was too great to permit her to accept the olive branch. "Who did you tell, Delia? You must have let somebody know she's your daughter. She's been kidnapped, you do realize that, don't you? And it's all your fault."

"I told no one but my lawyer, Maggie. I swear. And if she's been kidnapped, why haven't we received a ransom note?"

"I'm sure one will be forthcoming before long. Oh, why couldn't you have stayed away?"

"Maggie, we mustn't give up hope. I thought we could talk about what we're going to do when Patience comes home. Just the two of us, no lawyers, no one else. Perhaps it will help both of us to get through this. After all, I'm the only person alive who can even guess what you're going through. She's my flesh and blood, Maggie, and she's the only child I will ever have. I'm not telling you this in a bid for sympathy, but to try to make you understand my joy in finding her and why I need her in my life. But I realize that what I need, or even what you need, doesn't matter. We must do what's best for Patience."

"Are you saying you'll let her stay with me?"

"I was hoping she could be with both of us. No, wait! Hear me out, Maggie. When our lawyers suggested we share custody, I was at first horrified, as I'm sure you were. But then I began to think about it. We're both that aberration in our society—women who work, who do not devote our lives to husbands and children. Whether Patience lives with you or with me, she'll be left in the care of someone else while we're working."

"While I work she's with Jemmie, who adores her," Maggie said defensively. "Jemmie's been with us since Patience was a baby."

"And she's a very old woman," Delia pointed out. "How much longer can she keep up with a child? Maggie, what if we could put aside our differences and get together—I mean, live together."

"Two women in one house? You must be joking."

"No, I'm not."

"Your husband would have a fit."

"My husband is dead. I'm a widow."

"I'm sorry, I didn't know." Maggie noted that Delia was not wearing mourning, nor did she look particularly grief-stricken, but then, one could never really assess what Delia was feeling from her icily composed expression.

"Look, Maggie, I'm quite wealthy. Julian invested my earnings and doubled and tripled them—I have more money than Patience's children could ever spend. I've bought a large house, here in New Orleans. We could all move into it—

Jemmie, too. We'll hire some servants to run it for us, then we can devote all our energies to more important matters. Patience, first, then our work. Julian is restoring Courtland Hall, and I could perform there. I understand you have done some costume design—there are all sorts of possibilities for collaboration between us, if you'll agree."

"I can see you have given this a lot of thought," Maggie said grudgingly. "But it won't work. A house can't have two mistresses. A child can't have two mothers. Delia, I've thought about the future, too. Only Patience should have the right to decide with whom she wants to live. Now, I know I've had her for over six years, but I have to tell you that she speaks of you all the time and when she saw you onstage . . . well, I realized then I can't compete with you. She might very well choose to go with you. She loves music so—and she's bewitched by you. You are the fairy godmother who can make all her dreams come true. What can I offer except my love and devotion?"

Delia was silent, a tear trickling slowly down her cheek. Then, as if in response to an unseen cue, the two women were in each other's arms, crying.

Maggie had bathed and changed her clothes, attempted to eat a sandwich, sipped tea nervously, and watched the clock.

Hugo's telephone call had come hours ago, while Delia was still with her. He had said, "Patience is safe, I'll be bringing her home shortly. She wants to speak with you. Here she is."

Then Patience's voice, "Mama? I'm sorry you were worried. We left you a note. Didn't you see it?"

"No, I didn't! Oh, angel, where are you? Where have you been hiding? Are you all right?"

"I was with my daddy. He wasn't lost at sea after all; he just didn't know where I was."

Maggie heard Hugo's voice in the background but could not make out what he said, then he came on the line again. "She was at the Willows with Marcus. I'll explain when I get there. We're on the outskirts of town now. I stopped at the first telephone I could find."

"Delia's here—" Maggie began, and he interrupted her,

"Ask her to leave before we get there. I want to talk to you alone."

The line went dead before Maggie could question him further.

When she relayed the conversation to Delia, her face had become even more ashen when she learned Marcus had taken the child. She murmured, "Thank God she's safe."

"Is it true?" Maggie asked. "Is Marcus Van Courtland her father?

Delia nodded, confirming what Hugo had long suspected.

"Would you go now? Hugo said he wants to speak to me alone."

Delia hesitated, and for an instant there was a look of yearning on her face. She was desperate to see that Patience was unharmed, of course, but Maggie hardened her heart. "I'll telephone you later." She opened the front door, and Delia had no choice but to leave.

Maggie went straight up to Patience's room, although she had already searched every inch of it for a clue as to what had happened to the child. There was no sign of a note. Then she went to her own bedroom. The landing was uncarpeted, but a thick rug almost filled the bedroom, extending to the door. Bending, Maggie lifted the edge of the rug and found the envelope that had been mistakenly pushed under the rug when it was slipped under the door.

She read the adult script first.

Dear Mrs. Nesbitt:

I am Patience's father. We met briefly after Delia's concert. Since you and my brother have seen fit to deceive all of us about the child, and as I fear you may thwart any efforts on my part to see her, I have decided to take matters into my own hands. Have no fear for her safety. She wants to come and visit with me, and I will bring her back as soon as she asks to return.

Sincerely,
Marcus Van Courtland

Beneath was a brief note in Patience's childish printing.

Dear Mama,
   I'm going to my daddy's house. Be home soon.
   Love and kisses,
   Patience

Maggie awakened Jemmie from her exhausted slumber to give her the news that Patience was on her way home, then prepared to face Hugo.

Two hours later he arrived carrying the sleeping child in his arms. Maggie snatched her from him and covered her face with kisses. Patience murmured sleepily, but didn't open her eyes.

"She's fine, Maggie," Hugo said. "Let me carry her up to bed. She hasn't slept since he took her."

They put the little girl in her bed, and Maggie hovered protectively over her until Hugo took her hand firmly and led her downstairs.

"I want him put in jail," Maggie fumed. "He had no right to break into my house and kidnap her."

"Calm down, Maggie. When you talk to Patience in the morning, you'll learn that to the child this was not only an adventure, but the fulfillment of her most heartfelt wish. Hasn't she ever asked you about her father?"

"Well, yes, but—"

"Didn't it occur to you that all of her friends have fathers, and she had never received an adequate explanation as to what had become of hers?"

"How could I tell her? I never knew for sure who he was. I told her about my husband who was lost at sea—I didn't know what else to tell her. Then when Delia came, I promised her that Delia would tell her about her father."

"And did she?"

"I don't believe so."

"Marcus insists he left you a note."

"I found it a little while ago. He or Patience had pushed it under my bedroom door, but it got caught under the rug. He still shouldn't have broken into my house."

"No, he shouldn't. He claims he came to ask you if he might call on Patience some time and found you'd left the front door ajar—it was a hot night as you know—and on an impulse he decided to slip upstairs and look at his daughter.

But she woke up and—I suppose she was still half asleep—asked if he was her daddy."

Maggie remembered Patience asking Julian the same question.

Hugo continued: "He told her he was, and Patience said she was glad he wasn't lost any longer. According to Marcus, that was when, on another impulse, he asked if she'd like to visit his house so they could get to know each other."

"And why couldn't he have asked for my permission?"

"Would you have given it?"

"No, of course not."

"Maggie, the child went with him willingly—apparently Jemmie was in bed and you were working in your study with the door closed, so they decided to leave you a note. I know this was still wrong, and I'm not making any excuses for a reprehensible act, but, well . . . let me describe what we found at the Willows."

Maggie listened silently as he told of Marcus and Patience playing a duet, and how amazed he and Julian were that not only did the piano and flute blend in perfect harmony, but Marcus had informed them that the piece came from the mind of his daughter, who did not even know how to read music, let alone write music.

"Marcus was outraged at what he perceived to be a deliberate attempt to keep the child in ignorance of her true calling. It seems they had been up all night talking, mostly about music. They had one part of their histories in common, you see, in that they both received their first instrument—a flute—from Jemmie. Anyway, I have no doubt in my mind that Patience was thrilled and happy to have found a real live father who understood all her secret longings and who could listen to her play a tune and instantly memorize the notes in order to accompany her on the piano. Put yourself into the mind of the child—to her it was a miracle. I don't believe either of them understood the nature of the crisis they created or how frantic with worry you were."

Maggie was trembling. "I thought I would lose her to Delia. It never occurred to me to worry about the father."

"You haven't lost her, Maggie. Try to think of the situation in light of all that is being added to Patience's life—her world is expanding, with more people to love her, to teach her."

"I'm being selfish—is that what you're telling me?"

"No, not at all."

"I've heard that Marcus is mad."

"He isn't mad. Or if he is, it's the madness of genius. But in any case, he understands he can never take her away again without permission."

She stared at him. "Despite your protests to the contrary, Hugo, all you're really concerned with is preserving the Van Courtland name, isn't it? He should be prosecuted and you know it."

"Prosecuted, or persecuted? He didn't harm her, and I don't believe he had any intention of causing you and her mother anguish.

"*Her mother?* I'm her mother!"

"I'm sorry, I meant Delia. Look, Maggie, everything will look different to you in the morning after you've talked to Patience. Get some rest now, you're exhausted. Don't make any rash decisions tonight."

Maggie felt all of the tension of the past twenty-four hours burst from her in an angry torrent. "You want everything kept quiet, don't you? Let's not have anyone find out that Delia has an illegitimate child, or that your half brother is crazy and a kidnapper. And above all else, let's not upset your wife with a public scandal. I believed in you, Hugo, I thought you'd always do the right thing—"

"Maggie," he interrupted quietly, "think about what you just said and ask yourself if you would want anyone to say those things to Patience."

"You'd better leave now, Hugo, before I say something I'll really regret."

She was still trembling after she heard the door close behind him. Patience was safe; she should be rejoicing. Why then did she feel she had just suffered an irreplaceable loss?

When Patience came down to breakfast, Maggie saw at once that the child looked happy and excited. "Mama, I had such a nice time with my daddy. He can play the piano and he lives in such a big house. He let me eat anything I wanted to and didn't make me clean my plate or anything. There's a big river by the house, and he's got lots of boats, but he doesn't like the water, so we didn't go in a boat. Mama, when can we go to see him again? He told me he doesn't like towns, so it's best we go see him, isn't it?"

Maggie said carefully, "Honey, I was very worried about you."

The child's eyes widened. "But we left you a note."

"I didn't find it right away, honey. But in any case, you must never go anywhere, with anybody, not your daddy, not Delia or Uncle Hugo—*nobody*—without talking to me first. Do you understand?"

"But—"

"No *buts*, Patience. You must never leave with anyone again, not even someone you know. You shouldn't have gone anywhere with a stranger, no matter what he told you."

"But he is my daddy, isn't he?"

"Yes. But he could have been a bad man who would have hurt you. Honey, why didn't you come and tell me your daddy was here?"

"You were working, Mama. You had the door shut. Jemmie said we mustn't disturb you when the door's shut."

"You come to me any time you want to, angel, whether the door's shut or not. Now sit down and eat your breakfast."

Delia was on the telephone before they had finished breakfast, and Maggie remembered she had forgotten to call her after Patience came home as she had promised.

"Maggie? I couldn't sleep—is she all right?"

"Yes. Why don't you come over and see for yourself?"

Replacing the receiver, Maggie said to Patience, "Delia is coming. She was very worried about you, too."

The little girl's mouth drooped at the corners. "Delia's bad. I don't want to see her again."

"What? Why do you say that? I thought you were getting to know her, and you were so excited when we heard her sing at the concert, that's all you talked about."

"My daddy said she didn't want me, and she gave me away when I was a baby."

"Honey, Delia was very sick when you were born. She . . . she couldn't take care of you then." Maggie couldn't believe she was actually defending Delia, but all at once it seemed that she was less of a threat than Marcus, who'd had no difficulty luring Patience away from both of them.

"But why didn't she come back for me when she was feeling better?"

"Well . . ." Maggie was not about to attempt to explain the lies that had been told, especially not that Delia had believed her child had died, which might frighten Patience. "There was a big misunderstanding, angel. She came as soon as she could."

"My daddy says she doesn't have time for me and you don't, either. He says he would stay with me all the time and teach me to play the piano and read music."

Maggie felt her jaw clench. "Your daddy has no business telling you such things about Delia or me, which aren't true anyway."

"I *would* like to learn how to play the piano, Mama."

"We'll arrange lessons for you, then, sweetheart. Somewhere close by so you can go after school."

"I'd rather have my daddy teach me."

The doorbell was a merciful interruption.

"That will be Delia now. I want you to be polite to her, do you hear?"

"Yes, Mama."

In the hall Maggie whispered to Delia, "Marcus has completely ingratiated himself with her. She wants to see him—to take music lessons from him."

"That's out of the question. You don't know Marcus—he's unstable."

"So I've heard," Maggie said grimly. "He's already started trying to turn her against us."

"Marcus has always hated me."

Maggie blinked, wondering, but not asking, how they ever made a baby if that were the case. "We must be very careful what we say," she cautioned.

During the next hour it was painfully obvious that Patience had been thoroughly indoctrinated by Marcus, who had clearly given the child a glimpse of a world where her hours would be filled with music and she would have unlimited freedom to roam through a large plantation house and its extensive grounds. To a child raised in cities in small houses, the Willows probably seemed like a palace. And to a little girl who had never had more than a brief visit from a male, the prospect of an ever-present father was surely enticing.

Watching Delia's reaction to hearing Patience speak of

Marcus, while acting in a restrained if polite manner toward her, Maggie tried to assess Delia's reaction. She seemed to be frozen in a state of disbelief and said little to contradict the child's adoring description of her father.

At length Maggie said, "Why don't you go and see where Jemmie is now, Patience. She probably wants to tell you how much she missed you, too."

The little girl scampered from the room, and a moment later they heard her calling Jemmie's name.

Maggie looked at Delia. "What shall we do?"

"I know what we can never do. We must never let him be alone with her."

"Would it do any harm to let him see her—perhaps give her piano lessons?"

Delia was deathly pale. "I don't want him anywhere near my child."

Maggie felt a tug of resentment. "My child, too, Delia. If you're adamant that he not be allowed to see her alone, what if one of us were present? You have to understand how Patience has longed for a daddy of her own. I didn't even realize myself how much she wanted a father. Delia, we agreed that we'd put our own animosity out of it and think only of the child."

"I am thinking of the child. Marcus is mentally unbalanced. Oh, he can act as normal as anyone else when he wants to, but he becomes completely irrational without a second's warning."

"Are you sure you aren't letting your own feelings toward him taint your thinking? I mean, well, he didn't marry you, did he?"

"No," Delia said shortly. "He didn't."

"We're both going to lose Patience if we try to keep her from seeing him. Better to compromise, Delia."

"Compromise, Maggie? Or do you mean capitulate? Patience is six years old. Some decisions have to be made for her."

"Oh, dear. Marcus is a complication we didn't need, isn't he?"

"I'll go see him," Delia said unexpectedly. "And decide then whether Patience may take lessons from him—which will be supervised. On that issue I won't budge."

Chapter 44

*

Maggie had just put Patience to bed when Lucas Stone arrived. She was surprised by the lateness of the visit and even more surprised when she entered the parlor and saw that he stood stiffly in front of the fireplace, holding a bouquet of roses. He was flushed, his hair a little untidy, and his tie was askew.

"Why, Lucas . . . I wasn't expecting you. You must have worked late tonight." Knowing he had moved his widowed mother to New Orleans she added, "What lovely roses. Are you taking them to your mother?"

"No, Maggie. I brought them for you." His blush deepened. He thrust them into her hands and stood back, wearing a faint air of defiance, as if to say, *refuse them at your peril.*

Bewildered, Maggie murmured, "Thank you—I'll just get a vase. Would you like a glass of sherry?"

"Yes, I would. Thank you."

When she returned with a tray containing the roses and two glasses of sherry, he had seated himself on the sofa.

She put the roses on the table, then handed him a glass. "I suppose you came about Patience. She's fine, but I am concerned that—"

He interrupted, "I didn't come about Patience. If you recall, I already ascertained by telephone earlier that she is unharmed. Maggie, you always assume I come to see you on business, or for any reason other than the real one."

"Oh," Maggie said faintly.

"You know, in court I'm considered a formidable opponent. And I certainly have no trouble speaking my mind to my clients. I don't know why I become tongue-tied when I'm with you, but for once I'm going to tell you exactly what I think and how I feel."

"And how is that, Lucas?"

"I know you've never given me a passing thought, and I know you've never accepted a single invitation to go anywhere or do anything with me. If I hadn't contrived to run into you, or come seeking your advice, and believe me, I've about run out of excuses, I'm quite sure you would have forgotten all about me."

"Oh, that's not true," Maggie said gently. "You're the only man from Savannah I know."

"The truth is"—he seemed to be plunging on because he feared if he stopped speaking he might never again have the nerve to continue—"the truth is, I have cared deeply for you for years. Almost six years, to be precise. During that time I have never observed that you allow anyone else to court you, either, and—perhaps I'm a little slow—but I never speculated as to the reason for this. Now during this crisis over your daughter, I suddenly realized why you have never remarried."

"Oh? And why is that?"

"You built a dream, Maggie, wherein Hugo Van Courtland would come and make you and Patience his family."

She was all at once very still, very tense. She didn't speak, but knew her cheeks were flaming in concert with his.

Lucas continued earnestly, "But it was a fantasy that had no roots in reality. You waited for a man who will never create the family you dream of, because he was never yours, and you put all your hopes and dreams into a child, and she wasn't yours, either. We can rationalize away everything that you and Hugo did, but the fact remains, Patience is Delia's daughter, her flesh and blood, and nobody—*nobody* has the right to separate them."

Maggie's heart was thumping painfully against her ribs. "Why are you saying these things to me, Lucas? I thought you were my friend."

"I want to be more than your friend. But first I must make you understand that while you waited for the impossible to happen, life was passing you by. But it isn't too late. Maggie, answer me honestly—wouldn't you prefer to have a man who belonged to you alone? Don't you want to have a child that you would never have to worry would be taken from you? Wouldn't you prefer to live without lies and deceptions?"

"Yes, of course, I . . ." Her voice was a whisper. "Are you asking me to give up Patience?"

"I came to ask you to marry me, Maggie. To be my wife and, God willing, the mother of my children."

She felt her mouth drop open, but no words came.

He added, with a wry smile, "I haven't been very successful as a suitor, but I believe I'll do better as a husband, if you'll give me a chance."

"I don't know what to say."

"Say you'll come to the theater with me tomorrow night and come to meet my mother next Sunday after church. Say you'll seriously consider my proposal. You never know, now that I've got your attention, you might decide I'm not so bad after all. I make a good living, I'm sober, and—for a lawyer—reasonably honest. I'm a thirty-five-year-old bachelor, and of course, I'm from Savannah."

Then, to her complete astonishment, he rose from the sofa, placed his glass on the table, and took her into his arms. He planted a firm, and quite appealing, kiss on her lips.

During the following few days Maggie was bemused by Lucas Stone's determination to make her see him as a possible husband, and she reluctantly admitted to herself that his assessment of her relationship with Hugo had been uncomfortably accurate. Hugo had not been to see her since the day he returned Patience. He was probably afraid she might press charges against his half brother, she decided. The family name was very important to Hugo, he'd made that clear years ago.

Late one evening after Lucas brought her home, Maggie found Jemmie waiting up for her.

"Why, Jemmie, what are you doing up so late?"

"Y'all gwine marry that man?"

"I don't know."

" 'Bout time, if'n you ask me."

"Lucas has asked me, as a matter of fact. I haven't given him an answer yet."

"Say yes," Jemmie said. "You ain't getting any younger."

Maggie grinned. "And an old lady of thirty-three doesn't get that many chances, is that what you're saying, Jemmie?"

"Still time to make babies is what I'm saying."

"Yes, that's true. But—"

"But y'all's determined to wait for Mr. Hugo. Never mind he ain't never gwine leave his wife. 'Specially not now."

"Why *especially* not now? What happened?"

Jemmie leaned back in her chair, her eyes old and wise. "Gabrielle . . . she's got the consumption. Jes' like her cousin."

Maggie caught her breath. "How do you know? She didn't look sick at Delia's concert."

"She's got the gallopin' consumption. She won't linger for years like Mr. Alain. Oh, maybe she doan know yet, but she's got a maid who's the granddaughter of an ole friend of mine, and I heerd tell that Gabrielle, she's started coughing up blood and her clothes is all too loose. Now, them's sure signs of consumption, and if'n they come on that fast, then it's gallopin' for sure."

Maggie digested this news silently.

Jemmie said, "Now doan y'all go imaginin' that if she passes away Mr. Hugo will come looking for you. Ain't never gwine happen. He'll be all ate up with so much guilt he won't never come near you. Leastwise, not to marry you. Gabrielle will make sure of that before she goes."

But the possibility that Hugo might soon be widowed did not fill Maggie's mind with rosy prospects of the two of them being free to come together, as Jemmie supposed. In fact, Maggie felt slightly panicked that Hugo might expect her to fill Gabrielle's shoes.

Lucas was right, she thought. I waited all those years for Hugo . . . perhaps it was too long. Or perhaps I never really saw him for what he is. A man who never could make up his mind. He led me on, with veiled promises he never intended to keep. And he admitted to me that he was not faithful to Gabrielle.

"You listening to ole Jemmie, chile?"

"I hear you, Jemmie."

"Mr. Stone, he's a good man. More suited to you than Mr. Hugo."

"What an old busybody you are, Jemmie," Maggie said softly. "You know, you could have kept quiet about Gabrielle. If I really had been waiting for Hugo, telling me that she might have consumption could have made me more determined to wait for him."

"I jes' wanted y'all to think about it, before Mr. Hugo comes around, grievin' and looking for comfort."

"I'll give it plenty of thought. It's rather sad, isn't it?"

Chapter 45

DELIA

While we were at each other's throats, fighting for our child, he was lurking in the wings and, with no effort at all, won her.

Delia had to wait for what seemed a long time for anyone to respond to the door chimes at the Willows. At length a lanky mulatto clad in denim overalls and looking more like a gardener than a butler opened the door. His slack mouth, head drooping over his chest, and unfocused eyes told their own story. Delia remembered that years ago a Van Courtland parlor maid had given birth to a mentally deficient son, who had been put to work performing simple tasks in the garden.

"Oley?" she asked, "Are you working in the house now?"

"Yas'm," he answered proudly. "I is Mr. Marcus's houseman."

"You remember me, don't you? Delia? I used to stay here sometimes when I was a little girl."

He made no move to admit her to the house.

"Will you take me to him, please?"

Oley hesitated, chewing his lip in an agony of indecision. It was apparent he was unaccustomed to dealing with visitors.

"Just announce me as Miss Delia," she prompted and pushed past him into the hall.

Oley shuffled off, and she followed, appalled by the condition of the house. A week had passed since Patience had been found at the Willows, and neither Hugo nor Julian had mentioned the deterioration of their family home. It seemed obvious that Oley was probably the only servant left in the house.

He led her to the drawing room, announced her name in a high-pitched voice, and fled.

Marcus sat at the grand piano, idly drumming the keys. The French doors were open, and the previous night's rain had cleared the air. He looked up at she entered the room, his gaze brooding.

"Come in, Delia. Don't be afraid of me."

"I'm not afraid of you." A pearl-handled derringer, a gift from a San Francisco admirer, was tucked into her purse.

Marcus stood up. "I have never acknowledged the harm I did to you, Delia. Nor apologized for it. I do so now."

She was taken aback. "Did Julian tell you to say that?"

"Yes, but even he doesn't know the extent of my crime against you. He believes I seduced you and refused to marry you."

"I'd prefer that he continue believing that. I don't ever want my daughter to know how she was conceived."

"But she is a miracle child, Delia. A genius. Despite her beginnings," Marcus said wonderingly. "I couldn't believe that we created such a perfect little being. I was overwhelmed with feelings I have never experienced before. Her trust and innocence . . . oh, I have such fear for her, and a fierce need to protect her from harm."

"You will leave her alone, Marcus, do you understand? Because if you don't, I shall kill you."

He looked shocked. "I would never hurt her—how could you make such a threat? I adore her. I want to teach her—just as I once taught you. But more than that, I feel a bond of blood, a connection that I never felt to any other human being. Delia, don't you realize that between us we can give her so much?"

"We, Marcus? You've already begun to try to turn my daughter against me. Don't pretend what you have in mind is anything other than banishing me—and probably Maggie Nesbitt, too—from her life."

"The Nesbitt woman has no claim to the child, but according to my brothers she could be a nuisance. In your case, if you'll be reasonable—"

"I don't want my daughter to see or speak to you ever again. If you do, I'll have you arrested."

His eyes narrowed. "I have as much right to her as you do. After all, I didn't abandon her."

"Don't speak to me of rights. You lost all right to belong to the human race when you raped me."

His face was expressionless. "You're conveniently forgetting your own culpability in that."

Delia had never fought more for control than she did at that moment. "I only came here today," she said quietly, "because . . ." She choked on the words. *Because Patience has begged Maggie and me to let her see you again.* The two women had agonized over this, with Maggie believing that it would be acceptable for Patience to see her father providing either she or Delia accompanied her. But, of course, Maggie did not know Marcus as she did. No one did.

Marcus smiled knowingly. "My daughter wishes to see me. Of course she does. She knows that no one will ever understand her as I do."

"That's not true. She's nothing like you, Marcus."

"I didn't say she was. I said I understand her and I do. I understand the music she hears that no one else hears, I understand her joy when that music finds its own voice. But more than that, I shall never let anyone force her to keep her music from the world as mine was."

"And who do you blame, Marcus, for the rancor you wear like a shield?"

"My father," he answered bitterly. "Who thought it was not manly to prefer the piano to more rough-and-tumble pursuits, and who never tired of comparing me to my brothers. Who even bought this isolated house in order to hide me from the world. He was ashamed of me, of having given me life."

She looked around, at the faded carpet and dusty furniture. Spiderwebs, speckled with the shells of mosquitoes, festooned the windows. The ashes of a long-dead fire remained in the grate, and she had learned from Julian of the withered orchids that had once been his father's pride and joy. She suppressed a shiver. Marcus had turned the lovely old house into a sinister monument commemorating his loathing of his father.

"Your father is no longer here, Marcus. You don't have to live a hermit's life, shut away here. I shall never let Patience come here again. You won't turn her into a neurotic like yourself."

He looked into her eyes, and seeing the resolve there, some of his bravado faded. His tone became wheedling: "I could teach her to read music, give her piano lessons. Patience wants this, Delia. She begged me not to go away and get lost again. You can ask her yourself."

Why else am I here, Delia thought, *if not to please my daughter?* Reluctantly she said, "Maggie and I have talked it over, and we may allow her to see you provided you come to New Orleans and either Maggie or I are present. You are never to see her alone. You are also to stop trying to turn Patience against us. One derogatory word and the lesson will end immediately."

Marcus frowned. Delia added quickly, "You have no choice in this, Marcus. Supervised visits, in the city, or none at all."

He stood up and paced angrily around the piano. Delia slipped her hand into her purse, her fingers closing around the cool pearl handle of the derringer.

At length he said, "And if I don't agree to these terms, what then? I have no doubt I could persuade my daughter to come to me without your permission."

"Don't underestimate me, Marcus. You ruined my life. I'll see you in hell before I'll allow you to ruin my child's."

He shrugged, all at once ingratiating. "It would be better for the child if we could all get along, wouldn't it?"

"Yes, it would."

"Perhaps," he said softly, "Patience will civilize all of us."

Delia was sitting surrounded by trunks and boxes on the eve of her move into her new home when Julian found her.

"I've paid off Jacob Lacey. Tried to pay Maggie Nesbitt's lawyer, too, but he said he's a friend of hers and had not charged her a fee—" Julian broke off. "Why are you sitting on the floor in near darkness?"

"Nothing ever works out the way we hope, does it?"

"Sometimes it's even better than we hoped."

"I'm in no mood for your eternal optimism tonight, Julian."

He glanced at her sharply. "What happened?"

"Maggie and I are going to try to come to an agreement without the lawyers. At least for the time being Patience will stay with Maggie and spend some time with me. We'll let Marcus give her a music lesson once a week."

"And then?"

Delia sighed. "We're going to ask Patience to decide whether she wants to live with Maggie or with me. We've agreed to abide by her decision."

"Sounds reasonable to me. Why do you sound as though it's the end of the world?"

"I think I made a mistake in agreeing to it. I was in such a state when my daughter disappeared, I would have made a pact with the devil himself to keep her from harm. I probably have, in allowing her to see Marcus. But I wish now I hadn't given in on where Patience will live. After all, she's not yet seven years old—far too young to be capable of making such a decision."

"Delia, you're worrying unnecessarily. Even if she elects to stay with Maggie, you'll still be able to see her."

She was silent, knowing there was no way to make him understand how she yearned to be Patience's mother. After a moment she said, "Life is full of surprises. Perhaps Patience will decide one day she wants to be with me. I suppose I should be grateful that the two of us found each other again. I certainly didn't expect to find my daughter when I came looking for . . ."

Julian waited.

At length she said, "I found Thad Bouchet, you know."

"How disappointing for you. You were convinced either Marcus or I had killed him. Where is your handsome clarinet player?"

She told him briefly of her meeting with Thad in Daddy Lou's house, concluding, "But he's so obviously starving himself to death, and I don't know what to do for him."

"It seems pretty obvious to me. If he believes that the voodoo woman—what was her name? Abebe?—has put some sort of hex on him, then she should be found and told to un-hex him, or else. There are ways of dealing with such people—a threat of deportation is one. Where is she from? Martinique?"

"Could you do that? Persuade her to remove the hex?"

"Are you asking me to?"

"Yes."

"Consider it done. I'll talk to Jemmie, get her advice. She was always the conduit for black-white dealings in the old days when we all lived at the Willows."

She looked at him. He had always been there when she needed something taken care of, and she had never shown much gratitude. Strange, but since they returned to New Orleans, she had begun to see facets to Julian that she never dreamed existed. Or had he changed? She opened her mouth to say something but couldn't find the words to express what she felt. Besides, Julian might misinterpret any clumsy attempt on her part to thank him. The two of them had long ago assumed certain roles they performed for each other, and she suspected they would both be uncomfortable if one of them suddenly revealed that they occasionally acted toward the other with less than selfish motives.

Julian offered his hand to pull her to her feet. "Come on. Sitting here brooding isn't going to solve anything. I'm taking you out to dinner."

"I shouldn't go out—I'm supposed to be in mourning."

"Interesting turn of phrase—*supposed* to be."

She was on her feet now, but he kept her hands in his, and she was close enough to smell the faint aroma of bay rum he'd used after shaving. All at once she wished he would put his arms around her and hold her. The comfort of his touch might help alleviate her sadness. But he remained at arms' length, and so she said, "I miss Joe, and I do grieve for him, in the same way I would for a dear friend, which is what he was."

Julian raised a mocking eyebrow. "Are you inferring that you had that nineteenth-century abomination—a marriage of convenience?"

She willed herself not to flush but suspected she did anyway. She pulled away from him.

Instantly his expression changed. "You're really feeling blue, aren't you? I'm sorry—I shouldn't tease you."

"Do you realize that's the first time you've ever told me you were sorry about anything?"

He chuckled. "I must be getting old. Come on, I know a little place that's dark as a cave where you won't be bothered, and they serve a shrimp gumbo fit for the gods. It's not far, we can walk."

They lingered over the meal, finished an excellent bottle of wine, then walked back to the house. The Garden District was fragrant with the scent of magnolias and jasmine, win-

dows glowed like amber eyes behind filigreed wrought-iron
balconies, and Delia was all at once very much aware of Julian's presence in a way she had never been before. He
strolled beside her, his hand firm under her elbow, his voice
low and sonorous.

When they reached her house, he opened the door for her,
then handed her the key. In the dusk she could not see his expression, but he had been particularly charming all evening,
displaying none of his former sardonic humor, and he hadn't
teased her once.

She hesitated, half expecting him to kiss her good night.
He made no move toward her. She asked, "Would you come
in with me? The house is eerie now that most of my things
are gone."

"You're spending the night alone? Where is your housekeeper?" He pushed the door wide and preceded her into the
hall as he spoke.

"She's over at the new house, getting it ready."

He glanced at the empty rooms visible from the hall. What
little furniture remained was shrouded with dust sheets.

Delia said, "Some of these pieces belong to the landlord.
My bedroom furniture will be moved tomorrow morning."

"If your bedroom's still in order, then let's go up there and
have a nightcap. All this ghost furniture down here is going
to plunge you even deeper into gloom."

It was completely improper, but Delia didn't care. She felt
more relaxed, probably due to the wine, than she had for
weeks, and she was not eager for the evening to end. Since
Julian had walked over from his hotel, there was no telltale
carriage or motorcar parked outside to give the neighbors fuel
for gossip.

There was no electricity in the rented house, and she had
left the gaslamps in her bedroom turned low. There was a
chaise longue and a love seat in the window alcove, and she
gestured for him to sit down. "I can't offer you a nightcap,
Julian, the liquor cabinet is over at the new house. I could go
downstairs and make coffee if you like."

He took her hand and led her to the love seat. "Let's just
sit and talk until you're sleepy. That's what you really want,
isn't it?"

"Yes, but a gentleman wouldn't mention it."

"Shall I go and find a gentleman for you?"

"No, I'd rather have you stay."

She sat beside him, feeling his shoulder against hers in the confines of the love seat, the linen of his shirtsleeve pressing lightly against her bare arm.

"Do you realize this is a historic occasion in our long and stormy relationship, Delia? A quiet moment, just the two of us. Of course I realize that it's happening because you're slightly inebriated from a little too much wine, and a trifle maudlin about what you consider to be a defeat in regard to your child. But I'm grateful for any warmth you feel for me, no matter what the reason."

Feeling suddenly very lethargic, Delia rested her head on his shoulder and murmured, "I really hate you, Julian."

"Of course you do. I wouldn't be here if you were indifferent to me."

"Sometimes I wonder how my life might have been if you had not found me outside the Cajun Club. I would have been spared a great deal of heartache, but I would have also missed some rather heady thrills . . . Oh, dear, you're right, I must be tipsy. I actually feel . . . if not exactly friendly toward you tonight, Julian, then a little less hostile."

He slipped his arm around her shoulder, cupped her face with his hand, and turned her toward him. She didn't resist as his lips brushed hers, but he tantalizingly drew away again. "Careful, Delia, don't let your guard down too much. You might unleash feelings we both keep tightly under control."

"What feelings, Julian?" Could that be her voice, she wondered in silent astonishment, sounding husky and flirtatious?

His lips connected then, sending a thrill rippling down her spine. For an instant stars spun in the endless reaches of the heavens, and somewhere a distant orchestra began to play a throbbing introduction to an opera that must have been written long ago . . . or was it all an illusion, having no reality outside of her own mind? Could she be experiencing erotic longings conjured by her own thoughts? Her body certainly knew nothing of physical love, for it had never experienced it; yet in Julian's arms it not only seemed possible she could feel desire, but she found herself drifting away on a tide of sensual yearning that might plunge her into the rapids of a passion she could not imagine.

Julian's kiss, his tender caresses, were slowly coaxing her along a path she was eager to follow. Somehow it seemed inevitable that with the lateness of the hour and the intimate surroundings, they would find themselves on her bed, and, unhurried, bending to kiss each part of her flesh as he exposed it, he removed her clothes.

It was all so leisurely, he seemed to pause and savor each moment, until it was she who wanted to increase the pace, feeling the fever of desire sweep away all inhibitions. She was clinging to him, wanting to be closer, needing their flesh to fuse yet fearful that her body would betray her and the passion would be lost the way a dream fades with the morning.

Sensing that her fear was an echo of another time, Julian held back, murmuring that he would never hurt her, that even now when he wanted her so much that he was blinded by his desire, even now if she were to tell him to stop, he would.

"I love you, Delia," he whispered. "I never dared to tell you, but I do. I don't know what happened to you at the hands of other men, but I've always sensed something happened to cause you to hold back from an intimate union with a man. Let it go, Delia, let yourself go. Whatever it was, it's gone, in the past. You don't need it now. Tell me you want me to make love to you."

Sighing, she whispered, "Make love to me, Julian."

When Delia awakened the following morning Julian was gone. She lay in bed for a moment, memory returning. Her body still tingled, nerve endings reminding her of Julian's persuasive touch. How had he managed to sweep away all her fears and reticence and allow her to finally break free of the terrors of the past? How had it happened that she had learned what real lovemaking was from Julian? Was he a master lover, or had the magic taken place in her own mind? Had she been the power that released sensations in her body she could not formerly have imagined? And why had this happened with Julian, of all men? Her body felt languid, yet more alive than ever before, and after a moment she no longer wanted to analyze what had happened between them. She wanted simply to savor the memory.

The day ahead of her would be busy, she would have to supervise the arrangement of furniture and unpacking in the new house. But somehow all of the urgency and tension had dissipated, and she had to force herself to get up and bathe.

During the day she found herself thinking about Julian frequently and would catch herself staring dreamily into space. A disturbing question posed itself. Was it possible to hate a man and at the same time love him? She had submitted to his lovemaking—no, more than that, she had been a willing, eager partner. Surely feelings she had long buried must have surfaced, but she was unsure exactly what those feelings were, or what they might lead to in the future. Still, the anticipation was exciting and unlike anything she had ever felt for a man before. Had he told her he loved her? Or had that been part of the fantasy she had created in her own mind in order to justify her own wantonness?

By early evening the new house was in reasonable order and Delia was discussing with Ruby the possibilities of preparing a light dinner when Julian arrived carrying a picnic basket.

Delia felt herself blush at the sight of him as memories of the passion they had shared rushed back. She knew she would surely stammer if she spoke, but fortunately he was his usual debonair self.

"I figured you'd be hungry by now and probably didn't have much in the pantry, so I've brought cold chicken and fresh-baked bread and fruit. Ruby, why don't you put this bottle of champagne on ice and see if you can find a tablecloth."

He grinned at Delia. "You look mighty fetching. I think you should always wear gingham hitched up like that, and the streak of dirt on your fact definitely makes you look more approachable than a beauty spot, while your hair—"

Her hair was a tangled mess, skewered up on top of her head with a couple of combs. She burst out laughing and, tension gone, helped him unload the picnic basket.

"Sit down and join us, Ruby," Julian said easily. "You need to keep up your strength, too."

Ruby looked pleased by the invitation but demurred, saying she had things to do in the kitchen.

When they were alone, Delia's shyness returned. It was almost as though they were meeting for the first time and all of their past history had been wiped out. He was regarding her with an amused stare while she fussily attempted to cut a slice of chicken from the bone.

"Oh, pick it up with your fingers, Delia," he said after watching her struggle for a moment. "No need to stand on ceremony with me—especially not after last night."

She felt her face freeze into a mask she had so perfected over the years. Her hands rested on the table beside her plate, and after a brief silence he reached across the table and covered her hand with his.

"Don't be embarrassed with me, Delia. I always suspected that the lady in the drawing room would turn into a wanton in the bedroom. I'll keep your secret. Of course, if you're feeling morning-after remorse I could immediately propose marriage—for the umpteenth time, I might add."

She still sat immobile, afraid to speak in case she gave away her true feelings. Their lovemaking had been such a revelation to her, a remarkable and exquisite joining of two people that went far beyond the physical union to become a mystical spiritual connection; and she didn't want him to diminish it with casual banter. His offhand proposal indicated he was back into his teasing mode, and she was surprised by how much that stung.

She answered in a tight voice, "In view of the fact that I'm a brand-new widow, I guess you think it's safe to offer marriage, since I can't accept for at least a year."

His gaze was suddenly serious. He leaned forward. "And if I were to propose again at the end of your mourning period, would you accept?"

She muttered, "Why don't you eat your chicken and stop playing the fool. I'm well aware that rakes such as yourself have no intention of marrying the women they seduce. And, I might add, I knew that last night. Do you think women can't take their pleasure where they find it, just as you men do?"

He drew back, and when he spoke the old mocking tone had returned. "My dear Delia, I was most grateful for the crumbs of passion you tossed my way, and if my inappropriate babbling about making an honest woman of you offends you, then of course, I withdraw the marriage proposal immediately."

She pulled her hand free and picked up her knife and fork again, unreasonably angry; with herself for taking their love-making so seriously, with him for taking it so lightly.

A moment later she looked up to find him watching her, something dark and brooding in his gaze.

"Why are you looking at me like that?" she snapped.

"I suppose I'm trying to understand you, Delia. Last night I thought that . . . well, never mind what I thought. I can see that today it's back to business as usual between us, isn't it?"

She all at once felt too despondent to respond.

Delia's fragile connection to her daughter underwent a definite change after Marcus entered her life. Maggie had become much more cooperative about allowing the little girl to visit her, but whenever Delia suggested Patience might like to spend the night at her house, the child always politely refused. She showed little enthusiasm for Delia's gifts, and questions about her piano lessons or her father were answered with monosyllables.

"I'm like a favorite aunt to her," Delia told Julian despairingly. "She seems glad to see me, but even happier to bid me goodbye. Sometimes it's more than I can bear. I guess I'm never going to be able to wipe out the images Marcus planted in her mind when he had her to himself. We watch him like a hawk now, but the damage is already done. Maggie says Patience has changed toward her, too."

"You're trying too hard to make her love you," Julian said. "Why don't you relax and allow things to proceed at their own pace? Children sense it when adults become frantic."

"Oh, what makes you such an expert on children?"

"Believe it or not," he said gravely, "I was once a child myself. You might also try telling Patience as much of the truth about why you parted from her as she can understand. I'm willing to be the villain of the piece, and tell her what I did, if it will help."

Delia shook her head. "I can't do that. I'd have to tell her she's illegitimate."

"*She* isn't illegitimate. Your conception of her was."

"Perhaps when she's older . . ."

"Never underestimate the power of the truth, Delia. I only

wish I'd learned that lesson myself, years ago. By the way, you can begin rehearsing for opening night."

"What? Do you mean it?"

"The workmen have installed the seats and are presently hanging the chandeliers. We open in a month. I'm thinking of changing the name to the Courtland Opera House. We'll still put on plays and musical comedies, of course, but since you'll be the resident star, I want to emphasise that we are creating a cultural center."

"But isn't it too soon for me to perform? I mean . . . Joe has only been gone a short time."

"No, it isn't too soon," he said firmly. "Besides, don't you remember how impressed your daughter was the last time she saw you onstage?"

"But people will talk—"

"Delia, you can do penance for breaking Joe's heart in private. It's time you started thinking about your public, who adore you."

"You're such a callous beast."

"And you, my love, are a tyrant who would run roughshod over me if I weren't."

She pushed away the memory of shared passion, as she had so many times during the past days. Neither of them ever referred to that night, but although she acted as if it had never happened, she still responded to his nearness, feeling yearnings that now had a name; a state of affairs she had to go to great lengths to avoid revealing to him.

Plunging again into the excitement of preparing for opening night, Delia felt some of her gloom lift. On her next visit to pick up her daughter, she told Maggie of the planned reopening of the hall and impulsively added, "Maggie, would you design a gown for me to wear?"

Maggie looked pleased. "Why, I'd be honored. But you're sure you want me to? You're not just trying to throw some business my way? I mean, don't I remember reading that you used to appear in men's clothes in San Francisco?"

"I suppose I was rebelling against Julian in those days. He's always been both my mentor and my nemesis. No, I really want a new gown, and you are far and away the best designer in the city, maybe the whole country. I know I don't have to throw business your way; you've a waiting list of clients."

"Well, yes," Maggie answered modestly. "But none who'll make a name for me as you will."

They regarded each other with faint amazement. Delia said slowly, "Maggie ... do you think we're becoming friends?"

"I hope so," Maggie responded fervently.

They were so busy with the preparations for the opening of the Courtland Opera Hall that neither of them could spare the time to supervise Patience's piano lessons and had to cancel several of Marcus's visits. After several postponements, Maggie telephoned Delia.

"Patience is moping about not seeing her father."

"Yes, I know. I tried to explain that we're both busy."

"Delia, do you think it would be all right if I let Jemmie supervise the lesson?"

Delia was uneasy about the suggestion and tried to think of an argument against it. She knew that recently Maggie had been keeping company with her lawyer, Lucas Stone, which probably further cut into her spare time.

"I'm not sure, Maggie. Perhaps if we could get someone else to stay with Jemmie—someone we trust and who wouldn't be likely to send Marcus off the deep end. I'd suggest Julian, but he's working twenty hours a day to get the hall ready for opening night. What about Hugo? Do you think he would?"

"You haven't heard? Gabrielle is ill. Hugo has hardly left her side." There was something in Maggie's voice, a certain hint of resignation. They had never discussed Hugo, or Maggie's relationship to him. But whatever it had been, Delia suspected it was now over. Lucas Stone's courtship seemed proof of that. For herself, Delia had realized at almost their first meeting after she returned to New Orleans that her schoolgirl crush on Hugo had been simply that. She had outgrown whatever she had felt for him.

"Is Gabrielle seriously ill?" Delia asked.

"I believe she has tuberculosis. Her cousin died of it, you know. Delia, I must go. What shall I tell Patience? You know Jemmie was once Marcus's nursemaid, so she'll know how to handle him, and she'd never let any harm come to Patience."

"We could try letting Jemmie supervise one lesson, I suppose," Delia said reluctantly.

Maggie called a few days later to say the lesson had proceeded without any problems, and in fact, Jemmie had assured her that Marcus had been a perfect gentleman and Patience's delight at spending time with him had been a joy to behold.

Everything seemed to be moving at a lightning pace, and Delia's days were layered with activities and events that left little time to think, let alone brood that nothing had truly been resolved about Patience. Despite the cooperation between Maggie and herself, Delia felt empty every time she had to part from her daughter, but between rehearsals and fittings there were newspaper interviews, and Julian always seemed to be on hand if she had a spare moment, to whisk her off to some new restaurant or theater. He delivered her to her door, casually bade her good night, and left. Sometimes it was a long time before she fell asleep as she wrestled with longings she refused to recognize as being more than vague erotic impulses.

An ill-spelled and ink-blotted letter arrived from Danny in Los Angeles.

Dear Delia,

I red you was going to sing in New Orleens. I wish I was there. Everbody sez Mr. Zimmerman is a slave driver, but he's alright to me. He wants me to ask when yous coming to make a movie for him. The one I made will be out soon, its called something about an orphanage, F.L. keeps changing it.

If you can't come here, could I come there?

Your frend,

Danny La Rue

P.S. How'd you like my new name? F.L. gave it to me on account he didn't like my real last name.

"Do you really think moving pictures have a future?" she asked Julian.

"Yes, I do. Who knows, one day they may even have sound, then think of the audiences we could reach."

"Oh, what a dreamer you are!"

"How was your afternoon with your daughter?"

Delia bit her lip. "Distant. No warmth or closeness. I need to be with her all the time. I feel sorry for Maggie. She's a decent woman, but Patience is *my* child. I think once we get through opening night, I might go and talk to Jacob Lacey again."

"If it comes to a battle of the lawyers, don't underestimate Lucas Stone," Julian commented. "He may look meek and mild, but I hear he's a ferocious litigator. And he has a keen personal interest in Maggie Nesbitt."

The day before the scheduled opening of the Courtland Opera House, Delia had slept late as usual and was only half awake when Ruby brought her breakfast tray.

"Where's the newspaper?" Delia asked, sitting up in bed.

Ruby didn't look at her. "Honey, why don't y'all have your breakfast before you read the papers."

Delia was instantly alert. Ruby was well aware that she never touched her tray until she had scanned the headlines, and read the entire paper as she ate breakfast. "What's in the paper you don't want me to read before breakfast? Something about tomorrow's opening? About me?"

Ruby shuffled her feet.

"Get me the paper please, Ruby."

Minutes later Delia looked at Oscar Latimer's byline over an article in the Arts and Entertainment section of the newspaper. He had not named Delia, but there was little doubt it was she to whom he referred. His sensational revelations were couched in the proper euphemisms and vague terms required by editors of the day, and there was an irritating coyness to the article, which took the form of what he probably hoped would be a libel-proof question.

Which internationally acclaimed songbird recently returned to New Orleans in order to be reunited with her natural (out-of-wedlock) daughter?

Rumor has it that the father is a half brother to both the diva's agent and a prominent local businessman.

Chapter 46

*

Delia bowed to the scattering of people in the almost-empty house. Julian, the only occupant of the front-row stalls, was on his feet, applauding. His applause sounded like mockery, as the few curiosity seekers who had come to opening night were for the most part noisily making their way up the aisles to the exits. She did not take a second bow, but walked without haste to the wings.

In her dressing room her mirror reflected the beautiful ice-blue and lavender shot taffeta gown Maggie had designed for her, with its tiny waist and embroidered bodice. She had selected a necklace of sapphires and diamonds with matching earrings and looked, even to her own eyes, remote, cold, and unapproachable. Julian had tried to persuade her that although Maggie meant well, the gown seemed to beg for an audience's approval, and pointed out that Delia had captivated San Franciscans with her don't-give-a-damn appearance and attitude. But she hadn't listened. After all, she had been labeled a fallen woman and felt she must strive for ladylike dignity. Perhaps her defensive stiffness had also been reflected in her performance, for she knew she had not sung with her usual soul-wrenching abandon. She had been acutely aware of the small audience, and of their disapproval, throughout the evening.

A knock on the door announced Julian's arrival. His gaze flickered around the room, no doubt recalling the packed dressing rooms of previous opening nights.

She said immediately, "I'm not going out to supper."

"Oh, yes, you are. We're going to the most popular café in town, and you're going to sit where everyone can see you. But first get out of that dress. It makes you look like Marie Antoinette on her way to the guillotine."

"Maggie didn't come." It was a statement rather than a question.

"You didn't really want her to bring Patience, did you? Oscar Latimer and several other equally unsavory types were lurking in the back rows just waiting for an opportunity to pounce on them."

"We should have canceled my appearance. You could have postponed the opening and found someone else. As it is, I've tainted the theater with my name. You'll lose a fortune—"

"I'm fortunate to have one to lose. Here, I'll help you with the buttons. Wear that black dress with the ostrich feathers and your best go-to-hell sneer when we get to the café."

"Julian, I can't—"

"Buckle under to the philistines now, Delia, and you'll never be able to walk out on any stage in this country again. All Latimer put out is innuendo. If we ignore it, people will begin to question its veracity."

"Judging by the house tonight—"

He spun her around to face him. "You know what I always admired most about you? Your courage. Don't become cowardly over this. Latimer has besmirched your name and the Van Courtland name, but he doesn't know about Maggie and Patience. Whoever gave him his information at least had the decency to keep them out of the picture. So I'm not going to let you go to ground with the excuse that it's for your daughter's sake."

Delia reached up to remove her earrings. Julian was probably right that she must act as if the story of her illegitimate child was nothing more than an ugly rumor. She would drink champagne, laugh at his jokes, and if not another soul came near their table, she would pretend she didn't care.

As it turned out, they were besieged by reporters, all wanting comments on the meager audience for Delia's performance, and asking if they intended to sue for libel over the Oscar Latimer article. Julian had a standard answer for all of them.

"Obviously people were shocked by the innuendo, but we're certainly not going to lend credence to such outrageous gossip by taking the newspaper to court, or dignify it by arguing with Latimer. I'll just remind you that as reporters it's your job to sell newspapers, and some of your more unscrupulous colleagues have been known to stretch the truth, or even make up an outright lie if they felt the end justified the means."

Since they all knew he spoke the truth, most of the reporters quickly gave up and left them alone.

Shortly after being seated, several large bouquets of flowers arrived at their table, then buckets of champagne, facts which did not go unnoticed by surrounding diners and reporters alike. "I assume all of these are from you?" Delia asked, *sotto voce*.

Julian smiled enigmatically.

Delia sipped champagne. "Would it have helped if Hugo had come tonight, do you think?"

The closed expression he always wore whenever she mentioned Hugo's name slipped like a mask over his face. "Gabrielle is in a rapid decline. He doesn't leave her bedside. What a whip guilt is. He's neglected her for years, but now acts like a doting husband."

Delia made no comment. She understood only too well that guilt was a whip. At least Hugo had an opportunity to make amends to his wife, which was more than she had had with Joe.

At Julian's insistence, Delia sang again the following night to an even smaller audience, and, ominously, her appearance on stage was greeted by hisses and jeers. The house fell silent when she began to sing, but the jeers resumed when the aria ended.

Angry, Delia walked offstage.

Julian caught up with her before she reached her dressing room. She turned on him in controlled fury. "I'm not going back. I should have followed my instincts and canceled."

"You're making a mistake. If you'll brazen this out, the audiences will come back eventually."

"When do you think it will be time to return to San Francisco?" she asked wistfully.

"Not for quite a while. But if you're ready to leave, we could go to Los Angeles. Perhaps Zimmerman won't care about the hint of scandal and let you act in one of his moving pictures."

"It's more than a hint of scandal, Julian. And since it's out in the open, what have I got to lose? I'm going to get my daughter back."

"I want to take her to California with me," Delia told Maggie. "Just the two of us, so we can get to know each other. We'll tell her it's just a vacation, to make parting from you easier."

"But it isn't just a vacation, is it?" Maggie's eyes glistened with tears.

"No. But I don't want to remove you from her life. You can see her any time you wish."

"How am I supposed to do that? California is a very long way from here."

"Then pack up and move there," Delia said. "It's a place like nowhere else on earth. A grand place for new beginnings. With your talents you'd soon have a thriving business again. Julian believes the moving pictures they've started making there will soon catch on all across the country, and they'll have a need for costume designers. There'll be plenty of opportunities for you. Probably more than for me, now that I've been branded a soiled dove."

Something close to resignation appeared in Maggie's eyes. Delia thought, she knows this time I won't be deterred. There seemed little need to announce that nothing, not lawyers, not threats, nor guilt, was going to keep her separated from her daughter. Maggie was well aware that Delia had nothing to lose, since her reputation had already been destroyed and her career ruined. All of the papers had reported that she had been jeered off the stage at her last performance.

"When will you be leaving?" Maggie asked at last, brushing her fist across her eyes.

"Soon. I'll let you know. Julian can move into my house and arrange to sell it. He'll have to stay and take care of the Courtland Opera House for a while anyway, at least until he can find someone to manage it for him." That Julian would follow her to California was a foregone conclusion in Delia's mind.

At Maggie's door Delia turned and looked at her. "Think about what I said. You'd like California."

Maggie gave her a ghost of a smile. "A few weeks ago I wouldn't have hesitated. I'd probably be on the train with you. But you see, Lucas asked me to marry him and—I think I'm going to accept."

Delia walked home through the gathering dusk, feeling strangely content for a performer whose career lay in ruins. Julian would probably come over for a late supper after the Opera House closed, and for once she was looking forward to seeing him. They would discuss their plans for the future. Maybe it would be fun to make a moving picture, at least until audiences decided to forgive her. They could buy a house in Southern California, somewhere near the ocean. Then, when San Francisco had been rebuilt, they could go back and resume their old life. She had been happy there once, although not as happy as she would be now that she had found her child. Why, she and Patience and Julian could do so many wonderful things together . . . perhaps it was time to forgive his past transgressions and build an entirely new relationship with him. The prospect intrigued her.

She paused under a gas lamp at the corner of her street and chuckled to herself. Considering she had vowed to hate Julian Van Courtland for as long as she lived, he certainly occupied an important place in all of her plans.

A horseless carriage was parked in front of her house. It didn't belong to Julian, but perhaps someone from the Opera House had accompanied him.

The moment she stepped into the house, Ruby materialized from the shadows, pointing toward the closed parlor door and miming that she'd put the visitor in there.

"Julian?" Delia asked, opening the door and peering into the nearly dark room. "Why don't you turn up the lamps?"

"No . . . please, I'd prefer to remain in the dark." It was Hugo's voice, hoarse, ravaged with emotion.

Delia moved hesitantly into the room, every instinct warning that she was about to walk into something better avoided. "Hugo . . . what are you doing here?"

"Gabrielle's gone. She just slipped away as I held her. . . ."

"I'm so sorry, Hugo."

"The house seemed suddenly so empty—I couldn't stay there."

"No, of course not. Julian will be here soon. I'm sure he'll be glad to go back with you and help you with all the details.

Did you call a doctor to . . ." She couldn't bring herself to say to sign the death certificate.

He didn't answer for a moment.

She stood in the clammy darkness, not knowing what to do or say to comfort him. She moved closer to the sofa where he sat, and, feeling the movement of her skirt, he reached out and caught her hand, gripping it like a drowning man. "I've lost her permanently now. I should have fought for her, years ago. Perhaps we could have been happy together, for a little while anyway."

Her knuckles felt as if they were being crushed, and so she sat down beside him, hoping he'd let go of her hand. She was unprepared for him to throw his arms around her and pull her into a fierce embrace. His face pressed to her cheek, and she could feel the stubble of his beard and the wetness of tears. His broad shoulders heaved with suppressed sobs.

Delia was moved by the depth of his grief, but dismayed by its display. She who had always kept her own feelings under rigid control could not understand how a man of Hugo's apparent strength could allow himself to break down in front of a woman to whom he was not even related.

Awkwardly she patted his shoulder, and he buried his face in the hollow of her throat and clung to her. His tortured breathing seemed to fill the room.

Without warning, the hall door opened wide, sending a beam of light across the room, bathing the occupants of the sofa in a yellow glow that seemed as bright as a spotlight.

Delia, with her back to the door, heard Julian's sharp intake of breath, but Hugo did not raise his head.

Julian's voice, curiously devoid of anger, spoke. "You two might have waited at least until after the funeral."

The door was abruptly closed again, plunging the room into darkness more dense than it had been before.

Scrambling to her feet, Delia stumbled over Hugo's feet and almost fell. By the time she had recovered it was too late to call Julian back.

She turned to Hugo. "Go after him, Hugo. Explain that you were overcome with grief. He imagines . . . never mind what he imagines. Just go. I'm not the person you should be turning to now. I sympathize with your loss—but I'm not your family."

Hugo did not appear to hear. He slumped on the sofa, his face buried in his hands.

After a moment with no response from him, Delia said, "I'm very tired, Hugo, I'm going to bed. You can let yourself out."

She went upstairs, hesitating only a moment before locking her bedroom door.

Her dreams were troubled, and she spent a restless night, finally dropping into a deep sleep just as the dawn broke.

The sun was up, but it was still early when Ruby awakened her. "What is it?" Delia grumbled. "I don't have to get up yet."

"He's still here," Ruby hissed indignantly. "Sleeping on the parlor sofa. Y'all better get him out of here before folks find out you had a gentleman spend the night, 'cos nobody's going to believe he slept down there and you up here. Not with all them rumors flying about your love-child."

It was a moment before memory returned. "Pass me my robe. Then go and make some strong coffee."

Hugo was still asleep, sprawled on the sofa with his long legs on the floor. Delia shook him and when he didn't open his eyes, she slapped his cheek. "Wake up, Hugo. It's time to go home. Come on, pull yourself together. You can't stay here."

She managed to pull him into a sitting position, and he blinked open his eyes. "Delia? What are you doing here?"

"This is my house, Hugo. Don't you remember? You came here last night after Gabrielle . . . passed away. But you have to go home now. Come on, get up. Ruby will have a pot of coffee ready in a minute, but then you must go. You're ruining what's left of my reputation."

He sighed deeply. "So it wasn't a nightmare. I'm sorry, Delia. I shouldn't have come to you. I guess I wasn't thinking straight last night. I would have gone to Maggie, she's always been a good friend, but I was afraid Lucas Stone might be with her. Look, don't bother with the coffee. I'll just go. Delia . . . I'm sorry."

She walked with him to the door, and it was only then that she remembered his horseless carriage was still parked in front of her house, as it had been all night. She reminded herself that she was leaving New Orleans anyway, so what did it matter what the neighbors thought?

Joining Ruby in the kitchen, she poured herself a cup of coffee. "I'd like some hotcakes, Ruby. Maybe some sausages, too. I've got a lot to do today, and I'll need a good breakfast. I also have some news for you. I'm going back to California. If you'd like to come with me, you're welcome to. My daughter will be accompanying me, so if you have any reservations about my love-child . . ."

Ruby stammered, "Why, I'll have to think about it, ma'am."

Delia poured cream into her coffee, mentally listing all she would have to do before departing. Check on train departure times, supervise the packing for herself and Patience. Order a floral tribute to be sent to the church for Gabrielle's memorial service. She would not attend the funeral.

She did not call Julian. Better to let Hugo explain the situation about last night, she decided. But when she had not heard from him by early evening, she telephoned the theater and learned it was closed, probably indefinitely. She then called his hotel, and was informed he had checked out.

Puzzled, she hung up the receiver. But of course, he would have moved in with Hugo, in order to help him with the funeral arrangements and deal with the arrival of friends and relatives. She decided not to call Hugo's house. After all, Julian would get in touch with her sooner or later.

The next morning she went to Maggie's house to see Patience. "Have you told her?" she asked.

Maggie nodded. "She's wondering about her father, of course." She bit her lip. "I think she's going to miss him more than me."

Patience listened quietly as Delia explained they would be going away together so that they could really get to know each other. Did she seem too acquiescent? Delia knew that her daughter was as adept at hiding her feelings as she herself was, and worried about the child's reaction to the abrupt and all-encompassing changes in her life.

"You'll like California, Patience. I have a young friend there who is only a few years older than you—his name is Danny, and I'm sure he'll be happy to show us all the sights."

Patience asked in a small voice, "Will we be home by Christmas? I want to get my daddy a nice present."

"I'm not sure. But you could mail him a present, you know."

"Can I go out to his house to say goodbye?"

"Well ... we don't have much time before we leave."

"Could we call him on the telephone?"

"No, dear, he doesn't have a telephone."

Patience's lip began to tremble. "Why are you taking me away from my mama and my daddy?"

Delia couldn't bear it any longer. "I'm your mother, Patience. You were stolen from me when you were a baby, and I didn't know where you were all these years. But in my heart I've always searched for you. I didn't willingly give you away."

She grabbed the child's hand and pulled her closer. "Look at me. My hair is the same color as yours. Our eyes are the same. We both love music. Oh, my darling, I would have crawled on my hands and knees to find you if I'd had any hint of where you might be. Please try to understand. You're a part of me, no other two beings on earth can ever be closer than we are. You are flesh of my flesh. We're bound together by all the generations who went before us and all of those who will come after us."

She threw her arms around the child and held her. "You're my baby, and I will love you forever, more than anyone else can ever love you. There's nothing I wouldn't do for you. I'd die for you, gladly. Please, Patience, forgive me for not being here all these years, it wasn't my fault."

Never before had Delia ever allowed herself to show such raw emotion. Tears were streaming down her face and she was shaking.

The child was staring at her, as if at last sensing the truth. After a moment she asked, "Will we go on a big train?"

Delia had arranged to leave the day after Gabrielle's funeral. Julian still had not been to see her, or even called, but Delia didn't see any significance in this since Hugo obviously needed him more than she did.

The day of the funeral dawned unbearably hot and sultry. With all of her preparations to leave complete, the day stretched before her interminably. She didn't want to intrude into Maggie's last day with Patience, and as Ruby had decided to accompany her to California, Delia gave her the day off in order to finish her packing. Prowling restlessly through the house, Delia wished the funeral was over so that she could go to Julian.

The Van Courtlands had come into her life during a funeral, she recalled, for their butler Henry. She thought of Daddy Lou leading the procession through the narrow streets of the Vieux Carre, blowing his horn as only he could, and herself singing in the cemetery. How kind Hugo had been to her, from the very beginning, she thought. But it was Julian who had been there at her side, throughout triumphs and disappointments, keeping her on track when she wavered, cheering her when she was blue, guiding her, watching over her in a way Hugo never had. Why then, had she pined so for Hugo?

Now Gabrielle was dead, and Hugo was a widower. How ironic that once that news would have filled her heart with hope, but now all she felt was a passing sadness that a man she had once admired and respected was suffering. Had Maggie loved him, too? There was a strong possibility that she had. How strange were the whims of fate. There had been three women who loved Hugo, but in one way or another he had lost all of them.

Delia knew she had to do something to fill the empty hours stretching before her, and there was one person she had not told of her impending departure, perhaps because she did not relish the idea of seeing him again. But she doubted she would ever return to New Orleans, and perhaps a final goodbye was in order. She decided to go to see Thad and hired a carriage to take her out to the old house on the bayou.

A little more than two hours later she was again standing in front of the house, with its sagging porch and gnarled trees leaning perilously close to the peeling clapboard walls. Had Julian kept his promise to find Abebe and persuade her to remove the hex? Consider it done, he'd said, and with Julian that usually meant it would be done.

The front door opened before she reached the top step of the porch. Thad still looked gaunt, but his eyes were more alive than on her last visit, he wore a clean cambric shirt, and he had a pen in his hand.

"Delia! I hoped you'd come back. I was afraid you wouldn't, so I was just writing to you. What a coincidence—you must have left N'Oleans about the time I started the letter. Eulie would have said that we'd each received a spiritual message from the other. Come on in."

"Let's sit out here on the porch, shall we? It's so hot." She sat on a creaking swing and fanned herself with her hat. He sat in the ancient rocker that had once been Daddy Lou's favorite chair.

"You look a little more presentable than the last time I saw you," Delia said. "I hope that means you've decided to go on living."

He gave her a small smile. "Abebe came to see me. I have a feeling she was . . . coerced."

"I haven't seen her or spoken to her, if that's what you're implying. I'm leaving New Orleans, Thad. I may never return. I came to say goodbye." She told him briefly of recent events, including Marcus's abduction of Patience.

Thad's eyes flashed angrily as he listened, and she was reminded, unnervingly, of the time he had fought with the two hunters. The same bloodlust glinted in his dark gaze. But he said only, "You're wise to take her away. But I wonder if you'll ever be safe from him."

Delia shivered involuntarily. "I would kill him if he hurt her. I believe he knows that. But . . . but let's not speak of him. Tell me what your plans are. You can't go on languishing here forever."

"I'm going back to Paris," he said. "Perhaps to pick up where I left off, perhaps to start anew."

"Oh, I'm so happy to hear that! Will you write to me?"

He laughed softly. "That's my assigned role in your life, isn't it? Penfriend *extraordinnaire*. We never did know how to act around each other in person."

They talked a little while longer, and he offered to make lemonade, but she said she must return to town. The funeral would be over and she was expecting Julian.

Just before they parted, Thad took her hand and held it for a moment. "Be happy with your daughter, Delia."

"I will."

"Don't worry too much about what people say or think about you. Most folks are secretly envious of those who live by their own rules, you know."

She sighed. "I'm not sure that's true of women."

"What about Julian? Will you marry him one day?"

She was less surprised by the question than she thought she would be. "I suppose my feelings about him have undergone a change over the years."

"After you realized that what you felt for Hugo was only puppy love?"

"You're too perceptive by far, Thaddeous Bouchet."

He squeezed her fingers and smiled enigmatically.

Day had faded to evening by the time she reached her house, and the evening quickly became night. Julian did not come.

The following morning she telephoned Hugo's home. The butler told her he was not available for calls.

"May I speak to Mr. Julian then?"

"He ain't heah, ma'am."

"Do you know where he is?"

"No, ma'am."

"But he was there for the funeral?"

"No, ma'am. Mr. Julian he ain't been 'round heah." There was undisguised disapproval in the butler's voice.

Delia felt a chill. "You mean—he hasn't been staying with Mr. Hugo these past few days?"

"He didn't come near heah, ma'am, not even for the service."

Delia went straight to the Courtland Opera House, but it was barred and locked. A note tacked to the doors stated the theater would remain closed indefinitely. She waited until evening and then called Hugo again, giving the butler her name and telling him her business was urgent.

Moments later Hugo was on the line, "Delia? My man tells me you're inquiring about Julian. I'm sorry, he gave me a letter to give to you. In all the chaos I forgot about it. I'll send it around to you immediately."

"Where is he? Do you know?"

"He told me he was leaving New Orleans. He didn't say where he was going. I was hurt that he wouldn't stay for the

funeral and perhaps a little short with him, which in view of
the circumstances, I believe is understandable."

*He didn't explain about coming to my house the night
Gabrielle died,* Delia thought. *Is that why Julian is avoiding
me?*

Hugo's butler arrived at her house with a bulky envelope
half an hour later. She spilled the contents onto her desk.
Bank books, financial statements, stocks, bonds, trust deeds,
and, most ominous of all, a power of attorney she had given
to Julian, years ago, were spread before her. She unfolded the
accompanying letter.

> Dear Delia:
> Keep all the enclosed in a safe place. You can have
> Hugo take care of your affairs if you wish, but I strongly
> urge you to take charge of your investments yourself.
> I hope you'll sing onstage again one day. There truly has
> never been another voice like yours. I'll hear it forever in
> my soul.
> Good luck,
> Julian.

Chapter 47

*

Hugo's butler attempted to turn Delia away, but backed down when she refused to leave and took her to the study, where Hugo sat staring morosely out the window. He had not shaved and his shirt was creased and open at the neck. He looked at her with dulled eyes and spoke in a hoarse, sleep-deprived voice. "Delia ... I'm sorry I forgot about Julian's letter."

"Where is he, Hugo? Where did he go?"

He gave her a baffled look. "I don't know."

"He must have said something. Hugo, didn't you explain what you were doing at my house that night? His letter seems to indicate that he believes you and I ... that we ..." Her voice trailed away. Was he listening? He seemed to be looking right through her. She moved closer, and smelled the whiskey on his breath.

"I should go out to the Willows, I suppose," he said without conviction. "Marcus didn't come to the funeral, you know. I should be angry that neither of my brothers attended my wife's funeral, but what's the point?"

"Did you and Julian argue—the day after Gabrielle passed away?"

He looked at her with surprise. "No. He came to offer his condolences and said he had to leave town before the funeral. He asked me to give you that envelope."

"You mean you didn't talk about coming to my house the night before?"

"No. He didn't bring it up."

"Hugo, he must have given you some indication where he might be going."

He shook his head. "I thought you'd know. Aren't you

joining him? I thought . . . well, in view of the nasty articles in the paper and the fact that he shut down Courtland Hall?"

It was obvious Hugo didn't know any more than she did and neither did anyone else. She questioned theater employees, Julian's banker, and even telephoned his broker. But he had vanished without a trace.

So be it, Delia decided. Perhaps he's right. It's time I learned to manage without him. But one possibility remained. What if he had left the city, but not the state? What if he had gone home to the Willows?

Delia rented a buggy and journeyed through the Louisiana swamplands to the old plantation house. She went alone. She didn't want Julian, if he were there, to believe she was incapable of traveling by herself.

Since there was a possibility only Marcus would be in residence, her loaded derringer was tucked into the pocket of her skirt, and she had also taken the precaution of slipping into her purse a small packet of cayenne pepper. Flinging hot pepper into an attacker's eyes was a trick she had learned from Mignon. She might need the protection if only Marcus was in residence. The last time she came to the Willows, only half-witted Oley had remained of the servants, and he could have defected by now. She hoped Julian had retreated to his boyhood home, since then Marcus would be less of a problem when he learned she was taking Patience away.

The Willows appeared even more neglected since her last visit, and now an ominous silence hung over the house and grounds. There was no response to either the front or rear door chimes.

She walked around to the tradesmen's entrance and found that door, leading to the kitchen, open. Stepping into the littered room she called, "Hello? Marcus? Julian?"

How quiet it was. The complete lack of sound was unnatural, unnerving. She tiptoed through the downstairs rooms, afraid to break that deathly silence. Finding no one downstairs, she went slowly up the staircase, recalling how she had gone on a similar errand to Daddy Lou's house and found Thad living all alone.

But at the Willows there was no one in the house, and, judging by the undisturbed dust and cobwebs, no one had been there for days. Had Julian persuaded his brother to leave with him?

Delia's heart was beating rapidly. A prickly sense of urgency, a need to get out of the suffocating atmosphere of the house, sent her running back down the stairs. She picked up her skirts and fled through the drawing room, past Marcus's piano, out through the French doors. On the terrace she leaned against one of the great stone urns, gasping for breath.

Something flickered on the periphery of her vision. A shadow? Or had someone darted from behind the giant live oak near the river and disappeared into the boathouse?

"Marcus!" she called, "Is that you? It's me—Delia."

There was no answer. She reasoned that it was unlikely that Marcus would hide in the boathouse, or even go near it for that matter. He had always been afraid of the water, and the only time she had ever seen him in the boathouse had been the day she had gone on that fateful boat trip with Thad.

She had avoided considering he might be in the guest house. She had not set foot in it since the night Marcus had raped her there, and had no intention of entering it now.

It was clear Julian had not come here, and if Marcus had also left and the house was deserted, as it appeared to be, squatters could already be ready to move in. Or perhaps a thief was bent on stealing one of the boats. She decided her visit was foolhardy, and the sooner she left, the better.

But as she turned away, someone emerged from the boathouse. "Miz Delia . . . it's jes' me. Oley. I's Mr. Marcus's houseman."

"Oley? Where is Mr. Marcus?"

He wrung his hands and swayed from one foot to the other. "I's waitin' on him, Miz Delia. I doan know what to do. I done took out a boat and looked for him, but he ain't nowheres I kin find. I figgered he'd come back, but he ain't and I jes' doan know what to do."

"Are you trying to tell me that Mr. Marcus went out on the river? That's nonsense and you know it. Mr. Marcus never took out the boats and avoided going anywhere near the water. Where is he, Oley? You'd better tell me the truth."

He chewed his lower lip frantically. "Mr. Marcus, he done got up ever' night, playin' the pianny, all alone in the dark. But two, maybe three nights ago I wakes up, and he was stompin' up and down and shouting, sayin' the voices was telling him his daughter was a-drowin in the river and he was gwine to save her. Miz Delia, I done grabbed aholt of him and held him, I swear, and he done calmed down and went back to bed. But 'bout an hour after that I heerd sounds, voices, and scufflings, and when I got up next mornin' he was gone, and one of the boats was gone—that ole pirogue that was full of holes. So I took the skiff and I searched— found the pirogue, all tangled up in cypress roots and reeds and no sign of Mr. Marcus. I didn't know what to do, Miz Delia. I was skeered to tell 'case folks thought I'd done something to him. So I jes' hung around the boathouse and waited for somebody to come and tell me what to do."

Delia was thinking rapidly. Was it possible that Marcus had believed he heard voices that sent him out in a leaky pirogue to search the river for Patience? But Oley had said he later heard sounds—including voices. Had someone else arrived that night? But who would travel through dangerous bayou country in the dark of night? Certainly not Julian, who in any case had been in town three nights ago. If someone had indeed come that night, they had come with stealth and evil purpose.

Or . . . perhaps with a purpose he did not believe to be evil, but necessary and just. Someone who knew Marcus was a threat, not only to Patience, but to herself. There was only one man on earth who fit that description—only one man who knew the truth about Marcus, who cared enough about Delia to wish to remove any threat to her and her child. She thought of her visit to Thad and how he had tensed with anger when she told him how Marcus had spirited her child away and was now insinuating himself into her life.

Was it possible? *No, I mustn't even think it!* Everyone knew that Marcus acted strangely, professed to hear voices. Oley had just said that he heard Marcus shouting about the voices telling him his daughter was drowning. *But Marcus was terrified of the river. Would he have attempted to find her all by himself? Wouldn't he at least have awakened Oley?*

"Miz Delia? What'all we gwine do?"

"I'll go for help, Oley. You wait here. We need lots of men and boats and dogs to search the marshes."

*   *   *

After several days the search was called off. No trace of Marcus had been found, but everyone knew that bodies could vanish without a trace in the swamp, trapped under rocks or roots, or found by alligators or other predators.

When the hue and cry died down, Delia made her way to Daddy Lou's house.

Thad was gone.

She breathed a sigh of relief.

Chapter 48

*

Los Angeles, California
1910

Sixty gilded cupids watched the first-nighters who had come to the Grand Opera House at First and Main in the heart of downtown Los Angeles for the premier performance of a new light opera starring the great Cordelia in her first appearance onstage in four years.

Since the Opera House had opened, replete with ebony and gold railings, crystal chandeliers, and boxes that cost an unheard-of twenty dollars, it had been the scene of many notable performances, but none more eagerly anticipated than this one.

Few of the well-dressed patrons recalled all of the details of Cordelia's early singing career, but knew it had ended with scandalous revelations that she had not bothered to deny. She had disappeared for a while, then suddenly her name was on everyone's lips again due to the release of a moving picture in which she had a small but compelling part. In the film she played the mother of a boy who was already known for his haunting portrayals of waifs, Danny La Rue. Her name was listed below his in the credits. But critics and audiences alike were mesmerized by her expressive eyes and delicately beautiful features, and three more films appeared in quick succession, capturing a large audience barely aware that she had once been a singer.

Cordelia's producer, F. L. Zimmerman, issued a press release to finally put to rest the old rumors about his star's past. It was true she had a daughter, he said, but she had secretly been married at a tender age to the father of the child, they had separated, and he was now deceased. Adoring audiences accepted this. After all, there had to be tragedy somewhere in her past; how else could she convey such sadness with those large limpid eyes? Furthermore, she had a cherished little daughter, and it was a well known fact that she had unofficially adopted Danny La Rue years earlier. A woman who loved children must surely be worthy of their adoration.

"Delia, the house is packed!" Patience squeaked excitedly. "Every seat is taken, and they're standing at the back!"

She had never been able to persuade her daughter to call her anything other than Delia, but it no longer mattered. "Then perhaps you and Danny had better go to your box, before someone steals your seats?"

Danny scowled. "Just let 'em try! Anyways, the Zimmermans and the Stones are already there."

"Any*way*," Delia corrected automatically. "Take Patience up to the box, because it's time for me to put on my costume."

"Come on, kid," Danny said, taking Patience's hand.

Delia watched them go, and as always, a lump came to her throat. Danny had almost single-handedly built the bridge that closed the gulf between her daughter and herself. From the moment they arrived in California, he had taken them both in hand, refusing to allow them to withdraw from each other until they had, as he put it, talked the situation over.

When they first came to Los Angeles, Patience had been in a state of shock and grief, refusing to accept that her father was dead. "He's just lost again," she'd plead tearfully. "He'll come back. If he was dead there'd be a funeral."

No amount of explanation from Delia could convince her otherwise. But Danny spent hours with the little girl, and gradually her grief and denial diminished. She also missed Maggie desperately, and there had been a bad period when news of Maggie's marriage to Lucas Stone was received. But by the time their first baby was born, a year later, Patience was proudly referring to Danny as her brother and Delia as her mother. Maggie and Lucas now had a toddler girl and twin boys, who had fascinated Patience when the family arrived for their first visit to California to be present at Delia's opening night.

Alone in her dressing room, Delia donned her costume and

wig and permitted herself a moment's quiet reflection. The last few years had passed swiftly and had been productive and satisfying. She had created a family and built a home for them. She had enjoyed acting in moving pictures, but no camera could ever replace a live audience, and the silent flickering images on a screen were no substitute for the thrill of music and song and real people on a stage. She had not admitted, even to herself, how many hopes she had pinned on tonight's performance. She wondered if somewhere in the world Julian and Thad knew she had at last made her way back. She had not heard from either of them since she left New Orleans, but a telegram wishing her luck had arrived from Hugo.

It was like old times! The enormous bouquet thrust into her arms during her full ten minutes of curtain calls, the flowers tossed onstage until she stood in a veritable garden, the dressing room packed with floral arrangements, fawning critics, telegrams, well-wishers.

She had felt the adoration and enthusiasm of the audience throughout her performance, which had constantly been interrupted by applause, but her most treasured moment came when she walked to the wings into the hugs of Danny and Patience. Her daughter had looked at her with shining eyes and murmured, "Oh, Mother, you were wonderful!"

Mother, Delia thought, elated. Maggie may be Mama, but I'm Mother.

The ensuing party lasted almost until dawn. Patience fell asleep and was taken home by Mrs. Zimmerman, while Danny doggedly refused to leave until Delia did.

At last, as a silver dawn painted the eastern hills, Delia and Danny returned to their home on the bluffs overlooking the Pacific Ocean. Delia now owned a brand-new Oldsmobile, which she drove herself through southland streets filled with ever-multiplying numbers of Mr. Ford's cheap Model T. When she pulled into the circular driveway, she was surprised to see an unfamiliar motor car parked in front of her house.

Danny sat bolt upright beside her. "It's a Duesenberg!" he informed her excitedly. "Same kind that won the race. Nobody we know has one. What's he doing here so early anyways?"

"Any*way*," Delia said, as curious as Danny. "Why don't we go inside and find out?"

The boy raced ahead of her and disappeared into the house. By the time she reached the entry hall, Danny was emerging from the drawing room. "Now, Delia," he said, in the carefully conciliatory tone he cultivated when he believed she was about to be angered or upset, "don't get mad. I know you ain't seen hide nor hair of him in years, but why don't you just talk over the situation? Maybe he had a good reason for walking out on you."

Delia hid a smile. "Are you trying to tell me, in your own unique way, that Julian Van Courtland is in my drawing room?"

Danny's eyes widened. "How'd ya know?"

"The Duesenberg sounds like him."

"Y'know, if you had a husband, I could get myself adopted legally."

She looked at him in surprise. "Is that important to you, Danny? You've lived with me for years as my unofficial son. Besides, you're financially independent."

He stared at the floor and muttered, "I'd like it to be official. Anyways, do you want me to stay with you while you talk to Mr. Van Courtland?"

"No, you go straight to bed."

He hesitated. "Y'know, he sorta saved my life after the Frisco 'quake. I probably wouldn't have got out without him."

"Yes, I'm aware of that. Good night, Danny." She kissed his cheek and gave him a push in the direction of the bedroom wing.

On the threshold of the drawing room, she paused. Julian stood waiting for her. They didn't speak for a moment, each frankly scrutinizing the other for perceivable changes.

Julian looked almost the same as she remembered. He was tanned, as though he had spent time outdoors, more casually dressed than she recalled, and there may have been a few more silver streaks in his black hair. His dark blue eyes still regarded her in the faintly amused, quizzical manner she remembered so well.

"You missed my triumphant return to the stage," she said at last, as though they had seen each other only yesterday.

"No, I didn't. I was there—second row balcony. You were magnificent."

"Why didn't you let me know you were coming?"

"My presence wasn't important."

"You mean you'd have sneaked out of town again if I'd flopped?"

He laughed. "Probably."

"You could have come to my dressing room—joined us at the party."

"I didn't want to intrude. It was your moment, your shining hour. I might have been a distraction."

"But you didn't mind intruding into my home, or distracting me from my bed? I have another performance tonight, you know."

"I've been waiting since midnight; I didn't expect your party to last until dawn. But I'll come back later if you wish."

"No, sit down for a moment. I assume you had a reason for coming to see me. If you'd simply wanted to congratulate me on tonight's opening, a telegram would have sufficed. We might as well get this over with." She kicked off her shoes and curled up on one of the sofas flanking the fireplace.

"Doesn't sound promising." He sat opposite to her, leaning forward into the space that all at once seemed wider than it had before.

"Did you expect to be greeted with open arms, after the way you left?"

He pursed his lips. "I believed I'd left you in the arms of my brother."

"You were mistaken."

"Apparently so." He leaned back against the sofa pillows. "I saw Hugo in New Orleans a few days ago."

"Oh?" she responded coolly. "And how was he?"

"Lonely, I believe. Immersed in business, as usual. I would have thought he'd have married again, after his mourning period."

"Maggie married her lawyer, didn't you know? They have three children now."

"Look, Delia, if you're trying to tell me that Hugo never lusted after you, you're wasting your time. Besides, I didn't walk out solely because I found you and Hugo together."

"I don't really care why you left, Julian. I do feel it was

rude to go without a word, and heartless not to return when Marcus died. Hugo had to contend with a double loss all alone."

"I didn't know about Marcus," he said quietly. "I'd have come back if I had. I was on a ship to Europe by then. I didn't find out until several weeks later. By then there seemed little point. I couldn't bear the idea of coming back and seeing you and Hugo together."

"We weren't together, not ever."

"I know that now."

An awkward silence fell. After a minute Julian spoke in a lighter tone, "I saw you drive up in a new Oldsmobile. Not many women will tackle driving an automobile. And your butler told me that you supervised the building of this house yourself. Of course, I saw all the movies you made. Now you're singing in a new opera. I'm also aware that you've handled all of your own financial affairs—our mutual brokers and bankers kept me posted. I'm proud of you, Delia."

"I haven't tried to make you proud of me, Julian. Everything I've done, I've done for myself."

"Exactly. Which is the main reason I left four years ago."

"Let me see if I understand you," Delia said. "You now wish to take credit for what I've accomplished without you?"

"I'm going to take credit for giving you the opportunity to succeed on your own. You see, even before I stumbled into that touching little scene with you and Hugo the night Gabrielle died, I'd realized that I had moved into your life while you were still a child, and directed—guided—whatever you want to call it—your steps constantly. I never gave you an opportunity to make your own mistakes, achieve your own goals, *or to be on your own.*"

"And when did you reach that conclusion?"

"The night we made love. Or rather, the next day. That night I was too euphoric."

She looked away hastily, studying the Italian marble fireplace, not wanting to recall that night because it might weaken her resolve. She had been more successful than he realized, because her main accomplishment had been to stop missing him so acutely. It had been an effort, and there had been many times when she wished he would return, but she would, of course, die before letting him know that.

He leaned forward again, his dark blue eyes enigmatic in the pale dawn light. "Do you remember what we talked about, the next day? I offered to make an honest woman of you, but you pleaded propriety—your mourning period and all that rot—and I asked if I should propose to you again in a year."

"I don't remember any of this," Delia lied.

"Oh, yes you do," he said softly. "I decided then that my obsession with your singing career had destroyed any chance I might have of you seeing me in any other role—as a husband, for instance. I suppose I never knew how to tell you what you meant to me. How much I cared for you. Whenever I tried, you treated it as a joke, or sarcasm, and I could never figure out how to dispell that notion. I suppose seeing you in Hugo's arms was the catalyst, but I'd been thinking of going away for some time before that night. I had to leave, Delia, I had to try to forget you. But now four years have gone by, and you've surely come to realize you don't need me. It's difficult to explain, but I feel that fact is important to what might happen in the future. It's also significant that you haven't remarried."

"I haven't married again because I don't need a husband. I have my children, I'm independent in every way. I don't lack male companionship. Why should I complicate my life with a husband?"

The old teasing glint appeared in his eyes. "Oh, I don't know, perhaps for the sheer challenge of attempting to tame one? Perhaps simply for the fun of it. How about to grow old together when children and career are gone?"

"What nonsense. I shall never marry—" she broke off. "Why are you smiling like that?"

"I'm just fixing this moment in my memory. I have a feeling it's one I shall want to remember."

"You haven't changed one bit, have you, Julian? It's really too early in the morning to spar with you."

He stood up and said casually, "I shall be here for a few days before returning to San Francisco—did I mention I've rebuilt my opera house there? Perhaps we could have dinner and talk about booking you?"

"Oh, we don't have to do that over dinner, Julian. I have a booking agent, I'll give you his card."

He grimaced. "You're going to make me work for this, aren't you?"

Rising to see him out, she asked innocently, "For what?"

He reached for her slowly, one arm encircling her waist, pulling her close. "Don't worry, I'm not going to kiss you. I just wanted the physical closeness to remind you of a certain night so long ago. I never forgot it, Delia, although I roamed the world making sure I was always in the company of the most beautiful woman I could find."

"Then don't let me detain you from returning to your exciting life. If you'll remove your arm, I'll see you out."

He released her, giving her a mocking smile that indicated he saw right through her bluff.

At the front door the fresh brine tang of the ocean greeted them, and a breeze ruffled the bougainvilleas climbing the pink stucco walls of her Spanish-style bungalow, sending scarlet blossoms flying.

He raised her hand to his lips and kissed the inside of her wrist. "Congratulations on your performance, Delia. Goodbye."

As he started to walk to his car, she called after him, "I'm giving a small dinner party next Sunday." She kept her tone cool. She wasn't yet ready to forgive and forget, despite her racing heart and the dawning realization that Julian's reappearance in her life was the one element needed to make everything perfect. "Perhaps you'd like to come?"

He turned and looked back at her. "I wouldn't miss it."

She smiled. The old spark between them was still there. Perhaps the new Delia would allow it to ignite again.